A FLOWER AND FLAMES NOVEL

A Song Amidst the Storm

The Flower and Flames Saga: Book 2

Brett Shaffer

Double Infinity
PRESS

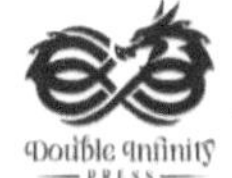

A Song Amidst the Storm

To Angie, for always offering a listening ear and encouragement to all my endeavors

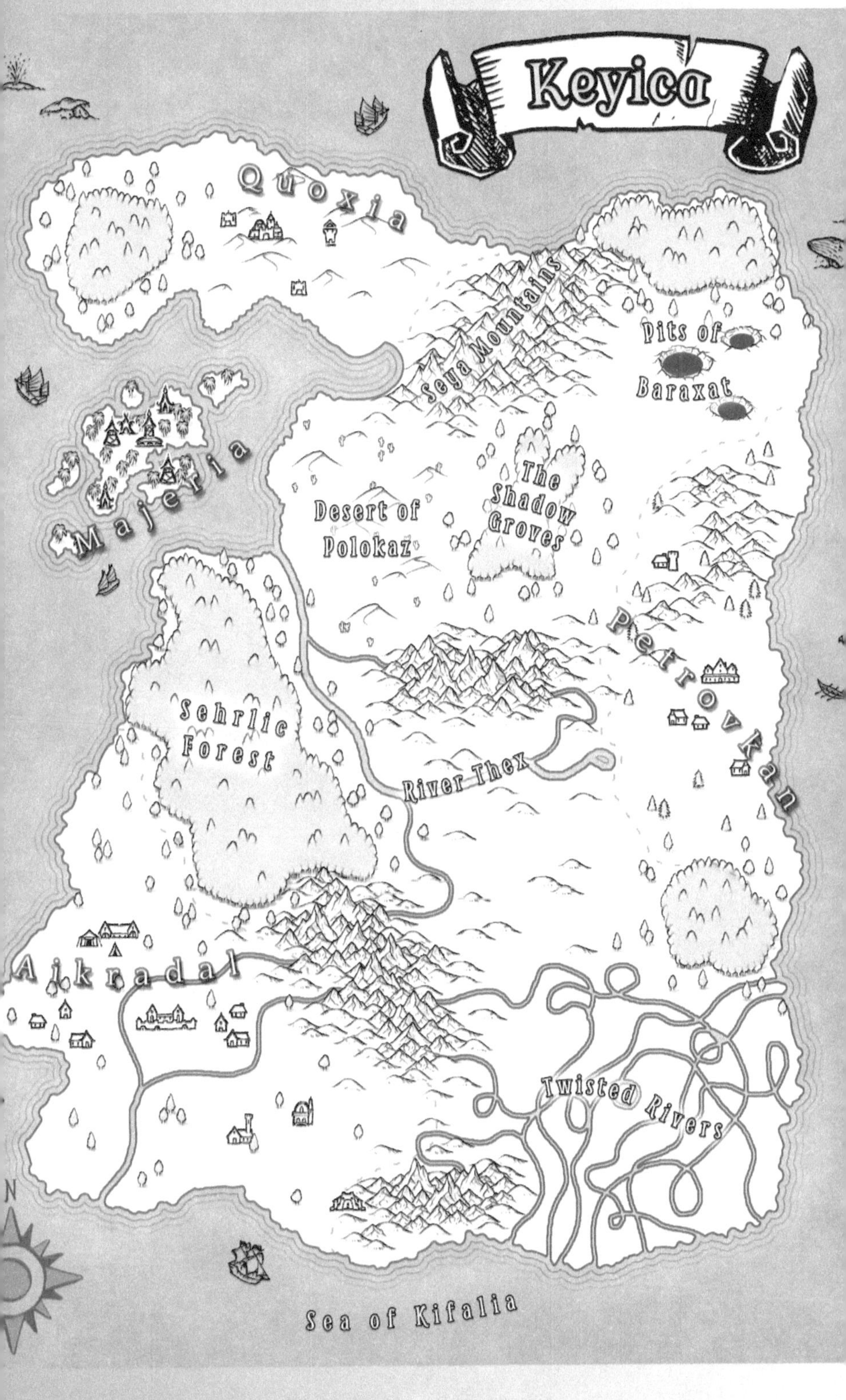

Keyica
Quoxia
Seya Mountains
Pits of Baraxat
Majeria
Desert of Polokaz
The Shadow Groves
Petrovian
Sehrlic Forest
River Thex
Aikradal
Twisted Rivers
N
Sea of Kifalia

ONE

B elyx knew storms far too well by now.

The sky was still. The violent clouds had passed, but the tempest's presence lingered...honoring a promise it would return and claim those lives it missed the first time.

Just like her mission tonight.

Belyx marched through a still puddle, following the lessons ingrained in her to stay hidden in the shadows.

Suppressing a shiver from the preceding rain, she continued her pursuit. The winding streets were full of bustling businesses that filled her with satisfaction. She found comfort in the sound of smiths hard at work, knowing they could keep their businesses *alive*.

At the market, an array of items flooded for sale. Baker's tables displayed bread of different varieties. Jewelsmiths produced delicate gems in every color and hue. Dressmakers offered dresses made of the finest fabrics; with embroidery, lace, and gem-encrusted belts in shades of pale pink to metallic gold.

With the Goldfinger smuggling brigades eliminated, the shops flourished as intended, although their leader put up quite a fight before meeting his end. The economy had prospered with tax revenues at the palace tripling in the six short months since Belyx ascended to the throne. No matter what life threw at her, she held onto one thing; a pledge she had made to rid the gangs from Aikradal. As the road twisted and turned, she was determined to keep it.

Wealthy merchants trotted by, boasting of their successes. With the Whispers timely exit, no one feared who might be listening. The only ones sneaking around now were the Order—currently led by Belyx. Remaining vigilant was the only option, fulfilling her promise to cleanse the streets of gangs.

The Order stopped the Cabarets with the same weapon that had ended Aydevko and swiftly vanquished Scandeni, another exiled male witch.

Despite the defeat of Aydevko, Aikradal still harbored a tumor that called for eradication. The majority of the people still blamed the fae for the attack...even though they were under a witch's curse, only exacerbating the discord among humans.

Belyx reminded herself to take one step at a time. Once the gangs were eradicated, she would redirect her efforts toward ensuring her people honored the returned fae. For far too long, they had believed the fae were responsible for her mother's death. They were deceived, and those who were behind it would face consequences.

The endless horizon of the Sea of Kifalia caught Belyx's gaze. Like a tempest, it stirred up memories of Majeria, the kingdom that had supposedly taken her mother away. In time, they would pay with their blood as well. A good queen was always deliberate in her decisions for her people, understanding that any kind of retribution needed careful planning. Too many precious lives were at stake, despite her thirst for answers.

However, tonight would satiate a different thirst; tonight she would see the last remaining gang dissolve into nothing.

The Berserkers, previously a formidable threat to the people of Aikradal, underwent massive changes over the past few months after their leader, Raul Fortan, and his general, The Scorpion, fell in battle. Despite Belyx managing to keep the latter out of her conscious thoughts, his name still sent shivers down her spine.

She wanted with all her being to trust that the intel was wrong—that there wasn't a new power taking charge of what remained of the Berserkers. Feelings only clouded matters in these dire moments.

Faint shouts and cries from afar thrust Belyx back to reality.

Running her fingers over her rose pin, her way of honoring her family before her kills; Belyx made sure each blade and venom were accounted for. Her nights became evermore frequent with using them...but hopefully, this time would be different. *This will be the last time.*

The savage cheers pierced louder air as she neared the outskirts of Aikradal by the isolated beaches—a sign of the forbidden fighting rings.

The two burly combatants were drenched in sweat, arms and legs faltering as their ragged breaths wavered.

Hoards of spectators sat perched on ramshackle stands, while Belyx stealthily approached, unsheathing her blades with a swift motion.

In a graceful hurdle, she appeared between the fighters, her agility allowing her to subdue them both and bring their sizable bodies to rest against the sandy mats. Some combatants they were.

The crowd erupted in boos, and Berserker guards closed in around her. Belyx raised her gaze towards them, deliberately lowering her voice. "Are you truly too cowardly to face me? I'm just a mere girl," she goaded their hiding new leader with spiteful words.

The guards were confined in their tracks, and he strode forward, proudly upholding his armor and letting his golden ponytail dance behind him in the breeze. He was everything Belyx remembered, but his eyes harbored an emptiness that petrified her to the bone.

Former Captain Thomas unsheathed his scabbard with ease, its heavy whistling sound hinting at its eagerness for battle. "Doneque...I must commend you for your efforts in dealing with the other gangs, although they are feeble when compared to us."

Adjusting her grip on her knives as if preparing for war, memories of their previous duel last year flooded Belyx's mind—recollecting the time when she had believed she was betraying her kingdom by fighting him...back when he fought for honor, truth and the kingdom.

How mistaken she had been. He was a different person now.

"It's not too late to reconsider," Belyx said in a determined tone as she eyed Thomas with caution. "You can still choose to rejoin Aikradal."

His raucous laughter echoed throughout the night air, damning her audacious proposal. "I would never return to that wretched place! It reeks of weakness, especially since that sad excuse for a queen took over."

Unwelcome memories and emotions associated with Freyja surfaced before Belyx willed them away. Freyja and Thomas's relationship had blossomed last year, but that faded away like a flower in a field of thorns. Freyja would understand. She needed to bring this confrontation to a close. Drawing a deep breath, she commanded with heavy authority. "Then I challenge you to the fighting rings!" No hint of doubt showed.

Those words were met with laughter from the crowd and the Berserkers alike, seeing her attempt as futile. But Belyx was unfazed by their jeers.

Thomas stepped forward, his armor glinting off the moonlight as he mocked her request. "How can I resist?" he asked with an arrogant smirk. In those moments, any fondness Belyx once held for him lost its luster; since she knew all too well what her mother had done for him when no one else would. She gave him a place in the guards and now he was squandering it.

She recalled how The Scorpion changed Thomas last year and remembered her part in it all; how she made him go against the beast. Her former captain won, but was irreversibly altered by a desire for power...

Her grip tightened around her daggers as Belyx discarded all pretense of their past friendship and embraced the identity of Doneque, the assassin who would stop at nothing to end the Berserkers...the final gang.

Without warning, Thomas lunged forward with rage burning bright in his eyes. Belyx remained alert and collected as she dodged his attacks with grace, flowing seamlessly between movements like a performance straight out of a play.

His relentless attacks, though daunting, were nothing but annoyances against her lightning reflexes. She would need to strike harder as his armor was impenetrable by her choice in weapons.

Stepping back, Belyx lashed her knife towards Thomas's eye, but the leader of the Berserkers moved like a wild cat and shifted his position just in time to dodge the attack. It grazed his cheek, leaving a faint line of maroon.

Satisfied she hit her mark, she pressed on with ferocity...

Waiting for her venom to take effect.

Crouching low to the ground, Belyx watched for an opening as Thomas swung at her. With a quick move, she flung sand from the dry earth into his face; the Berserker recoiled in surprise, instinctively reaching for his face in search of relief. This provided Belyx with the opportunity she needed; like a cobra, she struck at him with her remaining knife, poised to deliver a fatal blow.

Despite his temporary loss of vision, Thomas managed to skillfully countered each of her strikes. Belyx persisted relentlessly, attacking without ceasing in an attempt to end their fight. Yet he adapted to her technique, rotating his stance and delivering a forceful strike with the hilt of his sword, sending her sprawling across the ground. Why was the venom not kicking in? Even Belyx's limits and skills lessened in comparison to Thomas'.

In a moment of clarity, her grandmother's words echoed within her mind: *"Let them think they have won,"* she would say. *"Let them think they own you. Then...Strike."*

And so she did as instructed. Indeed, it seemed as if his cockiness took control as he stood above her ready to deliver the final blow. With her agility and flexibility to her advantage, she evaded his killing strike and twisted her body around, propelling her away from harm. The Berserker general was larger than her, so she had to rely on strategy and angles instead of sheer strength against him.

As he swung his weapon one last time, she stomped on it, disarming him momentarily before sending a forceful kick into his chest which sent him hurtling backwards.

He shot up, weapon blazing as he spun and slashed with a blur of deathly arcs. Belyx answered his offensive maneuvers, her hits blocking his as if she could predict each attack he sent at her.

"I must admit, assassin, you live up to your reputation," he muttered through gritted teeth. His words hung in the air like a murky fog as Belyx rubbed the bruises on her now tender hands.

She knew if she did defeat him, his Berserkers would for sure seek revenge for their humiliation. Taking a step back from him she tilted her head and lowered her tone. "This is your final opportunity to leave Aikradal. I have no desire for more bloodshed by my blade."

Thomas gave a wry smile as he twirled his scabbard through his fingers with a cavalier air. His eyes glinted malevolently as he sneered. "Well, I do" and once again hurled himself at Belyx in a silver blur of steel. The strike barely missed, the wind brushing past her skin. Movement from behind caught her attention and she ducked as a metal hammer soared over her.

The Berserker guards tried to outnumber her. Clearly, honor was not in their vocabulary.

A hammer attack nearly claimed Belyx again and she retaliated, taking out the guards one by one. Thomas was left as her last challenge. Drawing strength from her mother's courage, she stood her ground.

Thomas let out a roar of rage and pounced at her. His fists met her body with each blow, leaving an wound that matched his hatred. But as her mind surrendered to the pain, her heart refused to give in. Her demeanor remained defiant despite the ringing in her ears and the darkness clouding her vision.

With a renewed surge of energy, Belyx spun away and scrambled towards the cliffside overlooking the restless sea. However, he was not so easily fended off. He relentlessly pursued her with strikes from his sword, and she managed to avoid them. But in one swift motion, he pinned her to the ground and snatched off her short black wig, revealing her true identity concealed within. Her burgundy curls escaped onto the sandy grass as she looked him square in the eye.

Thomas gasped before retching onto the sand. "Belyx?" He croaked amidst his gasps, his face now drained of any ounce of color. The venom kicked in...she won.

Belyx scoured the area, ensuring not a soul was around to bear witness. She seized him by his bloodied ponytail and slammed him into the earth, sending his weapon clattering off the edge of the cliff. "You're correct. It is me," she said as he quivered beneath her.

"No!" He coughed into the grass patches.

With her fist full of his hair, she yanked him up again. "You were the pride and joy of this kingdom. My mother gave you a chance and you squandered it. You put dirt on her name!"

"How?" Limbs convulsing from the poison, he let out a whimper.

The victory was hers as she held her blade against his throat, pressing it deep enough into his tender flesh that the cold metal left a trail of crimson liquid on his neck. Flashes of his former life blossomed in her mind—of days long past when the people hailed him as a hero and beloved by all who knew him. Now, he served as a reminder that no one could be trusted and everyone was capable of evil. Aikradal was riddled with corruption and it was up to her to restore justice to her people.

"Your first mistake was underestimating us," she growled as he squirmed beneath her grip. "Your second mistake..." She pulled him to her, his hot breath coating her mask.

"Was thinking you could betray your queen!"

She plunged the knife into his neck without hesitation, warm blood dripping down her arm to her fingers. His once vibrant blue eyes were now glazed over in death and she watched with unease as his body slumped lifelessly to the ground.

He was dead...as were all of those who would dare cross Belyx and her kingdom.

Two

Enzo reached to the other side of the bed and agitatedly sat up.

Of course...Belyx had left without saying a word...again.

A sliver of light broke through the balcony door, bringing an inconvenient torrent to his eyes. There was a draft from the doors we well. Winter had lingered for too long this year. Getting up, he cupped his hands together and lit a candle with a few flicks of his fingers.

On his desk, lay the five books he had been flipping through in recent weeks. Belyx called him mad for reading so many at once, but sometimes he preferred a thriller whereas other days he leaned towards cozy mysteries.

She hardly read anything—although, her reading had increased, something she was picking up from him.

The joyous emotions he had for Belyx in that moment were squashed. He should be angry with her...yet why couldn't he ever stand up to her? After all these months, she still kept disappearing on her nightly escapades. Even though the council wanted The rest of the Order to handle things...not just her.

Enzo silently prayed to all the gods, even hers, that she would make it back safely.

Like a dry ooze—the gangs were stripped from the kingdom and the people were rejoicing. But still, he felt foreign in his own home; the dirty stares from the people were a mere reminder of it.

His fathers were encouraging, but they had been preoccupied at their home in Sehrlic Forest, readying their upcoming restaurant. Gink had said if he couldn't bring peace between the people with his cooking, he might as well just die and sprout grass instead. Enzo chuckled.

Though it had only been thirteen years since he thought to have lost them forever, last year Belyx and he had freed his tribe from Aydevko's terrible curse. Unbearable visions of lifeless red eyes and "fae killing" humans beleaguered in his mind.

He shook away the memories and continued his tale, glancing at the snoozing horned snake, Bruxos, by the dresser—it was its venom that gave them a chance to defeat Aydevko, yet there was an aura about this creature, making him want nothing to do with it. *Venom like that shouldn't exist in this world.* The thought of its venom in Enzo made him shudder.

The creak in the door told him it was time. Setting down his book, he tapped his foot impatiently. Getting caught was not in Belyx's wheelhouse. "Out for a nightly stroll?"

Belyx froze in the doorway, her eyes widened as if trying to process the situation. Enzo had to give her credit—she managed to successfully sneak out earlier even with his fae senses. She was truly something else. "It was lovely to see the moon after those stormy days," she said after some time, keeping her tone small and sweet, though laced with guilt.

As she limped by him into the washroom, he shook his head. Of course, she was limping. She had a hard time going one week without hurting herself. Their healer would not be around forever...especially given the implications that she was a witch. Enzo quivered at the thought. The fae and the witches were never supposed to cross paths again, but they *were* out there. As well as their exiled male counterparts.

Enzo grabbed Belyx's hand as she passed, they were still wet from dirt and gods knew what other things. "I thought we had an understanding. No more nightly missions?"

Belyx sighed, her eyes flickering away from his face for only a moment before settling back on him with determination. "The deal was after the gangs were dealt with." She shucked off her wig, her auburn locks cascading down her back, although they would not be enough to save her this evening. "They are still lurking around my kingdom."

"But why didn't you tell me?" He waited for her to explain further. After all, he was starting to learn that maybe if he gave her just enough space she might confide in him without having to get too personal with it all—which felt like progress between them.

With a lowered stare, Belyx continued. "You were so content in bed sleeping. I didn't want to wake you?"

For a second, Enzo wanted to call her out, but he nodded, understanding what she meant now more than ever before—but even she was not invincible and needed help. "I could have helped."

Belyx tore away, her leathers falling to the ground. "The storms prevented me from going out the last couple of days. But then the intel about the Berserker fighting rings came out and I couldn't resist. Some missions are easier alone."

Ouch. Of course it was the storms. It was always something.

After throwing her wig onto the floor, she exhaled. "Their new leader is dead."

Enzo knew that the former captain recently took over the role as leader of the Berserkers. However, Belyx's look indicated that wasn't the case anymore. He had never killed a friend before but if they fought for evil, then whatever had to be done was necessary. Slowly, he took her hand in his own, feeling the deep burn scars from when he hurt her, while also saving her from Aydevko, a guilt he still held onto.

With a hard swallow, he was grateful that Belyx had made it back alive once again. She had managed to save him in the past, even outwitting the fearsome Scorpion. His esteemed teacher and best friend, Ren, had been murdered by their treacherous hands. "Good, you can stop these dangerous missions then. That seems to be the last of the gangs."

"Yes, but I still need to be sure. After a couple more checks." The guise of an assassin was gone now, and she headed toward the washroom. "Can we talk about it after I freshen up?"

Enzo followed her. He could feel his cheeks burning with every glance at her bare body—now slick with various abrasions as she strode across the tile. "No. You keep dancing around this. I am done waiting and we must have this discussion now."

Her façade dropped as she slumped onto the stool...still brandishing her nakedness as if knowing it would affect Enzo's thoughts. "Fine... Let's hear what you have to say."

He breathed out, handing her a towel that she took with an eye roll; did she not realize the magnitude of her actions? "We agreed you would tell me when you leave on these assignments. I can help out too. It's my kingdom. I am the advisor, and also, you know, I control fire."

Refusing to look him in the eye, Belyx shifted away. "I am responsible for this kingdom."

"We all are. How can yo-"

"You don't get it. I am the queen. I get to make the decisions and I know these streets—"

She froze and for good reason, knowing full well he knew the streets better than anyone. Living on them did that to a person. "I didn't mean it like that."

A wave of anger rippled through him; she had been pushing herself too far the last couple of days. "This needs to end tonight. You have been using this as a distraction from your daily duties. At the council, you can barely open your eyes, your body is bruised all over, and you refuse to even throw a ceremony for your father and grandmother."

A flash of fury appeared in Belyx's bright hazel eyes as she snapped her gaze back on him. "That's easy for you. You sleep like the dead, heal quickly, and at least you still have a family. Mine is all gone! I have no one who shares my blood anymore!"

The hissing of steaming water filled the room as Belyx turned the faucet on. As if she could magically wash away her problems. Enzo hastened to her and shut it off, leaving mere inches between them. He studied her delicate face, marred with bruises and shadows beneath her tear-streaked eyes.

"You know that isn't true. You have us, your friends." She kept her head staring at the water.

Belyx's mouth dropped open at his words and slunk back, almost in remorse. "That is different. It isn't the same. I mean...you're right. I should have told you. I'm sorry and I am done from now on."

"This can't keep happening." Enzo stepped away from her, releasing her hand and gazing into her dark eyes for any sign of deception. His nostrils flared as her scent of beach sand and lilac engulfed him. Belyx looked up at him, fear sparking in her bright brown eyes.

The only way she would listen was an ultimatum. "If you continue this, I am leaving. I have things to do for my tribe." His words hung heavy in the air.

Belyx's expression remained stoic, her inner turmoil unmistakable yet unspoken. As a single tear slipped off her cheek, Enzo wiped it away with the warmth of his hand. "I'm sorry, Enzo. This is a problem I can't fix on my own. We have the rest of the Order. They can handle the threats too. I am so sorry for worrying you. I love you and I want to work on us."

She brushed the slick mud off her hands. "But it's done. They are no more. And I am sorry I don't talk about my dead family. I would rather focus on not failing their legacy. Normally, I would go to my grandmother for advice."

Enzo embraced Belyx and ran his fingers through her hair as he tried to give her comfort. "That's why I'm here. I could never leave you alone."

Belyx scoffed before averting her stare, the weight of what she said now apparent in her eyes. "You're right," she admitted. "It's not fair for me to keep putting you through this."

Enzo released her and looked deep into her eyes, trying with all his might to convey the truth hidden within his words. "I almost lost you to Aydevko once already. I couldn't bear it if that ever happened again. Besides…Aikradal needs its queen—and who else will protect our fae tribe when most people still view us like we have the plague?"

The hatred toward the fae had stayed the same, but as long as Belyx remained the kind person she was, there was hope.

Belyx glanced towards the tub and back to Enzo's eyes—her face revealing a twinkle of light that somewhere inside was still the woman he had fallen in love with before all this had happened.

She leaned forward and kissed him deeply…light and full of heat, but behind it there was an undercurrent of guilt about their passionate exchange; guilt that soon devoured Enzo too due to the ultimatum he had to give her. However, he tried his best to push his resentment aside and stay strong; for Belyx required more time to work through everything she had endured since losing two family members in such a swift and terrible fashion.

Irrepressible emotions surged Enzo as they embraced. All visible differences that had previously separated them melted away in the face of the profound bond they shared. The feelings they possessed for one another felt unassailable, irrefutable and timeless, like something which transcended their physical world. As they moved into each other's embrace with focused intensity, it seemed they were both determined to make up for lost time.

Soon, his clothes sailed across the room as the passion between them increased. Every frenzied moment glowed with a burning point of electricity that arced within them. Their bodies collided and tumbled together in ways so close and entangled that they were one. Belyx was an equal partner in this dance, allowing Enzo to explore and learn all her secrets. Time itself slowed as the sensation burst into each other's arms.

At last, Belyx went to take a much-necessary bath, leaving Enzo to lay on their bed and stare at the moonlight through the balcony door. He made a silent vow that no matter what challenges he may encounter along the way, he would stand by her side and shield her from any harm she might face in the kingdom. She was more than just his queen; she was also his partner, and he refused to fail her now when she needed him the most.

Three

The next day started way too early.

Wind still heavy from the recent storms, Belyx felt a strange mix of emotions on the way to the Sehrlic forest in the small carriage, silence gripping the air like an invisible force.

Belyx tossed a secretive glance at Enzo, who sat across from her, his expression distant as he gaped out the window. Not a single word had left his lips since they'd departed the palace that morning. She couldn't fault him; her bitter words from last night and his ultimatum still echoed in her ears.

She wished he could understand that her missions were necessary, but the truth was that she was not entirely sure why she had to do these assignments either. She knew it was her duty to her people that she'd have to risk her life—no matter the cost—so no one else would die.

The carriage rolled on, the crunch of dirt and gravel under its wheels the only sound to break the silence. Soon enough they arrived at the edge of Sehrlic forest and Belyx's pulse pounded as the silhouettes of those in front came into view. She inhaled and glanced at Enzo, signaling her readiness for whatever lay ahead.

The council had informed Belyx of some unrest occurring near the forest border. Freyja had suggested sending in the royal guard to resolve the situation, but Belyx said the people had to witness her taking action to ensure it was handled with care. The full support and cooperation of Aikradal's citizens was necessary for the fae to reintegrate into their home with success.

The morning sun was a relentless reminder of what Belyx faced through the night. Although she pretended to sleep, there was no rest for her soul as dread filled her being. Enzo, however, looked wide awake despite all he had endured...a trait unique to the fae that made them so fortunate. Her handmaiden, Onka, attempted to cover up any signs of fatigue on Belyx's face, but even that could not conceal the coal-like smudges under her eyes.

Enzo's hand squeezed her gloved one and she forced herself to look ahead. Word had spread that they were a couple and with it came cruel and unoriginal names hurled at them from every direction. Never had a human and fae been linked romantically, and yet here they were on the brink of setting an example.

Progress had been made—slightly. The two were able to journey about during daylight without fear of attack from the four menacing gangs that once threatened their kingdom. Although with Enzo's fire-wielding ability, along with a small brigade of guards, no one would stand a decent chance.

The guards and Captain, Freyja, stood rigidly as Belyx lifted her hand in a gesture of command to stop the carriage. It was exceedingly rare for her new captain to allow the new queen anywhere outside the castle walls without her vigilant presence at her side. Since she had no successor, she couldn't take any chances. Belyx had no qualms protecting herself, but dressed in only her travel gown; extra protection was more than welcome.

Once the brigade came to a halt, Freyja leaped off her chestnut steed, Wind Runner, and strode up to Belyx. "Are you sure you can't let us deal with them? They appear especially unruly today."

Before Freyja even finished her sentence, Belyx was already sliding out of the carriage. "No need. I will talk to them myself."

Freyja shot her a stern look, knowing full well it was futile to argue with her. The guards trailed after Belyx as she marched towards the protesters. Ten guards, her captain, and her fire-fae partner would be adequate protection.

The people yelled things across the way like "murderers don't deserve homes," "justice for the queen," and Belyx's new favorite, "traitors to the crown deserve death." If only they knew the truth.

As Belyx approached the group, their cries ceased as if they were awaiting her words. Many of those gathered were elders, most likely recalling the oppression suffered in times gone by - when malicious lies were whispered about the fae and her mother. Such anguish endured for far too long, never allowing space for mending.

Enzo leaned close enough for only her to hear him over the hush of the crowd. "Are you sure you want to do this?"

Squaring her shoulders. Belyx readied herself. "Stay here if you wish but I will not tolerate ignorance in my kingdom; these people are merely confused and need education on their errors."

Taking a deep breath and summoning all her strength, she pushed forward, sensing Freyja's steadfast presence behind her and Enzo's reassuring touch by her side; calming her racing mind.

Putting on her best queen smile, she faced the hostile gathering before her, their glares burning into her. The guards brought forward an elevated platform, on which Belyx carefully stepped one of her high-heeled shoes...praying not to fall. Her heart beat against her ribs like a caged bird as she tried to prepare the speech she had been practicing for moments like these.

"Greetings citizens," she began with a quivering voice, "I understand that it is natural to be wary of changes. Change is something we have all had to deal with recently. I know your pain. I feel it every day, but the fae are not our enemies."

The people spoke amongst themselves in hushed tones, but someone brazen enough called out, "Oh yeah? How?"

Belyx was thankful for the interruption; it gave her time to gather her thoughts. Composing herself once more, she continued with renewed confidence. "I'm sure you all remember how we assumed the fae were responsible for the death of the queen all those years ago? I was led astray by these misconceptions too. But now I am here to share with you what I've learned since —that the fae never did such things."

No sooner had she uttered these words than one of the protesters spat on the dirt. "Yeah, now you're in bed with one! They must have put some spell on you!" they jeered. All eyes were upon Belyx and the tension was palpable.

"Yea!" another chided. "The spell in his pants!"

Now discouraged and slightly flustered from the last comment, Belyx began to falter under their scrutiny when a comforting hand brushed against her backside surprised her. Enzo was standing tall next to her. With a gentle kiss on her hand, he silently conveyed his unwavering support and encouraged her to go on. That's when that fire burning inside her grew. A passion that had driven her to save Aikradal months ago.

"Your rage is understandable, but it is misplaced. The fae did not murder my mother," she said as her inner thoughts begged her to stop and step down. But a deeper part of her suspected the truth must be revealed. "Majeria did."

A collective gasp rang throughout. They were off the fae, and now spouting about the island kingdom. But a pit sank deep in the depths of Belyx's stomach. She had divulged information she wasn't meant to reveal yet, but with all the gossip and speculation, she couldn't keep it hidden any longer. What was the worst that could happen? Majeria was already aware Aikradal was searching for answers about what happened to her mother. Even if they had an inkling of what she was accusing them of, no Whispers were around to spread it.

Calming her apprehension, Belyx continued undeterred. "I understand your grievances. The council and I are working tirelessly towards justice being served. We need your help to accomplish this."

Freyja shot Belyx a glower, concern written across her face.

Belyx disregarded the distress from her captain and cast her gaze over the crowd and nearly lost her breath when a figure met her eye.

Standing tall amidst the masses of people was a woman, who looked oddly familiar despite her graying hair and worn-out features—it was none other than the witch she had run into just a year earlier. The witch shook her head slowly and gave an almost unspoken warning. Belyx squashed down her mounting fear as she turned to tell Enzo. But as she whipped around to catch the woman again, she had already vanished. A chill plummeted down her spine. After a dry swallow, she addressed her people once more. "Take care and stay safe on the streets. The gangs have fled and it is time to celebrate!"

The crowd dispersed back to their previous activities, yet some remained to protest further.

"You still good to head into the forest?" Freyja asked.

Belyx peered at Enzo. It had been a while since he visited his home and she needed to see how the fae were adjusting. It had gone anything but smoothly. *These things take time, Belyx.* "Of course," she managed to get out.

Enzo gleamed up at the sky, the rising sun glinting in his eyes. "I'm proud of you," Enzo said as they walked away from the square.

Belyx scoffed. "Addressing aggravated people is hard work. I don't know how my father did it all those years." And the people were always angry then.

"I think when someone has an imposing figure, they can control the masses. Those like you who are not so intimidating have to be creative when it comes to persuading a group."

Belyx arched a brow skeptically. "Like me? Not you?"

Enzo stuck out his cute tongue. "Okay, okay, me too. Us non-scary people have to stick together or we will get squashed by those who are naturally intimidating."

"I can be pretty scary," Belyx teased as she grabbed Enzo's hand in hers.

He laughed, pushing her away with his other hand. "Yes, but as queen, you can't just gut people when they wrong you."

She furrowed her brows. Such a thing could be done if she wanted it to be so. "Wouldn't that be something?" Although it would do more harm than good.

Enzo grinned slyly at her comment while hopping back into the carriage. "I could always burn them? Live up to my reputation for being terrifying," he said with a devilish smile on his face.

Leaning forward, Belyx gave him a long kiss on the lips and then pulled away with a mischievous gleam in her eye. "What was that for?" Enzo asked.

"Always giving me good advice," Belyx replied, following him into the carriage.

He eyed her with a narrowed gaze as they continued on their journey to his former home. "That isn't free though. I'll get my repayment later and not just some lazy smooch."

That embarrassing fool. Why was he with such a wild and impulsive girl like Belyx? He had something wrong with him as well. She turned away from Enzo, and of course, Freyja gawked at her like an old gossiping woman at tea through the carriage window. Belyx gave her an obscene gesture and they rode into the Sehrlic forest; past the remaining protesters who would hopefully come to understand the truth.

"Queen Belyx!" Gink cried out. Belyx had longed to be back in Sehrlic forest to aid in the fae integration, but her other duties kept getting in the way. After thirteen long years of imprisonment, the fae looked ecstatic to be released and return to their home.

Before Belyx could enjoy the sounds of birds chirping and the cool scent of minty air, Freyja instinctively stepped in between them. "Hold, please. Do a sweep!" The guards began their perimeter scan, seeming almost untrusting of the fae even though the fae were never intentionally dangerous. Belyx wondered if the guards still held grudges against them for what they did under the control of Aydevko.

"Frey, darling," Gink crooned. "Us fae are harmless. There is no need for all this drama. Queen Belyx is safe with us."

Freyja brushed him off and continued her inspection, barking commands to the palace security. Enzo approached from behind Belyx, a distant look on his face despite seeing his fathers. Why was he so cold to them? She had to remember his fathers tried to kill him when they were influenced by Aydevko's spell. It was a sight she could not stomach—family fighting one another like that. She recalled being forced to do battle against her father when they stumbled upon those catacombs so many months ago.

Thano, Enzo's other father, put on a friendly face and motioned for them to follow. "To our second home!" He laughed and he and Gink shared a stare. "Sorry, I just love the sound of that. Anyways, we have fresh treats and wine back there. Hurry so it doesn't get stale!"

Belyx and the others trailed deeper into the forest with the fae tribe, feeling the weight of multiple eyes on her back. The closer she drew to the center of the forest where the various huts had been rebuilt by the fae, the more potent their presence was.

Fae children played nearby. Elemental powers churned in the air, so present that Belyx had to veer out of their way multiple times to avoid getting splashed.

"Show some respect for our queen!" Gink bellowed at a group of children. Freyja also glared in their direction, and meek apologies were uttered before play resumed. Belyx didn't mind as she had no idea what they went through while trapped in that vault all those years ago. *Let them stay young and playful...before the world ages them.*

As they approached Enzo's father's hut, Belyx's stomach roiled as she saw what had been erected there: multiple statues of gods other than her own—which was strange to comprehend, as her God had saved her people numerous times and led them all to this great continent. Uncomfortable at witnessing other faiths being practiced, she felt Enzo's hand in hers and kept his grip, reassuring her.

Gink began babbling excitedly about the finished sculptures, one depicting a tall figure surrounded by flowers of red, blue, white and green—most likely each representing the fae elements. "To our right is the statue of The Original. The one who saved us centuries ago."

The Original? Why was that title so familiar?

Enzo squeezed her hand again as if sensing her discomfort. Taking yet another glance at the majestic sculpture before them, it occurred to Belyx that although the fae may have different beliefs than her own, they were still all connected in an inexplicable way—a collective family co-existing beneath this same sky. This was the most important thing.

"What is that story? Is he one of the gods you worship too?" Belyx asked, remembering now how the street witch last year mentioned how The Original was sent down from the gods and stopped the fighting between the witches and the fae.

Thano pursed his lips and eyed Gink, it appeared he wasn't as excited about this statue. "There is insufficient time for us to provide a full explanation, Your Highness. We are already here."

Belyx looked back to Freyja who shrugged.

Enzo tilted his head towards Belyx. She chose to ignore him and instead proceeded into the hut where a sweet yet musty aroma greeted her nose.

Gink cracked his knuckles and his leafy tattoos shimmered before materializing into multiple small vessels with various scones inside each one. Thano then swirled his arms in a circular motion causing all the scones to hover around. "Grab them while they are still hot!" Gink declared.

Belyx could not resist temptation and took a bite out of one with ferver. She earned a disapproving look from Freyja on account of suspicion of possible poisonings among other potential dangers. However, this was nothing more than an irrational fear as Belyx allowed the delicious flavors of mashed berries exploding across her taste buds in unison with the crumbliness that dissipated within moments upon touching her tongue. It was consumed in a matter of seconds.

"As usual, impeccable work you have both done here Thano and Gink."

The two fae waved off Belyx's compliments before taking their respective seats in their wooden chairs. "So now that we have you here, my Queen...we need to talk about our reintegration program," Gink said, scratching at his scalp as Belyx settled onto a chair next to Freyja. Enzo remained standing at the entranceway with his arms crossed. "This will prove difficult I am afraid. Many of the fae have returned home without issue, but there are still others...who remain unaccustomed to life outside the vault."

At this moment there was no longer any doubt in Belyx's mind regarding why things were so out of balance in the kingdom. No wonder so many citizens were struggling...deep down, Belyx was worried too.

As if sensing her discomfort, Thano shook his head. "Well, it isn't the biggest deal, and—"

"Quite a big deal, Than," Gink interrupted.

Belyx slapped her forehead and looked to Enzo for help but he only gave a helpless shrug in response. Her core sank as her mind raced with possibilities. Each worse than the previous.

"Okay. Okay," Thano continued. "Some of the fae aren't the same. Their curse somehow still...remains."

Belyx's eyes widened in disbelief. She knew all too well the consequences of a cursed fae. She recalled the memories of weaponized creatures who killed many guards and Order members not of their own free will. Had she failed to break the spell when she used the Dark Tome? *Patience Belyx*, she reminded herself. *Be calm like grandmother taught you.*

Gink rubbed his wrists while Thano elaborated further. "At first, we thought it was only temporary, but certain fae have fallen into some kind of trance...with red eyes."

Enzo coughed awkwardly and Belyx pinched her forehead as a wave of guilt washed over her. Had she been so blind to allow something like this to happen? She steeled herself and spoke up again. "Are they violent?"

Thano and Gink both said "no" in unison, as if rehearsed—no doubt because they were aware how desperate Belyx was for a lantern of hope amidst this tragedy.

Without warning, Belyx stood. "Where are they?" If this curse lingered, her people would revolt and she would be powerless to stop it.

Thano led her down a trail to their version of healing huts. The fresh herb scent tickled her throat; Freyja stayed close behind and Enzo kept his head down. Did he know about this?

Finally, they arrived at a tiny room where about ten fae rocked back and forth on the floor, chanting a language Belyx didn't recognize. Taking a deep breath, Belyx asked again, "When did this happen?" With caution, Freyja stepped forward with her bow/staff ready in hand; any sign of aggression from them would be met with swift action.

The water fae healer bowed before answering Belyx's question as her gaze towards Enzo's fathers were laden with dread. "It started only a couple of weeks ago. They are in some sort of coma and have done nothing else, but it has us wondering."

That chilled her to the bone. Her greatest fears seemed confirmed...again she had failed her people. Would these fae attack? And would their tribe stop them? Enzo would.

Enzo would.

The room filled with tension as Freyja stepped forward, her anger palpable. "What are they saying to themselves?"

Gink spoke solemnly, his melody no longer lingering in his words. "Kill the humans."

Freyja lunged, yet Belyx managed to halt her before she did any harm. "Captain. Please. They are not themselves. They are secure here." She hoped...

The healer attempted to explain further in desperation. "They are not physically able to cause any damage and I am certain if we just give it time—"

"There is no time! The citizens must remain unaware of this situation," she said, glaring at her partner, suspecting he had known. Why couldn't he trust Belyx to handle this? She was already struggling with being respected as queen and this was a knife to the throat.

It was about time Enzo found the courage to break his silence, splitting the unnerving void that had settled over the group. "This was some kind of witch magic," he said. Therefore, we do not understand this curse...which is far worse than anything we have ever experienced. Witch magic isn't supposed to infect us, remember? Let me investigate and find a way to stop it."

"Very well, I shall allow you to investigate this matter since you seem so intent on doing so. However," Belyx continued while addressing the entire chamber. "I want daily reports on how fast this plague is spreading...and if it has developed into violence...of any kind."

The healer and Gink bowed in unison and Gink placed his hands against his chest. "Your wish is our command, Queen Belyx. We will be sure to protect you with all our might."

That had to be enough, but Belyx found herself submerged in a murky wave of memories. The embers in the entranced fae's eyes were as red as blood. They were relentless in their pursuit, leaving nothing but destruction and death in their wake. Belyx shuddered, knowing that no one would survive an attack like that again.

Suddenly, a blood-curdling scream pierced through the healer hut walls. Freyja and her guards reached for their weapons, but just as quickly, a messenger on his white stallion galloped into view, the animal frothing at the mouth from exhaustion.

With labored breaths, he gasped out his message. "Queen Belyx. The council demands your immediate presence for an emergency meeting."

FOUR

"What the f—" Belyx cursed under her breath.

"Queen! I never! Language!" Lim Granald shouted. Even after all this time, she still hadn't learned that sometimes ladies were allowed to curse in dire circumstances. Especially ones like this.

Belyx slammed her fist down and Lim's new perm job sank with her. Her friend and Master of Trade, Maria Nebaka, consoled her as if that was the most pressing issue.

"Apologies council, but what?" Belyx seethed through clenched teeth.

Every member of the council—Enzo, Freyja, Lim, Maria, and Cook—kept their heads bowed downwards.

Cook pulled out a piece of parchment and read it aloud...again. "We, the kingdom of Majeria, officially declare war against the tyrant kingdom of Aikradal. It is expressed they have accused us of murdering their queen publicly and then killed one of our own at their ball last year. This comes as a sad notice, but we will be rallying with the other kingdoms to stop this oppression. Reach out if you would like to discuss the terms of your surrender. Kind regards, Majeria's King and Queen, Malanie and Rector Rochenda."

"Why would they do something this drastic?" Freyja inquired with disdain.

Belyx felt a wave of guilt wash over her...knowing what was coming.

"Well...you did tell our citizens that they killed the former queen today—with little evidence," Cook pointed out in her usual blunt manner.

"They did! But how did they even find out that fast? I said it this morning."
There may have been an earlier time she mentioned it...but council didn't need
to know. Belyx made enough mistakes as is.

"Who knows," Freyja added. "All we do know is they are retaliating against
us now. Let them try to storm our walls."

"Well, we didn't have any proof. This should never have been discussed."
Cook said. "A disgruntled male witch is not the best source."

"They have been refusing our summons. How suspicious is that?" Belyx
turned. "Lim, if you tell me to calm down, I will throw the curl out of her hair!"
Lim sank back in her seat. "Plus, we didn't kill Vivienne's cousin last year. The
gangs did."

Deep down, Belyx suspected something else, realizing it was far worse than
the tale they had been told. Princess Vivienne made it her mission to torment
and inflict misery upon Belyx. Her contempt for that woman ignited a rage
within her so intense she wanted to hurl her off the balcony.

"Belyx?" Enzo spoke up, his gentle tone doing little to ease her temper.
"Perhaps we could use the Order to stop Majeria?"

Cook scoffed, shaking her head. "We are still recovering our numbers from
when your people—" Cook froze as if noticing Belyx's scowl; her fingers trembling as she brushed them through her gray top knot. "Apologies, but we can't
just take over a whole kingdom like that. There are agreements in place."

"I certainly don't trust that kingdom. The lengths they have gone to increase
their slave trade and smuggling routes are deplorable. We have had to push it out
of Aikradal too many times!" Freyja added with venom lacing every word.

The headache from all this recent news intensified as a sense of hopelessness
washed over Belyx like an icy wave. With no family or guidance, she felt so
alone. She was desperate for someone to help her lead the kingdom, yet here she
was stuck debating instead of rallying the troops and taking action. She slowly
lowered herself into her chair before speaking, "I'll take responsibility for what
I said, but Majeria can't just expect us to surrender for nothing."

Cook nodded. "They figured out we are weakened. The gangs have only recently dwindled and a full-on invasion would cripple us."

Belyx clenched her fists until her knuckles turned white as despair filled her heart once again…reminding her why she was truly alone in this fight.

Thoughts of war raced in circles around her mind before finally coming upon an answer. Enzo was right. Sending the Order to stop them would work. Not only would it threaten the king and queen of Majeria, but it would also display Aikradal's strength and determination to win this battle without risking too many. Something Belyx wanted more than anything else. "Enzo has a point. Send the Order in."

"Good God, Queen," Lim declared. "You can't fix this situation with a sword and shield; you need to play the game of politics, using your eyes to study the opposition and making clever deals."

"But this isn't just some trade agreement, Lim," Belyx replied. "This is war. We have to stop it before it even begins."

"I'm with the Queen on that one," Enzo said, his dark eyes narrowed.

Cook scoffed, glaring at Enzo with disdain as she spoke. "I disagree. We can use strategies like diplomacy to protect ourselves from further losses we may incur if we must go into battle. Majeria is most likely trying to test your will as a ruler by seeing how you respond. They will be expecting a counterstrike and the Order is not ready."

Freyja's lips formed a thin line. "And also remember what happened when Queen Abigail tried involving the Order and fae in other kingdoms affairs…it led to her death." Her face paled.

"I agree with the Queen," Maria stated, but her eyes widened in fear as they met Lim's gaze. Though Maria had always followed Lim's lead, Belyx wished she had more courage when making decisions for herself. It was like Lim was in charge of two positions.

Belyx sighed as she fiddled with her hair. "What if Majeria decides to come here? How are we going to handle that?"

Cook snorted. "We should be able to prepare an adequate defense system while making arrangements for an apology if necessary. They are most likely offended by a female monarch. They are a sexist culture."

Freyja acknowledged Cook's opinion before continuing. "It would help if no one makes the same mistakes your mother did—involvement with other kingdoms and entities outside their realm proved too much for her and resulted in disastrous consequences."

Not knowing how to respond, Belyx looked away from Freyja as her thoughts raced back to her mother's demise.

Belyx hung her head down, suddenly feeling overwhelmed by the gravity of her responsibility as queen and leader of the Order. Could she make better decisions or would history repeat itself? As these thoughts ran through her mind, she subconsciously searched for her grandmother who used to give her strength during those dark days long ago...but no more comforting words remained.

Wishing for a moment alone, Belyx trembled before her council. "Let us negotiate this diplomatically. I put forth a motion to craft a response to them and I shall attend to some other matters." All the while, Enzo glared at her in clear suspicion.

She whirled away from them towards her chambers, knowing she had no other choice than to do what needed to be done. As soon as she was in her room, her handmaiden Onka stepped into her path. Belyx recognized the familiar concern on her face.

"My Queen, are you alright?"

Belyx disregarded her question and strode ahead, changing into her assassin leathers. Onka stayed rooted in place, still watching her every move with the same unwavering loyalty she had shown since she had become her handmaiden after Freyja became captain.

Onka had changed so much after the death of her twin sister Inka last year...an event that still seemed to haunt Onka in many respects. With hair touching her shoulders now, she sported more vibrant clothing too. Inka was literally her other half. What did that do to someone's identity?

Having finished changing attire, Belyx was about to rush off when Onka raised a delicate hand in protest. "Before you go," she started softly, tears glistening in her light blue eyes. "I wanted to make you aware that I would have given anything just to bring my sister back. Anything...even my life."

Of course, she was eavesdropping on the council.

Belyx paused mid-step, an inkling telling her she should say something that would help ease the pain of loss. "You can sit in on those meetings you know."

"I have duties to attend to." Onka then smiled despite the sorrow that clung to her heart and spoke again. "What I'm saying is if I died instead, I would not have known how wonderful and strong a queen you became." She laughed. "I guarantee you, Inka would have said otherwise."

The two shared a knowing look for a few seconds before Belyx looked towards the balcony. "I miss her honesty." Onka arched her brow in disbelief. "Okay, maybe not all of it, but Inka did great things for us. She was the best Stem here. No one had an eye like her...no offense."

"No offense taken." Onka stood emotionless like a marble statue, her russet eyes scanning Belyx's every move and gesture. "We have both lost too many people. Have you thought about your grandmother and father since?"

"Of course." A sense of guilt crept through her veins as Belyx uttered the lie.

She spent most of the time trying to forget them and how their tragic deaths were her fault. It was easier to push away the pain than accept their departure from this world. Belyx expected that one day, no matter how hard she tried to suppress her grief, it would come back to haunt her conscience when she least expected it.

Her promise to herself was simple; from now on she would be the sole person to take risks saving her kingdom...even if it meant her death. She didn't want others to suffer because of her anymore.

"Be safe. I will anticipate your return. Be smart as well." Onka leered at Belyx before turning around, not uttering another word.

As soon as Onka was gone, Belyx raced towards the balcony and yanked open its doors with newfound strength. The cool wind brushed against her skin like thousands of little fingers, providing solace and encouraging her mission. Without wasting more time, she scaled the wall and rushed to her destination with one goal in mind.

The temperature had plummeted to a new low that evening as if the chill in the air was perpetuating an age-old war between warmth and cold. Belyx, however, did not mind the needle-like frigidity as it numbed her fragile chest of feelings that would distract her from her responsibilities.

The main streets were empty since everyone from the day markets had gone home for the day, thereby providing Belyx with a momentary reprieve from having to blend in with the crowds and hide under the shadows.

As she made her way passed the bustling night markets and towards the docks, the sound of the sea called out to her like a quiet siren song. Anger surged through her veins as a singular thought looped around her head. Majeria had been so foolish to declare war on her peaceful kingdom.

Belyx's fists were clenched tight. It would be easy to use the Order to threaten Majeria. Yet she reminded herself that innocent families resided there too...this conflict was being orchestrated by Majeria's palace alone.

No matter how much temptation wrestled within her, Belyx could not bring herself to board a boat and take matters into her own hands. Her mother, although a timeless woman of wisdom, had made a grave mistake in attempting to single-handedly combat an entire kingdom. Belyx would not make this same error.

With a heavy heart, she turned away from the boats and sought refuge in another place—one that always managed to quell these confusing emotions swirling inside her blood. This haven had remained unchanged since being built six months ago. Standing proud near the center of Aikradal were three statues: one of Belyx's grandmother posed prim and proper while holding a rose, another of her mother, striking an elegant pose but also encapsulating strength, and then, her father's statue—serene despite all the turmoil he endured during his last thirteen years until his unfortunate death...a death caused by none other than Belyx.

Belyx pushed through her tumultuous memories of the night she had to battle him. Aydevko, a sinister and wily fake advisor to the throne, had deceived them all and tried to exterminate all humans. It broke her knowing her father was so consumed in his grief that he made a deal with an evil entity. *Grief wields a poison like no other.*

Kneeling at the flowers nestled about the statues, Belyx found herself praying for help as tears streamed down her face. No ruler of Keyica had ever dealt with a declaration of war before. Her limbs were heavy as she took in the enormity of the situation. Everything around her seemed to be moving faster than normal and she was unable to make a single decision or take any action.

All of a sudden, a faint scuffling sound broke through her thoughts. In an instant, Belyx had two daggers drawn. But when she peered closer into the shadows, familiar features illuminated in the moonlight—it was Enzo.

He poked his head out from behind the corner and slyly quipped, "thought you could go on a stroll without me?" Belyx rolled her eyes at his usual antics but couldn't help but smirk as she re-sheathed her blades. She took note of his simple black attire; like what he wore when they met a year ago, when he was still a thief running through alleys.

"Well, it wouldn't be complete without the dangers of the gangs lurking in every corner," Belyx replied as she wrapped her arms around his tall shoulders, noting how broad they were compared to their slimmer forms when he ate only one meal a day. "This almost feels like old times."

Enzo shrugged but stepped closer nonetheless, drinking up the warmth of their embrace. "Not quite...you would have to chase me around and betray your guards to save me." The two shared hearty laughter that echoed throughout the cobbled streets.

A shiver ran down her spine as he embraced her again. "Don't forget looking for body doubles in mausoleums," he whispered in her ear.

Belyx couldn't hold back a chuckle. "At least they didn't come to life like in Death Strikes." She *had* read the book...and surprisingly enjoyed it, hating Enzo for the book-loving now.

His mouth curved upwards in a smirk as he brushed back a lock of her wig. "That was the hottest thing you have said, my Queen."

She narrowed her eyes at him, faking offense. "Are you disrespecting your queen?"

Without warning, his lips crashed onto hers. He pulled away with that same condescending smile she both hated and loved. "What queen? I only see Doneque."

Belyx let out an exasperated sigh, taking two steps back. She had broken their agreement and he knew it.

Enzo lifted his hands, brows raised in amusement. "We agreed no more assassin work. Visiting a memorial? I don't think that counts. You found a loophole in my own ultimatum, love."

"May as well not waste the time it took to get here," Belyx replied, striding towards the night markets of Aikradal; Enzo's beloved spot where he could be himself—not solely her advisor. The fragrance of fish and spices greeted them as they drew near, and a feeling of warmth spread through Belyx's veins for the first time since long ago when they were normal people on the street and not queen and advisor.

Her attention shifted to a paunchy merchant whose specialty was Fire Lizards—grilled goat-eating lizards with a natural spicy flavor embedded deep within them. Enzo's treasured delicacy from years gone by.

Belyx purchased two of them on a whim, handing one over to him with a cheeky grin. Enzo's mouth and eyes widened as he caught sight of the treats, and he let out an excited yelp. "My favorite! You remembered."

"I remember many things."

The way the meat sizzled and oozed fat and oil around the stick made all sensations heighten for Belyx; her mouth was already watering before taking even one bite...though the spices were too strong for her taste.

They sat down together beside a charming fountain, its shining waters reflecting the night sky, contentedly feasting on the delicacy that brought so many fond memories flooding through her mind as they reminisced about stories from days long gone by.

Here, far away from court politics and strict royal decorum, Belyx and Enzo could be themselves again—the thief and assassin duo who had once worked side by side towards a common goal.

Enzo devoured his snack as though it had been ages since he last ate. Ignoring Belyx's protests, he proceeded to finish hers as well, her tongue already burning from a single bite of the dish.

Belyx recalled the time when they weren't royalty. A bitter memory came of how he'd "betrayed" her to save his family. Her fists clenched at the thought of what she wanted to do to him at the time for his treachery.

Enzo, who must have noticed her expression, asked, "What?"

"Nothing," she whispered, wishing that he didn't know her so well. It was like they shared a single mind between them.

"You have the face," he retorted, taking one last bite before speaking again. "The 'I am contemplating killing eighty people while also worrying about the future' look."

Not wanting to admit that he was right, Belyx shrugged, and continued, making sure no one else could hear her. "I don't want Majeria invading...what if they attack soon?"

Enzo placed a gentle hand on her leg in comfort and assurance, shaking his head at her words. "We talked about this before. They would need a huge invasion force. That would take months of planning. I'm a hot advisor now. I know these things."

Belyx sighed as she came back down from her anxious high. "I know...I'm just being...hyper-focused." She paused and took a deep breath by habit, trying to steady herself further to explain why she was on edge. "I want to be ready for anything...you know how I feel about sitting and waiting."

"One of your few weaknesses?" Enzo chided.

Belyx waved him off and looked out into the streets. Amidst the revelry and grief, she discovered a solution to their perilous predicament. The sorrowful melody of the older lute-playing man echoed in her soul, stirring her deeply. It struck a haunting chord but still held its beauty...as if finding a way out of the darkness.

"Got it!" Unable to contain her excitement, she leaped up.

Enzo glanced at her before quipping, "You're welcome."

"No, not you! Although your help means a lot." Enzo feigned insult and raised his eyebrow. "Enzo, we throw a ball!"

His eyes fluttered. "A ball?"

Belyx marched back to the palace, her pace increasing with each stride as if pulled by some invisible force. Enzo followed close behind attempting to keep up with Belyx's long strides.

"Wait!" he called out as he caught up with her. "Didn't a ball go poorly for everyone last time?"

With a halt, Belyx turned to him, grabbing both his hands firmly in hers. "We were in a gang conflict then." She tilted her head at the sky. "Now we are free...a celebration that will not only solidify the unity Aikradal has but prove we can handle any future threat like Majeria...Like a tribute to the death of the gangs."

Tightening his lips into a faint smile, Enzo replied, "that could work."

Belyx pushed him against the wall, leaning closer until they were a mere breath away. Feeling like messing with Enzo, she pushed away.

"Why the rush?" he asked, trying to pull her in again.

"Because I have plans to make." With a grin, she gripped Enzo close to her again and absorbed herself into him. Letting their mouths become one. "But first..." She kissed Enzo's cheek. "I need to repay my muse." She brushed her hand on Enzo's upper thigh and he shuddered.

"Guess, we better hurry then." Belyx took the lead as they hustled back to the palace.

Despite the menacing danger and uncertainty of what lay ahead, she knew how to do one thing for sure...how to throw one hell of a celebration.

FIVE

Her taste in dresses would always remain abysmal.

"Are you saying the sash should go across here?" one of the Seedlings asked, The God rest her soul as Belyx tried to add any sort of advice into these designs. Having the Aikradal fashion show a month early to coincide with the Gang Destruction Ball was another brilliant idea she had. It all had to be perfect, and right now, she craved an extra set of tedious eyes, like her former teacher, Madame Jewella. The thought of her shrewd comments and judging gaze made her shudder, but that woman had a talent for commanding a room.

Last Belyx had heard, Madame had fled to Petrovkan to pursue her writing career, and even released a book. Enzo said to avoid it because of its choppy flow and weak prose. That was no surprise knowing Madame.

Now, Belyx was in charge and would rather crawl into the Desert of Polokaz with no food or water than continue in this never-ending slog. "I trust your judgment, Serena. It was only a thought."

The young recruit with wisps of purple and black curls bowed and continued weaving the finishing touches on the gown, the last showpiece. The lilac hues split down the middle with a flood of shimmering tulle nesting between them. The sleeves were ruffled to the elbow with fine detail and the sash wrapped around the bodice in an asymmetrical line.

Asymmetry was foreign to Belyx as she liked things linear and neat, but the Seedlings claimed it was an alteration in fashion, so why deny their judgment?

After thanking the recruits, she moved on to the decorations, which Onka was knotting with deft precision. The idea of the ceiling having twisted clouds crossed Belyx's mind in her sleepless night, but it required more precision than she imagined.

"Blasted material, getting stuck again." Onka fidgeted and ended up setting it down, defeated.

"Let me." Belyx took the bedazzled silk and wet it with her mouth, letting the braids press on through. "No different than making my poison pellets."

Onka exhaled. "Only you could link something so graceful to poisons."

Belyx shrugged. "We all have our specialty." Although she struggled with party planning last year, she found a fondness for it....slightly.

More nobles and palace servants brushed by with table decorations and column swathes. The celebration would commence in no more than a week, so Freyja had a tricky time worrying about security with such little notice. Belyx assured her nothing would go wrong this time and she had total control. Who knew what guests Freyja would let in anyways. After bowing to a growling Onka, Belyx shuffled over to Enzo who wore his *I'm about to disappoint Belyx look.* "You better be in a kidding mood," she said with hands scrunching her sage green chiffon gown with a flowing sleeve cape for flourish...and to hide her knives underneath.

"Sadly, no."

"Why can't they?"

"You know how my tribe feels about human events."

Belyx tilted her head. "They used to attend Wakening Day every year and it wasn't even their holiday." They would celebrate a day when the settlers arrived on "their" continent, but not a celebration of Aikradal being whole again. These fae were starting to grind her bones.

"They aren't ready, especially with the current attitudes."

Belyx waved her gloved hand. "Those are getting better!"

Enzo returned a leaning head. "The protests say otherwise. They are still frequent by the way, even after your big speech."

So much for telling them about Majeria. "The fae were supposed to be our entertainment." Belyx pinched her nose. Their demonstration of their peaceful abilities would prove their solidarity with the people, not just being known as mindless slaves. Also the way they played their various woodwind instruments could calm a crocodile.

"Thanks for thinking of them as just decorations." Acid laced Enzo's typical soft tone.

"You know what I mean? Now what?" *Think, Belyx. A princess, no, a queen always prepares a backup plan.* "I will handle the music." How fast could she get a messenger to the music hall? They would require a hefty coin to perform on such late notice, but Lim would be on it.

Enzo gave her a peck on the cheek. "At least I will be there."

"To keep me safe or to party?"

He wiggled his eyebrows. "You don't need to know, but I do look rather dashing in a suit."

Belyx couldn't agree more.

She planned to flirt a little more with her partner, but Cook came storming in, sweat clinging to her brow and her gray hair in wads. When was the last time she slept? *Now I'm thinking like Madame.*

"Cook. How are the food preparations going?" Belyx asked with a tone as smooth as jade, trying to mask her frustration.

"This ball is foolish, Queen." Cook went right for the kill per usual.

Enzo's eyes widened as Belyx cleared her throat. "I beg your pardon?"

"Don't play dumb," Cook snapped back, almost unrecognizable now. "We should be pouring resources into defenses instead of this fantasy feat."

Letting her anger unfurl like the threads of twine, Belyx gritted her teeth. "It *is* strategic. It is to get people to stand with us *if* Majeria invades." Cook scoffed and turned away, but Belyx kept up her assault. "And who are you to decide anyways? You are not in charge last time I checked."

"I wish you would make things easier like your mother and grandmother did. They wouldn't even be at war. I knew this coronation was a mistake. You are not ready."

With fists almost ruining her favorite dress, Belyx shouted back, "We had no choice! They were both murdered and unluckily I survived!"

As if trying to reel her words in, Cook shook her head. "I only meant due to your youth. You have much growing to do and shouldn't have to manage an entire kingdom."

"Well, we didn't have a choice!" She pulled her arm away from a comforting Enzo.

"Your impulsivity puts this kingdom in danger. We agreed as a council to wait before striking."

"Waiting only brings disaster."

"No. Waiting brings clarity. Your mother lacked this skill. And look what happened to her?"

The palace workers were staring now and Belyx ignored them. "Don't act like you knew them. You abandoned my grandmother for decades until thirteen years ago, and my mother wasn't a coward like you, hiding in the palace all the time."

"Don't speak of things you know little about."

"Then tell me! Tell me why you left my grandmother!" She grew to regret these next words. "And tell me why you couldn't save them if you're so wise?." Was that unfair to say? Absolutely, but family members were out of bounds and Cook needed to understand.

"If you want to be a ruler who disregards her council, then maybe you should rule with Majeria. That is how they run their kingdom."

Belyx would slap her if she wouldn't lose an eye in return. Queen or not, no one attacked Cook. "I wish to be a ruler who the council respects and agrees with my ideas. I took enough shit from the all-men council as a princess. I won't stand for it here."

"Good luck planning this ball by yourself. You're right, I should go if I am such a burden. At least I wouldn't need to coddle a spoiled-brat queen."

With a dagger of poison...the one in her mind, she went for the kill. "Grandmother would be disgusted at what you have become. Why did you come back anyways? You should have stayed in retirement. You dishonor her legacy and she died for nothing if you can't even trust me!"

Cook stilled and Belyx readied for the counterstrike of words, anything to feel something for her dead family again, but Cook left through the kitchens without even a breath.

"Well, that was handled well, Queen," Enzo said with formality.

With a glare, Belyx said, "don't start. She was the one with the aggression."

Enzo shrugged, usually when he didn't agree. He was smart to avoid a fight. "I'll ask my father if he can cook for the ball. At least to prepare something."

"I think that will be best," Belyx said with a nod as she rotated for the stairs. "I will return in a bit. I need to check on things."

Like a festering itch, Belyx clawed her way up to her room and hurled a vase of flowers at the floor. The glass and water spread across the tiled floor; growing, like Belyx's irritation at this whole ordeal. Even after her declaration as queen, Belyx was still being treated like a princess. *I am not. I am Queen!*

Cleaning up her mess so Onka wouldn't have to, Belyx discarded the shards, only to have one slit her finger. It didn't hurt as much as the shock, but she let the blood flow down the sink, along with her tears. Cook had no idea what Belyx was going through. Sure, Cook had lost a friend, but Belyx had lost something more...her roots.

It was broad daylight, so she couldn't take to the streets to beat criminal heads. But there was another place where she could go and be alone...at least for a few hours.

As Belyx found herself sitting in the empty garden, she couldn't shake off the feeling that something had changed, drastically for the worse. It was as if a cataclysmic shift had taken place and it had gone unnoticed by everyone. The silence pressed against her. Did anyone care? The thought cut through her like a knife. With a heavy heart and a troubled mind, she knew deep down that no one did. This party was her burden to bear alone. But then again, perhaps it was better this way. Solitude was what she deserved after all the mistakes she had made. As much as it hurt, being solitary right now put Belyx on the path to making things right.

As Belyx went deeper into the rose gardens, now regrowing from burning down a year ago, she caught the Order healer Amenthya making her way back to her healing hut nearby. Her normal white hair was littered with twigs and her pale skin was splotched with mud. Was she just in the forest?

It had been a shocking revelation to find out her identity as a witch and her apprehension about the fae returning. She thought for sure the healer would quit, but she stayed. Although no one had mentioned what Belyx saw. Anytime she required a salve, Amenthya said very little.

Belyx handled her own injuries if possible now.

What was Amenthya doing in the forest if she loathed the fae? Perhaps she had some medicinal herbs with her, yet there wasn't a pouch or anything of the sort. Belyx waved to her. Amenthya paused and even from a distance, those piercing yellow eyes sent a warning. Hand now dripping with sweat, Belyx quickly lowered it and Amenthya carried on in the other direction.

There was only so much time in a day to handle *that*. If Amenthya wanted to be weird and traipse around the fae-infested woods, then so be it. As long as she continued healing for the Order.

With a sigh, Belyx inspected the disheveled garden, hating Aydevko more for laying waste to it. The plots and shrubs had just started to return, serving as a reminder of the trauma which still lingered. Like the flowers, everyone's resolve was not grown to the beauty they once were. However, the plants were still thriving and so would her people's spirits. A sting of guilt nabbed at her. Cook was only doing her job and Belyx made it personal. Her grandmother always said, *"if you fight dirty, you get mud under your nails forever."*

"What have I done?" Belyx whispered to herself.

Holding a short bud in her hand, she realized there was hope. With time and nurturing, a flower grew to be anything. Cook would be fine, but for now, Belyx had work to do.

The Order passageway groaned open as the stairs revealed themselves. Belyx shuffled down and closed it behind her. The hideout was the only place where her thoughts froze. And she would stall this thaw as long as possible.

The poison flowers were growing nicely. The hemlock had sprouted a couple of white buds and the monkwood ripened to a rich chocolate brown hue. Gathering her vials, she chopped and crushed the plants into them.

The belladonna was another struggle. After some of the smoke fumes snuck into the lair, it hadn't grown the same. If it died, she would need to make a trip up north to gather more seeds. But that would be difficult and Belyx had little time for such tasks..

She missed her signature plant. The once vibrant crimson leaves were now the color of ash. She gave it some water, saying a quick prayer. Although a plant wasn't a person, it was living and provided Belyx an earned comfort.

Entering the next room, she held her breath, each time expecting something else to have died. She released a breath as her black mamba, Gwyar nestled about in her cage. Over the last couple of months, she had been getting slower and slower. Belyx had to give the mice a sedative so Gwyar was able to catch them. Her venom was the most lethal and Belyx ran dangerously low. But how could she harvest from her when her body was giving out?

Gwyar flitted her tongue at Belyx in a greeting, a dead mouse lay in the cage. "You need to eat. It will give you strength." Losing another loved one would devastate her, even if it was just a snake. Black mamba venom saved Belyx countless times and she remained thankful for it.

The other snakes slithered with glee at their dinner. Kali, the pink cobra, gobbled hers down with ease, while Jay, her blue viper, teased her meal, before swallowing it whole.

Mira was smaller, so a slighter catch worked fine, plus Belyx required more of her venom. Its less dangerous of the venoms provided more effective interrogation and a non-lethal escape.

Belyx opened the cage and Mira twisted across her arm, a subtle warmth to the scaly body. Holding the vile she pressed Mira's fangs on it and squeezed. Mira was only a minor krait and couldn't penetrate human skin, meaning she didn't have to be as cautious. She still had trust in all her pets, but the other three were too deadly to risk handling.

After getting her vile filled, she stroked Mira's head as the snake nuzzled against Belyx. "If only you could talk, maybe you could offer some helpful advice after your many years alive."

Mira gave Belyx the best response she could, a slight hiss, and Belyx put her back. The krait dove into its mini pond, relishing in the cold embrace.

On her way out of the hideout, she stopped by the Seedlings in the middle of self-led drills. The older Seedling froze as Belyx stepped in. Belyx didn't come around as much and never wore a gown. "Queen," the dark-skinned Seedling said.

"Carry on. I was only finding some comfort in your training. What rank do you hope to achieve at the next Budding?"

The girl's eyes widened. "I think Stem your grace. I brought my family over from the slave ships and kept them safe. I want to do the same here. I want to be a protector."

Leaf and Stem work would bore Belyx to death, but she respected that some people wanted to do it...like Cook...who she called a coward for it earlier. "I wish you luck then. But I will not give any special treatment for you in the Budding." Belyx labored to say it with a serious face. It would be her first time running the Budding ceremony, where Seedlings were tested and ranked into Thorn, Leaf, or Stem. She would most likely pass everyone. How could she deny anyone missing out on this chance to help the palace when it was so needed as of late?

Aydevko and the fae decimated the Order, but they were working to rebuild their reputation. This group was formed from a time of tremendous sorrow in Aikradal's history. Who knew a team of angry, but determined women would have turned things around. This group would continue to do so as well.

While watching the fresh recruits train, another idea manifested in Belyx. The Order remained unexpected and her mother was killed because she used the fae against Majeria, not the Order. If Majeria truly brought their armies here, then nothing would prepare them for what her assassins would bring. They would have the king and queen of Majeria down in days.

Wait, Belyx.

It was a good plan, but Cook was right. Belyx had to observe before attacking. She would handle the ball first, and then once that entitled and murderous kingdom showed its hand, she would be the first one to cut it off.

Six

If Belyx was allowed to have her moment, then Enzo deserved one tenfold. There was no getting through to her sometimes. What frustrated him the most was how she still clung to her old habits of running away to her Order hideout when things got too overwhelming to handle.

I wish she would come to me.

All last year, she was the one saving and helping him, but now he had a hard time repaying the favor.

After saying farewell to the planners, he set off to check on his family. The idea of Belyx hosting a ball was daring, and it meant Enzo had little time for them. After years in isolation, he found it difficult to spend enough time with his tribe.

His parents weren't in their palace chambers, meaning they had to be back in the forest. Enzo ran his fingers through his hair; it was getting a bit long and he'd need a trim. He hadn't intended on visiting his old home on his own, yet it would be pleasant to inspect things and maybe inquire about the still-infected fae.

Etched into Enzo's mind were the blank expressions on his father's faces, like black ink that refused to be erased. He, a fae and son to them, found it difficult to trust them—no wonder others were skeptical. All he wanted was for them to comprehend this curse was abnormal; fae had been peaceful since the dawn of time.

The fragrant air enveloped Enzo as he slipped out of the palace grounds and plunged into the forest. Captain Freyja had urged him to take an escort, but Enzo was certain his powers would protect him.

My abilities.

A warm coil snaked through his veins. For years he had been powerless on the street, living in fear of using his abilities. That mistake would never be repeated. His flame was a part of him, like a second heart. Not calling to it again would be like never seeing a lover again. *I couldn't imagine if I never saw Belyx.*

She loved him before and after the truth of his identity was revealed. She didn't care if he was a thief or a powerful fire fae; Belyx cherished him. Why didn't she show him more of her love during these difficult times?

Rebuilding a kingdom proved to be a slow process, but he knew the streets better than anyone and improvements had been made.

The sun shone over the day's hustle and bustle of factories and carriages. He heard children's laughter coming from the academy and people appeared happier...until Enzo walked by.

Belyx claiming most of the people had regained their respect for the fae, was exaggerating. Enzo understood too well what it felt like to be stared at for being different. His pointed ears, angular features, and an array of tattoos marked him out. Back in the street times, it was a wonder how he kept his identity hidden. He absentmindedly touched his ears—the thought of what he had to do to them every couple of days still filled him with dread. *Never will I hide again.*

The people cleared the way as if Enzo would roast them all alive if they came too close. It wasn't that the people were rude to his face, but Enzo had studied human habits as a thief and they all closed up like he would steal their souls.

Enzo continued with a nod and smile, needing to show them he was peaceful. One day, they would understand.

When he arrived at the forest's edge, his fathers' almost-opened restaurant awaited. They'd built it on the border of the forest with a desire to share their fae cuisine, Gink insisting food united even the wickedest beings.

"Enzo!" Gink shouted as he embraced his son. Thano came out of the building too, hands covered in paint. The outside had a modern touch to it with high widows and carved flower trims. It was painted a mint color with lavender swirls. They named the restaurant A Taste of Sehrlic. It was catchy while staying original. How many would indulge in fae-made delicacies?

"It looks great."

Thano waved a purple and green hand. "Of course, you came after the hard labor. Nice one."

Gink swatted his partner. "Enough of that, Than. Come on Enzo, come in and try some samples. You still love Pala Cake right?"

With one mention of the sweet, yet savory pastry, Enzo was a child again, scarfing every piece of it. Were they going to make that for the humans? It was considered a true fae delicacy. "You know I'm in."

The inside of the restaurant was almost finished. Comfy chairs, carved from wood and tables adorned with lush foliage surrounded him—a more luxurious version of the Sehrlic forest. This experience was truly immersive.

"You can be impressed. It was all me," Gink said while fanning himself. "Hidden nature fae talents."

"I have to say I think the people will enjoy this." The walls caught most of Enzo's attention; carved with beautiful paintings of trees and fae glyphs.

Thano cooed. "I know your unsure voice. It hasn't changed even after all those years." Enzo stilled. How could they talk about that time when they were trapped and Enzo was out on the street?

Enzo swallowed. "I am not seeing an attitude improvement from the people. Don't tell the queen though."

Gink poked his head out from the kitchen. "Don't worry about it. This food will reassure them we have a place here."

If only it were so easy. "It will take time."

Gink came out with the steaming Pala Cake and set it down. "It is always business with you. Relax a little."

Enzo took a bite of pastry, almost too upset to eat now, but no bad mood could resist that flakey crust. The berries and spices were an epic book series on his tongue. His taste buds churned with the flavors of every fruit in existence, as if he had drunk from a jar full of cranberry juice mixed with blackberries and chocolates. He felt as though he was tasting things for the first time, but at the same time, it all seemed familiar. The sweetness swirled around his teeth and into his gums before sinking deep into his stomach.

Shaking off his trance, he responded. "Well, sorry my partner is worried about an invasion and you all refuse to help."

Thano shook his head. "Enzo. The tribe agreed we wouldn't show performers for this ball. We need to stay cautious for now. Unveil this hate slowly, like an old salve."

"I have a favor then." They raised their eyebrows with matching green eyes fluttering. "Can you cook for the ball at least? Belyx's cook, um, fell ill."

The faes eyed each other and smiled. "Now that we can do!" Gink replied with a squeal. "I'll prepare a menu!"

"Try not to make it weird," Enzo said. Don't spook them with Esara in the beginning."

Thano scoffed. "They don't know snails like the ones we cook."

Although Enzo used to enjoy them too, he ate more human food than anything.

He downed the last of the cake and Gink took the plate. "We are proud of you, En. You saved us after all that time."

"And even went against his own identity and lost his abilities. You're lucky the gods gave them back to you. That is very rare," Thano added.

"I never lost it...for good. I mean I pulled Belyx from Scandeni's spell with no powers. That had to be something."

His fathers grew quiet, most likely recalling the time he stole from people as a thief, a severe immoral crime to their gods, but Enzo had to do it to survive. "Fae magic is rather finicky," Thano replied. "Anyways, how about you assist us with the last of the embellishments? The day is still young and you hardly see your fathers or tribe."

Enzo groaned to himself. Decorating for the ball had taken up a lot of his time. "Advising is not easy. Especially for Belyx."

Gink cooed. "She is an amazing queen." He handed him some dirty pots and he proceeded to wash them.

"You both seem to be the only ones to think so. Everyone is underestimating her youth."

His fathers laughed while chopping and stirring a stew. Kern soup, made from fresh onions and carrots. "Humans are strange about age," Gink said. "Why do they match wisdom to a number? I've seen kids say the wisest things. Even better than mature beings."

Enzo shook his head as he dried the pot. "She can be...impulsive."

Thano chuckled. "What effective ruler isn't?" He blew some hair out of his hands to speed up Enzo's drying. "A little help over here. I hate the flint."

Of course, they declined newer stoves and still used an older model one. With a snap of his fingers, a spark lit the kindling; the soup already bubbling.

"Definitely gonna serve that at the ball," Gink said as he tried some.

Enzo smiled, but it went down as a thud came from the front of the restaurant.

"Can you check on that?" Thano asked. "I think some customers are curious! Invite them in!"

Enzo rushed over, where the glass had shattered, and a small flame roiled on the wooden floor. Someone had thrown a fire bomb!

"Get a water fae and fast!" He burst out the door and scanned the way, focusing on his fae hearing, which never let him down on the streets.

"Quick, this way!" A kid said to another. It came from the west. Enzo slipped off his hard-to-run loafers and sprinted after them.

No human could outrun him thanks to his increased speed and stamina. He found them, shoving one another as they attempted to flee. They messed with the wrong fae this time! The people gasped as he pushed by and he smiled when the criminals were in sight. No one would hurt his family again.

The two boys were in their teens and were slowing down. One of them screamed when he approached. "Enough. You will report to the palace for your crime!" Enzo shouted.

The people around him whispered derogatory things about what he was doing.

Wait until they see what they did.

One boy spat. "Go back to the swamp, monster!"

He was no monster. Humans showed it more often than not. *Now I sound like Aydevko.*

Enzo closed the distance and the people swarmed him. "Aikradal business. I am the royal advisor, taking these criminals in."

"Leave those boys alone!" a woman in the crowd hollered.

The boys were panting with nowhere to go. "Come back with me and we can discuss punishment." He reached for them when a glass bottle slammed into his face. The shards left blood as he grunted in pain. The boys tried to slip by him, but he grabbed one of them, who kicked and clawed to escape. *Stop fighting.*

More people closed in on him, shouting vulgar remarks he had never heard before.

"Get away from me!" Enzo yelled, but the people came to the boy's rescue. A wave of fear washed over him as he recalled his helplessness on the streets, hopeless and vulnerable to marauding thugs. He was on his own then, without anyone to save him - until Ren showed up. Even though Ren had given him such hope at that moment, he was still unable to save them from being killed years later.

His body shuddered, and his head pulsed with agony. His breathing came in ragged gasps. The people around him shrank away from his torment, their eyes open with terror. Their alarm spurred the fire inside, summoning it to life. It ripped through his skin and burst forth as a sheet of orange flame.

The boy collapsed on the floor, his mouth hanging open in a devastating scream reverberating through the air. His right wrist pulsed with sweat and his skin turned a deep crimson red, matching the panic in his eyes. *I burned someone...again.*

Enzo reached out to offer assistance, but the boy retaliated with a handful of dirt, stinging Enzo's eyes. He recoiled in shock as the nearby people backed away from him, horrified by what had just occurred. Tears brimmed his eyes and a tight knot formed in his stomach as he turned away and ran back to the safety of the forest. This was far from over.

Seven

Cook had been behaving oddly since her grandmother passed away, and there was only one person who could explain why.

She realized Cook and her grandmother were close, but she sensed something deeper between them—a mystery that she was determined to uncover.

Ponka, a woman from her grandmother's past, provided cosmetics and disguises for the Order until one day she quit without explanation. Belyx had enlisted her services for several Order missions after. Like last year, when Enzo and she had to mislead the leader of Whispers into believing the leader of the Berserkers was dead—for which they contrived a fraudulent head. Their attempt almost succeeded; however, the Whispers figured it out...barely.

Belyx would never forget what Ponka said about Enzo. *"No potent feelings are pleasant...even the good ones."* That was an understatement of history. The emotions she felt for him were intense...especially as of late, but she thanked The God they had found each other. Enzo was her partner, her everything. A yearning told her to go to him for assistance, yet she had risked enough lives through her rashness. If she was to end any danger, it would have to be by her own hand.

If Ponka was right about him, then she wondered what other life advice she could bestow upon her. The absence of her grandmother lingered; even Madame's peculiar proverbs were strangely missed. A shudder ran through Belyx as she pondered it, praying that her mind would forgive her.

The streets were clearing out for the evening as Belyx ventured to Ponka's home, where she resided in one of the lower rings, as was customary for most artists. A musky scent settled around the vicinity. As her rule endured, the separation of classes would fade piece by piece. It was unfair to expect individuals to live in poverty due to their employment. Everyone had a significant and equal role to play.

The house greeted Belyx like an old friend, with worn doorknobs and faded bricks built in it. She knocked on the door. Nothing. She tried again, shifting uncomfortably on her heels. Where was she? It was too late for someone of her young age to be out at night. Maybe she had retired for the evening.

The door opened…unlocked, which was also unlike the cautious ally of her grandmother's.

Unsheathing her knives, she stepped into the doorway. Her breath hitched. Ponka's stuff; all of her plaster tables, her stacked-up canvas, and even her herb collection…was gone. What remained was worn-out furniture and the stench of death. Ponka had forewarned about a final farewell from her, though she often gave obscure statements. Something had happened here.

A sudden chill coursed through Belyx as she bent down to inspect the broken dish. Before the scream left her throat, a tight cord wound around her throat, strangling her desperate attempts to breathe. She struggled to grasp for anything to stop the person behind her. With each gasp of air blocked by the ever-tightening noose, Belyx's fingers edged closer to their unknown attacker whose height matched her own.

The assailant had her in a vice-like grip. Who was it and why were they here? As lights danced across her vision, she surveyed for something to save her. She found a pot of gooey adhesive and with one swift motion she sloshed both herself and the assassin into it. The assassin howled in fury as Belyx twisted to the front and kicked them away with a force like thunder, breaking the deathly cord from around her neck.

The attacker moved with a sinister grace, her black clothes reminiscent of the Order's garb. The attacker's hood concealed any detailed features from view. Fear and adrenaline filled every cell of Belyx as she readied herself for a fight. In a blink, the assassin sprung from her chair like a wild animal and kicked Belyx with all her might. She braced herself, but was still hurdled into the wall, crashing against it with a sickening thud.

The assailant maneuvered like a dancer. *Petrovkan dance fighting.* She had witnessed a similar style last year when she and Enzo infiltrated the Whisper hideout. Was it a Whisper here now? Or was the Kingdom of Petrovkan in Aikradal territory in search of information? If so, what had they come for? What secret did they seek from Ponka?

Her questions had to wait as the woman twirled to the ground and sent a stern kick right into Belyx. She grabbed an abandoned pot and slammed it against her face. With a flip, the assassin was up, a knife spinning in her deft hands like a miniature cyclone.

Voice still raw from the cord, Belyx flung her knife at her opponent, but the agile dancer kicked it aside and charged forward, undeterred. With a sidestep out of the way, Belyx hooked her arm around the attacker's neck, pulling her off balance. Seizing the opportunity, Belyx pushed her into a nearby wall with a powerful throw.

The assassin was quick to recover, another hidden blade now prominently displayed in her hand—most likely coated in poison. Belyx weaved through a flurry of strikes before maneuvering to the left, smashing her elbow into the girl's face with an echoing crack. The woman drifted back momentarily, giving Belyx just enough time to take hold of her entire body and fling her like a ragdoll across the room—straight into an empty table that shattered under her weight.

With a breath, Belyx held the attacker down as she squirmed. "Who do you work for and why are you here? Belyx ripped the mask off to reveal a girl no older than sixteen, her pale face still soft from inexperience; her eyes fluttered with fear.

Belyx reached for her non-lethal venom when the girl snatched a dagger and pointed it towards her, but Belyx slammed her arm away and the blade dropped to the floor. In the blink of an eye, the girl popped something in her mouth: a pellet of some sort.

"What was that?" Belyx tried to pry it away, but it was too late. If it was poison, she would be dead in minutes. Before she could use her antidotes, the girl tackled Belyx into the wall.

A dazed feeling crawled up Belyx as the girl's lips turned purple, most likely dying from Myrtux poisoning. Whoever this assassin worked for had a tight hold over her psyche or she was loyal beyond measure. Whichever it was, the Order would need to hear about it quickly if there was any risk of espionage or invasion.

Despite the heavy ache in her bones and muscles, Belyx rose to her feet and peered outside for anyone else witnessing the incident. Thankfully it was only her.

Adrenaline coursing through her veins like fire, Belyx sprinted as fast as her battered body could carry her. With every labored step, a burning gaze prickled the back of her neck sending shivers down her spine. She felt certain someone was watching her.

Although the tea was as nasty as sludge, it helped to dull her ache; both mental and physical. Belyx forced herself to swallow the rest of it before handing the cup back to Onka. She returned her attention to the dress designs. They had a couple of finishing touches remaining—almost ready for the ball in a couple of days. Invitations were sent out earlier that morning and Belyx hoped the citizens would attend. She longed for some sort of victory.

Belyx had a servant summon Cook to break the news of the spy. She thought this was a well-timed opportunity to bury their quarrel and concentrate on the kingdom's needs which mattered most.

The poor Seedlings were struggling with some simple finishes on the gowns. With her grandmother and Madame Jewella gone, not many people with such impeccable design skills were left besides Enzo's fathers.

Which was another issue...Enzo had not come back the previous night and she became apprehensive. He was with his fathers, so perhaps he stayed out of nostalgia. It was refreshing to observe him re-bonding with his tribe...luckily, he still had one.

Belyx helped hand sew some hems and stitches, but needles were never her forte, despite her deftness for knives.

"Mind if I assist?" a familiar voice called from the design room. Cook had shown after all, wearing her customary apron and skirt. Her hair was up in a neat braid and her face appeared more alive than usual. Belyx rushed to hug her without giving her time to think.

Cook held her for a while. "I see we have come to our senses."

Belyx pulled away. "I am still proceeding with the ball." Were they going to fight again?

"No, flower. I meant me. You were right and I'm sorry."

In every disagreement, there are always two sides. "I shouldn't have said those things about you and grandmother. It was unfair. You both were so close. It was like you were family."

Cook waved a struggling Seedling away and went to work on the needle and thread. Who knew she possessed these talents too? "You had a brilliant idea that I was unable to see due to my fears. Fears of losing anymore Velenas."

She and Belyx shared the same anxieties. It was amusing how two opposing forces often had similar thoughts. Belyx laid her needle aside as she knew she couldn't be of assistance. "I was so desperate to learn more about you and grandmother, I went to visit Ponka last night."

Cook kept sewing. "She was gone, wasn't she? She always liked to run."

"I didn't mean to sneak around, but it seems as if my wisdom is fleeting here."

Cook laughed. "I know. I am not helpful either in that sense. I prefer to handle things with force, but that seldom works."

Now for the part Belyx dreaded. "There was an assassin there looking for her, using a Petrovkan fighting style."

This made Cook freeze. "You're joking."

"What does it mean?"

Cook licked her lips and leered at Belyx. "It means there are other players in this game. Ponka was smart to escape."

These answers were getting them nowhere. "What can we do then?"

Cook stitched up a dress and moved on to the next one. "I have some contacts in Quoxia, where I was raised. I will look into it. In the meantime, you need to make sure this ball amazes the citizens. These dresses are splendid. Dara would be pleased." Even the mention of her name made Cook waver.

"You were the best of friends."

Cook laughed, fighting her tears. "We were as close as friends could be. We did everything together; growing into older adults, working for the Order, doing missions, stopping tyranny. It was all a jolly time."

"What made you leave then?"

Cook let out a colossal breath. "Your grandmother married and became queen. So she had little time for the Order. She had to raise a family...run a kingdom. I couldn't work without her anymore. So I went back to Quoxia."

Belyx couldn't imagine such a friendship like that. To watch a friend separate like sap on a hot day was unthinkable.

So that was why Cook left. "What forced you to come back then?"

Cook chuckled again, wiping her brow. "She asked me. Said that dangers were afoot after your mother's death. How could I say no to Dara?"

No one did. Belyx had learned that the hard way

"It was a difficult task to do. Just remember your relationships, Belyx. Never stop listening to your heart and fight for love. Always."

They sat in silence for a bit and Cook brushed off her apron. "Well, let's call these Seedlings back in here and maybe have a proper sewing lesson. Including yourself, Queen. Madame Pompous may be gone, but I think you are teachable yet."

The Seedings came back and Cook showed them some basics while Belyx still struggled, but at least the recruits were successful.

After finishing up, a Leaf approached Belyx with a face as pale and stark as the wintery snow blanketing the ground. "Your Majesty. There was a fae attack yesterday in the markets. A citizen was burned."

Belyx's heart thudded in a staccato rhythm as the fear of the infected fae consumed her. She had get to the forest before it was too late. Gasping for air, she sprinted past the Leaf, but she stopped her. "Queen, wait."

Taking little time to pause, she turned. "What?"

"The fae who burned the boy. It was the fae advisor...your umm partner, Enzo. He is up in your chambers now."

Belyx didn't bother to ask any more questions as she made her legs move, each step a painful attempt at regaining faith in what she was about to do. What had Enzo done this time?

EIGHT

Belyx was right on time.

Enzo barely had time to change before she barged in, with that look of fire in her eyes...*and I thought I was a fire fae.*

"What happened?" Belyx began the fight as usual.

"It isn't what you think. They started it!" Enzo let his emotions fly.

"Who? The kid you *burned?*"

"They vandalized my fathers' restaurant!"

"So you used your power on them?"

Enzo closed his fists. Why was she not getting it? "I was trying to take him in for punishment and he fought back, along with *your* citizens." That was a low blow, but she needed to hear it.

"Enzo. The people are respecting the fae again. How could this happen? You didn't need to burn them. Who knew you had such anger?"

"You're one to talk, acting out of anger. You nearly killed me last year."

"I thought you were a traitor, Enzo."

"The people surrounded me and called me all kinds of nasty names, but you never see it or believe it!" Even his fathers refused to think rationally about this, saying the attack wasn't that bad.

After he ran back to the forest, his fathers had already fixed the mess and went on like nothing had happened. Enzo wracked himself in guilt for how he yelled at them for not doing anything. They were the almighty fae, why would they let the people do something like this? He hoped Belyx would be on his side, but that hope failed like a flame in the rain.

Belyx kept her arms crossed, scratching them as she did in her anxiety. "So where did you go after? Why did I have to find out what happened from a Leaf?"

"To avoid a situation like this, Belyx."

"Well, now I have a major mess to clean up. The people are scared of another fae attack...I—I thought the fae were zombified again."

"Well, at least my tribe has to be under a spell to do heinous things. What are the human's excuses for acting that way?"

"That is my kind you're talking about, Enzo," Belyx replied with acid. "Are you saying all humans are bad then?"

"No. Of course not." Belyx was nothing like the other humans. "But, I think you are having a hard time seeing how the people do not like the fae."

"I wonder why?"

"Excuse me?"

"You heard me." Belyx was ready for blood in this duel. "They killed so many people last year."

"Under. A. Curse."

"Enzo. I know they were, but the citizens don't."

"Why can't we tell them? Oh right, your precious family name."

"If they found out my father was making deals with a dark force, they would usurp the kingdom. We would have more than just a takeover. It would be ten times worse than the gangs. Please, set your feelings aside."

"At least I have feelings! I am not some lifeless statue who can shut them off at a flip of a lever."

"I feel things, but I can't afford to show them. If I do, our enemies grow closer and closer and use it against me."

"Then let me help you." Enzo stepped toward her, but Belyx kept her distance, as if afraid of him...like everyone around here.

"I don't need anyone's help to stop this threat. I have my plans for Majeria."

Enzo pretended to look around. "Oh? I didn't realize all of the people setting up this stupid ball weren't helping, or the guards keeping us safe day in and day out. My mistake…"

Belyx lashed a finger at him. "You know I didn't intend it like that. I meant no one else needs to die for me. And also…" She marched passed Enzo to the balcony. "If this ball is so stupid, then perhaps you don't need to attend. Join the rest of your tribe and be unhelpful."

Belyx was only lashing out—she did that more often than not. "You don't mean that. We work so well together."

With a long gulp, Belyx avoided eye contact. "I am finding your loyalties lying elsewhere. I get they are your tribe, but Aikradal is mine and I will protect it too. Leave."

Meeting her challenge, Enzo stayed. She fought well with blades *and words*. "Don't do this, Belyx. You just don't understand what I have been through."

"Don't I? I lost everything. All my family. You still have yours. Go stay with them…forever."

She always brought that up, like a bullet she saved on her person…waiting for the right moment to fire it…and every time, it went right into Enzo's heart.

Slamming the heavy door behind him, Enzo stormed out of the palace. He wanted to scream and shout his frustration into the sky, but he had to maintain his composure. As he reached the walls, he saw the hustle and bustle of vendors, planners, and decorators all hard at work preparing for the ball that he wouldn't attend.

Good riddance.

Belyx was blinded by her false sense of privilege and unwavering hope that failed to recognize the blatant injustice embedded in the streets. As tensions began to rise, it became clear that humans would take sides with other humans, disregarding morals or truth, leaving Belyx hopelessly vulnerable to the prejudice and bigotry of an unjust society.

Enzo couldn't help but wonder when the time came if he had the choice, would he side with the humans or the fae?

A pit wrestled in his stomach as he stepped out. Faint whispers caught his attention. Someone was talking, but the words were lost in the wind. He spun around, scanning the crowd for signs of anything unusual. But all he felt was a sick tightening in his stomach, warning him that this ball would bring about something evil.

You're just being paranoid. Let Belyx have her plan and her perfect world.

All would work out, but for right now, Enzo needed to be away from the humans.

Nine

The ballroom was alive with anticipation as the crowd of elegantly dressed people formed a ring around the makeshift runway. Voices hushed in excitement as the first model stepped onto the platform, ready to showcase Belyx's newest collection.

Belyx stood with trembling hands, her nerves on edge. No matter how hard she had worked these past few days to make sure everything was back to normal, it felt like it would never happen. Enzo was still angry and things were different than they used to be. She wished that somehow, someway, he'd come back and everything could go back to how they were previously. But deep down, she knew nothing would ever be the same again.

She had roamed the streets the previous night, hoping to find him; even considering a venture into the forest. But she was sure he would come back when he was ready.

Eyes straining, she scanned the ball crowd for his delicate but handsome face, and that smirk he always gave when he was right—he may have been correct this time. Aikradal was still recovering and she remembered her grandmother's positivity which helped her through it—she now understood why. The reality was like a light in a window, offering only one clear view of what was hidden. The darkness was hers alone to face.

Stepping onto the dais, Belyx surveyed her guests. Hundreds of eyes shone back in enthusiasm, eager to hear what their beloved Queen had to say. "Thank you all for coming this evening. I am glad you were all able to make it on such short notice. We will start with the dress showing. It is slightly early this year, but I assure you, it will be worth it. Get ready for ten fresh styles to add to the stores for purchase. Thank you for supporting our shop vendors. Let the show begin!"

Belyx stepped back, a cue for the start of the music. The band began to play, their passionate strings echoing off the walls of the room. Lim's face had drained of color at their steep cost, but it was necessary—the melodies had a way of captivating an audience like a spider in a web.

The models walked to the beat and showcased the designs. The colors were vibrant like brilliant stained glass, and the shapes were intricate and delicate with patterns emerging from within them. A gasp of awe left her throat as she examined each piece, realizing that these artworks were beyond anything of her abilities. *Nice work, Seedlings.*

The opening look turned many heads; it was a tight, emerald-green gown with gold sequins that sparkled in the lights. Leaf-like motifs ran along every seam to give it a unique botanical pattern. It was daring and unexpected for the fashion line, and a plethora of jaws dropped at its sight.

The rest of the dresses impressed, but the final look was incredible. The audience erupted into cheers and applause as the model stepped onto the runway in the most exquisite gown of all. It was an asymmetrical sash dress, the one Cook had helped her with. The delicate lavender silk shimmered in the spotlights, and the arms were encrusted with sparkling jewels that glittered like stars. The sash was tied around her neck and flowed in an arc behind her like a royal cape.

The crowd applauded and the shopkeepers exchanged hopeful glances as Belyx approached the podium again, letting the cheers empty her sadness.

"To my staff. You have all done an exceptional job with the finishing touches on my designs. I could not be more proud of the result!" Lying was despicable, though it was her name on the dress line. She made a note to reward them all later. "Now that you are all here, I would like to announce what we are celebrating this day."

The citizens of the upper ring looked up at her, the palace's last thread of hope. Their faces were no longer worn with sorrow but instead beamed with joy for the first time in months. Her grandmother always said that sunshine was the brightest after a storm. If only the rain would never come again.

"We celebrate tonight," the queen declared, "for the evil that had plagued our streets is now vanquished. The gangs are no more!" The people clapped and smiled, united in purpose.

"They threatened our very livelihoods and the values we hold dear to The God. I have made it my duty to protect every one of you from any threat that knocks on our gates." She gazed at Cook who gave her a reassuring nod.

"The continent is ever-changing and there will be kingdoms who don't agree with us and what we do. But when they come to end us, we will stand together—as Aikraldal, the first and strongest kingdom. Let's drink to this unity!"

Onka handed Belyx a glass of sparkling wine and she held it up. "To Aikradal. May we stay strong and never give up the fight."

The crowd echoed her, all sipping their drinks. A quenching feeling embraced her throat as she gulped down the wine. "Cherish the rest of the night here, indulge in Cook's tempting treats and the delightful dishes from one of our fae advisors."

The room went quiet at the mention of the fae, but the next song filled the awkward silence with an upbeat tempo and catchy melody. *I should not have said that,* Belyx thought.

Colorful platters of exotic foods overflowed the nearby tables. Skewers of glistening meats and ripe vegetables piled high, along with trays of delicate pastries and steaming pots of soup. Although she was tempted to try some, her stomach felt taut and distended beneath her gown; it seemed like it could rip open at any moment.

Gink was interacting with the others to Belyx's shock; even managing to make them laugh with his charm. Enzo had exaggerated the situation; the people were slowly becoming accustomed to the fae again. Freyja had handled the vandalism incident by arresting the boys and making them admit their faults. Would it be enough? *Hopefully for now.*

Onka came closer to Belyx, in a simple peach gown, but only to hide her weapons underneath. She was a protector after all. "Great speech, your Highness."

Belyx shrugged. "I feel like I want to melt into a puddle."

"Well, I wouldn't worry too much. Freyja says there are no protests or any active threats tonight. I think we are safe."

Thankful for the guards, Belyx knew the palace was in good hands, but she was more than capable of protecting herself. She donned one of her protective dresses crafted for her the last year—they came in many colors. Tonight, she had the silver one with chiffon twirling around her; yet it could be removed to reveal a leather dress that had a slit along the side for added mobility. And light armor concealed within her bodice. The poisons and knives lay hidden beneath her person too—should anyone try something, they'd receive an unwelcome surprise.

Onka and Belyx continued conversing until a high-pitched scream went through the air, shattering the stillness. Lim's panicked cries reverberated off the walls, shaking Belyx at her core. As Lim ranted about her latest irritation, Onka rolled her eyes in silent protest. "I got it," Belyx said with relief; it was only a "minor" incident.

"I've ruined this brand-new dress I purchased last week!" Lim's hands were balled around a section of her red dress and a tray of food lay scattered across the floor. The Order member servants went into cleanup mode. Belyx counted her breaths as Maria tried to comfort her friend.

Lim shoved Maria away. "No, you old coot. The stain will not come out. I saved up so much money tryin' to buy this."

If this was the worst occurrence at the event, Belyx would take the win. "Master Lim. You are making a scene." Belyx looked to Maria for help who only shrugged.

Tears befell Lim's face. "We just haven't had any events lately and I wanted it to be special."

Belyx grabbed Lim's hand as her tears continued to flow. "I miss your aunt so much," Lim lamented. "We used to do everything together."

Last year, another family member was taken from her, but it didn't feel real until now.

Maria took Lim's other hand and said, "Come on, let's get you cleaned up." Lim nodded in agreement.

"Here." Belyx handed her the key to her chamber. "Take one of my dresses. Pick anyone you like and come back down. It isn't a party without Lim Grenald."

Lim took it and laughed. "Flattered you think we are even remotely the same size, your highness." And there was the old Lim again. "But, I'm sure I can find one that won't swallow me. Lead the way, Maria."

Maria mouthed a thank you and followed her friend.

Those two would never cease to entertain her.

Belyx chatted with the locals, marveling over all the new stores that now thrived without any illegal activity. The prospect of these establishments brought a spark of hope back to Belyx after the recent coolness.

After her feet had nearly given out from dancing, she stopped to catch her breath and take a much-needed sip from her drink. Suddenly, the music shifted and in walked Enzo, wearing a navy blue suit that clung to his body in all the right places, and a bright smile across his chiseled face.

Without a thought, Belyx jumped into his embrace and kissed him in front of everyone, scandalous queen be damned! "You came back." Belyx released her partner and he tilted his head.

"I think I was done with my pity party and wanted to glimpse a new one."

She hugged him again. "I'm so sorry I didn't take your feelings seriously. I don't know why I do that, but I just let the pressure get to me and—"

"You talk too much. Right?"

"Make me stop then?" With a nod to Onka, whose eyes rolled to the ceiling, Belyx dragged him away from the party where they could be alone. She clawed into him with a hunger she didn't know she had. These last couple of days had been hell without him!

He pulled himself free. "Slow down there, your Highness. I wanted to say something first." Belyx tapped her foot and Enzo giggled. "Okay, I'll hurry. I am sorry that I overreacted and endangered lives. I need to have better control of my abilities in those situations. It is still new to me after being gone all those years and it's like a second brain sometimes."

Belyx felt a twinge of envy as she watched Enzo's power grow and protect them from danger. Though she could never possess it, it didn't matter—she was confident in her skills and strength to defend herself.

"You do have control, Enzo. I'm so sorry for not believing you—for not trusting you first. You are my partner, and how could I ever doubt that? All this time I was too busy worrying about the kingdom when it's more important to trust you."

"You only wanted to make sure your people respected my tribe again. That made you a little more spirited when there was a snafu."

She loved it when he used fancy words. *Now, enough talk!*

He crashed into her, their bodies dancing in a tempest of kisses. She clung to him tighter, as their tongues explored each other with eager intensity. He was the heat that melted her frozen heart, like a blazing fire on an icy day. And the blade that kept her safe and strong in moments of peril. With him by her side, Belyx was invincible and ready to conquer the world. His beaming smile warmed even the darkest souls.

Belyx sealed them inside a decadent room and their hunger for each other ignited. Enzo grabbed her waist with an eagerness and tossed her against the wall, their lips melding together as she ran her fingers through his thick locks of hair. His tongue moved in languid circles, trailing down to her neck as warmth spread through Belyx's chest like wildfire.

The two of them released their fervor in a flurry and fell back, chests heaving with verve. With skillful grace, she adjusted her outfit and hair, alluringly looking back at Enzo. "Let's saunter out there first and then we can complete the night in bed. I think I'm not ready to part ways with you yet."

Enzo wiggled his eyebrows. "Not even close." *The fae and their stamina!*

They shuffled back to the party, avoiding eye contact with other people. As far as everyone was concerned, they suspected exactly where they had been and it was written all over their faces—that unmistakable afterglow of guilt.

While conversing with a few more attendees, an older lady with a kind face and a gorgeous robe dress kissed Belyx's hand. "You inspire greatness, your highness."

Belyx put her hand to her chest. "Thank you, so much. That means the world to me. What is your name?"

The old lady smiled. "Death."

In a second, a cacophony of shrieks and shattering glass pierced the air. The old woman whipped her head downward, snatching up a cruel dagger from her side. But before she could thrust the blade forward, an arrow flew like lightning into her chest, sending her lifeless body to the ground.

Freyja appeared, pulling Belyx from the chaos that engulfed them. The cries of citizens filled the room as more smiling masks showed up, putting innocent lives to a bloody end. Ichor stained the ballroom floor, and the haunting ringing in her head grew louder as she counted over ten masqueraded figures carrying out these unspeakable acts.

The people screamed in terror as they surged toward the exits, desperate to escape. But the masked assailants slayed anyone who dared to move, their blades dripping with fresh blood while ruin and destruction reigned supreme.

Two attackers advanced on Enzo and his group, but he unleashed a fearsome torrent of fire that incinerated them in an instant. His face determined and unyielding, Enzo declared, "I must find my father!" The flames licked hungrily at the floor around them.

"Wait. The queen—" Enzo took off before Freyja could finish. "Come on, Belyx. Let's get out through the secret entrance."

"How did they get in?" Belyx's eyes widened in shock at the sea of masked attackers, rushed towards them with menacing intent.

Freyja spun into action, her staff whirring as it slashed through the air. Each attacker crumpled to the ground like paper dolls, unable to withstand Freyja's power. "They were disguised as guests."

"Who do they work for?"

Belyx's throat closed as the sound of children screaming pierced her eardrums. In a flurry of motion, she ripped off her outer gown and prepped her battle dress with lightning-quick speed. Nothing would stand between her and the distressed Seedlings that were being slaughtered by these hooligans at the entrance. She was in no mood for Freyja's worries—"Belyx, no!"—as Belyx took off in a sprint, her mind focused on one thing only: saving her people.

"I can't let them die!" This was a stupid idea. The air reeked of death and a crimson hue filled the room, where bodies were strewn like rag dolls. She charged at them in a flash of silver blades, her fury unleashed and she ripped through the attackers. Their wide eyes stared in horror as they barely had time to scream before their throats were torn out. "Go!" Her screams reverberated around the chamber as she commanded her recruits, urging them into battle. Belyx leaped forward, ducking under a slicing blade and plunging her knife into an unsuspecting attacker.

There was too much going on as her mind raced to where Enzo, Onka, Cook, and Freyja were. An assailant swiped at Belyx, but she blocked the blow and sent a counter strike into his nose.

Two of his friends grabbed both of her arms, but she dropped low and slammed their heads together. There were too many for her to fight alone. Why hadn't Freyja followed her?

She flung her knife through the nearest one's heart while dropping the other one with a kick.

Plate in hand, she smashed another's face. How many of them were here? *It doesn't matter. I'm here to kill them all.*

A quiet applause came from the entrance and Belyx recognized those manicured nails anywhere. "Now that, I didn't see coming," Sewek, former leader of the Whispers said. Her hair was cropped to the side and lighted; and of course, she fashioned a cream pantsuit, still pristine as ever.

"You!" Belyx charged, but an imposter slammed her face with his hilt and Belyx fell. With her vision clouded, two more attackers hoisted her up, restraining her.

Sewek clacked closer in her heels. "I recognize that fighting style. Here I thought we would be taking down a precious princess, I mean queen, but it turns out to be the assassin, Doneque to be exact."

Who knew this vermin was still around? Belyx assumed Sewek and her band of clones had fled to whisper in a new place, far from Aikradal. The pain they had caused the kingdom for years was devastating. They knew every detail that transpired here—until Belyx and Enzo found their hideout and Belyx prevented them from killing her partner. Her eyes blazed with rage as she remembered Enzo dying on the ground, about to succumb to death. That would never happen again. Sewek was now facing a different queen; one who would not hesitate to take her life this time.

Belyx spat. "I have no idea who Doneque is. I just know how to fight."

A smile formed on her mostly-nosed face. "I study fighting styles as an art. You fight like that bitch who ruined my precious face last year."

Belyx smiled through bloody teeth. "And I would do it again." Honing all her weight, she fell and took her captors with her. With a roll, she gave them both a clean kick to the face with good measure.

Sewek stood, in her confident state as usual. Belyx didn't know how Sewek managed to plan this attack, but Belyx would end her now. Charging, Belyx took a blade and went straight for Sewek's throat. Sewek stayed still and Belyx found out why.

The wall exploded around her with a deafening crack, and the shattered pieces cut into her skin like jagged knives. She fell to the ground as her vision started to spin, right as a hulking figure made its way into view—The Scorpion! Memories of his hulking spear came flooding back, paralyzing her with fear. His presence loomed over her like a dark cloud, filling the space with an oppressive sense of dread. *Stay calm. you have bested him before.* However, that was the former captain, Thomas, whose body now rested in the ocean.

"My pet is a valuable asset to me. It's too bad that Berserker's leader was so foolish to let him go. Now, he will never know what he could have had!"

This couldn't be! The Scorpion was meant to be dead. But now, he was being controlled by Sewek—the most malevolent person imaginable. "Why?" Belyx gasped out as she struggled to stand from her aching ribs.

Sewek ran her hand over the Scorpion's tarnished armor. He hovered like a statue, and his spear seemed all the more menacing after all this time. "Do you remember your accusation at Majeria?"

It couldn't be.

Sewek laughed. "One look at your face and it was obvious you had no clue about our scheme. Although invading the ball was a snap decision, why not have some fun with a spectacular entrance?"

Belyx hobbled forward and more assailants surrounded her. "So you abandoned your followers? What will they think?" *I need to buy time for the others to escape.*

Sewek scoffed. "They still have their undying loyalty to me!" She shifted her neck, snarling. "We had no choice but to retreat after your little escapade, and I'm sure you know about Majeria, who are just biding their time before they seize control of this so-called kingdom."

Belyx's hands clenched. Sewek was working with Majeria now, but Belyx refused to go down this way. "Where is Princess Vivienne then? Hiding behind her pretty face as usual?"

A smile unfurled from Sewek's sharp features. "Oh, she is on the way and has other plans...especially for you."

Sewek was making a bad deal if she ever trusted those Majerian water snakes. "She won't give you the throne. If she says she is, she is lying."

"Oh, I have no intention of ruling *here*, but I am promised another kingdom. I have waited this long. How do you plan to win now, Belyx? Or are you Doneque?"

With the final strains of her strength, she put one of the masked people in a choke hold, holding a knife to his throat. "I will kill every last one of you if you think you are going to take this kingdom!" She had struggled to reclaim it, yet now it was destined to crumble like everything else.

"Kill them. We have plenty more. Majeria is hungry for revenge." Sewek snapped her fingers and The Scorpion drew his spear.

Belyx let out an ear-splitting wail as she thrust her blade through the man's chest, his blood splattering across her hands and staining her pale skin. A fierce heat barreled towards them from afar; it could only be Enzo—they had a fight on their hands now, a battle against a fire fae of immense power.

The Scorpion's menacing face was hidden behind his onyx mask, but Belyx sensed the eagerness that he was coming for blood.

Her knife pinged off his armor. He swung his spear down and Belyx moved back expecting a counterstrike, but he held still.

"We don't have death planned for you, just yet, your Highness," Sewek said as she snapped her fingers.

Throat closing, Belyx knew this was a trap. In a desperate attempt to escape, she shifted on her feet but was seized in The Scorpion's iron grip. Before she could utter her partner's name, a jarring thud pounded into her skull and she dropped like a stone into the crushing embrace of nothingness.

Ten

Enzo's flames flickered and waned under the relentless onslaught of the horde. For every enemy that fell to his fiery blasts, two more clawed their way forward. The odds were insurmountable, and it was only a matter of time before they would be overrun. With gritted teeth, he fought on, knowing that he might not survive this battle. But even in the face of certain doom, he refused to back down. He would fight until his last breath, cost be damned.

The members of the Order moved into assault formation. They had removed their disguises and stood tall and proud with weapons in hand. Their opponents were numerous, but the Order battled with courage and skill; parrying and thrusting as one cohesive unit.

Snatching a blade from the corpse of a masked figure, Enzo sliced through the nearest assailant. Five more rushed toward him. Two members of the Order blocked their advance, their steel ringing as they collided. One member with long red hair was a ferocious force, felling two enemies in each stroke, letting their blood blot the walls. Enzo spun around, the flames of his power flashing in the night air as he spotted three menacing figures looming behind her.

With a cry of rage, Enzo thrust his power outward and engulfed one of them in embers, but the other two surged forward, knives glinting cruelly in their hands. Before Enzo had a chance to do anything, one of them had plunged their blade into the girl's back. Enzo had no idea how old she was, but he guessed she was not much older than eighteen. He wished with all his spirit that he knew her name...Belyx would have known.

Escape was impossible—the attackers threw him into the wall, his vision blurring from the pain. Then, from nowhere, two vines shot out of the ground, wrapping tightly around each attacker's ankles, and dragged them screaming through an open window.

Gink, stood tall amidst the chaos, beads of sweat rolling down his forehead, glowing arm tattoos blazing an emerald hue as he thrust away enemies with every powerful swing. Every opponent Gink fended off, two more swarmed in to take its place.

"Father!" Watch out! But he was too late as an attacker lashed him in the back.

Enzo unleashed a cascade of flames that destroyed the trespassers. He hastened to his father on the ground and embraced him. "Go, Enzo," Gink whispered. He would recover, but he required time and rest. These invaders were fast and well-trained; where had they come from?

Belyx's shriek riveted Enzo. He singed an assailant as Gink whipped a vine around another foe and hurled him to the floor. After finishing off the adversary, his energy waned. "I love you, Father." Then he pushed past the other defenders when Freyja fell from the top balcony of the stairs.

She rolled forward and quickly regained her footing, her arrows already nocked. With a smooth motion, she raised her bow, drew taut the string, and sent an arrow hissing through the air to strike an enemy's throat. The one who most likely pushed her off. "Where is Belyx?" she asked as more attackers began to appear from the upper stairs where Freyja had been thrown.

Flames swarmed Enzo now as held back more enemies. "She was by the front last I checked!"

Sweat beaded on his forehead as the assassins advanced, and he cursed himself for being so foolish. He summoned all the courage and strength that he could, feeling its power course through him like a fiery current.

Two assailants approached Enzo, but Freyja dashed in and blocked them with her staff. With a resounding thwack, their skulls smacked against the wood.

Another strike came, yet she ducked out of the way. At the same time, an arrow flew off her bow towards another attacker far away. Then Enzo blasted a fire bullet that immobilized another.

They wasted too much time with this fighting. They needed to get Belyx and retreat!

Freyja wheeled around, but more masked foes blocked her path. "You'll never defeat me!" she bellowed as she fired arrow after arrow into the fray.

Surrounded, Enzo wouldn't give up. He'd fight through all of them with his last breath to reach Belyx.

With a scorching blaze, Enzo rushed to the front of the room, sidestepping the motionless bodies of citizens. When he had an unobstructed view of the chamber, his heart plummeted.

The Scorpion held an unconscious Belyx in his massive arms, with the former Whisper leader, Sewek standing by. She met eyes with Enzo and waved while more attackers piled in.

So, the Whispers were behind this attack, and getting their takeover after all this time. They were outnumbered and Enzo had no power left.

Give me more power. Save us. Please.

Belyx was in peril and his gods were silent to his prayers. He stood in a corner, determined not to give up. Heat surged from his fingertips towards the intruders, their piercing screams drowned out by their burning. "Belyx! I am coming!"

A masked figure barged in and cut Enzo's arm. He gnashed his teeth in agony as he grabbed the woman's face, her shrill scream reverberating through the air. His bloodlust rose as he watched her flesh melt away. It felt good to do that—to slaughter all of them.

Enzo unleashed another blow, but a hilt to his jaw sent him crashing to the ground. Harsh kicks pummeled him while he was down and all that raced through his mind was Belyx. Shutting his eyes...perhaps he would be with her once more.

The onslaught ceased and, when Enzo opened his eyes, tendrils of vines were dragging them away. Freyja yanked him upright. The Order women charged for Belyx, but no one could triumph over The Scorpion in combat. The Order assassins dwindled on the main floor as Freyja blew a shrill whistle. "Retreat! Now!" She quivered like she was reluctant to leave her queen behind. After devoting so much to her safety...now it was crumbling.

They trudged back toward the kitchens and Enzo grasped for any hint of fire, but it never answered.

When using your power, if you overfill your well, you may never be the same. Know your limit and never go over it.

Enzo attempted to summon more flames, but it was only a faint spark. "Belyx," he muttered as Freyja pushed him towards the kitchen, firing off more shots at their enemies.

Cook snatched Enzo's hand and dragged him through the door. His father stayed close behind them, panting as if he'd run a hundred miles, and slammed the door closed. As soon as the latch clicked, Cook securely locked it.

As they marched him through a hidden tunnel, Enzo's mind raced. Perhaps this was all a dream and he'd wake up next to Belyx. In his head, he could still see her smiling, teasing him about the book he was reading, then him chiding her in return—embracing and lounging in bed until late in the morning. As if on cue, Belyx appeared in his thoughts, walking towards the balcony. He followed but as he drew closer, her face changed to one of dread—Enzo tried to scream out, yet nothing came out as she plummeted off the edge.

Enzo's vision wavered, and he realized this was no dream—it was reality. A reality that promised to alter his entire world. He attempted to call for Belyx, but she had disappeared. Once more, he had failed her. His agonized cries soon gave way to total darkness.

Eleven

Belyx's eyelids fluttered open, the darkness of her surroundings pressing down on her like a shroud. A throbbing pain pulsed at her temples, and she let out a soft groan, her throat parched. With every breath, the salty tang of the sea air cut through the fog in her mind, bringing her back to consciousness.

"Where am I?" she whispered, her voice carrying above the distant sound of waves crashing against the wood. Her fingers grazed the rough rope that bound her wrists together, and the memories came flooding back: the attack, her capture, and the fate of Aikradal now uncertain.

Her body swayed beneath her, the subtle rocking motion leaving her feeling lightheaded. She was on a damn boat! Belyx forced herself to focus on her surroundings, trying to make out any details that might help her understand where she was...or where she was going. Gone was the dress she'd worn for the ball, replaced with plain attire. What had happened to her?

The moonlit night provided just enough light for Belyx to discern the outlines of barrels and crates piled high around her, casting eerie shadows across the wooden planks of the ship's deck. This was a Majerian vessel, one that had been designed for long journeys through treacherous waters...the only ones that could venture the Sea of Kifalia without being destroyed. As The God intended for some unknown reason.

The ropes they had bound her with bit into her skin as she fought against them. Her breathing came in shallow gasps, and sweat beaded on her forehead. She clung to the spark of rage inside, knowing it was the only thing that kept her alive—that and the knowledge they had underestimated her. Someday they'd pay for that mistake.

Think Belyx. There must be a way out of this.

As she struggled to sit up, the motion sent a wave of dizziness crashing over her, but she gritted her teeth and stayed resolute. She scanned the dark deck, searching for anything that could aid her escape. In the distance, she caught a glimpse of a faint orange light, flickering like tongues of flame. It was the glow of lanterns, positioned strategically by her captors—probably to keep watch over her. The way they were spaced out suggested that they weren't being very careful or competent in their surveillance.

As despair threatened to close its icy grip around her bones, Belyx felt the familiar fire of defiance burn within her. The spark that had driven her to train tirelessly, to master the blades she wielded with lethal grace, refused to be extinguished. The fire that reminded her of Enzo, who she craved to get back to...or was he captured as well—or worse?

Failure is not an option. I will find a way out of this. For Aikradal.

Her gaze locked onto a small piece of broken wood on the deck, sharp enough to cut through rope if she could just reach it. Belyx knew her life and kingdom depended on her ability to escape from these scumbags. Also understanding that biding her time would work, waiting for the perfect moment to make her move. If she tried too early, they would knock her out again.

As the guards paced the front, their lanterns casting eerie shadows, Belyx began inching toward the piece of wood. Emotions surged like a symphony as fiery streaks of adrenaline rushed through her veins.

The pain of her scarred hands was almost unbearable, but she forced herself to keep going. Sweat poured down her face and salty tears streamed from her eyes as she reached out with a trembling arm, struggling to grasp the splintered instrument that would free her from her ropes. With one final push, she grabbed the wood and brought it to her grip in triumphant agony.

"Hey!" one of the guards shouted, his eyes narrowing as he caught sight of her movement. "What do you think you're doing?"

"Nothing," Belyx replied, forcing a tone of innocent confusion. "I'm just trying to get more comfortable."

The guard snorted. "You think we're fools? We know what you're capable of, Queen of Aikradal. Or the former Queen I should add." He laughed with his comrades.

"Then you should also know that I will not be held captive by the likes of you," Belyx retorted, her anger like molten lava.

"That's it!" the guard snarled, stomping towards her. "No more of this goading. We have strict orders to get you to Majeria alive."

"Good to know," Belyx challenged, her eyes locked onto his as she managed to slice at her ropes. *I have nothing to fear then.*

But before she could use it to free herself, the first guard lunged at her, his fist connecting with her temple. Pain exploded and darkness flickered in her consciousness, leaving her crumpled on the cold, wet deck.

Damn them, she thought in the fleeting moments while sleep claimed her.

I will not let this be my end.

As Belyx's world faded to black, she clung with every fiber of her being to the hope that Enzo would come to her rescue. She knew that together, they could overcome any obstacle—even one as formidable as the Majerians.

Belyx held tight to the thought that her courage was shared by those who believed in her, vowing to escape and kill anyone who opposed her; determined to reclaim her kingdom and prove she couldn't be defeated. With that final thought, she drifted into unconsciousness.

The cold, damp floor was Belyx's new bed.

Her eyes struggled to focus in the dim light as they twitched open. Reality seeped into her psyche like the fog that permeated around her as she blinked. The cell she found herself in was a dismal space, walls stained with grime and mold creeping along the crevices, a testament to the neglect and despair that lingered here.

She held her breath and gagged as the fetid odor of decaying flesh and sickly sweet decay assaulted her senses. The air was so humid it felt like a physical presence clinging to her body, suffocating her in its embrace. Every step she took stirred up more of the stench, making it harder for her lungs to expand.

"Awake at last, are we?" a voice echoed from the shadows, startling Belyx. She glanced around, searching for the source, her hand instinctively reaching for the knife that was no longer at her side. *Right, I'm a prisoner.*

A figure emerged from the darkness, his features obscured by the dusk. "I thought you'd never wake up."

"Who are you?" Belyx demanded. her pulse was like thunder, but this unfamiliar prisoner wouldn't see her fear.

"Call me Mave," he replied with a cautious tone. He stepped closer, allowing the faint light to reveal his face—sapphire eyes, cropped blonde hair, and a scrawny build. He reminded her of someone, but Belyx pushed any recognition aside, focusing on what he wanted.

"Where are we?" Deep inside, she knew they were most likely on the island kingdom of Majeria, but she had to hear it.

"Welcome to Majeria's finest accommodations," Mave said with a bitter laugh. "We're in the dungeons right beneath the palace, reserved for only the most distinguished of guests." His humor was getting old fast.

"Great," Belyx muttered, her anger simmering under the surface. "How did the likes of you end up here then?"

Mave hesitated for a moment before answering. "My parents were...taken from me when I was younger. They stood against the tyranny of the Majerian royalty and paid the price. Like they all do." The sorrow seemed genuine, but Belyx couldn't shake the thought there was more to his story than met the eye.

"Sorry to hear that," she replied with a shaky tone, unsure if she should trust him. Her instincts told her to be wary, but his presence also brought an unusual sense of comfort—a reminder that she was not entirely alone in this nightmarish prison.

"Thank you," Mave murmured, his gaze dropping to the floor. "But we must focus on the present. I have been plotting an escape for a while now, but I needed another person. You in?"

Belyx nodded, her mind racing. She knew that time was of the essence—every moment spent in captivity dragged her kingdom closer to ruin.

"Listen," Mave whispered, leaning into Belyx, his eyes alight with a fierce determination. "I've been in this cell long enough to have discovered a weakness in the bars."

"Really?" Hope fluttered like a bee at the prospect of escaping this dank prison. The meager five minutes spent in this dump was enough.

A sly smile played on his lips. "Yes, but it won't be easy. We'll need to act fast and remain quiet."

"Tell me what to do." Her body tensed with anticipation.

"Here." He revealed a small, sharp rock he had somehow brandished despite the close watch from their captors. "We can use this to weaken the bars further. It's slow work, but I've already made some progress."

Belyx marveled at the resourcefulness of his plan and took the stone from him. Together, they worked in silence, chipping away at the weakest points in the iron gate. As they labored, Belyx felt a growing sense of companionship with her fellow prisoner...a bond forged in the shared goal of escape.

After what seemed like hours, the bar gave way with a muted groan, allowing just enough space for them to squeeze through.

"Stay low and follow my lead," Mave instructed as they slipped out of the cell. Shadows clung to them like an old friend as they crept through the dim corridors of the prison, their footsteps muffled by the damp, moss-covered stones underfoot.

As they rounded a corner, Belyx caught sight of two unsuspecting guards, their attention focused elsewhere. Silently, she signaled to Mave, who waved in understanding. With a predatory grace, they each lunged at a guard, subduing them with swift, precise movements before they could raise alarm. Belyx thanked The God for her years of training and experience in hand-to-hand combat, and she couldn't help but admire Mave's skills as well. She would return home before the week was up.

"Come on," he urged, his breath hot against her ear as they pressed on toward the heart of the palace. Most likely the throne room.

As the ornate double doors loomed ahead, Belyx felt a cold knot tighten in her stomach. *Why are we going to the throne room?*

She stopped and Mave shook his hand. "Belyx, come on."

"This seems like a bad idea."

He grasped her hands and a surprising comfort befell on her. His hands were also rather smooth for a prisoners. "There is a secret escape route through the throne room and the king and queen are fast asleep. Don't you trust me?"

Not really, but what choice did she have? Go back to that humid trap? Fat chance. Her thoughts swirled like storm clouds, but she couldn't waste a second; he had led them this far and would carry them the rest of the way to safety.

With one final shared glance, they pushed open the doors, ready to face the unknown together.

The room was a cavernous expanse, its high ceilings lost in dark shapes. Columns of polished black stone stretched up into the darkness, giving the illusion of endless height. A single shaft of moonlight cut through the gloom, illuminating the throne—an imposing seat crafted from bone and ebony. It was empty...the King and Queen must be asleep at this hour.

"Isn't it lovely?" Mave murmured, making Belyx shiver. Maybe she made a grave error. Who was this man? He stepped forward, leaving her standing at the entrance to the chamber.

"Mave, what are you—" she began, but he silenced her with a raised hand.

"Ah, I suppose it's time for the truth to come out." He turned to face her with a cruel smile. "You see, my dear Belyx, I'm not the innocent prisoner you thought me to be."

She stared at him, confusion and fear twisting her insides like a vise. "What do you mean?"

"Allow me to introduce myself properly," he continued, his icy blue eyes glinting with malice. "I am Prince Vincent Rochenda of Majeria, twin brother to Princess Vivienne, who recently...acquired Aikradal."

Belyx's core swirled as the realization dawned. *How could I have been so blind?* She fought back the urge to vomit, bile spiraling in her throat.

"Betrayal suits you well, Prince," she spat, her anger flaring hot against the cold double crossing that gnawed at her core.

"I'm flattered." He drew closer. "But now, I'm afraid it's time for your part to come to an end."

With a swiftness that belied his slight frame, Vincent lunged at her, his fist connecting with her jaw. Pain broke across her face, stars flashing behind her eyes. She staggered but resisted falling, pulling on every ounce of strength she possessed. Vincent came at her again, his martial arts training evident in the precise strikes that aimed to incapacitate her.

Surrender was not an option as she retaliated with gritted teeth, the bruises staining her skin and her split lip leaking blood. She drew on all of her lessons, seeking out his weaknesses—but he moved with god-like speed, thwarting each one of her attacks. Her muscles burned as if on fire; the boat ride combined with inactivity had caused her joints to ache. He was as agile as seaweed in the current.

Despite his slight frame, he caught her leg and sent her crashing to the cold ground.

Vincent stepped away. "Give up, *Queen*. Your reign is over."

"Never," she gasped, springing back up in a fighting stance. She would fight until her last breath for Aikradal. "You won't break me."

"Ah, but I already have," Vincent taunted. She went for a strike, but he landed a final, devastating kick to her abdomen, sending her plummeting to the stone floor. Writhing in pain, she clutched her stomach as bile rose in her throat once more.

"Like my sister and I, you were born for greatness." Vincent loomed over her. "But unlike us, you lack the ruthlessness necessary to seize it."

"You...you're monsters," Belyx spat out, her vision swimming as tears welled in her eyes.

"Perhaps," he paused, a twisted smile curling his lips. "But we are monsters who rule. And monsters who will control all of Keyica by the end of the year."

So that was part of their plan the whole time!

Belyx's broken form remained on the floor, her breathing labored and sluggish. The arrogant prince stood over her, his face illuminated by a sickly green light.

"You must know the truth," he began. "Vivienne and I had planned this for years. We even overthrew our parents and older brother just to take control of the throne. Our people are stronger now because of it. And soon we will conquer the whole continent." How did Belyx not know Vivienne had a twin? She tried to comb through her memories of the academy, but only Princess Vivienne's face remained.

"How long ago?" Belyx croaked, trying to get up again, but her body stilled.

"Young enough that we were tired of taking shit from people older than us. Ten years." He laughed.

What a demon! They would have been nine years old when they planned this. How could literal children be able to accomplish such a task? Belyx's brain spun. What had she gotten herself into? Suddenly her problems back in Aikradal paled. This plot had been going on for ten years! All while they were dealing with the gangs and the fae, Majeria had been quietly plotting, like a twisted chess game.

"Your resistance will crumble," he cooed as if reveling in her despair. "And when my plan is complete, you'll bow before us, just like the rest."

Belyx's hands curled into fists as her stomach churned with sorrow and rage. Images of her mother's kind face flashed in her head, followed by the dark memory of how she had been taken from her too soon. A sob threatened to bubble up in Belyx's throat, but she swallowed it back down, determined not to give him the satisfaction of seeing her cry.

"Never. I will never bow to you."

Vincent's twisted smile widened, casting an eerie glow in the dimly lit throne room. "But enough about our grand plans, Belyx. You must be curious about what awaits you." He circled her like a predator, his boots echoing off the cold stone floor.

"Since you're so special," he continued, "we've decided not to send you to the Pits of Baraxat. No, we have something far more...entertaining in mind for you."

With a breath caught in her throat, she tried to ignore the tendrils of dread snaking through her chest. The Pits of Baraxat, a place where the continent sent its most ruthless criminals to suffer and die at the hands of The God. If whatever Vincent had planned was worse than that, she knew it wouldn't be pleasant.

Refusing to let him see her fear, she spat out, "I'm not afraid of your sick games."

"Ah, but you should be." Vincent leaned down to whisper in her ear. His breath was hot on her skin, making her shiver with disgust. "You see, dear Queen, this little competition will be unlike anything you've ever experienced."

"Enough of your riddles!" Belyx snapped, her throat cracking under the strain. "Just tell me what you want!"

"Patience, my dear." Vincent straightened up and stepped back. "All will be revealed in due time. But first, there's one more thing you should know."

His eyes bore into hers, dark and merciless. "Thirteen years ago, your beloved mother, Queen Abigail, meddled in our affairs. As you can imagine, we couldn't allow such insubordination to go unpunished."

No.

The world seemed to freeze around Belyx as the implications of Vincent's words began to sink in. Her breath came in shallow gasps, her lungs constricting with the weight of her dawning realization.

"You...you killed her," she choked out. "You murdered my mother."

"Well, technically mother and father did, as we were only six, but that was their last noble accomplishment," Vincent confirmed. "It was quite unfortunate, really. But as I said before, we cannot abide disloyalty. She was poking around in places she shouldn't have. Sound familiar? The rumors that you shared about us with your people only accelerated our plans. You messed with the wrong family, Belyx." He let out a sinister laugh. "I mean, we killed our own blood! What do you think we would do to a bitch queen and her pathetic kingdom for straying too far into the sea?"

Belyx's entire body trembled, her vision blurring as tears threatened to spill over. She could feel the faint burn of rage igniting within her, fueled by the unbearable pain of her loss. How many nights had she lain awake, tormented by the mystery of her mother's death? And now, to finally know the truth...and be too weak to do anything.

"Psycho bastards," she snarled, clenching her fists so tight that her nails bit into her palms. "You may have taken my kingdom and destroyed my family, but you will never stop *me*."

"Ah, Belyx," Vincent sighed, shaking his head in feigned disappointment. "Always so defiant. It's a shame—your spirit would have been such an asset to our cause."

"Go to hell," she fumed, the venom in her words contradicting the hopelessness threatening to engulf her.

"I'll leave you to your grief. But, my dear, your suffering has only just begun."

The tears Belyx had been holding back spilled over, streaming down her cheeks as hot and bitter as the rage that roiled within her. She gritted her teeth, her nails digging crescent moons into her palms, trying to focus on anything but the awful truth of her mother's fate.

"Guards," Vincent commanded. "Escort our dear former queen to her new accommodations."

As the guards stepped forward, their faces hidden behind iron masks, something inside her snapped. The grief and fury that had been building like a storm inside her erupted, and she lunged at the nearest guard with a feral snarl.

"You fucking monsters!" she screamed. "You'll pay for what you've done in blood!"

Her bare hands gripped the guard's throat, her fingers clenching around it like a vice. For a moment, she reveled in the feeling of his pulse pounding beneath her fingertips, the power she held over him in that instant.

But then another guard was upon her, wrenching her away with brutal force. Her grip slipped, and she found herself gasping for breath as she was shoved against the rough cold stone wall.

"Enough!" barked the second guard, his words muffled by his mask. "You will not resist us, girl."

Belyx's chest heaved as she fought to draw air into her lungs, her vision swimming with the effort. But even as she struggled for air, the fire of her anger only burned brighter.

"Your cruelty cannot extinguish my spirit," she lashed at the guards, defiant despite her weakened state. "You may chain me and beat me, but I will not be broken."

"Ah, Belyx," Vincent said, his tone mocking. "Your stubbornness truly is a marvel to behold. But I fear it will only make your suffering all the more exquisite."

"Your arrogance will be your downfall," she shot back, her vocals shaking. "You cannot control me, Prince. You never could."

"Perhaps not," he conceded, his eyes narrowing as he studied her. "But then again, I don't need to break you, Belyx. All I need is for you to bend...just a little...like a weak twig in a rainstorm.

"Go to hell," she whispered, her throat tight with unshed tears.

"You need a new insult. But for now, I have other plans for you."

With that, he turned on his heel, leaving Belyx in the hands of the guards. As they dragged her away, she vowed that no matter what horrors awaited her, she would not yield. She would fight until her last breath, and when she stood before her enemies, she would make them pay in blood for all they had taken from her.

TWELVE

"Prisoners!" bellowed the guard outside. "Free time begins now!"

Free time? What an illusion in a prison. What kind of place was this? As Belyx sat on the cold, hard floor of her cell, she contemplated other ways to escape. Perhaps she could try the way Vincent did. Maybe his arrogance would betray him. Her mind still refused to acknowledge Vincent and Vivienne's plot. They had this planned for years, all while Aikradal falsely imprisoned the fae and were almost killed by a human-hating male witch. It was ironic, to solve such a major dilemma, only to be thrust headfirst into another typhoon.

The narrow shaft of light that filtered in through the high window traced patterns on the stone as she lost herself in thought. Just last week she was a queen. Now she was just another prisoner, locked away and stripped of her former glory.

The door to Belyx's cage swung open with a creak, revealing the dimly lit corridor beyond. She hesitated for a moment before pushing up to her feet, using the wall for support. Though she longed for the solitude of her cell, she knew that staying here would only weaken her resolve. No, she needed to face the other prisoners, to remind herself of her purpose: to escape, and stop this plot that threatened her kingdom.

As she stepped out into the common area, Belyx couldn't help but feel exposed. The prisoners' gazes weighed on her, scrutinizing her every move. She clenched her fists, the pain in her burned hands grounding her. They were a silent comfort and reminder that Enzo would find a way to save her...like he always did. But in the meantime, she wouldn't let them see her falter.

"Hey, I know you," called a deep voice from across the room. Belyx turned to see a tall, handsome man leaning against the far wall, tattoos snaking up his caramel skin. His eyes were dark and intelligent, a playful smile dancing at the corners of his lips. He approached with unhurried grace, his confident stride almost cat-like.

"Zephyr Kop, at your service," he said with a theatrical bow. "And you must be Belyx Velena. Your reputation precedes you. Youngest queen in existence, Freeing the trapped fae after all these years. I am impressed."

Belyx eyed him, remembering her most recent encounter with a charming prisoner that had ended in her beating.

Rumors of who she was spread fast. Although her reign was an oddity in their male-favoring continent. But no matter what this man claimed to know, she couldn't afford to trust anyone here, especially someone who wore charm like a necklace. *The serpent charmers should be approached with extra caution, for they too are snakes.*

"Am I flattered or concerned?" she retorted.

"Neither," he replied, his smile never faltering. "Just observant. You're not exactly easy to go unnoticed in a place like this."

"Is that so?" Belyx raised an eyebrow. "And why is that?"

"Fiery hair, fierce determination, and hidden deadly skill," Zephyr listed, ticking the points off on his fingers. "Enough to make anyone take notice." Belyx wondered how he found out about her skills, but left it alone. Her assassin identity mattered little here and he didn't need the satisfaction of being correct. The longer this conversation went on, the more danger she was in. If this ruffian figured out who she was, then Predator One and Predator Two hiding in the corner did as well.

"Sounds like you've been watching me too closely," she snapped, feeling her anger rise. "What's your angle?" She sensed other eyes on her...circling like vultures to fresh carrion.

"What?" He feigned innocence. "I have no game, Your Highness. Only a mutual interest in survival."

"Call me 'Your Highness' again and we'll see how long you survive," she threatened. She was no queen here.

"Apologies." Zephyr raised his hands in surrender. "No offense meant. I thought that perhaps we could help each other out."

"Help each other?" Belyx scoffed. "How? By stabbing me in the back when it's convenient for you?" As they all did. Why would he want her assistance anyways? This was a prison...for common criminals like him...and her.

"Believe it or not, not everyone in this place is a psycho murderer." His tone shifted serious. "Some of us want to escape this hellhole alive."

"Then I suggest you focus on yourself and leave me alone," she shot back, crossing her arms and pivoting away from him, refusing to trust another male here.

"Alright," Zephyr said with a roguish grin, "I can see you're not entirely convinced about me. So let's make a deal."

"Deal?" Belyx scoffed as she turned back, her eyes narrowing. "What could you possibly offer?" *Disengage from this waste of time, Belyx.*

"Information." Zephyr leaned in closer. His voice was low and smooth, like honey. "You're scared, aren't you? Worried about what's going to happen to you?" Belyx bristled at his accuracy but remained silent. "Well, I've been here long enough to know how things are done. And I believe you deserve to know your options." And he had been here awhile...which meant his crime must have been quite egregious. All instincts told her to retreat, but then she recalled a time when she had to trust a shady figure. Now, she was in love with him. She hated it, but she would need help if she was to escape in one piece.

"Options?" Belyx raised an eyebrow, intrigued despite herself.

"Instead of the Pits," Zephyr began, "Majeria offers all prisoners a chance to compete in the Trials of Rain. Four deadly competitions where only one prisoner makes it out alive."

"Sounds...delightful." Her grip tightened on the material of her sleeve. "I want to enter." All this time, Majeria had been making the prisoners compete in these stupid games? It was unbelievable until she remembered children took over this place years ago...psycho and unhinged children. Kids were supposed to be innocent souls without a care in the world. What happened to them that would turn them into feral beasts?

"Ah, there's the catch," Zephyr's grin shifted. "I plan to enter as well. And only one of us can come out alive."

"Then why tell me about it?" Belyx asked.

"Because," Zephyr sighed, his expression turning somber, "I have a sister in Petrovkan I need to rescue from their slave mines. That's why I became a pirate, to find her and bring her home. But now, I'm in here, and she's still out there, suffering." Of course, he was a pirate. He fit the description to the letter; she had heard of them only in stories, usually tales of plundering ships and ports — though they stayed clear from Aikradal.

Belyx's heart ached for him, but she couldn't let sympathy cloud her judgment...he was still a stranger with secrets. With a clenched jaw, she struggled to keep her emotions in check. "Why should I trust you?"

"Because we both have something to lose if we don't make it out of here." Zephyr's dark eyes met hers. "And maybe...just maybe, we stand a better chance together than apart."

Belyx hesitated, her mind racing with the possibilities. Could she afford to trust this man? Was he genuinely offering an alliance, or was this another deception like Prince Snake? Also, how would they both make it out if the rules stated only one could?

Whatever the reason, she stood a higher chance with someone, even if they betrayed her later. Her grandmother believed that any bridge of value was worth taking the time to traverse. "Fine," Belyx conceded but shook her head. "If you betray me—"

"Trust me," Zephyr interrupted, his grin returning. "You'll never see it coming."

Belyx marveled at his stupidity, but couldn't help smiling at his audacity, feeling a spark of hope ignite within her. She stared into Zephyr's eyes as the weight of his story pushed on her chest. Swallowing the lump in her throat, she nodded. "What happened to you and your sister?" His story saddened her, but she had her reasons for needing to escape this wretched place.

He licked his lips as if debating what to say. She knew that look...the look of guilt. "I know why *you* need to escape." Skillful dodge on his part, already proving he couldn't be trusted. "Your kingdom and your people, right?" Zephyr replied.

Belyx decided not to press him further. "I agree. I can't let them suffer any longer under the tyranny that has taken hold." She curled her fists. "Princess Vivienne and Prince Vincent took over my kingdom. I won't rest until it is mine again and they answer for their crimes."

Zephyr's gaze held understanding and sympathy. "We all have our battles, Belyx. Understand that even though you just met me, I'm willing to help you. I know there is a way and until now, I felt so hopeless. With you, I have hope again."

Belyx fought the heat rising in her cheeks. "Perhaps, but first, we must focus on surviving these Trials of Rain." Her feelings clouded her judgment and her impulsiveness would not beat her this time.

"Agreed." Zephyr extended a hand toward her. "For now, let's part ways and prepare ourselves for what lies ahead. We'll need all our strength and cunning to succeed."

"Agreed," Belyx repeated, taking his hand and giving it a firm shake.

"May the winds be ever in your favor, Belyx Velena," Zephyr offered her a wink before turning away.

"Likewise, Zephyr," she replied, watching him disappear amongst the throngs of prisoners. Once he was gone, Belyx couldn't help but think about Enzo and the way Zephyr's sassy attitude reminded her of him.

She missed Enzo desperately, his warmth and humor, his unwavering loyalty. The weight of grief gripped like a heavy cloak draped over her shoulders, threatening to suffocate her with its oppressive darkness. Belyx fought back tears as she retreated to her cell, knowing that she had to push through the pain if she wanted to reclaim her kingdom.

"Enzo," she murmured. "I promise I'll make things right again. For you, for our people, and Aikradal." She circled her burned hands again…like his heat was still with her, watching over her. His power saved her more times than not and even without him here, the symbol was enough for her to keep fighting.

With renewed perseverance, Belyx began to plan her strategy, preparing herself for the brutal challenges that awaited her in the supposed trials. No matter what sick games those bastards came up with, she would survive them and escape this prison.

Thirteen

The somber and dark forest provided a calming comfort as Enzo, Cook, Onka, Freyja, and his fathers headed deeper into the woods. How would they take Aikradal back from the Whisper's grasp?

The aroma of smoky damp earth filled Enzo's lungs as he stared up at the moon and felt its intensity. He clenched his fists by his side, letting his warm fae power bubble beneath his skin. Though only a couple hours had passed since their takeover, the team had nothing. Spies hadn't seen Belyx and no real plans from the Whispers had been discovered yet. Enzo was beginning to lose hope in the Order.

"Where is this place?" Enzo asked, praying it was close. His powers had only just returned and he yearned for a long rest. Any fae pushing their ability limits were at risk of life-threatening problems, although Enzo seemed fine at the moment.

"Soon," Freyja responded, not letting her emotions show. The palace lost many lives tonight. Betrayed by the people and fooled by a former gang leader. How had Sewek orchestrated this? And, more importantly, how had she managed to retrieve The Scorpion—Enzo assumed the beast to be dead, yet there he was, blocking their way into Belyx.

"Here," Cook said as she pulled a switch by what looked like a normal tree, but on closer inspection, it was made from stone—a fake one!

With a creak, the heavy ground shifted, revealing a hidden door and a set of stairs leading down into the darkness. His breath quickened; he had been forbidden to enter the old hideout because he was a male. What things had the Order kept down there?

"In," Freyja commanded and they all headed down, except his fathers.

"We need to talk to the other fae. Maybe convince them to help," Thano said.

Gink put his bleeding hand on Enzo. "We will figure this out, son."

"Be safe," was all Enzo could say with the little vocal strength he had left.

After going their separate ways into the night, Enzo trudged down a narrow set of stairs into a bunker below. The smell of wet earth crept up his nose as he descended, and the enclosures were moist with patches of moss.

"Hide that scowl, fae," Cook said. "We only made this a couple of months ago. Belyx was paranoid about another attack, so she had another Order hideout built. It still needs some fine-tuning."

Enzo was about to answer when they went further into the darkness and soon reached an illuminated chamber. The walls were coated with dust, and cobwebs draped in every corner. A dozen women, battered and disheveled, were gathered around a crackling fire pit discussing their predicament.

"Petal Rajabi!" one shouted as she sprang up from one of the many cots laid about the dusty floor. "Where is Belyx? We retreated here after she was forced back."

Freyja shook her head. "She was taken."

"But not for long," added Onka. "I have already deployed my Leaves to find out where she is and how to get her back. By nightfall tomorrow, she will be rescued and we will retaliate against the Whispers."

The Stem agreed and returned to the others. The lavish room boasted tapestries of roses and portraits of Belyx's mother, grandmother, and great-grandmother. The likeness to Belyx was uncanny, with the same burgundy air and striking hazel eyes.

Freyja strode to the wall, where a multitude of weapons were piled, and filled her quiver with arrows. Cook followed her. "Freyja, try to stop! We can't do anything tonight—"

"I can! I have enough strength to march down there and slay them all. No one touches Belyx."

Cook blocked Freyja's path once more and he wondered if a fight was about to break out. He wagered that Cook would come out on top. "Those who recklessly rush in often find themselves tumbling in the mud."

"Save it. I'm the Captain. It is my responsibility."

Onka shifted on her feet. Being Belyx's new protector, it was her's, but Enzo wasn't going to point that out right now.

"We have to wait for the fae to make their decision and for whatever intel the Leaves can get. Also, Enzo has no power left and we need his help," Cook added with urgency.

Freyja shot a glance at Enzo before locking her gaze with Cook, slowly putting down her weapons. "Fine."

Cook gestured to an empty cot, but Enzo remained on the ground; he felt out of place and didn't want to make it worse. "Get some rest," she said, her eyes lingering on Freyja, who was slumped with her hands in her head. "We'll regroup tomorrow and figure out what comes next."

Onka lay away from the others, still silent. Enzo wanted to tell her it wasn't her fault; he, too, had failed Belyx. If only he hadn't been so focused on how humans viewed him he might have noticed the looming danger sooner.

As Enzo sat in bed, his eyes wide open as he stared at the ceiling; he repeated his promise to bring Belyx home—but he could not help but wonder what dark obstacles stood in his way.

"Enzo, we must be strategic in our attack," Cook urged. "We cannot simply rush in to save Belyx without a solid plan."

"I know," he growled, clenching his fists. His mind was filled with thoughts of Belyx—of her blazing red hair, her fierce courage, courage that wouldn't back down. He ached to rescue her from the Whisper forces now, but Cook's words rang in his ears—they couldn't risk more lives rushing in unprepared. He wanted to burn them all down himself. If only his strength was enough.

The next day came and still no news. Cook wouldn't grant them release until they had additional information. Enzo had conferred with his people and the results were equally discouraging.

Freyja and Onka exchanged glances before addressing Enzo again. "We all failed to protect her," Onka admitted, her voice heavy with guilt...at least she was speaking today, ready to face the threat at hand. "We cannot forget that Belyx is strong and independent. She always does her own thing, whether we like it or not."

"True," Freyja agreed. "She has a way of defying expectations. She is a survivor. The Whispers are playing a dangerous game. That will be their demise."

Enzo couldn't help but smile at the thought of Belyx's stubbornness. As much as it frustrated him at times, he admired her resilience and tenacity. Those were the traits that would keep her alive. "You're right," he conceded. "Belyx can handle herself. But that doesn't mean we have forever to wait."

"Of course not," Onka said. "But we need allies, and unfortunately, the fae are unwilling to help. They're determined to remain neutral in all conflicts." A whiff of snark laced her words and Enzo glanced away. It was all true. His tribe refused to do anything. So much for vowing to protect Belyx at all costs. However, the fae would fight if the humans entered their forest home, but his would be foolish for the Whispers to do.

The Order was all they had. The Whisper forces never discovered the old Order hideout, but Belyx had one built on the outskirts of the forest for this very reason. Most members made it...while others weren't so lucky. After last year's decimation, the Order had barely recovered and now, like ashes, it was scattered once more.

"Neutral." Enzo scoffed, his anger flaring like a spark igniting kindling. "My tribe are cowards, then." He looked around the circle of faces, each one solemn in the wavering torchlight of the hideout. "We need to plot some type of rescue team, to be quick and quiet."

"Agreed," Freyja said, her eyes sagging from lack of sleep. However, she appeared determined as ever. "We'll gather our forces and strike when the time is right. The recruits are still pretty fresh, but I will work with them. It will take time."

Time was not their ally. He knew they needed to be patient, to prepare carefully if they were going to save Belyx and reclaim Aikradal. But every moment that passed seemed like an eternity, and deep down, he worried it might already be too late.

"Alright," he said, forcing himself to focus on the plan. "Let's figure out our next steps, and pray to the gods that we can reach Belyx in time."

As if on cue, the heavy bunker door creaked open. A hooded Leaf emerged in billowing leathers and advanced towards them. Her demeanor was faint as she leaned in close to Onka's ear, and the handmaiden's expression shifted to terrified alarm. "It is worse than we thought." Onka's eyes teared. "They took Belyx to Majeria."

Enzo stood up, but Cook waved him down.

No. No. No!

She couldn't be in that awful place...all alone and suffering. Why would they do that? Why not kill her here and save the trouble? His flames bit at the surface of his palms. They would not win.

"So Majeria was behind this. Not the Whispers," Cook added. "That...complicates things. This is not some minor coup, but a full-on invasion."

"Why would they take her there?" Freyja asked.

The Leaf stilled. "I overheard the guards. They said she was being taken to the Pits."

The Pits of Braxat were where they sent the most notorious of criminals. They were thrown in and no one knew what came after, but no prisoner ever returned. Belyx would never survive. "We need a boat. We need to attack them. Now!"

Onka shook her head. "There is other bad news. Majeria has taken over our trade ports as well. They're using them to ship in goods and...slaves."

"Slaves?" Enzo's eyes flared with fury. He clenched his fists, the flame tattoos on his arms seeming to dance as his anger grew. "We have to do something."

"And now!" Freyja declared, her brow knitted. Enzo remembered how she had been a slave once—those memories were still torturous for her. Enzo could hardly conceive the indescribable suffering she endured. "We must act swiftly."

Cook sighed. "If we take back the ports and steal a ship, maybe we can rescue her. It is the only way, but I'm afraid it won't save Aikradal. We will need to plan that after she returns."

Freyja tied up her hair, wasting no time for battle. "We will. Sewek thinks she is so smart sitting on Belyx's throne, making some kind of deal for a kingdom...I'll kill her."

Onka and the Leaf exchanged a glance. "Sewek is not the one on the throne," the Leaf said. "Princess Vivienne of Majeria is."

Enzo's face heated. Vivienne, Belyx's rival from the academy who one-upped her at every opportunity. She declined to help Aikradal last year despite Belyx throwing a lavish ball in an attempt to persuade them. It was no shock she was responsible for this. She'd messed with the wrong fae this time. "When do we leave?"

Freyja stood. "Tonight. I'll prepare the recruits. Tonight we destroy their garbage ships and save Belyx. Then rid our kingdom of that slaving and stealing mess of a kingdom."

Enzo could see the ferociousness in her eyes, and he knew that together they'd be a formidable force. They had to be if they were going to rescue Belyx and reclaim their kingdom. "I'm ready," he told her, the fire within him fully recharged, begging to be unleashed.

"Good," Freyja replied, gripping her bow/staff to her chest. "Let's go."

As night fell, Enzo, Freyja, and a few recruits they could find crept through the shadows toward the port, their hearts pounding in unison. The salty tang of seawater filled Enzo's nostrils, while the distant cries of seagulls echoed across the waves. The sight before them was chilling: Majerian soldiers patrolled the docks like predators stalking their prey, their movements deliberate and sinister.

"Look at them," Enzo whispered, unable to keep the disdain from his words. "Arrogant bastards. Think they can take over our kingdom and then bring this filth here."

Freyja stilled. "I made a vow to never let slaves hit my land. Let's just say I become pissed when I can't uphold my promises." She turned toward the recruits, some were trained Thorns, while others were only Seedlings. "Listen up. We have ten ports total and they control all of them. We need to commandeer a boat and prepare to sail for Majeria. Your queen was taken there. Our priority is those guards." She transformed her staff into a sleek, deadly bow. "Then we move onto the ships. The one we are going to steal is on the farthest end, as it will be hard to shoot down once it is in the water. Any questions?"

The assassins all stilled as if bracing themselves for whatever came next. "You good, fae?" Freyja asked.

Enzo felt the familiar spark of heat that ignited in his chest, spreading throughout his body. He closed his eyes and welcomed the warmth of the flames which wrapped around him like a comforting embrace. "I'm ready."

They crept closer to the patrolling guards and Enzo raised his hands. "Allow me," Enzo murmured, focusing his gaze on one of the unsuspecting guards.

With a flick of his wrist, a whip-like tendril of flame shot forward, coiling on the man's throat and yanking him off his feet. His scream was quickly silenced by the fire that consumed him.

"Nicely done, but—" Freyja loosed an arrow that found its mark in another guard's chest. The man crumpled to the ground, lifeless. "You missed one."

The Order members moved to their targets as well and only slight grunts indicated they completed their parts. The guards were down and now it was time for the boats.

"To the last one, we go. Stay alert," Freyja commanded as they crept across the ports, keeping to the shadows. "I have to say, you would make a decent Rose member if you weren't a male." Freyja kept low as people went by.

Enzo arched his brow. "Thanks, I guess. Having to steal to survive sharpens a person's assassin skills."

"Couldn't agree more."

The group stayed in silence for a beat, taking in the details of the massive ship moored at the docks. The sound of light conversations echoed from nearby patrols. "I count around five on the boat, give or take," Enzo said, shrugging his shoulders. This was their best chance for a heist, but if anything went wrong they were far away from any retreat.

"Real specific," Freyja chided as she notched an arrow. "Order. Move out with Enzo and I will pick off any stragglers."

Enzo's fingers swelled as he followed them, his body shaking with anticipation. They were so close to their goal and the danger only seemed to grow closer. He could almost taste success, but still, they went forward with careful steps, rising above a crouch as they moved ever closer to their destination.

A scream set Enzo's hope ablaze. One of the Seedlings had a blade inside one of the Thorn's, a twisted look setting on her face.

"For Majeria!" she sneered, her steel carving out swathes of the opposing recruits. Enzo unleashed a burst of flames, but she backflipped with ease and hurled a knife right at him, but he ducked in time. As he was preparing his next flame attack, an arrow flew true and pierced her throat—her blood painting the docks in a disconcerting hue.

Freyja was by Enzo before he could comprehend. "I knew that Seedling was too skilled for her rank. Come on! Let's get to the sh—"

Bells clanged like a death chime, setting Enzo's pulse striking in terror. But they were too late; Majerian soldiers appeared from all sides and shouted orders in unison. There was no escape now—they'd never sail a boat out of this harbor alive.

"New plan?" Enzo asked.

Freyja readied her bow for the attackers, the blood of Order members soaking her feet. It had to have taken intense training to block off those feelings right now. "Retreat, but while we are here—" She launched an arrow into a running guard's heart. "Burn these ships to the ground."

Enzo didn't have to be told twice as he fired a torrent of flames straight into the hull of the vessel they were supposed to take. Its wood caught ablaze and the people on deck jumped overboard. The flames illuminated the night sky, indicating their intrusion.

Freyja slammed a guard in the face while loosing an arrow into another.

With each guard that fell, Enzo's confidence grew back. Although their plan had failed, they could still create some mayhem.

But as they continued their assault on the port, it became clear that there were far too many ships for them to destroy on their own.

"Damn it," Enzo cursed under his breath, sweat trickling down his temple as he surveyed the numerous vessels. "There are too many."

"Focus," Freyja urged, her eyes sharp and determined as she slew another soldier. "We can do it if we keep going. Belyx wouldn't give up. Now is the time to strike." Enzo looked up, knowing she was right. This was just the beginning of their fight to reclaim Aikradal—a fight they couldn't afford to lose. With renewed boldness, he let loose a barrage of flames, watching as another one of the ships went up in smoke.

Tonight they would launch a blow against Majeria. And soon, they would have their kingdom back...one step at a time. The Order recruit may have betrayed them and now they had no chance of getting to Belyx. But these ports would never be used again.

Enzo's lungs burned as he drew in ragged breaths, the air hot and heavy with ash. The sweat on his brow stung his eyes, but he blinked it away, determined to keep moving. He sprinted passed soldier after soldier, setting each ship ablaze. He approached the next ship when a loud boom filled the space.

"Get down!" Freyja screamed and over his head, a large metal ball flew and exploded into the water near him.

Freyja took out more soldiers, her chest rising and falling rapidly, her bow/staff back in its original form, gripped in her hand.

"Cannons," she panted. "Any other powers you care to have?"

"Attack the closest cluster." Enzo's voice was hoarse from the smoke and exertion. Courage coursed through his veins like molten steel. They had managed to destroy two ports, but more appeared with so many others. "The flames will spread to the rest."

"I'll handle the infantry," Freyja said, concern etched on her face. "You burn those damn ships to the ground. No slaves shall walk this ground again."

"Trust me," Enzo insisted, "I'll give it everything I have."

Freyja charged more men, her anger shining through her exhaustion. Enzo followed while dodging cannon fire as well and sent the next ship to ashes.

Enzo, reeling from his victory, found Freyja locked in a deadly duel with a general of some sort. His armor glinted in the sun and his fish insignia revealed his rank. He was agile and matched Freyja's speed. With shoulders heaving, she fought to keep up. She would soon be overpowered! With a burst of energy, he switched direction and encircled both combatants with flames.

The general sneered at Enzo, but Freyja was ready. She clocked the man right in the face and sent him staggering back towards the wall of blazing fire. He reached out his hand to catch hold of her, gripping her by her braids. Freyja's fury only grew, yet she was well prepared for this kind of attack. In one sweeping motion, she threw herself to the floor while he jerked down. She followed up with a powerful kick to his side, sending him flying into the crackling inferno. His screams echoed through the night.

Enzo lashed a couple of attackers with his flame and Freyja ran to him, out of breath. "Thanks for the save. We can't give up now."

It became apparent that this wouldn't be a simple repeat of their previous plan. The Majerian guards were more numerous and better armed, their movements disciplined and precise. There would be more as skilled as that general too.

"Enzo," Freyja whispered, her eyes dilated with alarm. "We are surrounded."

"Follow my lead," Enzo instructed, his thoughts drummed. "We can run past my flame, but you must stay close."

Freyja cracked her neck, eyeing the charging soldiers. "We'll have to do this quickly."

"Ready?" Enzo asked, his fire abilities crackling at his fingertips.

"Ready."

They sprang into action, darting between crates and barrels as they closed the distance to their retreat. The flames flickered and crackled as he led the way, a fiery shield that melted anyone who attempted to block their path. Freyja uncoiled her staff transforming it into her bow, notching an arrow with ease while running. Her breathing was steady but her eyes were wild as she let out a breath through pursed lips before aiming. The arrows flew true, piercing soldiers' throats.

Enzo summoned a fierce gale of embers, targeting the soldiers themselves. But as he did, a skilled Majerian fighter lunged at him, his sword slicing through the air with deadly intent, slipping through his flame shield. Enzo barely managed to dodge the swipe, the heat of the blade singeing him as it passed too close to his face.

"Enzo!" Freyja shouted. "I can't keep them away for long!" More surrounded them while he was preoccupied.

"Go!" he yelled back, gritting his teeth as he unleashed another blast of fire at the encroaching soldiers. "Get out of here! I'll cover you!"

"Enzo, no!"

"Trust me!" he roared, his chest constricting with the weight of his decision. "Go!"

Freyja hesitated for only a moment before she sprinted away, her steps muffled by the chaos surrounding them. Enzo fought on, fending off the skilled Majerian fighters with fury who seemed to appear from every shadow.

Finally, when he was certain Freyja had made her escape, Enzo ducked behind a stack of crates and used the last of his strength to summon a pillar of fire, momentarily cutting off his pursuers as he slammed it down in a devastating explosion, sending him and the soldiers back.

Coughing as he slouched up, he seized the opportunity to flee, each breath like sandpaper against his throat as he stumbled back into the safety of the forest.

"By the gods," he swore, his entire body shaking from exhaustion and fear. *I will find a way to take back Aikradal and rescue Belyx. I swear it.*

He met with Freyja back in the forest and they both fell with a thud, their symphony of heavy breathing filling the chirping woods.

They had failed. They had failed Belyx and she had no one to save her.

She will be fine for a little more time.

Belyx was a survivor...she had to be. Right now, they had a bigger mess to clean up.

Enzo collapsed to his knees in the ink-blackness, unwavering in his purpose even as his strength ebbed away.

FOURTEEN

The stench of rotting fish clung to Belyx's nostrils. Even as she forced herself to breathe through her mouth, the taste of decay settled like smoke on her tongue.

They served the hapless prisoners limp, week-old cod. Belyx loathed seafood with every ounce of her soul and now it appeared the penitentiary was hell-bent on tormenting her more so.

"Ugh! Isn't being in prison bad enough, now we have to eat this trash? Nothing that swims in the sea should be eaten."

Zephyr chuckled, his caramel skin glistening with sweat in the dim light of the prison. "You know, cattle and pigs aren't any cleaner than fish. The land is no less dirty than the sea."

"Then perhaps I'll become a vegetarian after all this is over," Belyx retorted, trying to suppress her laugh.

Zephyr took a bite from one of her meals and waved past Belyx. "Gelina. Over here!"

Belyx spun around and locked eyes with an older woman in a wheelchair. As Gelina wheeled herself towards them, her dual-colored irises—blue and brown—radiated a kindness among the shadows of these dreary hallways. Belyx had never seen someone with two-toned eyes; even before Gelina opened her mouth, she was an alluring marvel.

Belyx was also chilled by this woman's situation as well. What had happened to her? It couldn't be easy, in this wretched place where guards weren't jumping for joy to accommodate her.

"Ah, Belyx, let me introduce you to my good friend, Gelina," Zephyr said, gesturing toward the woman. She had a smile on her face, even though she too was trapped in this desolate prison.

"Hello, Gelina." Belyx approached her cautiously. "It's nice to meet you."

"Likewise. Zephyr has told me so much about you," Gelina replied. If peaceful had a sound, it would be hers. Its cadence was almost song-like and nestled a certain comfort in Belyx's brain. "I'm glad to finally meet the woman who has managed to give him hope again." Zephyr blushed at her comment, but Belyx could sense the appreciation in his eyes. As she grew to converse with Zephyr more, it was clear he was just as troubled as she. And this friend of his gained her trust with little effort despite all of her instincts. Her presence proved that perhaps not all hope was lost.

"How did you both find each other in such a lovely place?" Belyx asked.

"Zephyr and I go way back," Gelina continued, turning more serious. "We met while working on an escape route for the sex slaves in Majeria. We were able to free many of them before we were caught and thrown in here."

Maybe these prisoners weren't all violent criminals like she thought, but mere citizens going against Majeria's sick rules. Belyx ached for the woman. It was clear that she had a gracious soul, one that was willing to risk her freedom for others. "You're very brave." There was a time when she too, would fight with all her might to keep slaves out of Aikradal. It was a wonder if they were there now since Majeria was in control, but she couldn't let those thoughts cloud her.

"Thank you," she replied, her eyes shining. "I had planned on entering the trials, to ensure that Zephyr emerged victorious. But then I changed my mind—I want to give you a helping hand as well. If you can restore our hope and save his beloved sister, it must mean you are extraordinary."

Belyx's heart swelled with gratitude for Gelina, who despite barely knowing Belyx had offered to assist her. She glanced at Zephyr and saw that his cheeks were now a deep shade of red, his lips curved in a proud but bashful grin. Warmth spread across Belyx's face, and she found herself blushing too.

The remaining foul-tasting seafood was a struggle to choke down, its rancid aroma and slimy texture making her gag. A couple of the prison guards approached and Belyx instantly stood.

The taller one stalked to the center of the bustling prisoners. "Attention. His Highness, Prince Vincent has declared sign-ups for the Trials of Rain open. Head over to the front to put your name in. Remember, while you are participating in the Trials, you must in no way harm any other competitor outside it. Also, you must understand the risks. Those who enter will die, and we will not spare anyone. Participate at your own risk, trash." He turned to leave when another guard whispered in his ear. "Ah yes. Don't forget about the offering you make to His Highness, Prince Vincent, for giving you dirtbags a chance of freedom. You know the rest." With measured steps, the guards pivoted back where they came from.

"Offerings? You never mentioned that! What do they want? We have nothing." Belyx's insides panicked. She was also floored by the dangers of entering, but that was expected.

Zephyr laughed and Belyx thought it odd to laugh at such a dire moment. "They mean more of a promise to The God, like your soul will rot in the afterlife if you don't follow the rules, blah blah blah."

Belyx scrunched her nose. "I don't find that funny. Don't be blasphemous here."

Gelina waved her hand. "Don't bother. I've given up on him."

"I just don't understand," Zephyr replied. "The God is nowhere near this pit, or else all these innocent people like us wouldn't be here." Before Belyx could respond, he was heading to the table.

Gelina grasped Belyx's hand. "Don't worry. My prayers are still with him."

"As are mine." Belyx and Gelina followed to a booth surrounded by Majerian guards. Prisoners were lined up for what appeared like forever. How many of them were so desperate to escape, and would risk their lives? *You are one of them, Belyx.*

Belyx's hands trembled as she placed the quill on the parchment and signed her name at the small ornate table. The priest watched, his eyes full of pity and understanding, as she made her promises to The God. Her stomach churned with acid and fear—she was aware of what breaking this promise would mean, but it was the only way out.

On her way back to where they were sitting, a tall man with messy, dirty blonde hair approached them. His intense, steely blue eyes glared at her as he clenched and unclenched his fists. He pulled his arm back and struck Belyx's shoulder with great force. She stumbled backward and hit her head on the floor, feeling a sharp pain course through her body.

"Velena," he snarled, hatred spewing from his lips. "I know who you are, what you stand for. You and everyone like you ought to be dead." His companion grimaced at Belyx with yellow eyes filled with malevolence. Her face was contorted in disgust and her white braided hair whipped around her head menacingly as they disappeared into the prison. She had made more friends here...

Zephyr was on his feet, helping Belyx up with a firm grip on her arm. "Are you alright?" Concern etched into the lines of his face.

Belyx brushed herself off. "Who was that?"

"Soren Blackthorn," he said, jaw clenched. "He's here to compete in the trials too. He was a former Majerian soldier. But no one knows exactly how he ended up here."

"His friend is Luo Pina," Gelina added, her gaze following the retreating figures. "A prisoner they found up north. Also, no one is sure why she is here. Be careful around her, too."

"Thanks for the warning," Belyx murmured, rubbing her shoulder where Soren had struck her. The pain was already fading, but anger burned hot within her. She had never met this man, yet he despised her. Why was she unable to not have any enemies? Whoever he was or whatever he thought of her, it only made her more determined to win the trials.

"Here, let me get you some water," Zephyr said, and Belyx agreed gratefully. As he disappeared to fetch it, Gelina turned her wheelchair to face Belyx.

"Zephyr had a difficult past," she began. "He was on his own as a child, forced to trade his sister into slavery just to survive. He ran away and joined a crew of pirates, hoping for a better life. But he never stopped fighting against the injustices in Majeria, to free his sister for his mistake."

Belyx listened carefully, trying to reconcile this image of Zephyr with the charming man she had come to meet. That must have been why he hadn't spoken of his sister because he was responsible for her being sold.

"Don't judge him too hard. Yes, I see it in your face, dear." Belyx looked down, she had been scowling. To trade a life for things was something she would never consider. "Remember, you have grown up with the privilege of not having to make those decisions. No offense to you, but it is hard living where you don't know where your next meal comes from or whether you'll be locked up for doing something about it. It is a cruel world. Remember that."

Gelina was right. Belyx's chest tightened at her guilt for judging him. She realized that her feelings for him were growing deeper, more complicated than she had anticipated. She wanted to win the trials for herself, but now, she wanted to help Zephyr too. If it came down to it, who would she choose?

"His heart is in the right place," Gelina continued, her eyes softening. "But he's still learning to trust others. I think that's why he's so drawn to you, Belyx. You're different from anyone else he's met."

As Zephyr returned with the cup of water, Belyx inhaled a deep breath and accepted it. The road before them would be hard, with difficult decisions to make. But she wasn't alone any longer—not with Zephyr and Gelina by her side.

Maybe, together, they could find a way to win the trials and help those in need. Belyx had the strength to do anything; she had defeated a deadly magic user last year, against all adversaries. There had to be some way for more than one person to succeed in these trials. She'd do it for Zephyr's sake.

Fifteen

As Enzo and Freyja emerged from the shadowed underbrush back to the Order hideout, their expressions were grim as they took in the devastation that was once the vibrant Sehrlic forest. Enzo's chest tightened, a mixture of anger and grief welling up inside him like a raging storm. The lush green canopy he'd always known was now a ragged mess of torn branches and leaves, a scar on his home.

"By The God," Freyja whispered, her brownish-red eyes wide with horror. "Majeria did this."

"Those bastards," Enzo spat, clenching his fists. Weak flames danced around his knuckles, mirroring the fury that threatened to consume him. He only wished he had a scrap of power left. Then he would burn all of them away like they did to his forest. He scanned the wreckage of burned trees and found a group of fae huddled together, their faces etched with despair. Gink approached them, his tattered ponytail swaying as he walked.

"Enzo, Freyja," Gink said, his usually expressive hands hanging heavy at his side. "We have terrible news. Majeria attacked the forest while you were away. Someone must have told them about the hideout. They came and took Cook back to the palace."

"Damn it," Enzo muttered, his mind racing. He couldn't stand by with another ally in danger. "We had a double agent in the Order. We were betrayed on our mission too." Belyx cared so much for Cook and now that was another thing he had to deal with. The pressure of this entire situation weighed on him like a printing press.

"We were too late," Freyja stilled as if trying to keep her composure as captain. "Is everyone else all right?"

Gink looked behind him. "Yes. Quite shaken up, but the Order is with our tribe deeper in the woods now."

Freyja nodded, her face hard as steel. "Where is Onka? She can sneak us to the palace. We need to find out what is happening."

Gink guided them to the rest, and as they advanced farther into the forest, the less damaged it was. Majeria was scared to move further into the abode of the fae...so why hadn't the fae come to Cook's aid? They'd said once Majeria intruded upon the woods, they'd lend a hand—but it hadn't been enough.

"Ah, Enzo," the fae leader, Sycamore, said. "I take it you weren't successful in your endeavor?"

Clearly. "No thanks to you," he spat, having no patience for their pacifist bullshit right now.

"Enzo. We are bound by our gods and our ways. We cannot assist in human affairs." *Aaand there was the pacifist bullshit.*

"Whatever!" Enzo slipped past him and the other cowardly fae, looking for anyone who wanted to do something about the invasion.

Onka was already dressed in her leathers and approached him. "This has to end."

"Agreed," Freyja responded as she walked by Enzo. "You two get into the kingdom and find out more about Majeria's big plans. I'll interrogate the rest of the Order and make sure we still don't have a traitor. I am tired of being blindsided."

Enzo glanced at Onka with a hint of apprehension. "Are you up for this?" he asked her. Onka peered at them both with intense scrutiny as if she could read their minds.

After an extended pause, she declared, "nothing worth having is ever easy. I'm ready—are you?"

"Yes," Enzo affirmed without hesitation, already beginning their walk to the palace.

The morning sun glinted off the cobblestone streets and Onka pulled Enzo closer to her side, leading him through alleyways and backstreets. They moved like whispers in the wind, blending into the shadows until they reached the center of the kingdom. The people were heading toward a once-grand palace that had been reduced to rubble by Majeria's forces. Tears pricked at Enzo's eyes as he looked upon their gaunt faces and tattered clothes—evidence of Majeria's cruelty melding itself into their expressions. He thought of Cook suffering, wherever she was, under such oppression, and his heart burned with rage.

"Look at them," Onka whispered. "Majeria has forced this life of sex slavery and smuggling onto them. It was worse than I imagined."

"Then we'll take it back," Enzo vowed, a steely lump settling in his stomach. "For Belyx, for all of Aikradal."

"Agreed," Onka said. "But first, let's find Cook."

With Onka's guidance, they continued deeper into the kingdom, each step bringing them closer to the palace with the rest of the citizens.

The Aikradal people were gathered in the courtyard of the palace, gathering in silent masses around the balcony. Sunken faces and despair shone on every destitute face, as they waited for their new despotic ruler to make an appearance.

Princess Vivienne stepped onto the balcony, her slender frame silhouetted against the sky. She began uttering words that Enzo couldn't catch due to the protests, but soldiers struck them down and Enzo's flame flickered at the surface. He was still too weak to fight. Once the screams of beat citizens subsided, a hush descended on the them as they gazed upon the "Queen." Her piercing ice-cold blue eyes scanned the mob before she began to speak.

The woman smirked, her ruby lips parting ever so slightly.

"Thank you my fine guards. Where was I? Oh yes—Dear citizens of Aikradal," she continued, sending shivers down Enzo's spine. "It is clear to me, as it should be to you, that Majeria is the strong and invincible force in Keyica. We are your rulers now and forevermore. You will accept your place within our new world order or suffer the consequences."

She stepped closer to the railing, her eyes glinting like daggers in the light.

"For those of you who refuse to comply, let me assure you that we have ways of making you change your mind. Painful ways."

The crowd gasped as she continued speaking, each word dripping with hostility. "So I suggest you fall in line, or else..." The guards brought in a man who was in chains. His weeps were like a sad ballad.

One guard gripped the man's throat with an iron grasp, lifting him off his feet and brandishing a weapon in one smooth movement. Enzo shut his eyes as he heard the sickening crunch of bones surrendering to steel, and the man's anguished screams stopped all of a sudden.

She trailed off, letting the weight of her threat hang heavy in the air. The silence was deafening.

She smiled. "You'll regret it for the rest of your pitiful lives."

Enzo's fists clenched at her words, anger simmering beneath his skin. Standing next to Vivienne was The Scorpion, with his black armor, his face hidden and carrying his life-taking spear. Pulse quickening, he remembered his near-death encounter with the monster a year prior.

"Resisting our rule would be foolish," Vivienne continued. "The Scorpion is only too eager to demonstrate what happens to those who dare defy us." She paused, letting her gaze sweep over the downtrodden faces below. "Any opposition will result in your head on his pike."

The crowd remained silent. Enzo could feel their crushing defeat weighing down on him, but he knew they couldn't give up. Not while Cook, Belyx, and the others were still suffering.

"Come on," he whispered to Onka. "We need to let the others know what happened here."

They retreated into the shadows and made their way back to the Sehrlic forest, where Freyja, Gink, Thano, and the rest of the fae and Order awaited their return.

"What did she say?" Freyja asked, her stare intense as she met Enzo's teary eyes.

"Vivienne declared that Majeria is the new world order," Enzo replied, struggling to keep his voice steady. "They won't hesitate to kill anyone who opposes them."

A heavy silence descended upon the group, the weight of Vivienne's words hanging in the air like a dark cloud. Desperation and concern squeezed Enzo's thoughts as he searched for any possible solution. His gaze landed on the statue of The Original, an ancient fae figure who loomed over the forest.

"Wait," he said. "I have an idea. It's risky, but maybe...just maybe it could work."

"What are you thinking?" Thano asked, his eyes narrowing with concern.

"Don't legends say that The Original can be revived?" Enzo asked, a flicker of hope licking at his soul. "If we can bring him back, perhaps he could help us defeat Majeria and save Aikradal."

The others exchanged uneasy glances. At this moment, faced with insurmountable odds, Enzo knew they had to take a chance, no matter how dangerous or uncertain it might be.

"Reviving The Original?" Thano's voice quivered. "You can't be serious, Enzo. Those are mere tales to give us hope in dark times. Strictly metaphoric."

"Father, you used to perform that play when I was younger. When The Original returned and gave us peace again. It might be our only way," Enzo pleaded, his chest filled with desperation.

"Enzo, listen to yourself." Gink stepped forward, his wide frame casting a shadow over the surrounding fae. "The Original has a...complicated history."

"Indeed," chimed in Sycamore, his silver hair glinting in the dappled sunlight. "He was created by the gods long ago, tasked with stopping the civil war between the witches and the fae. But when he did so...he wanted to destroy the witches. He was hungry for complete domination."

"He then drove the witches out and claimed the land for the fae," Thano continued, his fingers tracing the intricate designs on the statue before them. "His—our tribe flourished as they drew upon his power. He was never intended to rule, but soon, The Original began dictating the lives of every fae and witch under his command."

"Until the witches intervened," the leader said. "They banished him for his arrogance, but the curse wasn't perfect. It left behind his relics that could re-summon him. Many fae still revere him as a hero. but others see him as a tyrant who fostered hatred between fae and witches. And the witches themselves—they view him as an apocalyptic figure, destined to destroy the world."

"Regardless of which side is right," Thano warned, "reviving The Original would be a gamble of the highest order. We don't know if he would even assist us. What if he continues his previous mission."

"Why make his statue if he was such a tyrant?" Freyja asked, always the logical one.

The leader sent her a look of ice. "Humans sometimes honor rulers who aren't so clean either. The Original serves as a reminder to never forget our faith. Which is why we still can't involve ourselves now."

Enzo locked his fists together, the panic rising inside him. It was like a storm brewing—one that he could no longer ignore. He knew how dangerous this path was, but Vivienne's tight grip on Aikradal left them few choices. With the fae tribe unwilling to act, what other option did they have?

"Please," he begged. "We need to take back the palace. We need to save Belyx. Help me. Use your powers. Our gifts from our gods. It is the only way."

His fathers exchanged anguished looks, but their silence spoke volumes. They couldn't—or wouldn't, help him. The other fae murmured amongst themselves, their faces were a mix of fear and uncertainty.

"Fine." Enzo straightened his shoulders, determination burning within him like wildfire. "If no one will step in, I'll do it myself."

The ground beneath his feet cracked with each heavy step, and Enzo's skin tingled as the shadows of the forest engulfed him. He drew in a deep breath. He felt ready for anything that lay ahead—even if it meant risking all he cared for to restore peace to Aikradal. There was no time to hesitate or second guess himself; this was his passage to make alone, and there would be no turning back.

Sixteen

Hands still shaking with adrenaline, Belyx wiped the sweat from her brow. After the intense sparring session with Zephyr, her lungs craved a reprieve. The colliding of their fists echoed through the dimly lit training grounds as if a symphony of heavy breathing played only for them. As she caught her breath, Belyx's gaze slowly settled on an elderly man shuffling his way down the corridor. His skin hung loose from his frame and his amber eyes were dull with exhaustion. As he reached the open cell, he propped himself up against the doorframe.

"Who is that?" she asked Zephyr, nodding towards the elder prisoner, wondering what kind of thing a man his age had done to be imprisoned for such a time.

Zephyr's smile flattened. "Ah, you noticed the infamous Aurelius." He wiped the sweat off his hands. "Quite the story behind that one."

"What happened?" There was a familiarity to him she couldn't place, like a long forgotten friend. He was old enough.

"Well." Zephyr took a deep breath before beginning. "Aurelius was once a revered Majerian martial arts master, rumored to be a part of some secret assassin society." Belyx caught her gasp. "They were known for their escapades all across Keyica, fighting to end tyranny wherever it reared its ugly head."

Belyx's breath hitched at the mention of an assassin group. It couldn't have been her Order since he was a male, but were there others too? "So, why is he here? What happened?"

"Rumor has it," Zephyr continued, keeping his voice low and cautious, "one day he just...snapped. Killed all the other members of his group for unknown reasons. It's a tragedy, really. They say he turned himself in afterward and ended up here in the Majerian prison."

"Killed them all?" Her mind raced with questions. She couldn't help but wonder what could make a person crack like that, to betray their order in such a brutal manner. "Do you think it's true?"

"Who knows?" Zephyr shrugged, his tattoos dancing with the movement of his muscles as he stretched. The intricate designs had stories behind them no doubt, but Belyx had to stop herself from staring too long. "Maybe he couldn't bear the weight of the secrets he carried or perhaps something darker took hold of him. What I do know is that people generally try to steer clear of him."

Belyx stared at Aurelius, now hunched over in his cell, his white hair tied in a top knot and scars criss crossing his worn face. A sudden blizzard ran down her spine as she thought about the mysterious man and the violent past that surrounded him. Yet, even amidst the darkness of those rumors, she felt a strange connection to the old master, an inexplicable pull towards his story.

"That changes things," Belyx said, feeling the weight of this new knowledge settle like a cannon on her chest. Her impulsiveness might be leading her astray, but Aurelius had something about him that made her believe she needed to learn more about his group and if he had any link to the Order or her kingdom.

"Be careful," Zephyr warned, his eyes littered with concern. "There's no telling what someone like him might be capable of."

"Of course." Though she couldn't quell the curiosity burning within her. Before she turned around, she glanced back at the old man one last time, her mind already spinning with possibilities.

A vivid memory surged into Belyx; the history of how her great-grandmother had been taken under the wing of an elite Majerian warrior. He had trained her in hand-to-hand combat, stealth tactics, and poisons. These skills were then passed down through generations to create the Order of the Rose. Was Aurelius the same teacher? Her eyes fluttered as she pondered this possibility.

"Do you know where he went on his missions?"

"Your guess is as good as mine," Zephyr said with a shrug. "Some say he spent most of his time in Aikradal. Then he lost it soon after. Why? Do you know something?"

Belyx shook her head, her lips pressed in a thin line. A shiver of trepidation ran through her body as her gaze remained locked on Aurelius. Something deep within told her to take the risk—even if it meant allowing her pain and fear to be exposed.

"I have to talk to him," she said. "I have this feeling that he can help us win the Trial and save Aikradal. I need to learn from him. Also, there is a slight chance he knew my great-grandmother. He would know my Velena name."

"Are you sure? I mean, the guy's a killer, Belyx."

"Sometimes we must risk everything for the greater of the world. And if that means talking to a murderer, so be it."

With that, Belyx strode towards Aurelius's cell, her sensations a labyrinth in her mind. A mixture of fear and anticipation swirled as she approached the old man, his amber eyes meeting hers with an unreadable expression.

"Hello," she began, trying to keep her voice steady. "My name is Belyx Velena."

Aurelius regarded her in silence, his eyes narrowing ever so slightly. Belyx swallowed hard but continued.

"Are you the master who trained my great-grandmother in combat and other things?" Her throat trembled with hope. "Because if so, I could use your help. I am at an impasse in these trials and I need to get back and save my kingdom."

He remained silent, his face inscrutable. It was as if a wall had been erected between them, and no matter how much Belyx tried to breach it, Aurelius refused to let her in.

"Please," she implored, desperation creeping into her tone. "Aikradal is under Majerian control, and I need all the help I can to save my people. If there's anything you can teach me—"

"Enough!" he barked without warning, his throat dry and scratchy, like he seldom used it. "You have no business here, girl. Leave me be."

Reeling back, she ached with disappointment and frustration. But she wouldn't give up without a fight. The fate of her people depended on her being able to pass these trials, even if it meant learning from a far-gone master.

Determined, Belyx kept at him. The dim light flickered across Aurelius's worn face, revealing his sunken eyes that seemed to hold a millennium of secrets.

"I was taken captive while trying to protect my kingdom from the Majerian forces."

Aurelius remained silent, his gaze unyielding as if daring her to continue.

"Is there anything you can teach me? Anything that could help free my people?" Her eyes pleaded for an answer.

Still, he said nothing, his jaw clenched and eyes cold. Belyx took a deep breath, the weight of the soon-to-be trial bearing down on her shoulders. She knew she had no choice but to reveal the secret she had been guarding.

"The Order of the Rose needs your help," she whispered.

At her words, something in Aurelius snapped. His eyes blazed with fury as he slammed his hands against the bars of his cell, a loud clang coming from them.

"Give up on your foolish quest, girl!" he roared like thunder echoing through the prison. "The Order has no place in this rotting world!"

He threw his door shut, cutting off any further conversation. Belyx stared at the closed door, her chest tightening with a mixture of frustration and fear. Fighting to regain her composure, she realized that her goal was tarnished like a rotten apple.

Belyx dragged her feet back to Zephyr, who was pacing ten yards away. Each step echoed against the concrete floor and added weight to her already heavy heart. As she approached him, a sudden loud clang reverberated throughout the prison, its metallic tone ringing in her ears like an alarm. Sweat poured down her forehead as she looked around, trying to determine where it had come from.

"What is happening?" Belyx asked.

Zephyr shook his head. "The signal for the beginning of the first task for The Trial of Rain. It comes at random times so no one can be prepared."

"I'm always ready."

Both Belyx and Zephyr exchanged anxious glances, knowing the challenges that lay ahead.

"We work together on this, no matter what," Zephyr said, his body steady despite the uncertainty in his eyes.

Belyx nodded, her tenacity unwavering. "Stay safe and stay smart." Her skin trembled with a new cold sensation. Whatever these tasks were, she would win them all...and free her kingdom.

The hair on her neck standing up, she and the other prisoners were led underground, through a damp tunnel that opened into an immense, dark cavern. The air was heavy with the scent of saltwater and the sound of echoing waves lapping against the cave walls. A massive cliff loomed before them, its heights disappearing into the shadows above. Around fifty contestants huddled together, including Zephyr, Gelina, Soren, and Luo. Her confidence flushed at the sheer number of people...all vying for the same taste of freedom from this dingy place.

These trials were held once a year and every time, many people were killed. *All that killing. For some sick game.* The thought set Belyx's teeth on ice.

"I don't see rain," Belyx muttered, her gaze locked on the daunting rock face. She couldn't help but wonder what the other tasks might be, but she allowed herself a small smile. A wall meant climbing, and if there was one thing she had confidence in, it was her ability to scale heights.

"Attention, prisoners!" Prince Vincent's said as he approached them from his ship, which was anchored nearby, his presence stirring a maelstrom of anger within Belyx. She remembered his deception all too well and silently vowed to gut him for it. But for now, she would have to play his twisted game.

"Welcome to the Trials," he said, smirking. "I won't sugarcoat it—the rules are simple: you will die."

The area stayed silent as he chuckled like some demented puppet master.

"Only one or none of you will make it out alive after these four tasks. And believe me, by the end, you'll wish you'd been thrown into the Pits of Baraxat instead."

Belyx clenched her fists, struggling to keep her temper in check as she listened to Vincent's cruel words.

"The first trial is called The Rising." He motioned to the overhanging cliff, now foggy and ominous like a call to death. "You must climb this, while my numerous ships fire at you from above, attempting to knock you into the shark-infested waters below." He paused, his eyes gleaming with malicious delight. "Consider it the first step of rain, when the water evaporates. The rest of the Trials will follow a similar pattern. As I said before, there are no rules. Good luck."

"Shark-infested waters?" Zephyr whispered to Belyx as they stared at the crashing waves underneath the jagged rocks. "Well, at least we won't have to worry about drowning."

"Very funny." She couldn't shake the image of being thrown into the churning sea, at the mercy of the hungry sharks that lurked beneath the surface.

"Climbing is just...lovely," Gelina said. "We'll need each other's help to survive this."

"What choice do we have?" Belyx responded. Well, she could stay locked in prison forever, but that wouldn't save her kingdom. They were stronger together. She locked eyes with Gelina, then glanced over at Zephyr before returning her focus to Prince Vincent, who stood smugly on his ship. "Let's show them what we're made of."

"Enough chatter!" Vincent shouted, holding his hands up while his guards twisted their weapons in excitement. "I am in a giving mood so anyone who would like to back out can."

Everybody stayed and Belyx considered her chances of escaping without these trials, but now she had Zephyr and Gelina to think about. She had to protect them now.

The guards pulled Belyx from Gelina and Zephyr, forcing them into different lines of others. Panic clawed at her chest as she lost sight of her friends in the chaos, but Belyx swallowed her fear and focused on the task ahead. Vincent knew to separate her. *That sick bastard will get his!*

"Whoever makes it up the cliff alive advances to the next round!" Prince Vincent's twisted grin gleamed in the dim light. "Best of luck, prisoners. It is all you have."

Belyx wiped the sweat from her palms. She would need everything in her tank to push through this in one piece. The silence cut through the air like a well-made dagger. Restless prisoners shook next to her.

Vincent held up a pistol and with a smug smile, fired it. "Begin!" he barked, setting off a flurry of movement as the contestants surged forward toward the cliff face. Belyx's vision danced, her hands trembling with anxiety.

As they rushed on the bridge to the cliff, Belyx took a deep breath and began her ascent, her fingers finding purchase within the cracks of the rock face. Her mind blurred, calculating each move, while her heart thundered in her ears. As she climbed higher, the sounds of cannon fire and screams filled the cavern, an orchestra of chaos and terror.

Prisoners from all over were falling like rocks and the sharks feasted on their mid-morning meal. Holding the stones tight, she counted her breaths. Climbing was easy, but this proved challenging. Belyx continued and had a solid groove going when an explosion interrupted her thoughts. On instinct, she rotated her body and a fiery projectile slammed next to her, sending debris into her face.

She glanced down at the array of ships firing cannons at the wall, slamming into screaming prisoners. Prince Creep locked eyes with her and he gave a little finger wave. Another cannon propelled her way and she narrowly dodged again, feeling her muscles fail. She had to find her allies.

As she scanned the giant face, she climbed up and parallel. They had to be around on the other side. She made a promise and she would keep it.

Remember your training, she thought to herself, focusing on each movement, each breath.

You can do this. You will survive.

"Hey there, pretty thing," a gruff voice growled beside her, making Belyx's skin crawl. A burly man with a scarred face smirked down at her, his fingers curling on a jagged stone...a makeshift shiv. "How about I save you the trouble of climbing and just cut your throat right here?"

"Sorry," Belyx said with frost, her eyes flashing with defiance. "I don't plan on dying today." With a swift, fluid motion, she kicked out at the man, her foot connecting with his hand. He roared in pain and lunged at her, but Belyx dodged his grasp and sent him hurtling into the shark-filled waters. As his screams echoed through the cavern, she allowed herself a grim smile of satisfaction before continuing her climb.

"Skilled move," a person called from above, drawing her attention to a slender woman with silver-blonde hair. "But don't think I'll go down as easily." The woman's fingers flicked, and a barrage of knives hurtled toward Belyx.

"Damn it," Belyx muttered, twisting her body to avoid the deadly projectiles. How did they get weapons in here? She gritted her teeth as one grazed her arm, leaving a stinging trail of blood in its wake. Her rage flared, fueled by adrenaline and fear, and she hurled herself at the woman in a daring move that left them both dangling precariously from the cliffside.

"Get off me!" the woman screeched, her eyes wide with terror as Belyx's grip tightened around her throat. Belyx hesitated for a second, then released, watching dispassionately as the woman plummeted into the water below.

"Two down," she murmured, pulling herself back onto the cliff face. "But there are still so many more to go."

"Hey, Velena!" a mocking prisoner shouted from somewhere nearby. *Now what?*

Belyx's fingers dampened as she recognized Soren's taunting tone. "You're doing pretty well for a little princess! Don't worry, though—I'll make sure your kingdom remembers you fondly after you're dead!"

"You're fighting a losing fight, brute!" Belyx snarled, trying to ignore the dread coiling in her stomach. "I'm not going to die today, or any day soon. Remember that as you breathe your last breath."

"Ooh, scary!" Soren laughed. "We'll see how long that bravado lasts, Your Highness."

Belyx shot back a rude gesture, refocusing on her climb; needing to push through this trial, to find her friends and make sure they were safe. And if that meant taking down anyone who stood in her way, so be it.

Sorren lunged for her, but two prisoners came crashing down onto him and sent him down a couple of feet, giving Belyx room to escape. *Thank you, The God.*

"Almost there," she panted, her fingers aching with the effort of gripping the slippery rock. Her eyes darted around the cliff face, searching for any sign of Gelina or Zephyr. A sudden shout caught her attention, and she spotted Zephyr locked in combat with a hulking brute of a man, while Gelina clung to a nearby ledge, her face pale with fear.

"Zephyr!" Belyx cried out, adrenaline spurring her on as she scrambled toward her friend. With a fierce yell, she launched herself at the man, her knee connecting with his jaw and sending him plummeting into the water below. "Are you okay?" She reached out to steady Zephyr as he swayed over the rocks.

"Thanks to you," he replied, his skin glistening with sweat. "Gelina's fine too, but we need to keep moving. The cannons and other prisoners are getting closer."

"Right," Belyx agreed, her being blossoming like a garden as they resumed their climb. Shark-infested waters churned below them, and cannon fire threatened to tear them from the wall, but Belyx wouldn't give in. She would survive this trial, and she would protect those she cared about—no matter the cost.

Cannon's exploded around her, showering Belyx with jagged shards and blurring her vision. She gritted her teeth and dug her hands into the cliff face, trying to find footing on the slippery surface.

In a panic, Zephyr and Gelina were nowhere to be found. Her eyes scanned the chaos below, searching for any of their falling bodies, but they hadn't fallen.

"Zephyr!" she shouted over the cacophony of battle cries and rock debris. "Where are you?" They were just here!

"Over here!" he said. She spotted him several feet away, one arm wrapped around Gelina's waist as he struggled to climb with her weight slowing him down.

"I'll cover you!" Belyx called before leaping across a gap in the rocks, dodging a cannonball that left a trail of white smoke behind it. As she reached Zephyr and Gelina, she noticed three other prisoners closing in on them, their faces twisted with malice.

"Stay back," Belyx warned, pulling out a jagged stone from the cliff. The prisoners laughed, unmoved by her threat. With a surge of courage, she lunged at the nearest one, sinking her rock into his shoulder. He screamed in pain and stumbled back, losing his grip, and plummeting into the waters. The other two hesitated, casting wary glances at their fallen comrade.

"Try me," Belyx snarled, her gaze blazing with fury. She turned to Zephyr, who was still struggling to keep Gelina safe from harm. "Can you climb up?"

Gelina's blue and brown eyes widened, but she nodded determinedly. "I can do it."

"Good." Belyx faced the remaining attackers, her fighting spirit undeterred. "You two want to join your friend down there?"

They exchanged uneasy looks before backing away, unwilling to risk their lives against Belyx's fierceness. She breathed a shaky sigh of relief, her sensations flowing like a river as she turned back to help Zephyr and Gelina.

"Thanks, Belyx," Zephyr panted, his tattoos standing out starkly on his sweat-slicked face. "I don't think we could've made it without you."

"Neither do I," Gelina agreed, her thinning brown hair plastered to her forehead. Her kind smile was strained but genuine.

"We are not there yet," Belyx replied. They had little time for sentimentality. They had to keep moving if they wanted to survive this deadly trial.

The trio resumed their climb, Belyx's body ached from the effort and the relentless barrage of cannon fire.

Just as they neared the top, Soren appeared above them, his dirty blonde wisps whipping around his face as he leered down at Belyx.

"Didn't think you'd escape me so fast, Velena."

"Get out of our way," Belyx spat, her muscles trembling with fatigue. He lunged for her, aiming to throw her off the cliff, but Gelina swung her arm out just in time, striking him across the face. He stumbled backward, losing his footing, descending toward the water below. He underestimated the wrong woman.

"Is he...?" Gelina began, breath shaking.

Belyx shook her head. "No." Soren caught hold of a rocky ledge, his eyes burning with anger. "He'll be back."

"Let's go," Zephyr urged, pulling them onward. Finally, they reached the top of the wall, joining the other panting, battered survivors.

Soren and his accomplice, Luo, followed close behind like a disease. This wasn't over.

Belyx's arms felt like they were on fire, her body drenched in sweat and exhaustion.

"Thirty of you trash made it. Congratulations," a guard waiting announced as he spat on the ground, his eyes devoid of any warmth. "Your reward...cell time." The remaining prisoners were dragged back to their cells, and although Belyx was thankful to survive, the looming knowledge they still had three more of these grueling tests cast a heavy cloud of dread over her.

After Belyx was thrown into her cell, she staggered back against the stone wall. Its coldness seeped through her clothes. But she welcomed the cold, drawing strength from it. She closed her eyes as a wave of relief washed over her. *One down*, she thought, letting a fierce resolve surge through her veins.

And three to go.

SEVENTEEN

Enzo loved to read, but these kinds of texts were just ridiculous. As he sat hunched over the ancient fae history tome, his eyes scanned the pages as the flickering glow of candlelight danced on the faded ink. The parchment crackled beneath his fingertips. The words were written in fae dead language and it translated to common about as well as a toddler telling a convoluted story.

It had been almost a day and so far he made little progress on what he needed to revive The Original. His tribe had turned its back on Aikradal, but he wouldn't do the same. The Original would help free this world from the clutches of Majeria, like he did long ago with the fae and witch war.

The text said The Original would be honored and serve those who revived him from his slumber. A pit sunk in his stomach.

The Original had forsaken the gods, but only due to his fixation on power. Perhaps the fae did require strong leadership, Enzo mused. Anything was better than remaining idle and inactive. After all, neutrality only benefited the oppressors. It was something he'd read in a book once, and it had stamped an indelible impression on him. Therefore, he knew that standing up for justice was crucial.

Enzo traced his finger down the yellowed page. Three objects had been left behind, embedded within The Originals magic, ready to revive him when a determined and powerful fae called to him.

I guess that's me.

The text said these items were hard to find and retrieving them equally deadly. Many had tried and paid the ultimate price.

As Enzo squinted his eyes at the tattered sheet, a familiar voice cooed, "I can lend a hand you know."

Enzo turned away from his father, not wanting to speak to any of his tribe right now...especially his fathers.

Gink turned down the gesture and bent over, his brown ponytail brushing Enzo's arm, a missed comfort from when Enzo was a child. "Where are you supposed to find the first object?" Gink asked, leaning in closer.

"The Lake," Enzo replied. "In the forbidden part, where no fae dares to venture. Where your worst fears will be recognized."

"Sehrlic Lake? Only fools go there. It is cursed," Gink interjected.

Enzo recalled the stories, but he had handled worse. "The second object, his quill, is through the mists of—what?"

An audible gulp left Gink. "Memories. Ones you wish were forgotten."

How bad could that be? Enzo had nothing but good memories...repressing his bad ones. It was his present that threatened everything.

Gink took the book again. "And the third one, a sacred key, is in the caves with creatures that no fae dares challenge."

"What does that mean?"

Gink shrugged. "I have no idea about any of it, but are you sure you need to do this?"

"It is the only way. You all won't do anything."

He regretted the stab, but Gink had to hear it. As if diverting the attack, Gink replied, "do you think you can do this without Belyx?"

Enzo paused, his lips pressing together as doubt crept through him. Belyx had always been there for him, guiding and supporting him. But now she was a captive far away. He had to do this alone—for their people. So that when she returned, it would be to a restored home.

"I have to try." He closed the book and tucked it into his messenger bag. "Aikradal depends on it."

"I wish we could help more, son I—"

Enzo stormed away from his father but turned his head. "Save it. Once again, I will do things myself." He marched on, letting those be the potential last words to his father. The fae had free will, they could help. They were cowards. Enzo would be the one to do something about this.

The ominous expanse of the Sehrlic Lake stretched before Enzo, its dark waters churning restlessly under an iron-gray sky. A shiver crawled down his spine, not from the cold but from the palpable sense of foreboding that hung in the air, filling his nostrils with the scent of danger and decay. He had recalled trying to play here as a child and his tribe pulling him away, stating how no faes came back from this lake.

Enzo's shoulders tightened, a drumbeat of doubt threatened to drown out the resolve he had mustered. He missed Belyx with an ache that could shatter him, and the thought of plunging into the depths of Sehrlic Lake without her left him feeling more alone than ever before.

Maybe he couldn't do this. His mind cracked under the weight of his fears. But Aikradal couldn't wait any longer. Even if it meant facing his fears on his own, he had to do this…like when he had lived on the streets.

Summoning what little courage he had, Enzo stepped forward, his bare feet sinking into the muddy shoreline as he stared out across the forbidding waters. The lake seemed to beckon him, daring him to venture forth and confront the unknown that lurked within its depths.

Enzo plunged into the dark depths, hoping that he would emerge victorious—or at least stay alive.

Enzo's fire flickered inside his veins, casting a warm sensation while under the murky water. The cold tendrils of fear crept up his spine as he swam towards the small island in the middle of the lake. The lake weighed like a ship upon him, threatening to drag him down into the abyss below.

Keep going, he thought as the water rushed around his head.

As soon as Enzo reached the island, he pulled himself onto the slick, moss-covered rocks. His lips trembled, despite it not even being cold. He was so close now—he couldn't afford to hesitate or second-guess this plan.

Globs of cold liquid left his throat as he scanned the shadows for any sign of the journal. What kind of task was this? It didn't appear too dangerous. But he knew the story wasn't over until the final page.

He barely took another step when something sharp pierced his skin. A searing pain sliced through him, snuffing out his fire like a gust of wind extinguishing a candle. Panic clawed at his chest as he realized his flames were gone, leaving him vulnerable and exposed. He tried for a spark, but his hand stayed bare, no flame in sight.

"Damn it," Enzo hissed, cradling his pierced foot. He had gone without shoes. The memory of last year's powerlessness washed over him, a chilling reminder of how he had hidden his true self for thirteen long years. He forced himself to breathe, slow and steady, unwilling to give in to the fear threatening to consume him.

You've come this far without your powers before. You can do it again. He needed to remain strong and pull from the Enzo he was on the streets...just a common thief.

His mind galloped as he tried to remember everything he had learned during those dark years, relying on his wit and cunning to survive in a world that sought to erase his very existence. With a grim resolve, he pressed on, navigating the treacherous terrain with a heightened sense of awareness.

Each step he took grew with a newfound purpose. Belyx was counting on him. His foot throbbed like no other. He wondered what the spike was made of and if he'd ever recover from what it had done to him. As he walked away, he promised next time he would be more vigilant.

Enzo crept along the path, legs tightening as he tried to identify and avoid all the hidden dangers. His eyes darted around, searching for tripwires or pitfalls that could put an end to all hope. Exhausted, he still felt a glimmer of strength deep within himself, despite the overwhelming terror surrounding him.

Your fire isn't gone, he thought desperately, willing his powers to return. It was only a poison...just an odd anti-fae toxin. But what if it had been more sinister? Were there other deadly things lurking here on the island? Recalling his tribe's warnings from when he was a child—this lake was cursed—he now believed it.

As he neared the center of the island, the oppressive darkness began to lift, replaced by a soft, ethereal glow. The source of the light called out to him, guiding him through the shadows like a beacon of hope. It couldn't be this easy.

As he crept closer to the siren light, his fingers fidgeted with clothes; he reached out towards the mysterious object, praying that it was the object he needed.

The flicker changed and led to a firefly-lit path spanning deeper into the island. Enzo's breath hitched as he continued moving through, now more vulnerable than ever. Despite his lack of fire power, he refused to give up. Sweat dripped down his furrowed brow as he scanned the environment for any sign of danger.

I'm still a skilled thief, he thought, tapping into his extensive knowledge of traps and snares. A sudden snap echoed through the air, and Enzo narrowly avoided an arrow that whistled past his ear. Suppressing a shudder, he pushed onward.

He muttered a curse, focusing on each step. His fingers twitched with anticipation as he disarmed another hidden trap with deft-like precision, the intricate mechanisms clicking into place beneath his nimble touch.

"Almost there." His feet bounced on his heels.

With every fiber of his being focused on survival, Enzo leaped over a pit of sharpened spikes and rolled out of the way of a swinging log adorned with vicious barbs. The copper tang of blood filled his mouth as he bit his lip, steeling himself for the final stretch.

Enzo drew from a deep well of tenacity and pushed through.

Hurtling between a series of concealed dart launchers, Enzo finally reached what appeared to be the last obstacle: an enormous stone wall covered in razor-sharp vines. He eyed the treacherous growth with apprehension but knew he had no choice but to scale it.

Here goes nothing.

Enzo clenched his jaw as he clawed and scrambled higher up the rock face, his bloodied hands slipping on the jagged vines. His skin ripped away under the unforgiving thorns, yet he gritted his teeth and stubbornly pushed forward, refusing to quit before he reached the top. He fell onto the hard ground, exhausted from the effort, and gasped for air as a crimson river of blood rolled off his aching limbs.

"Made it," he wheezed, a triumphant grin spreading across his face despite the pain that wracked his body.

In the center of the small clearing, nestled among the moss and ivy, lay a weathered leather-bound journal. Enzo's hands were suddenly sensitive as he gingerly picked it up, fingers tracing the faded gold lettering on its cover. The worn pages crackled beneath his touch, filled with secrets of a time long past.

He smiled, clutching the ancient tome to his chest. One down. Enzo sprinted back before more traps could come.

Steel entered his gaze as he rose to his feet, adrenaline coursing through his veins. Enzo was a fighter, and he was a good runner too. With renewed purpose, he sprinted back the way he had come, dodging the traps he'd already navigated earlier. Each stride brought him closer to saving Aikradal, and he swore he wouldn't let them down.

His muscles burned for relief.

Enzo pushed himself through the pain barrier and refused to give up. His tribe needed him, Belyx needed him, and he would not fail them now.

Enzo burst through the water's surface, air greedily rushing into his lungs as he swam away from the treacherous island. The oppressive weight of the forbidden part of Sehrlic Lake seemed to lift with each stroke, though the knowledge that he carried one of the three objects required to revive The Original weighed on his mind like lead.

I'm one step closer, he thought, casting a look over his shoulder at the receding island. His fire powers had not yet returned, but he couldn't afford to waste any time. Aikradal's fate rested on his shoulders now, and he would not fail them.

The shore drew nearer, and Enzo swam faster, the strain in his muscles and the chill of the lake gnawing at his bones. With one final, forceful stroke, he hauled himself onto the rocky sand, panting for breath.

Enzo gritted his teeth against the exhaustion threatening to pull him under. He glanced down at the ancient journal in his hand, its pages seeming to whisper secrets of ages long past.

On shaky legs, adrenaline fueling his spark; he sprinted back toward his tribe. Dirt kicked up around him, and the sinking sun cast an eerie glow over the landscape. Every step brought new urgency to his mission. As he neared the outskirts of the forest, shouts and cries pierced the still air.

Enzo's eyes fluttered as he climbed the hill overlooking the Aikradal docks. Majerian guards marched in formation, their cruel faces twisted in triumph. More slaves were being herded like cattle from the docked ships, their shackles clanking in a sickening symphony of despair.

"No," he said, horror twisting his gut. "This can't be happening."

At the edge of the Sehrlic Forest, the wind tugged at Enzo's brown curls as he watched in shock.

Like a long-lost friend, his flames flickered along his fingertips. In another miracle, his powers had returned, and he would burn them all.

Freyja approached him, her determined gaze locked onto the ships.

"Did you find it?"

Enzo nodded, his wounds now seeping with his fae healing. "We can't let more slaves come in."

"We can handle this. I promise you, slaves will never be part of Aikradal." Her throat hitched, as if she was trying to drown her emotions.

He clenched his fists, letting the fire inside him be unleashed. "But I want to help," he insisted, unable to shake the disappointment in his fathers and the fae for not aiding the cause.

Freyja placed a reassuring hand on his shoulder. "Your skills are required elsewhere. Find the second object. We'll take care of this. Majeria has the advantage, but if this Original is what you say, they are in for it." She let a smile across her face.

After the heavy from the burden of his task, Enzo glanced back at the forest.

"Fine," he muttered, turning away from the chaos unfolding before him.

The Order would handle Majeria for now. The more he waited, the more powerful Majeria would become. Right now, he had one goal.

"Two more objects," he whispered to himself as he ran, the wind whipping through his hair and stinging his eyes. "Just two more, and I can save us all."

He pushed himself harder, muscles straining and lungs burning, knowing that every second counted. Aikradal's future hung in the balance, and Enzo would stop at nothing to ensure their freedom.

Eighteen

"Are you alright, Belyx?" Gelina asked. Her wheelchair creaked as she leaned closer, offering a comforting presence. The first trial had been over for a day now, but she couldn't shake the cannon blasts and sharks eating people out of her mind. The sun dipped low, casting long shadows over the training grounds as she stared at the dirt beneath her feet. She was drained from the last challenge they had faced and couldn't help but wonder if her skills were enough to win the rest of the trials.

"I don't know," Belyx admitted. "I'm not sure I can do this."

Gelina's kind smile never wavered. "You're stronger than you think. Don't doubt yourself now."

"Maybe there's another way," Zephyr piped up, his eyes flickering in the fading sunlight. He twirled his fingers idly, his recent wounds haphazardly covered standing out against his muscles. "We could try breaking out of here. It couldn't be too hard."

"I have thought of that," Belyx mused. "Majerian guards are nothing but morons."

Gelina shook her head. "It has to be the trials.

"But why?" Belyx asked, heat lacing her tongue. "Surely, you know we all can't survive it."

Gelina stared off into the distance, closing her eyes. "I do. And I have made my peace with it."

"No!" Zephyr turned away. "No one dies here. No one!"

Gelina only responded with a shrug and Zephyr shifted to Belyx. "What do you think?"

With a glance, she saw Aurelius sitting in his cell staring at a wall like he did every day. The knowledge he possessed could be rarer than a diamond. Should she try convincing him again? Her grandmother always said a flower planted once never grows...or something like that.

It didn't matter though, as he wanted nothing to do with her.

Belyx frowned, considering her new plan. "I think I need to talk to Aurelius again."

Zephyr hung his head in his hands. "Not this again. Belyx. I don't know what you could learn from him."

A high-pitched sound left Gelina.

"What?" Zephyr asked.

"His past, Zephyr."

Zephyr shook his head. "No way. That is why they are rumors."

Irritation licked at Belyx. "What now?"

Zephyr eyed Gelina and she shrugged. With a groan, Zephyr said, "Aurelius is rumored to possess some kind of ancient magic. He apparently has never lost a fight."

Belyx's eyes widened. "What magic?"

"Why don't you ask him? I think it is dog-wash," Zephyr growled.

"Hog-wash," Gelina corrected, getting an eye roll from Zephyr.

Standing up, she headed for him. "I think I will."

If such a thing existed, she was determined to learn it. Images of Enzo flashed through her mind—his reassuring smile, the warmth of his touch. He was depending on her, and she would do anything to keep him safe.

As she set off, Belyx couldn't help but feel dread. The master was about as approachable as a cactus, but if he knew some ancient magic, she would win these blasted trials and get the hell out of this prison. The first trial was horrendous and it was sheer luck they all made it out alive. And if Prince Vincent held to his nasty demeanor, then the next three would morph progressively worse.

Belyx approached Aurelius, a newfound fire surging through her veins despite the ever-present ache in her heart. The elderly man sat on a worn wooden stool in his cell, his attention focused on a small leather cup and a handful of dice.

"Master Aurelius," Belyx began, "as you can see, I won the first trial, but I need to win the rest as well. I have to get back to my kingdom."

Shockingly, he said nothing.

"I understand this prison has been hard, but I know about your secret. How did you become unbeatable in combat? Is it some sort of magic?"

Aurelius's amber eyes looked up for a moment before returning to his game, a single dice rolling across the dirt floor. He offered no response, the silence between them heavy and oppressive.

"Please," Belyx tried again, desperation seeping into her tone. "What is this ancient secret you possess? I have never asked for much, but right now, I need it. I can't watch anyone else die. Teach it to me so I can protect my kingdom and those I love."

Aurelius continued to ignore her, scooping up the dice and shaking them in his cup without a word. Belyx felt her frustration boiling over as she clenched her hands into fists.

"Fine," she spat, "if you won't help me, then I'll just have to find another way." As she turned to leave, she couldn't resist one last stab. "Pathetic old man. I bet you weren't a master, just a drunk!"

The old master remained silent, rolling the dice once more. His refusal to acknowledge her only fueled Belyx's relentlessness—she would not be defeated by his stubbornness. What a waste of breath from a lousy old coot!

Belyx found Gelina and Zephyr sitting together at a rough-hewn table, sharing a meal of unappetizing fish. Her stomach churned at the sight...what a strange day it had been. She was too consumed by her thoughts to care about eating.

"I can't believe it," she muttered, slumping down onto a bench between her friends. "He won't even talk to me. At least he didn't slam a door in my face."

"That's progress in my eyes," Gelina added.

"Always positive, Gelina," Zephyr said, tearing off a piece of cod with his teeth. "Remember when there was that Majerian blockade and you said the sun was shining, so we would be okay?"

Gelina shrugged while offering Belyx a meal. "What can I say? Positivity breeds positivity."

If only that were true.

She still envied her attitude. "Well, I'm glad you are hopeful," Belyx said, picking at the greasy fish on her plate. "But I'm starting to lose hope."

"Hope is something we can't afford to lose," Gelina said, her tone lightening. "Without it, we have nothing. It is the air we breathe, and the food we eat. Hope separates us from evil."

Belyx looked into Gelina's eyes, her despair reflecting on her. But there was also strength—a resilience that had carried her friend through unimaginable hardships.

"I think it's time I tell you," Gelina said. "How I started doing what I do and how hope saved me."

She paused to take a deep breath before beginning her story. Belyx leaned in closer. Zephyr refused to share about her; why she was injured and how she ended up here. Some much-needed inspiration would do Belyx some good in this place. "When my entrance into the world was announced, the elders of our village warned that I should never have been given life, and should be killed, for I would never be able to stand without assistance, nor use my legs as others do. But instead of following their orders, my parents chose to defy them and embrace me for who I am. They taught me that despite my disability, I could still dream and fight for all that I believed in."

As she spoke, Belyx saw a wistful determination shining through Gelina's angelic features. "My best friend was sold into sex slavery at a young age. I hated how they forced women to do such heinous things. That's when I started an underground rescue trail for sex slaves. It was easy at first, as no one suspected a dainty dame in a wheelchair to be so sneaky." She fluttered her eyes up and down. "Zephyr," Gelina continued, a sad smile playing at her lips, "was one of the first people who volunteered to help me. He was a famous pirate and made a great asset with his ships, as well as a fantastic friend. He began smuggling food for the slaves, and together, we saved countless lives."

Tears pricked at the corners of her eyes. "You were so brave. Maybe there is hope after all." Belyx said.

"Told you so," Gelina said, reaching out to squeeze her hand. "We are stronger together."

Belyx nodded, the weight of her friends' support uplifting her. The road ahead would be treacherous and fraught with danger, but with their help, she was determined to face whatever challenges came her way.

With a renewed spirit in her, Belyx strode back towards Aurelius. The old man was still hunched over his one-player dice game, the harsh lines of his face illuminated by the flickering candlelight.

He must know something, she thought.

Something that would give her the edge she craved.

"Teach me," Belyx demanded, staying firm and unwavering. "Teach me your ancient secret." In her fear, she recalled Gelina, fighting for her beliefs despite all who stood against her.

Aurelius scoffed, not bothering to look up from his dice. "A pathetic Aikradal queen could never learn such a thing, especially one whose emotions are clouded." His breath dripped with disdain as he rolled the dice once more. *So there was some kind of technique after all.* What kind though?

"Please," Belyx said, her patience wearing thin. She balled her fists at her sides, a familiar heat of anger rising within her. "I need this. I have to win...haven't you cared for something once?"

"Ha!" Aurelius laughed without humor. "You think I don't know what it's like to be desperate? To want something so badly it consumes you?" He finally cranked his head up at her, his eyes cold and unyielding. "But I will never train an Aikradal queen again."

"Wh-what do you mean...again?" Belyx stammered, taken aback by the venom in his tone. An odd sensation crept down her spine, as though an ancient memory were trying to claw its way to the surface. Marjorie, her great-grandmother, *had* trained with him, hadn't she?

"Your family is cursed," Aurelius spat, focusing his attention back on his dice. "Their blood runs through your veins, tainting everything you touch. You'll bring nothing but ruin...Aikradal was doomed from the start."

"Enough!" Belyx screamed, her vision blurring with hot tears. She wanted to lunge at him, to make him understand the depth of her pain, her desperation. But as her throat constricted with the pressure of her emotions, she couldn't force him to help her.

"Fine," Belyx hissed, turning away from the old man. "I'll win without you." Despite the setback, she was certain success was within reach. Last year, she liberated the fae and vanquished an infamous witch. She could do anything and she would triumph.

With barely a step, the sound of a bell echoed through the prison, its heavy clang sending a shudder through her body. She clenched her teeth and held her head high, determined not to show any sign of fear or weakness. The second trial was starting already.

Nineteen

As he ventured deeper into the abandoned part of the Sehrlic Forest, the shadows grew darker and the air colder. Enzo felt the pull of the tunnel of memories, where fae had lost their minds to the ghosts of their past. He shivered, grateful for the fire that surged through his veins once more. Losing it to the traps for the last object had left him vulnerable and exposed, but now he was whole again.

Why won't they fight this? Thinking of his fathers and the fae who resisted standing against the injustice that Majeria had placed upon Aikradal made his blood simmer.

The wind howled through the trees as if echoing his frustration. The fae's pacifist code would ironically cost more innocent people their lives. Aikradal had now become a hub of sick and oppressive people. Reviving The Original. ..was the one way to help.

The entrance to the tunnel loomed ahead, its darkness beckoning him like a siren's call. He hesitated, unsure of the dangers that lay within. But he had a mission to complete, and he refused to let fear stand in his way.

"Here goes nothing." Taking a deep breath, he stepped into the unknown.

As Enzo ventured deeper into the cave of memories, he could feel the dampness in the air, and a chill that seeped through his clothing. He braced himself against the wall as slick, slimy moss grew in patches along the sides. Shadows crept closer, like fingers reaching out to him, and an intense pressure bore down on him. But he wouldn't give up. Holding tight to his courage, he pressed forward, willing his ember to push away the darkness.

"Don't lose your cool, Enzo," he murmured, navigating the twists and turns with practiced ease. He laughed. "I've never lost that...except now I appear to be talking to myself. Oh boy."

The dim light in the cave was slowly fading, enclosing Enzo in shadows as he stumbled through the crevices. It had been about an hour since entering and he found nothing so far.

His thoughts lingered on Belyx as a heavy sadness weighed him down. Was she still alive? Would he be able to revive The Original and save her before it was too late? He missed the sensation of her lips against his and her over-enthusiasm about little things like poetry. That would always make Enzo stop and take notice.

As he continued down the dark tunnel, using his flame as a light source, his body ached at the thought that perhaps she was already lost to him. But he couldn't let himself dwell on that possibility, not when there were still tasks to be done. Gritting his teeth, he pushed onward.

Belyx, stay strong, he prayed, as if she could hear him through the trees. *I'm coming for you.*

The mouth of the cave gaped before him, swallowing all light like an endless void. Taking a deep breath, Enzo stepped inside, feeling the chill air wrap around him like a shroud. At first, the tunnel appeared calm—almost too much, given the tales he'd heard of fae losing their minds within its depths.

"You're here for a reason...And stop talking to yourself." With that, he pressed forward, allowing his guiding fire to lead him along the winding passages.

But as he crossed deeper into the inky blackness, a menacing quiet shook his bones. His vision distorted and morphed until he felt as if the cold, hard walls of the cave were crushing his chest. Like an icy hand was shaking him awake, he found himself back on the cobblestone streets of Aikradal—but this time in his twelve-year-old body, sobbing helplessly as his tears iced over.

"Please...please don't hurt me," he cried.

Two men, brandishing metal bars, advanced on Enzo as he clutched the apple in his palm. He had tried to earn money the honest way, but his hunger got the better of him—now he was going to be beaten for a mere piece of fruit.

Tears welled in his eyes as they closed in, but then a mysterious figure appeared and sent them both sprawling to the ground. Enzo went to flee—what he was best at—but the stranger held out their hands, halting him in his tracks.

"Hey, kid," a gentle voice called out, cutting through the haze of his terror. The person stood over him, their short purple hair glistening in the moonlight. They helped him up. "My name is Ren. What is yours?"

Enzo shivered, still holding the apple over his chest. Like it was his last meal.

"I won't steal that from you. I promise. In fact, I can teach you how to steal a lot of things and not get caught by worthless brutes like them."

Nodding, he took Ren's hand.

"Come on, let's get you out of here."

"Thank you," Enzo said shakily, grasping Ren's hand and letting them lead him away from danger.

The vision shifted to two years in the future and Enzo fell to the floor, shaking, knowing full well what came next.

"Enzo, I need you to watch my back," Ren called out. "I won't be in there long. Just make sure to give me the signal when the Berserkers show. Okay?"

"I won't let you down," he promised, his eyes already scanning the shadows for any sign of threat.

Ren saluted Enzo as they always did and dipped into the warehouse.

Time seemed to stand still as Enzo waited impatiently. He was growing increasingly restless, but kept his gaze fixed on the horizon for any signs of Berserkers. Despite the risks he faced by doing so, he found himself drawn to the market stalls—the same stalls that had been his respite from danger for many years. Those times when they stole from the markets were countless, but Enzo always made sure to repay the favor. The fae had taught him balance and he intended to keep it that way.

A few minutes went by of his daydreaming and a commotion caught his eye. Ren! He sprinted back to find multiple hulking men screaming inside the warehouse they were stealing from.

Ren!

Ren would be okay. Ren would be okay. His mind raced with fear as he desperately searched for them. Then, his shoulders sank as he saw them at the end of an alley, their lifeless body surrounded by a haunting pool of blood. "Ren!" He dropped to his knees and wept with helplessness as he clutched Ren's frail frame in his arms. Tears streaming down his face, he whispered like an echo. "Please... I'm so sorry. You deserved better."

He held his mentor the whole night as Ren's eyes turned cold. He had only drifted away for a few minutes, but even a second could change the fate of a life.

"Enzo." The whisper was faint, like a breeze rustling through leaves. It was enough to pull him from the darkness of his memories, bringing him back to the tunnel. Blinking away tears, he realized it had been the light from his fire that had drawn him out of the flashback.

"Ren...I don't want to lose anyone else," he said. However, deep down inside, fear clawed at him and threatened to make him turn back.

A chilling sensation crept up Enzo's leg, rousing him from his stupor. He glanced down, horror gripping his heart as a shadowy tendril coiled around his calf, trying to feed on the lingering despair from his memories.

"Get off!" he snarled, igniting a flame in his palm and driving it into the darkness. The shadow recoiled with a soundless scream, retreating into the depths of the cave.

Enzo panted, sweat beading on his brow. He had failed to save Ren with his powers then, but failure wasn't an option now.

He clenched his fists, needing to find the second object and leave here before more weird shadows tried to have him for dinner.

As he wandered deeper into the tunnel, its gloom pressed in around him like a thick fog. His fire cast eerie shapes onto the walls, their flickering forms giving life to his mounting anxiety. Every strange shadow made him jump. The space was closing in too fast.

As Enzo rounded a bend, his gaze fell upon an ancient, wooden table nestled against the cave wall. Atop the dusty surface sat an old quill pen, its silver nib tarnished and weathered, yet still elegant in design. A single crimson feather protruded from the base, glowing faintly under the firelight. He reached out, fingers trembling with anticipation.

After a quick exhale, a wave of relief and triumph washed over him. But before he touched it—

"Enzo...," Belyx's voice whispered from behind him, her tone laced with contempt. Clenching the quill tight, he spun around, his voice tight at the sight of her— something was wrong.

"Can't even keep me safe, can you?" Her eyes were cold as a night storm. She fell into an unfamiliar man, his tan skin adorned with tattoos, and pressed her lips hungrily to his.

"Who is this?" Enzo demanded, the fire in his hand flaring with fury. "What have you done with Belyx?"

She pulled away from the attractive male but looked hungry for more. "Your incompetence allowed me to be captured," she sneered, pulling away from the stranger's embrace. "And now, I've found someone better." The man smirked at Enzo, a glint of malevolence in his amber eyes.

"Stop it!" His flames surged forth like a tidal wave, engulfing the false vision before him. As the deceptive figures vanished, he staggered back, gasping for breath. His throat parched, but this had been just another trick of the shadows.

Clutching the quill close to his chest, Enzo steeled himself and pressed on, determined to overcome the darkness of the tunnel and the haunting memories it provoked.

Enzo's feet dug into the damp earth beneath him, trying to anchor back to reality. He knew the sight was a lie, but the pain in his being was too real. Gritting his teeth, he shifted back onto his feet, searching for a way out of here.

But as he stepped too far forward, the shadow struck again. The world around him faded, replaced by another false dream. Belyx was there...again. Her fiery hair was a stark contrast to the darkness.

"Enzo, how could you let this happen?" Her voice was adorned with accusation. "You were supposed to protect me."

"I know...," he replied, the weight of guilt settling heavily on his shoulders. His forehead coated in sweat at the sight of the stranger from before, sliding his arm on Belyx possessively.

"Because of you, I'm dead," she said, her once vibrant eyes turning grey. "You failed me." The man pulled her again. "At least *we* can be together in the afterlife. Sad you are still fighting your games here. But I am free.

"No!" Enzo's screams echoed.

Belyx and the man laughed. "Face it. You are a fae, I am a human. Your kind will betray us and I know it. I've been preparing for a while haven't I?" The stranger nodded and Belyx clawed at him with passion again. Enzo tried to close his eyes, but the vision stayed. This wasn't real!

"The fae will betray us all," she said. "Your kind is nothing but trash. Go join them."

"Enough!" Enzo's flames emerged from his hands like a wild inferno. They would not tempt him again. What was this magic?

The heat scorched the air, the intensity of his emotions feeding the fire. The apparition of Belyx and the man evaporated in the blaze, leaving only the smell of burning behind.

Panting, Enzo dropped to his knees, his arms trembling from the effort. The quill pen lay unharmed beside him, untouched by the firestorm he had just unleashed. He hesitated before wrapping his fingers around it, relief flooding through him, praying that no more awful visions afflicted him.

But even as he clung to the triumph of finding the second object, Enzo couldn't shake the lingering images from the vision. Belyx's accusing eyes and the way she had leaned into that man's touch haunted him, gnawing at the edges of his heart.

Enzo held back tears, trying to push the memory aside. *That was not the real Belyx. She is out there, waiting for me.*

With renewed determination, Enzo rose to his feet, clutching the quill as if it were a lifeline. The unknowns of anger controlled him no longer—he would face whatever challenges awaited him head-on and return to Belyx's side again. No one else would die for his mistakes. Once The Original returned, the fae would see reason and help with his conflict. One object to go.

TWENTY

The prisoners were herded up the side of a towering mountain, its peak shrouded in an eerie fog, like talons reaching out to snatch them. She glanced at Zephyr, who grimaced but nodded resolutely, his messy hair tied in a back knot.

"Promise me we won't get separated this time," Belyx urged over the howling wind around them.

"I promise," Zephyr replied. "We'll stick together."

"May the God protect us," Gelina murmured, as she kept her head heavenward.

Only thirty prisoners remained in these sick games. All with the same goal...to win. Whatever this foggy pass was, it cast an eerie prophecy that more would perish.

As they crested the top of the mountain, Prince Vincent emerged from the fog, his usual sapphire eyes cold and calculating. He looked down upon the ragged band of prisoners, a curl growing on his tiny lip, before addressing them all. "Welcome to The Clouding, the trial that will test your wits and survival instincts." His voice carried on the frigid air, sending shivers down Belyx's spine. "This labyrinth is filled with dangers both seen and unseen, and getting lost within it is not the only way you might meet your end."

He paused, letting the terror sink in, and then his gaze fell heavily upon Belyx. A cruel smile played on his lips. "Take what weapons you need." Belyx clenched her fists, the anger boiling within her like a volcanic eruption waiting to happen.

She imagined slicing Vincent open with one of the knives, watching the life drain from his eyes as they dulled like tarnished silver.

"Let's keep moving," Zephyr urged as he took a curved scabbard from the pile while the other prisoners pillaged them. Belyx could kill them right now, but guards were still everywhere. *Save the killing for the Trial.*

Belyx grabbed a couple of blades and Zephyr arched a brow. "It is all I need," Belyx added...her palms clenched the handles of the knives, knuckles turning white with tension. A vibration ran through her body on what they would face in there.

"I believe it," he responded with a smirk. "Gelina, take one."

Gelina shook her head. "I don't fight. The God will protect me."

"You mean us?" Zephyr chided and Gelina shot him a down-faced glare.

Belyx shivered as they stepped up to the labyrinth. She couldn't help but feel as though they were walking straight into the gaping maw of some terrible beast. But she steeled herself, the idea that they were one step closer to freedom pushing her onward. She would face whatever horrors lay ahead.

"Begin!" Prince Vincent's command echoed through the fog, and the prisoners surged into the maze. Belyx expected instant pushback from the others, but they sailed on.

"Stay close," Belyx said. The thick air obscured everything beyond a few feet, turning the labyrinth into a twisted, confusing nightmare.

"Left or right?" Zephyr asked, his hand resting on the hilt of his sword.

"Right," Belyx decided, her instincts guiding her despite the oppressive fog. As they ventured deeper into the maze, Belyx clutched her knives, preparing for anyone...or anything to attack.

"Watch your step," Gelina warned, her wheelchair bumping over uneven ground. A pit yawned open mere inches from where they stood, and Belyx shuddered at the thought of what might be lurking below.

"Thanks." Her hands shook. She glanced over at Zephyr, who offered her a tight smile. "We can do this," he told her, and she struggled to agree, trying to ignore the dread coiling in her stomach.

As they continued through the maze, Belyx couldn't shake the feeling they were being watched. The other prisoners stumbled through the fog, but there was something else, too—a sinister hissing sound that followed them no matter how fast they moved.

"Did you hear that?" Gelina asked, her breaths struggling as she pushed herself over uneven ground. Belyx exchanged a worried glance with Zephyr before nodding. They rounded a corner and came face-to-face with a grisly sight: a prisoner's remains, picked clean down to the bones.

"By The God," Zephyr choked out, his face pale.

"Let's...let's go the other way." Belyx trembled. They reversed course, only for a deep growl to echo through the fog.

"Something's coming," Gelina said, her hands gripping the arms of her wheelchair.

"Get behind me," Belyx ordered, holding out one of her knives as Zephyr held up his sword. The growling grew louder, and suddenly a massive lion materialized from the fog, its golden eyes locked on them.

"Run!" Zephyr shouted, but it was too late—the lion lunged like an arrow, sinking its humongous claws into a hiding prisoner who never stood a chance. Blood splattered across the ground as the beast roared in triumph.

"Stay back!" Belyx snarled, placing herself between the lion and Gelina. Her muscles tensed, ready to strike. She knew she couldn't defeat such a creature alone, but she would die trying if it meant keeping her allies safe.

"Help her, Zephyr!" Gelina cried, and he obeyed, slashing at the lion with his sword. As the lion reared back, Belyx moved in, her knife slicing through the air in an arc. The blade connected with the beast's side, but not deep enough to cause any real damage. The lion swiped at her in retaliation, leaving a stinging gash across her arm.

She threw her blade and nailed the beast in the eye as a counterstrike and the lion whirled away with a howl. Belyx sank to the ground, holding her oozing wound as hot blood clung to her fingers.

"Are you okay?" Zephyr asked, his breaths coming in ragged gasps.

"Fine," she grunted, gritting her teeth against the pain while standing tall. The wound was only a scratch. She had endured worse. "We need to keep moving."

"Agreed," Gelina said, her gaze flicking between Belyx's injury and the lion. "We can't afford more injuries."

We...She adored Gelina, but that was a bit much right now.

As they hurried away from the deadly predator, Belyx couldn't help but wonder what other horrors awaited them within the labyrinth. And as the hissing sound grew louder once more, she knew the source would be equally as bad as the lion.

Belyx's licked her dry lips. The air turned colder, her breaths forming ghostly wisps. She clutched her injured arm, blood seeping through her fingers. Her mind raced, only thinking of Gelina and Zephyr, praying they would survive this ordeal together.

"Guys, listen," Zephyr whispered, his sword still at the ready. "Do you hear that?"

The hissing she heard before turned real, and even though she had a fondness for snakes, her stomach twisted with dread. "That doesn't sound like any snake I've ever seen."

Gelina shuddered. "Not a damn–I mean darn snake."

Was swearing the most pressing issue right now?

As if on cue, a monstrous serpent emerged from the fog, its scales glinting an eerie green in the dim light. Its enormous head reared above them, its tongue flicking out to taste their fear. Even Belyx's love for snakes couldn't quell her terror at the sight of this behemoth.

"Okay, Belyx, you're the snake expert," Zephyr said, gripping his sword tighter. "Any ideas?" Belyx forgot she confided in Zephyr about her strange pets. This was much different and bigger than anything she took care of, but alas, she had to be the experienced one.

"Stay calm," she replied, forcing her body to remain steady. "Maybe it's more afraid of us than we are of it."

Belyx recalled her black mamba, Gwyar, being deadly, but always ran away from people first.

"Unlikely," Gelina muttered.

The snake lifted its head and lunged at them, its fangs bared. Belyx rolled out of the way, barely avoiding its lethal bite. Zephyr swung his sword, nicking the creature's thick scales, but it only enraged the serpent further.

Its tail slammed Belyx into the jagged wall and she stayed down, gasping for breath. Zephyr's grunts echoed as he faced the beast down. Belyx turned to help when something caught her eye.

"Zephyr, don't!" Belyx shouted, her eyes darting to anything that could save them. "We need to outsmart it!"

"Outsmart it? How?" he yelled back as the snake snapped at him again, narrowly missing his leg.

"Trust me!" Her eyes locked onto a tripwire hidden in the fog. "Lead it this way!" It had to be something...or they would all perish and become snake food. They were nothing but glorified mice now.

Zephyr hesitated but followed her instructions. Belyx held her breath, praying her idea would work. As Zephyr neared the wire, he lunged to the side. The snake, unable to stop its momentum, pulled on the string, releasing a barrage of swinging blades from the labyrinth walls. It *was* something after all. Majeria's traps helped their survival.

"Get down!" Belyx screamed, pushing Gelina to the ground as the deadly weapons slashed through the air. The serpent wasn't so lucky. The creature writhed in agony as the knives made contact, its hide splitting from the force of the attack. With a thunderous roar it slumped to the earth, draining its last breath of life as it lay still and lifeless.

"Is everyone okay?" Belyx asked, her blood pounding in her ears.

"More or less," Zephyr replied, wincing as he clutched his now-injured leg. "That was...intense."

"Indeed," Gelina said. "We must keep moving. The God will guide us through this dark labyrinth if we have faith."

Belyx admired Gelina's unwavering devotion, even in such dire circumstances.

Zephyr helped Gelina back up. She, once again refusing to let Zephyr push her. "Nice thinking with that trap. We better watch out for more. I, for one, don't plan to be ground beef today."

"Traps and monsters," Belyx added. "I fear what else is in this demented maze."

They pressed on, and Belyx's confidence slowly returned. But as they began to relax, a familiar chuckle protruded from the thick fog,

"Thought you could escape us?" Soren and Luo materialized out of the mist, their faces a mixture of sadistic glee as they slumped toward them. "Did you really think you could escape?" Soren sneered, giddy for a kill. Luo let out a savage laugh.

"Never," Belyx spat, her rage flaring. She faced Soren, knives ready, while Zephyr limped toward Luo, sword in hand.

Soren held his basic sword. "Gut them all," Soren ordered his crone.

Luo tilted her head, her yellow eyes sinking like a determined killer. They would need to fight through them. Belyx readied. This would be the last time Soren staked his claim on them in this competition.

The enemies attacked and Belyx was overwhelmed by Soren's vicious onslaught. The sound of their clashing weapons echoed against the damp stone. Blood dripped from Belyx's wounds as she struggled, her blade clanging against Soren's. The brute shoved her and knocked the knives from her hands. Belyx went to retaliate, but Soren proved effective at hand-to-hand combat and slammed Belyx into the wall.

He put his face in hers...close enough to smell his rotting breath. "It's over Your Highness."

Belyx winced at the ringing in her head, but Zephyr's screams fueled a fire in her. She made too many promises to fail now.

Before Soren could react, she dug her thumb into his eye. He lurched back with a scream and Belyx snatched another one of her knives from the ground.

Soren wiped his face, huffing like a bear about to attack. "Your tricks are over you pathetic bitch!"

Belyx twirled her knives. "Watch yourself, Soren. Ladies don't take kindly to such insults." She went on the offensive, striking him where she could and landing a few quick slashes on him. It made little difference as Soren kept up his assault.

Gritting her teeth, she screamed in pain as Soren attacked her mercilessly. With each blow, Belyx felt her strength dwindling. But as Soren appeared to have the advantage, Gelina surged forward with all her might and plowed into him, sending him flying off a short ledge.

Gelina helped Belyx up. "Not a fighter, huh?" Belyx asked with low croak.

Gelina shrugged. "A girl's gotta beat these jerks somehow, right?"

A scream from Zephyr cut them off.

"Get away from him!" Gelina bellowed, rushing to Zephyr's side as he faced off against Luo.

"You'll lose more than just those legs!" Luo cooed, maneuvering her blade for Gelina.

Gelina stood between Zephyr and her gaze met Belyx's, followed by a wink. What was she planning?

Luo was on Gelina, but she rotated her chair and deflected the strike, following with a slam into Luo, sending her toward Belyx. Belyx dodged Luo's counterstrike and kicked the woman over the same edge as Soren.

"Come on!" Belyx screamed, but a curse rang from the ledge. Soren had managed to climb up already, Luo close behind.

Belyx stepped up, ready to kill them both when Gelina pushed Belyx to the ground.

What are you doing—?"

With expert precision, Gelina skillfully triggered another hidden trap, causing a hefty door to fall and block the path between her and Zephyr.

"Go!" Gelina urged Belyx. "I'll hold them off!"

As Belyx stumbled back, she knew that the cost of surviving this trial had risen exponentially.

Belyx's lungs thundered in her chest as she scrambled to reach Gelina, the labyrinth's fog swallowing her vision. The sound of scuffling from behind the rock trap fueled her desperation. "Gelina!"

"Stay back," Gelina called through the door, her tone strained. "I'll be fine. Just protect Zephyr and get out of this wretched place."

The ground quaked beneath her feet as the monstrous lion roared from the other side of the door, its growls like a symphony of nightmares. Soren and Luo cursed loudly. Hopefully, the beast would end those monsters for good.

"Damn you!" Belyx snarled, her hands blistering against the chill metal of the door handle. Her knuckles whitened, but the door remained shut.

"Belyx," Gelina urged, her voice weakening through the stone. "Promise me you'll take care of Zephyr and free the rest of the slaves when you escape."

"Gelina," she choked out, tears burning down her cheeks. "I can—"

"Remember our vow." Gelina's tone softened. "Protect Zephyr and free the slaves. No matter where I am, we will always be together in spirit. It had to be like this. Now go!"

The finality in Gelina's words hit her like a carriage. She knew it was coming, yet she wouldn't accept it. Her fingers trembled on the stone door, no handle in sight, the coldness seeping into her bones.

A pained shriek from Gelina ripped through the fog like a jagged knife, slicing through the stillness and paralyzing Belyx with fear. The air thickened until it was almost too heavy to breathe as if all life were suspended in time. Then, quietly, Gelina's screams melted away into the oppressive air, leaving nothing but an icy chill behind.

"No!" She screamed into the void. Her knees buckled, and she collapsed to the ground, her sobs echoing through the labyrinth.

She felt Zephyr's hand on her shoulder, his touch warm and steady. "We'll make it through this...For Gelina."

Her chest tightened, her body suddenly weightless. Gritting her teeth, she wiped her tears away, only streaks of grime remained on her cheeks.

Rising to her feet, she pulled Zephyr close, steadying him as they moved forward. "Let us finish these trials." Her eyes stared ahead, unable to find a focus. "Then we will avenge Gelina and free the slaves." *And I will decapitate everyone who gets in my way.*

Together, they disappeared into the fog.

Belyx's hands were shaking, her nails biting into her palms as she fought to control the storm of emotions raging within her. The fog swirled around her and Zephyr, a thick, suffocating blanket that seemed to press down on them, mirroring the weight in her chest.

"Damn them," she muttered, her throat raw from screaming Gelina's name earlier. "I swear I'll make them pay."

"The time will come," Zephyr added. His eyes were red-rimmed and shadowed with grief, but there was a spark of anger burning in their depths. "Hopefully they died in there too."

As they continued through the labyrinth, the fog began to thin, revealing other prisoners stumbling out of the mist. How many had died though? She knew at least one.

After everyone made it through, Belyx did a quick count of the prisoners. "Twenty of us left." Belyx scanned the faces around her. Her teeth numbed as she spotted Soren and Luo among the survivors, their smug expressions cutting through her like a knife.

"They survived..." she whispered, her anger flaring anew. But as she looked at her fellow prisoners, she realized there was someone else responsible for her death...someone who refused to help her.

The guards escorted them back, and Belyx suppressed all of her rage. She left without letting Zephyr know where she was headed. A fury she'd never felt churned in her chest. Gelina had been kind and righteous—she didn't deserve to die. Everyone else here did...including Belyx. It wasn't right that Gelina had been taken away so soon. Why had she sacrificed herself like that?

Belyx headed to her destination, ready to kill.

Aurelius wouldn't teach her the skills she needed.

It could've saved Gelina's life.

He was responsible and he would pay.

Taking a breath, Belyx stormed to his cell, about to show the old bastard what his stubbornness had cost them.

Twenty-One

Enzo's shoes crunched against the rocky terrain as he approached the forbidding mountain pass. The wind whipped through his brown curls, carrying with it the scent of impending danger. Clenching his fists, he embraced the comforting warmth of his flame control abilities at his fingertips. They would keep him safe as they always did in the past.

"Alright, Enzo," he muttered to himself. "You've got this." He thought of his fae tribe, their fate hanging in the balance as Majeria's forces grew ever stronger. Failure wasn't an option.

As he stepped into the shadows cast by the looming mountains, the chill air pounded his ears. With a shudder, he continued onward. He scanned the area for any sign of the last object...a small key.

The farther he ventured into the mountain, the darker his surroundings became. His thoughts were flooded with memories from a year prior when he had searched and searched for another key—one to free his family. To obtain it, he had to betray Belyx. His trust issues were a problem then, but he hoped he and Belyx grew from that time. He had hardly known her after all.

Did she ever truly forgive me?

The weight of his past actions bore down on him, making each step feel heavier than the last. But there was no time for dwelling on regrets; he had a mission to complete. Whatever this final test was...it couldn't be any worse than losing the ones he loved.

He blinked away painful memories, determined to shape a new future. Enzo pressed on into the darkness, clinging to hope that he could make things right for his tribe, the Order, and Belyx.

Deeper into the mountain, Enzo found himself in a cavernous chamber, its walls adorned with distorted rock formations and faint metallic smell...blood. The unnerving echoes of his footsteps were accompanied by the scuttling things hiding in the shadows. He had heard rumors of the creatures that guarded this place, and now, it seemed, they were all too real.

He shivered under his breath, the temperature making a surprising drop.

Enzo gasped as a creature emerged from the shadows, a spider-like monstrosity with a body compared to his own. He clenched his fists, desperation rushing through his veins as it approached him. Driven by instinct he released a barrage of fire bolts towards it, but they were deflected off its hard shell like harmless pebbles before it pounced at him. Enzo backed away as the beast landed, its razor-sharp fangs gnashing hungrily together like a quill scrawling across paper.

The monster lunged at him again and Enzo forced up a shield of flames, but the spider leaped through like nothing, its beady eyes inches from his face. So, they were immune to fire after all! That was what the warning had referred to about these creatures being impervious to the fae. Could they resist all the elements? He'd never encountered an enemy invulnerable to his powers before—the thought sent a chill down his spine. But he couldn't allow fear to paralyze him.

The creature sprung again, a tiny shriek emanating from it, Enzo sidestepped and kicked at it, but it wrapped its hairy legs around Enzo. With a scream Enzo pushed it off with his other foot, but fell into a stone, banging his head.

As his vision came too, more tapping filled his senses. More spiders were coming his way and they looked hungry for his delicate fae flesh!

He blasted a couple with his flames, but the fires died out, leaving even more pissed-off monsters approaching him. Scanning the cave, he took off in the other direction praying he was heading the right way.

The sound of his steps reverberated with their swarm of legs catching up to him. He was raised to love nature, even the ugly parts, but this was too far!

Something crashed into him from above and he hit the rough ground below. A spider stretched its fangs right at Enzo. He pushed it away, but it held on. The creature's hair prickled his hands as he kept it away. How could he handle them all when he struggled against one?

Summoning a flame like no other, Enzo forced it on the spider, but nothing happened. The sounds of the others approaching sent a panic throughout his body. With gritted teeth, he summoned more flames, thinking of Belyx, his tribe, and the kingdom. With a scream, he stretched out his arms and a gale of embers burst from him. The force launched the creatures into the surrounding mountain walls.

They may have been fireproof, but his power could still send them flying. The creatures vibrated on the ground, still not dead, and angrier than ever. He took off passed them through a couple of other passageways, praying he would be able to find his way back.

A cavern with a faint bright light caught his attention. With a quick look over his shoulder, he made sure no creatures were still on his tail and turned in. It had to be the key.

"Enzo Prekaro." A voice slithered through the darkness, cold and poisonous as venom. "You've come a long way."

"Who's there?" Enzo demanded, He strained his eyes, searching for the source of it.

"Or perhaps I should say, you've returned." The voice laughed, and a figure materialized before Enzo—a tall, pale-skinned being, with white hair and black eyes...Aydevko, the male witch who had enslaved the fae and tried to annihilate the humans last year. He was here!

"Impossible." Enzo backed away. "You're dead."

"Am I?" Aydevko smirked, spreading his arms. "You're hoping I'm merely a figment of your imagination, a manifestation of your deepest fears."

"You're just a vision." Enzo tried to steady himself. "But what do you mean *I've* returned? And why are you here?"

"Ah, that is the question, isn't it? Why *am* I here? Perhaps to warn you, Enzo. You have returned to that mental place. That place of fear and hate for humans. Don't worry...I understand." He even laughed the same way despite it being an illusion.

Enzo curled a flame in his palm. Aydevko wouldn't win this time either. "Warn me about what?" He wanted to protect the humans...not harm them. Most of them were good. It was Majeria who were the invaders and had caused all this turmoil.

"To tell you that seeking The Original will bring nothing but ruin to the world, and put your kind through far worse than what they've already endured."

"Your words mean nothing to me," Enzo spat, clenching his knuckles. "I didn't come here for your counsel."

"Of course not," Aydevko sneered. "You came for that." He pointed at a small, glinting object nestled among the rocks...the key. "But consider this, Enzo; your kind would have been better off without the humans. You should have joined me when you had the chance."

"Never," Enzo hissed, beads of sweat traced his forehead. He grew tired of these games. "I won't succumb to hate like you...blaming others for all of my problems."

"Suit yourself." Aydevko shrugged, fading away into the shadows. "Just remember my words when everything crumbles around you."

With a final burst of courage, Enzo lunged for the key, snatching it up before sprinting toward the cave exit. The spiders were waiting, and advanced, their spindly legs carrying them closer and closer with each step. He could hear their venomous fangs snapping hungrily, ready to inject their deadly poison into his vulnerable skin. But he was determined not to let them win.

Almost there, he thought, desperation propelling him forward. As the cave entrance loomed ahead, he used every ounce of energy he had left, just managing to escape the monsters' clutches.

Clutching the key tightly in his hand, he looked back to make sure Aydevko wasn't following him. Whether the male witch's warning held any truth or not, Enzo couldn't be certain. But one thing he knew: he would do whatever it took to save the people, even if it meant jumping into the unknown.

Enzo turned and almost dropped the key with a shudder. Aydevko reappeared at the entrance, fiddling with his talon-like nails. "Always a runner, boy. Well, you can't run from the hate that humans will send you."

"Your vision of a world without humans is warped, Aydevko. They are not our enemy."

"Are you sure about that?" Aydevko spoke in a whisper, like wind rustling through wilted leaves. "Remember how they treated your kind after the fae were rescued? The fear and hatred in their eyes?"

Enzo clenched his fists, his fire simmering beneath the surface, useless against the fireproof spiders beginning to surround him again. The memories of discrimination and mistreatment stung like a fresh wound, but he refused to let Aydevko see his doubt.

"Enough!" Enzo shouted. "Leave me be. You are dead!"

"Very well." Aydevko sighed, his image flickering before vanishing altogether. "But heed my warning, Enzo Prekaro: The Original will bring nothing but destruction for all you love. You'll learn this soon enough."

Silence reclaimed the cave, and with a deep breath, Enzo held up the key—its metallic surface shimmered in the faint light, intricate engravings weaving around its delicate frame. Pressing his fingers along the design, strange energy emanated from it, sending a numbness down his spine.

Maybe Aydevko's words hold some truth, Enzo thought, his brow furrowed with worry as he slipped the key into his pocket. But there was no turning back now; his tribe depended on him.

As Enzo left the mountain pass behind, haunted by the male witch's warning, he found himself questioning whether reviving The Original was the best course of action. Was he dooming his people to a worse fate than the one they currently faced?

His inner ramblings were interrupted by a sudden flash—a vision of Belyx, eyes open with terror, reaching out for help. Enzo staggered under the weight of the horrifying image.

"By the gods," he gasped, his chest tight with panic. Belyx was in danger! He had to get back and recite this ritual before it was too late. Almost losing Belyx last year devastated Enzo, but he would save her this time.

Enzo broke into a sprint, his feet pounding against the rocky terrain as he raced toward the forest. As he neared, the sky turned an ominous orange, thick plumes of smoke billowing above the tree line. The forest was ablaze even more than earlier, and every fiber of his being screamed that he needed to reach his tribe. This was an all-out war.

He panted as he spent the last of his energy running down the mountain face, his legs burning from exhaustion as he urged himself to run faster. He prayed he would make it in time.

The scorching forest dried Enzo's tears, his lungs heaving with each breath. The flames licked at his skin, but he pushed back the heat, creating a barrier of fire around himself. He could hear the cacophony of battle echoing through the trees—the clash of metal, the cries of pain and fury, the roars of elemental powers unleashed.

His fae tribe was finally fighting back. Enzo swelled with pride as he glimpsed his fellow fae using their abilities on Majerian soldiers. Water fae raced among the inferno, extinguishing the flames that threatened to consume the forest.

Wind fae soared above, guiding gusts of air to scatter enemy arrows and buffet would-be attackers off balance. Nature fae stood still, commanding vines and branches to ensnare their foes.

"Enzo!" A young voice called out over the torrent. Several members of the Order struggled against a group of Majerian soldiers. They were outnumbered and outmatched, exhaustion etched onto their faces.

"Stay back!" Enzo shouted as he dashed towards them, summoning the full force of his fire powers. Flames danced along his fingertips, the tattoos on his arms glowing brighter with each heartbeat. "I'll handle this!"

He released a torrent of fire upon the Majerian fighters, searing their armor and forcing them to retreat or be incinerated. The smell of burning flesh mixed with the scent of charred wood made Enzo's stomach churn. Yet, he couldn't afford to falter now. Lives depended on his actions.

More Order members fought side by side with the fae and struck at Majerian soldiers while avoiding the flames threatening to circle the forest.

The Order launched arrows for the remaining guards while the other fae used their elemental attacks to subdue them.

Enzo rushed down to help, sweat clinging to him and his lungs heavy. More Majerian warriors broke out from the embers and charged them. The Order and fae met the assault with weapons and elements drawn. At the front, Enzo sent the guards away with a pulse of fire, but it wasn't enough. They were cutting the Rose assassins down and impaling the fae with their swords. They were prepared. The Order and fae wouldn't stand a chance.

A large soldier smacked a younger girl to the ground and went to kick her when Enzo snapped a blast of heat right into him as she slit his throat, blood mixing with ashes.

He helped her up as more soldiers overtook them.

"Go!" Enzo commanded the weary Order. "Get to safety! I've got this."

The grateful fighters exchanged quick nods with him before taking off.

With renewed determination, he steeled himself for the next wave of attackers. He took the flames from around him and created a wall in front, keeping them at bay. It wouldn't last long, but he had to find his fathers.

He sprinted through the burning forest, his lungs aching from the acrid smoke. Flames rubbed at the trees, but his fire immunity protected him from the heat. He spotted his fathers, fending off a group of Majerian soldiers with their combined wind and nature powers. The desperate urgency in their movements set Enzo's pulse thundering.

"Enzo!" Thano shouted, his green eyes blocked by the floating ash. As Gink launched a barrage of thorny vines at their opponents, Thano used his wind power to whip the air around them into a fierce gale, knocking several guards off balance.

"Where are Freyja and Onka?" Enzo yelled as he scanned the area for any sign of his friends.

"Taking down the front-line soldiers," Gink replied out of breath. "They went that way!" He gestured eastward with a hand wreathed in foliage.

"What happened?" Enzo asked as he forced a soldier into the burning bushes.

"They ambushed us from all sides of the forest and lit it on fire!" Thano said as he sent a gale into more Majerians.

"Sycamore should've done something earlier. Look at our home!" Enzo whirled around to be surrounded by five soldiers, but vines and winds pressed them back.

Gink embraced Enzo. "He should have. The fae have direly messed up. I wish we could've done more, En."

After pulling away from the hug, Enzo's fire whipped an enemy away. They had no time for pleasantries. "Keep holding them here. I will save the others!" Enzo called out, already turning in the direction Gink had said. His pulse raced as he summoned his power.

He soon found Freyja and Onka, sprawled on the ground near the imposing figure of none other than The Scorpion. The sight of his fallen friends cut deep into his chest, and he felt his skin boil at the memory of his past defeat at the hands of the monstrous general. This time, Enzo swore it would be different.

"You monster!" he roared, launching a searing torrent of flames in the creature's direction. The Scorpion raised his massive spear, effortlessly deflecting the attack. His soulless black eyes pierced straight through Enzo, sending shivers down his spine despite the inferno surrounding them.

Come on, Enzo. You can do this. He threw himself into the fight, using every ounce of his firepower and agility against the towering monster.

The Scorpion shifted, drawing his attention away from Freyja and Onka. He swung his enormous spear, but Enzo narrowly dodged the deadly weapon by twisting out of the way.

The Scorpion lunged for him again. Enzo barely managed to evade the strike, his shirt burning from the heat that radiated off the sharpened metal tip. Sweat poured down his face as he summoned another wave of flames. They engulfed The Scorpion, but the beast was impervious to the inferno.

"Impossible!" Enzo gasped, his disbelief now turning to frustration. It was as if this creature had an unnatural resistance to his power. But he couldn't let that stop him—not when the lives of his friends were at stake.

The Scorpion turned his helmeted head, his spear glistening in the flickering light of the burning forest.

Gritting his teeth, Enzo dodged yet another attack. He reached deep within himself, searching for any hidden reserves of strength. *I have to save them*, he thought. *I can't lose here.*

The Scorpion brought his weapon down and Enzo rolled to the side, evading the crushing impact. His breath came in ragged gasps, and his muscles ached from the fierce battle.

Enzo summoned one last surge of flames. No matter how hopeless the situation was, he couldn't abandon his friends to this monster. He would fight until his final breath—for them, for their freedom, and for all the people who had suffered at the hands of Majeria.

The Scorpion somehow managed to dodge, his dark silhouette moving through the wall of embers like a phantom. The spear in his hand cut through the air, aiming straight for Enzo's heart.

"No!" he screamed, as he tried to summon his power once more. But this time, nothing came. He felt drained, and empty, his strength depleted by the intensity of the fight and the merciless heat surrounding them. At that moment, he knew his fire had failed him. The arc of the blade missed, but the hilt slammed Enzo into the ground.

The Scorpion approached Enzo with deliberate, predatory steps.

Enzo struggled to get up, but his limbs were heavy, his body betraying him. Desperation clawed at his insides. He couldn't help but think of Freyja and Onka, and his tribe. They were counting on him, and he was failing them, just as he had lost against The Scorpion last year.

The Scorpion towered over him. His lifeless eye sockets showed no emotion, and the tip of his spear pointed menacingly at Enzo's throat.

Before Enzo could react, or even attempt some last-minute effort to save himself, Majerian soldiers swarmed him. Their hands gripped his arms, pulling him to his feet and restraining him. Freyja and Onka were being led into a carriage, their faces were a mixture of pain and defiance.

Wait, Enzo thought, recalling the three objects of The Original. If they fell into the clutches of the enemy now, all would be lost. Gritting his teeth, the objects: the journal, the quill, and the key--disappeared from his pockets, hidden safely somewhere else, but he could somehow sense them.

He breathed a deep sigh, but it was short-lived as the guards came and secured him. Enzo's mind raced, desperately trying to find a solution, some way out of this nightmare. But as he was dragged away by the soldiers, he couldn't help but take on the crushing weight of defeat settling over him like a suffocating shroud.

After he was thrown into a carriage, now bound and shackled, Freyja locked wet eyes with him. "Stay strong," she whispered. "We'll find a way out of this."

She coughed from the smoke and leaned toward an unconscious Onka. They had failed.

The door slammed shut, plunging them into darkness.

As the wagon began to move, the world spun, exhaustion claiming him. He fought against it, straining to remain conscious, but he fell into a cold dark abyss.

TWENTY-TWO

The prison corridor echoed as Belyx stormed through it.

The blackened stone walls seemed to close in on her as she pushed past her fellow prisoners, their curses were merely noise to her. Let them try to attack her. She was an inferno of rage, refusing to be contained any longer.

"Out of my way," Belyx snarled at a hulking figure who dared to block her path. The man shrank back, pressing himself against the wall as she continued toward the cell holding Aurelius. Before she proved herself in these trials, they would have tried to fight her. Now they knew her strength and her willingness to kill.

Aurelius sat in his cell, legs crossed and hands resting on his knees like a meditating priest. His lifeless eyes gazed serenely into the darkness, betraying no emotion or concern for his situation.

"You!" Belyx screamed, thrusting her now blood and dirt soaked finger at him. "Gelina's death is on your hands!"

Aurelius didn't flinch or look away from the wall, remaining as still as a statue. The only indication that he had heard her was a subtle furrowing of his brow.

"Because you wouldn't teach me your secret fighting art, she's dead!" Tears streamed down her cheeks. "You're nothing but a murderous failure! I wish it was you who died instead!"

A tense silence settled over them, but Aurelius remained unresponsive, his calm gaze locked on the darkness beyond his cell bars.

"Answer me, damn you!" Her voice cracked with anguish.

But there was no reply, and something inside her snapped. With a wild, desperate cry, she lunged at him. In her grief-stricken haze, she failed to notice the calculating glint in his eyes.

Aurelius sprung into action with a grace that belied his age, sidestepping Belyx's charge with ease. He caught her wrist in a vice-like grip, twisting her arm behind her back and forcing her to the ground in one swift motion. The cold, hard stone floor bit into her cheek as she struggled against him, but it was futile—his strength was unyielding.

"Let me go!" Belyx screamed.

Aurelius held her down for a moment longer before releasing her, allowing her to scramble to her feet. Belyx glared at him, emotions blazing with fury. As she drew in a shiver, a fierce tenacity took root deep within her.

She was tempted to strike again but feared she would end up in the same predicament as the last attempt.

Inhaling a cold breath, Belyx turned away from the master. "From now on," she whispered through clenched teeth, "no one else will die for me. I am my own strength. I will win these trials. You are a sorry old man with no fucking excuse, but a past failure. Rot in this prison cell where you belong. I hope all your limbs fall off and burn!"

He still sat there, staring into the wall once more. He was a sad and pathetic man who had given up on the world.

Chest heaving, she struggled to control her breathing; her heart pounding with a blend of anger and humiliation. She turned back toward him, now nothing more than the embodiment of her pain. The silence of the prison felt suffocating, broken only by the distant echoes of dripping water.

"Fine." Venom laced her tone. "You didn't deserve to know my family or be part of our lives. I'll win the Trials on my own, and I'll do it without your precious secret fighting art. You can rot in here forever."

Aurelius met her glare with an inscrutable expression, his eyes betraying no emotion. Why didn't he answer her? He said nothing, simply inclining his head and turning away from her, dismissing her as if she were nothing more than a nuisance. It stung, but Belyx refused to give him the satisfaction of seeing her falter.

"Remember this, Aurelius," Belyx whispered. "I will succeed. And when I do, it will be because of my strength, not yours."

Spinning on her heel, she stormed from the cell, the cold air of the prison biting at her exposed skin like a thousand tiny needles. As she walked, she could feel a passion that had ignited earlier spreading through her veins like a lightning storm. No one else would die for her sake—not when she had the power to prevent it.

In the dim light, Belyx could almost see the spirits of her grandmother and mother walking alongside her, their love and wisdom infusing her every step. They had made sacrifices for her, given their lives so she could rise to greatness. She owed it to them and to herself, to carry their legacy forward.

Belyx clenched her hands into fists, letting Enzo's heat radiate through. The pain was a reminder of her care and affection for her partner. She would honor their memory by emerging victorious in the Trials, no matter what it took.

From that moment on, she was her own weapon.

TWENTY-THREE

"I can't believe she's gone." Belyx could still feel the ghost of Gelina's touch, the warmth of her embrace when she'd protected them from harm.

"Neither can I," Zephyr murmured, drained with sorrowful words. "She was one of the kindest souls I've ever known."

Belyx's gaze drifted toward Soren and Luo, who stood at a distance, their expressions unreadable. Her blood burned with anger as she glared at them. "Why is it that only the good people die?"

Zephyr shook his head. "I ask myself that every day my sister is trapped with the slavers."

"We will save her," Belyx reassured, but Zephyr only turned away.

"Only one of us can make it out. How can we both?"

Belyx hadn't gotten to that part of the plan. She would cross that bridge when they came to it. There had to be a way for them both to win. *Would I save his sister if I made it out?*

After saving Aikradal, I would. Belyx couldn't promise him anything. Promises were like a burning candle. No matter what someone did to keep it alive, it would eventually burn out. There was no room for such promises. Her only goal right now was to win and shove that bitch off her throne. "We will find a way, Zephyr. Gelina's death will not be wasted."

He tightened his grip on her, the tattoos coiling around his strong arms like a comforting net. "I know it will, Belyx. We'll make sure of it."

For a moment, they stood in silence, mourning the loss of their friend. Then Zephyr began to speak, his voice low and steady. "My parents died in a boating accident when I was younger," he said softly. "I thought I would hate the sea after that, but instead, I learned to embrace it. It was my way of honoring them—of keeping their memory alive."

Belyx listened with all her focus, admiring his resilience. "I'm so sorry, Zephyr."

"I'm not," he replied and Belyx arched her brow. "The dead shouldn't be felt sorry for. They were here for a reason and their time was up. I refuse to believe their legacies go unnoticed. Death should be celebrated. Good memories are what separate us from those who harm this world."

"I wish I could find a way to get over my family's deaths, too." Belyx's fingers dug into her palm. The thoughts of her dead loved ones coiled into her mind, but she pushed them away.

"Maybe you will, in time. You are strong, Belyx. Stronger than you realize."

She fought back tears. "My mother...the fae were framed for her death. But it was Majeria who was truly responsible. They've taken so much from us, Zephyr. From everyone."

Zephyr's grip tightened around her once more, his dark eyes filled with turmoil. "Then we'll make sure they pay for what they've done. For Gelina, for your family, for my sister, and for all those who have suffered at their hands."

As they stood, united in their grief, Belyx knew that together they would find a way to bring justice to those who had been wronged—no matter the cost. Even if it was short-lived by this competition. They were stronger as a team. Gelina had planned it from the start.

Zephyr's his hand reached out to grasp Belyx's burned one. "How did you get these?"

Belyx pulled her hand away. "Just an accident saving my kingdom last year. It's nothing."

Zephyr took her hand back and a familiar heat rang from them. "Don't hide your scars, Belyx. Cherish them. Don't you know why I got these tattoos?"

Without asking, he took off his tunic and his carved muscles glinted in the prison light. "See?" He pointed to the one on his shoulder of a dove and beyond it, near the wing, was a long gash.

Belyx felt the wound, the bump tingling her fingers. "What happened?"

Zephyr shrugged and put his shirt back on while Belyx fought the red in her cheeks. "Pirate and street life. Whippings and lashings were a common punishment."

"This kingdom is full of tyrants." Too many decent people had died in the clutches of this monstrous kingdom. That would end. "Gelina's dying wish was to free the slaves here. How is that possible?"

He took her hand again and a breeze whispered through the courtyard, ruffling Belyx's hair. "I haven't a clue, but that seems to be my life. Lots of unpredictability."

She stared at their intertwined fingers. "You're telling me." A feeling of numbness rolled up her arm. Zephyr released her hand and she put it away as if it were a weapon. This prison was making her desperate for attention.

Zephyr's chiseled jaw calmed as he looked the other way. "You know, despite the dreariness of this situation, I am glad I met you."

An awkward cough left Belyx's throat as she locked his eyes. She was with Enzo, and yet she couldn't shake the temptation of Zephyr's soft eyes and comfort.

"You and Gelina have done so much for me here. I would surely be dead without you."

Zephyr tried to nod, but something in his face sunk...like disappointment? "Too bad that old master won't help you. I know you feel like you need him, but all that magic stuff is fake anyways."

If only that were true.

"You're right," she said, though uncertainty gnawed at her insides. "We will honor Gelina's name. The slaves in this kingdom and every kingdom will be freed. We can do it." Would freeing the slaves bring about change? There were so many and did she have it in her to free them all?

Zephyr smiled solemnly and reached out to grasp her hands again, his touch calming yet suddenly determined all at once.

"We will," he said firmly. "Majeria will not continue to oppress us and those we care about any longer."

Belyx gazed up into Zephyr's alluring eyes, and a wave of courage washed over her. With him beside her, she felt like she could conquer any obstacle—even the wickedness that reigned in Majeria's court.

Squeezing his hand, a smile graced her lips.

In the stillness of their encounter, Zephyr moved towards Belyx, his face coming closer to hers until their mouths were but inches apart.

Belyx wanted nothing else than for them to collide in a passionate kiss, but instead, she turned away.

"Zephyr, I... I can't," she whispered, a sour pit in her stomach. "I'm with Enzo."

"Right." he stepped back, his face flushed with embarrassment. "I'm sorry. I didn't mean to assume...I mean I got caught up in our moment."

She shook her head, attempting to regain her composure. "It's fine. We should...we should get ready for the third trial."

"Of course," Zephyr replied. "I'll see you there."

As Belyx walked away, a flurry of emotions churned within her—fear for the upcoming trial, grief for Gelina, and an overwhelming confusion about her feelings for both Zephyr and Enzo. The familiar walls of her cell offered no comfort, but as she prepared for the challenge ahead, she knew she couldn't allow herself to be distracted by what-ifs when so much was at stake. Why was it that she was with Enzo, the most loving and loyal partner she could find and yet, she had some kind of desire for Zephyr?

Her emotions clawed at one another and she cringed at the thought of a horrible love triangle. *I only miss Enzo,* she thought. *I will find my way back to you my love.*

The walls of the cavern dripped with condensation as the prison boat glided over the inky black water. Belyx gazed up at the stalactites that stretched down from the ceiling like rows of jagged teeth. The iron chains around her wrists bit into her burned flesh, and she flexed her hands, wincing.

"I'm sorry about last night," whispered Zephyr. He stood beside her on the swaying deck, his eyes bearing dark circles. Had he regretted that attempted kiss? "I am sure Enzo is an amazing guy or male...I'm not sure what to call a fae as I've never met one."

"Male is fine, but he won't care." The thought of them ever meeting chilled her blood. It would be a battle of snark though.

"Plus. I don't want to be burned to death by his jealousy." He laughed as Belyx side-eyed him. "Kidding."

Belyx glanced at him, his jaw was tight, but something about that angle made Belyx lose all senses. *Stop! You are with Enzo you fool! Love triangles are for children!*

She surveyed the guards surrounding them—their swords glinting menacingly. "I understand. We just need to win these damn things."

"We will," Zephyr replied with a hint of a shake. He was unsure as well.

As they emerged from the cave into the open air, Belyx's chest sank. They had been brought to the top of a colossal underground river that twisted and turned around Majeria, its waters churning like a bubbling soup. It seemed impossible to navigate. Was this where the third Trial would take place?

"Attention, prisoners!" Prince Vincent's yelled, and Belyx resisted the urge to flinch. The scrawny prince stood at the edge of the water, his blonde hair as poised as ever. More guards lined up behind him, their faces cold and impassive. "The third Trial shall now commence: I call it The Falling!"

A murmur of dread rippled through the crowd of prisoners. Belyx clenched her jaw and glared at the prince. She would not let him see her fear.

"Four teams of five will sail ships down this treacherous river to the bottom of a lake," Prince Vincent continued with an unsettling glee. "Along the way, you will encounter Majerian vessels and other traps and such."

"Most likely aimed at me," Belyx whispered, her breaths pounding in her lungs. She had survived his cheating thus far and would continue to do so until his head was raised on a pike.

"Surviving teams will proceed to the final Trial," Vincent concluded, a wicked smile on his lips. "Try not to die."

Belyx glanced sideways at Zephyr, who looked as calm as ever. They could handle whatever they faced together, but she couldn't shake the fear that something terrible awaited them on this river. The guards unshackled everyone and the other prisoners formed their teams and began to board the ships. She took a deep breath, clutching at a rose pin on her chest that didn't exist.

"Well, we couldn't have asked for a better competition, right?" Zephyr asked, his eyes locked onto hers, filled with hope, hopefully enough for both of them.

"I wouldn't think so. We need more than two people to crew this vessel." Fear gnawed at her insides. The boats sat ready for them. They were sturdy...barely. Although Zephyr's eyes widened like a puppy, most likely missing the open sea.

"Then let's find some." He grinned.

Belyx choked on bile as she glanced at the dwindling pool of potential teammates. Only mere minutes remained to form their crew.

"Zephyr," she whispered urgently, "I've never sailed before. How are we going to do this?"

"Relax, Belyx. I was a pirate, remember? I know my way around a ship."

"Great, well I hope you have experience with a novice crew," Belyx muttered. Despite her sarcasm, his confidence was reassuring.

"Come on." Zephyr pulled her along as they scanned the crowd for any potential recruits. Most of the teams had already been formed, and the remaining prisoners seemed less than promising.

"Wait," Belyx heard herself say, staring at a young man who stood apart from the others. He was fidgeting with his clothes, obsessively adjusting the fabric. "Him. He might have some useful skills."

"Are you sure?" Zephyr raised an eyebrow, but Belyx nodded. She could see something in the young man's eyes—a fierce courage, hidden beneath layers of anxiety. It reminded her of Onka. The anxious ones always had an unseen strength that pushed them beyond what anyone thought possible.

"Trust me."

"Alright, let's go talk to him."

The young man sat up straight as they approached. "Name," Zephyr asked. "Also, any special skills?"

The man stumbled a bit but got his words out. "Edric. I am also valuable because I practiced knot tying all my life making nets."

Just like Gelina did. How did such a soft-spoken man—or boy more like it, end up here?

"That will be fine," Zephyr said. "I will have you man the ropes. Can you handle that?"

He stared back as if his brain didn't have anymore to say as he fidgeted with his sleeve and bowed. He followed them as they went to the next prisoner.

"Told you so," Belyx chided Zephyr who smirked with defeat.

"Only one more," Zephyr said, glancing around the rapidly emptying space. "What about her?" He jutted his chin towards an older woman who sat alone, her milky eyes.

"Wait. Is she...blind?" Belyx hesitated. How on earth did she make it this far? But then she noticed the woman's hands, their fingertips dancing over the rough surface of a wooden carving with incredible precision.

"You underestimate, Belyx. I knew a person with blindness who was quite adept. They say when one sense goes, the others heighten."

They approached the woman and Belyx wanted to believe what Zephyr said. She also wondered what *she* did to end up in prison.

"Hello," Belyx began cautiously, "I'm Belyx, and this is Zephyr. We're looking for one more crew member."

"Ah, yes," the woman replied, almost as if a melodic tune left her mouth. "I've been waiting for you. My name is Mira."

The lady was up and joining their crew before they could inquire anymore.

With Edric and Mira now part of their team, Belyx couldn't help but hope they had a fighting chance. As they gathered together, Prince Vincent strode to the front again, ready to witness the carnage.

"Good luck," he said, his eyes glinting with cruel amusement. "You'll need it."

As he pivoted away, Soren's stare clashed with Belyx's from his vessel, his features twisted in a malicious scowl. His menacing intent was unmistakable—he wanted her death. But she refused to be defeated. She had ventured too far, battled too much, to surrender now.

"Alright, team." Zephyr clapped his hands, drawing their attention. "Let's get ready to sail!"

Belyx took a deep breath, trying to calm the storm of fear and rage rising within her. She steeled herself for what lay ahead, knowing that to survive, they would all need to rely on each other's strengths.

"Here goes nothing." And as one, they stepped onto the ship that would carry them into the jaws of danger.

Zephyr, with the air of a seasoned captain, barked orders at their small crew. "Mira, you're on rigging! Edric, you'll be our lookout and repairs. Belyx, you and I will handle the sails and navigation."

The creaky vessel they found themselves aboard was sturdy and well-built, though it had some minor damages. Its once-proud navy blue paint was now faded and chipped, while the intricate carvings that adorned the bow were worn by time and weather. The sails, patched in places but still strong, were hoisted up with Zephyr's expertise. They spared little expense on these vessels.

"Alright," he said, clapping his hands together. "Let's set sail!"

A heavy burden slammed on her shoulders as she adjusted the rope. This time had to be different; failure would mean more than letting herself down. It would put others at risk—more lives lost because of her. And as the doubt and fear began to creep up, a reassuring hand squeezed her shoulder.

"Hey." Zephyr's said. "You alright?"

"Fine," she lied, forcing a smile. "Just nervous about sailing. Water is not my strength."

"Trust me," he said, his gaze searching hers. "We've got this."

The sudden blast of a horn signaled the start of the challenge, pulling Belyx out of her thoughts.

With a mighty heave, they pushed off from the rocky shore, the current capturing their boat in an instant and sending them careening down the treacherous river.

"Keep an eye on the sails, Belyx!" Zephyr shouted over the breeze. "We need to catch every bit of wind we can get!"

She formed a tight lip expression, gripping the ropes under her calloused hands. The water churned beneath them, frothing whitecaps threatening to swallow their tiny vessel. Jagged rocks jutted from the water, some hidden right below the surface, ready to tear their vessel apart.

"Hard to starboard!" Zephyr yelled. Belyx eyed him with confusion and Zephyr shook his head. "Go left!"

Belyx yanked on the ropes, adjusting the sails as they narrowly avoided a lethal-looking boulder.

It wasn't long before enemy ships came into view, their sinister silhouettes cutting through the mist that clung to the water. As they drew nearer, the deafening boom of cannons filled the air, making Belyx flinch. She hated cannons—the noise and the destruction they caused.

"Brace for impact!" Zephyr roared as enemy cannonballs sliced through, barely missing their boat. A nearby ship wasn't so lucky, its mast splintering under the assault, while another was struck and disappeared beneath the churning waters with a sickening crunch.

"Keep pulling, Belyx!" Zephyr urged her as they raced to outmaneuver the relentless barrage.

"Mira, faster with those ropes! Edric, keep us informed of what's in front!"

"Rocks up ahead!" Edric called out.

"Port side, now…right!" Zephyr commanded, and Belyx heaved on the ropes, sending the boat veering just in time to avoid the deadly obstacle.

Another enemy ship appeared out of the mist, its crew shouting taunts and threats as they fired their cannons at Belyx's boat. "Incoming!" Edric shouted, and Belyx ducked instinctively, feeling the rush of air as a cannonball whizzed past her head.

"Zephyr!" she cried. "What do we do?"

"Keep going!" he yelled back, his expression fierce. "We've come this far—we're not giving up now!"

As they raced along the treacherous river, Belyx felt a surge of pride for their ragtag crew. They were working together seamlessly, each member focused on their task and trusting in the others to do their part. If they could just make it through this, they would be one step closer to freedom.

"Keep your head down, Belyx!" Zephyr warned her as yet another cannonball soared past, grazing her shoulder.

"Thanks," she breathed, nerves fraying as the relentless assault continued.

"Almost there!" Edric called out encouragingly.

"Let's make sure we get there in one piece!" Zephyr shouted, his eyes scanning the water for any signs of danger.

The river seemed to grow angrier as they approached the end of the treacherous course, its roiling waters churning and frothing like a living beast. To Belyx's horror, two nearby ships collided with a sickening crunch, their shattered hulls disappearing beneath the waves with screams of terror from their doomed crews. She gripped the railing of their battered boat, her knuckles white as she struggled to keep herself steady. Mira was repairing a rope with ease and carving something else into the railing.

"Zephyr! We need to do something!" she shouted over the roar of the water. The ship cracked like it was falling apart under them, the relentless pounding of the rapids threatening to rip it asunder at any moment.

Soren's vessel drew ever closer, looming ominously behind them like the sinister shadow of a predatory bird. With every passing second, the gap between them narrowed. If Soren managed to catch up to the boat, it would be the end for all of them. That monster never gave up!

"Alright," Zephyr yelled back, his head locked on the approaching enemy ship. "I've got an idea, but it's going to be dangerous."

"More dangerous than letting Soren gut us?" Belyx snapped. She couldn't bear the thought of losing anyone else, especially not Zephyr.

"Maybe," he admitted, his expression grim. "But it's our best shot at stopping him." He looked at Belyx, lines forming on his face. "Listen to me, Belyx. You have to keep going, no matter what happens. Get Edric and Mira to safety—promise me. Save my sister."

"Zephyr, what are you planning to do?" Her voice shook, a sinking feeling she already knew the answer played in her mind. She prayed that she was wrong.

"Stalling Soren," he replied. "By breaking our ship in half."

"Are you insane?" Belyx grabbed his arm. "You'll be killed!"

"Better me than all of us," Zephyr said fiercely, gripping her shoulders. "Now promise me, Belyx. Promise me you'll keep going."

"No!" Tears filled her eyes. "I won't leave you behind! We promised to stick together!"

"Listen to me," he said urgently. "You are a queen, and your people need you. Our crew needs you. I need you to survive this. We knew there was no way we could both survive. Belyx. Please."

Hot, salty tears streamed down her face as her heart broke. "I promise," she whispered. The roar of the river cut her off.

"Good." With that, Zephyr wrapped his arms around Belyx and kissed her with such intensity, that she felt like a million little stars were exploding inside her. He pulled away and smiled. "Thanks for the adventure." Then with a sudden jerk, he threw her across the deck towards Edric.

Mira jutted back toward Zephyr. What was she doing?

"Zephyr! Mira!" she screamed, her stomach in her throat as she watched him dash into the center of the ship. She struggled to rise, but the boat shuddered as if an earthquake hit, throwing her off balance once more.

"Keep going!" Edric shouted, gripping the helm with white knuckles. "We can't help them now!"

Belyx's vision blurred with tears as she looked back at Zephyr and the older woman one last time. He had managed to wedge his sword into a weak point in the ship's hull, and with a mighty heave, he wrenched it apart, splitting the boat in two. Mira spun around, muttering something to him. Why wasn't he forcing her back?

Save her!

The front half, carrying Belyx and Edric, lurched forward, propelled by the raging current.

"Zephyr!" Belyx sobbed as the rear of the ship, along with Zephyr, slammed into Soren's vessel, halting its progress and sending both ships careening off a waterfall into the churning waters below. But She gasped in horror as only

Zephyr and Mira's vessel fell all the way, swallowed by the frothing maelstrom and over a hulking cliff. Soren once, again, dodged death.

"No!" she screamed again. But there was no response, no sign of him resurfacing amidst the chaos and destruction.

"The task!" Edric called out over the sounds of splintering wood and crashing waves. "We have to make it to the end!"

Numb with grief, Belyx forced herself to turn away from the wreckage of their ship. As she took the wheel and spun it to their destination, she vowed silently his sacrifice would not be in vain. No matter what it took, she would see this through to the end—for Zephyr, and for all those who had placed their trust in her.

Soren's vessel clawed its way out of the currents, but the rest of their crew were not so fortunate. As Belyx stared at Edric, her eyes filled with rage and sorrow, she would never forget the cost of this terrible trial.

With the finish line in sight, Belyx pushed their disheveled ship forward. Every creak and groan of the vessel's timbers was like a harbinger of doom, but she wouldn't back down now. She had already lost too much.

"Almost there," urged Edric, the boy's voice surprisingly calm despite the chaos around them. Her fingers danced across the splintered wheel, sensing the ship's movements through subtle vibrations.

"Keep it steady!" called out Belyx, and Edric adjusted the sails, her eyes darting from one task to another. The treacherous river had taken its toll on them. Belyx had come too far to turn back now.

Belyx ached as she recalled Zephyr's final moments. She clenched her hands on the wheel until they stung, the pain serving as a reminder of all she had sacrificed for this moment.

"Look!" shouted Edric suddenly, pointing towards the horizon where the river finally emptied into a vast end where Majerian guards awaited. "We're here!"

"Let's make it count."

As they crossed the finish line, she allowed herself a brief pause of triumph before her thoughts turned once more to the friend she had lost.

"Zephyr," she murmured, her eyes welling with tears. *I promise you, this won't be for nothing.*

A wave of dizziness came over Belyx, blurring the image of Zephyr lying still and lifeless at the bottom of the sea...the sea he loved. She crumpled to her knees, exhausted by the weight of grief.

As the darkness came in, her vision twisted and turned. Tears rolled down her cheeks and she felt a slight twitch of her lips, as if she was trying to will herself to stay conscious. But it was no use. Her mind and body had reached their limit—she couldn't fight anymore. With one last deep breath, she let go and allowed unconsciousness to take over.

TWENTY-FOUR

Belyx's head pounded with such ferocity that she thought the world might be splitting in two. She opened her eyes to a cold wash rag over her head, panic roiling in her chest like a swarm of angry hornets.

"Easy there," Aurelius murmured, his slender form standing tall–something she'd never witnessed before. His words were the most kind he'd ever spoken to her. She must have been dreaming.

"Wh-What happened?" Belyx attempted to sit up but her throbbing head reminded her to stay down.

"Exhaustion and a minor head injury." He soaked the cloth in a canister of muddy water. "You need rest."

"Rest?" Belyx scoffed, trying to ignore the nausea that surged with the simple act of speaking. "I can't just lie here. There's work to be done. Where are the others?" She caught her error as soon as it dropped from her lips. There were no others left. Zephyr and Mira were dead.

"Safe." Aurelius, as if detecting her sorrow, continued, "Edric is hiding in a corner somewhere. About ten of the prisoners survived. Congratulations."

Why was he talking to her all of a sudden? It was too little too late as she wouldn't forget his part in Gelina's death.

Aurelius paused, looking up at her with a wry smile that seemed out of place on his scarred face. "You are just like your great-grandmother." An unfamiliar warmth emanated from him.

"Wait," Belyx shook her head, her heart suddenly pounding for different reasons. "You...you *did* know my grandmother?"

"Ah, yes." His gaze grew distant. "Marjorie. We were...in love, once upon a time."

Belyx couldn't process this news fast enough, her head still reeling from the pain. "Love?" Her mind raced to this new revelation, but it couldn't be possible. "How? She married a king." Her great-grandfather, Titus.

"Many years ago, my Order, called the Order of Dancing Flowers, sent me to Aikradal." His tone shifted softer and slower. "The kingdom was suffering under the weight of oppression and they needed someone to train them to fight it. That's when I met her."

Belyx's mouth hung open as she listened with wide eyes. So this *was* the Majerian master that had trained the Order.

"Marjorie was a force like no other storm," Aurelius continued, his eyes shining with every mention of her name. "I arrived there to help the soldiers, but she had other plans. She insisted I only train the women servants and such, as she believed men couldn't be trusted. Shockingly, I agreed. Most of our problems in Keyica were caused by men; wars, famine, slavery. I had never thought of it before until she made me realize." He laughed. "It was quite unexpected to see how fiery she was given her soft nature. I fell in love instantly."

Belyx's felt pride for the great-grandmother she'd never met. This woman had defied tradition and fought for her people, even if it meant putting herself at risk.

"During our time together, our feelings for each other grew." His words cracked slightly. "It was...complicated, with Marjorie being married to the king and my Order forbidding any romantic entanglements. But our hearts refused to listen to reason."

Belyx knew that feeling all too well as she held onto every word, her own heart aching for this love story out of a song. She thought of Enzo and the way his embrace sent her mind spinning with sweet delight, despite the dangers that lurked around them.

"Then why are you helping me now?" Letting a stronger wave of strength pull over her, Belyx sat up. "Why bother with someone like me? After all my pleading and insults." All at once, a pang of guilt crept up her back. Why had she been so mean to this man?

He still refused to help you. Don't let your guard down.

"Because I had a vision," Aurelius replied solemnly, his wrinkled eyes locking onto hers. "You are destined for great things. That's something I believe in, even if you don't. I am sorry for the way I treated you. It is not often an Aikradal queen passes through. You reminded me so much of her and I allowed my feelings to cloud my judgment. You spend enough time in this infernal place, your training is bound to waver." She let out a choked laugh. "Joking aside, Belyx. You have the talent to make a difference."

"Everyone keeps saying that." She rubbed her temples, the headache still knocking within her skull. "But what if they're wrong? What if I'm not cut out for this?"

"Trust in yourself, Belyx. You're descended from a line of powerful women, and that strength resides inside you."

"Enough about destiny," she grumbled, pushing herself upright and swinging her legs over the edge of the cot. "Tell me more about my great-grandmother and the Order." Perhaps this would calm the swirling in her head. She was only a queen who had to save her kingdom...nothing more.

"I owe you that much." Aurelius sighed, leaning back against the cold stone wall. "As Marjorie and I grew closer, our love caught the scent of my Order. They commanded me to kill her...to kill all of the girls I trained. As my punishment, of course, they would punish the women and keep me alive."

Belyx's eyes widened in shock, lurching at the thought of such betrayal.

"But I couldn't," he continued. "Instead, I declined and they sent others to the job." His crinkly hands rubbed together. They never even made it through the gates." Belyx gulped. How many people had he killed to protect her family?

"I used my secret art to kill every one of the Order who came after her."

"Secret art?" Belyx repeated, curiosity momentarily eclipsing her fear. So there was something he knew after all. If only she had learned it earlier.

"An ancient technique is known only to the elite few within my Order…well now just me." A shadow crossed his face. "It allowed me to strike down my enemies with just a singular blade."

What kind of power was this? "How?"

"By manipulating time. Or at least the perspective of it."

Belyx's mind flashed to multiple possibilities. "If you killed the threats, then why didn't you stay with Marjorie?"

"Because the cost of my rebellion was high. I had to leave Aikradal, knowing I could never return." His eyes were downcast with sorrow. "I left Marjorie behind. She would be safer without me. Plus she had a kingdom to run and a family to raise."

Belyx ached for the star-crossed love that had come before her own, but she couldn't help the flicker of anger that ignited within her at the thought of Aurelius abandoning her great-grandmother. "Then surely you understand why I can't rest now. I have to fight for those I love and for the kingdom that needs me. If I'm truly meant for life-changing things, then it's time I start living up to that destiny."

Aurelius studied her for a moment, his gaze piercing through her bravado. Then, he nodded. "Indeed, Belyx. Let us start your training. I regretted my whole life not teaching your great-grandmother the skill and look what happened to her kingdom…to your kingdom."

"Wait," Belyx interrupted. "You never taught Marjorie this sacred art. Why not?"

Aurelius halted mid-step, his golden eyes meeting hers with an intensity that sent shivers down her spine. He appeared to be choosing his words carefully as if they held power beyond her understanding.

"Marjorie was already a formidable force in her own right," he began, his tone low and measured. "My intentions were too, but she said no, saying no one deserved such power." He paused, head shaking. "Then she called me a murderer and said I wasn't welcome in Aikradal."

Belyx frowned, her fingers unconsciously tracing the outline of her thigh. "I never realized. Why would she refuse something like that from you? I thought she loved you."

"Love is a complex thing, Belyx." A hint of sadness touched his features. "Sometimes, we must sacrifice what we previously found important for it. My guilt overwhelmed me, so that was when I came here. To serve a life sentence...until now."

"Then what is it about me that makes you believe I can handle this art?" Her hands clenched against the bed frame as fought against the frustration boiling within her. "Why do you think I'm ready when Marjorie wasn't?"

"Because the world has changed." He shot his head into the distance as if his words were borne from a vision only he could see. "The time for balance has come, and you—" he paused, his eyes narrowing as they bore into hers with an intensity that made her vision race, "—are the key to achieving it."

"Balance?" Belyx echoed, her mind reeling with questions and possibilities.

"Indeed. You have the potential to bring about a harmony that has long been absent from this world. But first, you must master the sacred art—and embrace all that it entails."

With a hard swallow, Belyx let the weight of his words settle upon her shoulders like an invisible mantle. She had always known she was destined to do well, but hearing it from Aurelius, someone who had trained and loved her great-grandmother, made it more real than ever before.

"Show me." She steadied her words. "Teach me this sacred skill so that I can restore balance to Aikradal and fulfill my destiny."

"I will." A ghost of a smile touched his lips as he resumed his stance. "But remember—the path you are choosing is one fraught with peril and sacrifice. Are you prepared to face whatever challenges may lie ahead?" Belyx had already faced the worst things that could have happened to her. Nothing else would stop her. Fear would not consume her anymore.

"Whatever it takes." Her eyes blazed with hope as she mirrored his position, ready to learn the secrets that would shape her future and the fate of her kingdom.

The sun dipped below the horizon, casting a warm orange glow across the prison courtyard as Aurelius led Belyx through the shadows and to the outskirts of the compound, where the crumbling stone walls met the fierce embrace of wild ivy.

It was refreshing to see such vibrancy after the dampness and dread of the prison. No other prisoners were here either. It must have been where Aurelius sat and contemplated the world. *To live a life alone...as a recluse.* How much of his guilt weighed down on him? To think he and her great-grandmother had a secret love affair. The threads of her family's history were unwinding with care, giving Belyx a glimpse into her legacy.

Only time would tell what that was.

They settled on a patch of soft earth, dampened by the evening dew, and rested side by side as the last vestiges of sunlight surrendered to twilight.

"Listen now," Aurelius said, his voice like gravel crunching beneath a boot. "This skill comes from a questionable history and I need you to be present and willing to do whatever it takes."

Belyx's breaths quickened with anticipation, her eyes darting over the old man's worn face.

"This art came to my Order during the beginning of the settlers. They broke off after the formation of Aikradal because we believed no hierarchy was free of flaws." He eyed Belyx as her eyes widened. "No worries. We didn't believe in the old place's teachings."

Belyx exhaled. The old place, or Morag, where her people escaped, had a belief that total control meant worshiping a heinous deity, in which no crown would rule. Aurelius's ideas were similar despite his reassurances.

"After my ancestors fled and formed their Order, they stumbled upon the Twisted Rivers, where the witches reside."

A gasp left Belyx's throat. "They *were* there?"

Aurelius stared down. "They *are* there. They live in their tribe, torn away from the rest of the continent."

Tales of terror from Twisted Rivers and the witches that roamed fermented in her mind. None who ventured to that wretched place ever returned.

"The Order were captured by them, but given a chance to prove their worth. They were able to and the witches shared a piece of their magic with them. The art of balance. As I explained before, it is a technique that allows one to slow down time by focusing on a weapon of some sort...At the time, it was our simple daggers."

Trying to remember what he said, Belyx's mind raced with possibilities. She imagined herself wielding her knives with supernatural speed, outmaneuvering even the deadliest foes. Was such a thing possible? "How does it work?"

"Balance, my child. Physical and emotional balance." Aurelius met her gaze, his own amber eyes gleaming with knowledge. "The witches thought all physical and emotional feelings held us back. To perfect their craft, they had to let go of all human emotions that restricted them. Only then could they unlock their true potential."

Belyx's excitement waned, replaced by a cold sense of dread that settled in her stomach. Emotions? She frowned, trying to push away thoughts of her mother, father, and grandmother, their faces etched in pain. "I don't have any feelings holding me back," she lied. "I can do it." She was more determined than ever. Pushing aside her grief, she was unfeeling as she built the wall inside of her.

Aurelius studied her, his expression impassive. "We all have sensitive spots, my dear. Even the strongest among us." He leaned closer, the scars on his face casting sinister shadows in the dim light. "If you wish to learn this technique, you must be prepared to confront your grief and let it go."

Belyx's froze. How did he know what she felt?

She couldn't do it.

She couldn't face the memories of her family, their lifeless bodies haunting her every waking moment. But if she wanted to save those she loved, and to protect her friends from suffering the same fate, she had no choice.

"Very well." She lifted her head. "Teach me."

"Remember, Belyx," Aurelius cautioned, "emotional balance is key. You must feel the weight of your grief before you can release it. No hiding."

She tilted her head, throat tight, and braced herself for the journey into the depths of her pain. All the while, she clung to the hope that this newfound power might tip the scales in her favor and help her avenge the ones she'd lost.

Aurelius raised his hand, signaling for Belyx to close her eyes. "Breathe deeply and clear your mind...focus on the energy within you."

Inhaling slowly, she filled her lungs with air before exhaling with more force. The tension in her shoulders began to dissipate, and a sense of clarity washed over her.

"Listen again," Aurelius continued as he whispered ancient words into her ear. They sounded like the rustling of leaves or the gentle murmur of a stream—soft and calming, yet full-bodied. Belyx repeated the words to herself, letting the magic weave its way through her being.

"Open your eyes," Aurelius commanded, handing her a makeshift shiv. She raised an eyebrow at the weapon, surprised that he had managed to keep it hidden within the prison walls. He winked at her, and she couldn't help but smirk in response.

"Focus on the aura of the weapon. Feel its energy, its purpose. Let it become an extension of yourself. Even the most simple of weapons harness an energy us humans cannot see."

Obediently, Belyx concentrated on the shiv, her gaze tracing its sharpened edge. A faint shimmer surrounded it, and she imagined it pulsing with life. As she did so, the world around her slowed down, each breath she took elongating into infinity. Was it really that easy? Why had this technique not been more common?

For a moment, she reveled in the sensation, feeling both numb and untouchable. But then, without warning, her feelings plummeted like they were falling off a cliff, and she was assaulted by images of her deceased family members.

Belyx felt her body plunge as the visions of her family slammed into her. Her mother's accusing hazel eyes, her father's desperate outstretched hands, her grandmother's agonized expression; all of their faces were overlaid with a deep sorrow that filled the room with an oppressive energy. The pain ripped through Belyx like a physical force, and she almost dropped the shiv in her shaking grip.

"Belyx." His voice was still calm but insistent. "You must let go of your grief if you wish to master this technique."

"Let it go?" she croaked. "How can I? They're gone, and I couldn't save them. I don't want to feel it. I don't want to feel anything. How is that not letting go?"

"Releasing your grief does not mean forgetting them," Aurelius reminded her gently. "It means accepting their loss so that you can continue to live and fight for those who still need you."

Belyx closed her eyes again, allowing herself to be lost in the memories of her loved ones for a moment longer. With each gasp, she tried to release the pain that weighed her down, letting it seep from her body like ink into water.

"Good...now, once more, focus on the weapon. Focus on you."

Determined to succeed, Belyx took a deep breath and turned her attention back to the shiv. She would honor her family's memory by becoming stronger. And with this newfound skill, she would ensure no one else she cared for would suffer the same fate.

Belyx's gut roiled in her chest as darkness threatened to consume her. The world slowed, and then...a vision popped into her mind.

Enzo stood before her, his familiar green eyes large with surprise as the blade pierced through his neck. His flame tattoos flickered weakly like dying embers, unable to protect him from the cold steel that shredded through his chest. Crimson blood seeped through his shirt, staining his tanned skin.

"Enzo!" Belyx screamed, reaching out for him, but her fingers grasped at nothingness. Helpless tears blurred her sight as she watched the life drain from her partner's eyes.

"Enough," Aurelius's command cut through the haze, stern and commanding. There was a sharp sting on her cheek, bringing her back to the present with a gasp. "You're still holding onto your grief and fear. You can never master this if you don't let go."

Tears of frustration pricked her as she fiercely denied it. "I don't feel the grief. I've buried it deep within me." *Where it belongs.*

"Ah, but there lies the problem." His resolve softened with understanding. "Burying it is not the same as letting it go. If you wish to master this technique, you must face your pain and allow yourself to feel it all at once."

"Feel it? All of it?" Her hands trembled as she clutched the shiv. The thought alone was terrifying—like standing on the edge of a cliff with darkness swirling below, waiting to swallow her whole.

"Yes," Aurelius insisted, his age-worn features furrowed. "Only by facing your fears can you conquer them. You have the strength within you. Now you find the courage to use it."

Belyx hesitated, her breath catching in her throat as she stared down at the makeshift weapon in her grasp. The thought of fighting the pain that had haunted her for so long was nearly unbearable, but she knew what was at stake.

"Alright," she whispered, steeling herself against the storm of emotions that threatened to engulf her. "I'll do it. For them."

"Good," Aurelius's expression was resolute. "Now, focus on the shiv and let your grief flow through you. Let it crash over you like a wave, and then recede into the ocean of your soul."

With a final deep breath, Belyx closed her eyes and braced herself for the torrent of anguish that would come crashing down upon her. She would face this pain, for Enzo, for her family, and for the kingdom that depended on her strength. And when the storm passed, she would emerge stronger than ever. She did have those emotions. Each night before bed and each time she required help. Her longing was like a scar, never to fade, never to heal. How was that not embracing it? She felt the hurt worse than anyone. Her family was gone...and so was the rest of the ones she cared about. Zephyr, Gelina, and most likely everyone at Aikradal.

Like a lightning strike, her eyes opened and a large breath escaped her throat. The weapon remained untouched and her teacher shook his head.

"Come. We must try again," Aurelius said, guiding her to a more secluded corner of the prison. "Lie down and relax your body."

Belyx did as she was told, feeling the cold grassy floor beneath her. The air was damp and heavy, filled with the distant echoes of rain and guards yelling from the inside. She closed her eyes, attempting to block out the sounds, but it wasn't enough.

"Remember the good times you shared with your family. Let those memories fill your heart."

Taking a deep breath, Belyx began to recall memories she hadn't dared visit for a long while. She remembered her mother's laughter as they baked together in the palace kitchen, their hands dusted with flour and faces smeared with batter. And recalled her father's strong arms around her, holding her close after reading her a magnificent story, telling her how proud he was of her progress as a princess.

A smile tugged at her lips as she thought of her grandmother's warm embrace, her soft, lilting voice recounting stories of ancient battles and magical creatures. The scent of rosewater and fresh herbs clung to her skin, comforting Belyx even when she was miles away from home.

"Good," Aurelius encouraged. "Now let the sadness come. Let it wash over you, but remember that it, too, will pass."

The grin faded from Belyx's face as a twisting knot of pain formed in her chest. It grew tighter and heavier, threatening to suffocate her. Her breath hitched as images of her father's lifeless eyes and her mother's broken form flashed before her, quickly followed by her grandmother's pale, blood-streaked face. Belyx's clenched her clothing, tears streaming down her cheeks as she finally allowed herself to embrace the full weight of their loss. She awoke again, breathing harder.

"Enough," Aurelius said quietly, placing a hand on her shoulder. "You've made progress, today."

Sitting up, she wiped at her tear-stained face, her chest heaving with the effort of each ragged breath. "I don't know if I can do this, Aurelius." She trembled. "The pain is too much."

"Without mastering this skill, you may not be able to save those you love," he reminded her. "It's a difficult path, but one you must walk if you wish to protect your kingdom and those you love."

Belyx kept a straight face, her resolve returning as she thought of Enzo and all the others who depended on her. She would face this pain, for them and herself.

"I need to do this on my own." Tears welled in her eyes.

Aurelius acknowledged her and as she rose from the ground, marched off in search of solace. Yet, despite the foreboding that loomed, she didn't need this power to overpower her foes. She had her strength; she'd battle till the end to ensure those she loved were safe.

The dank corridors of the prison were like a siren call, each step echoing in the dimly lit stone passage. Her still bruised head ebbed with raw pain, and her mouth burned with the intensity of her emotions. The grief clawed at her insides, as relentless as a tempest.

"Damn them all," she muttered under her breath, wringing her hands together. *Why did everyone who died have to leave me like this? Alone?*

A sudden scream tore through the air, slicing through Belyx's thoughts like a sharpened dagger. A young boy, no older than thirteen, was being dragged down the corridor by two burly prisoners. His face was a tapestry of terror and confusion, and his eyes—wide and pleading—locked onto Belyx.

"Please! I didn't do anything!" the boy cried out, struggling against the iron grips of his captors. "Help me!"

"Quiet, you little rat!" one of the prisoners barked, smacking the boy across the face. Belyx winced at the sharp sound, her rage simmering beneath the surface. She glanced around the prison, looking for any familiar faces who might be able to assist. But no one was there.

Why was a child in this godforsaken place?

Belyx followed as the boy's pleas continued. What could he have done that was so unforgivable for two grown men to be picking on him?

"Hey, let him go! What did he do to deserve this?" Belyx demanded. She stepped closer to the trio, her poise that of a queen unafraid to wield her strength...despite her being a prisoner within these walls.

"Crawl away, bitch," the other prisoner sneered, tightening his hold on the boy's arm. "He's a thief and a liar."

"Is that so?" Her eyes narrowed as she examined the boy. He was small and scrawny, with dirt-streaked skin and ragged clothes. The sight of him stirred something deep inside her, a memory of another young thief— Enzo—whose childhood had also been cut too short. She blinked away at the thought, despair threatening to swallow her whole.

"Again. Let him go," Belyx ordered. "Or else."

"Ha! You? Don't make me laugh," the first prisoner scoffed, his laughter echoing through the prison like the cawing of a crow. "You are nothing but a spoiled queen whose mommy and daddy had to help her all her life."

"Let him go." Her voice turned ice-cold, trying to ignore their jabs as her determination flared like a beacon in the darkness, fueled by the burning desire to protect those who were innocent.

A cacophony of jeers and taunts erupted further down the prison corridor, snapping Belyx out of her reverie. More prisoners surrounded her now, their faces twisted into cruel sneers. They threw the boy down, his body still, but his breathing faint. This was some sort of gang fight the boy had gotten in the middle of. There was no going back now.

The prisoners leered at her, ready to make their claim of flesh. With resolve marked across her features, Belyx backed away from the commotion, her hands shaking. This would not be easy.

One prisoner...Bald head, started kicking the boy on the ground. "You should've thought twice before stealing our food."

"Enough!" Belyx snarled, shoving her way through the throng of prisoners. Her pulse quickened like a staccato, a war drum urging her forward. They were blocking her way. This prison would be the boy's coffin if she didn't do something.

Laughter rippled through the prisoners, but they stepped away, leaving the boy gasping for breath on the cold stone floor. Belyx crouched beside him, shielding him with her body as she glared up at the towering prisoners.

"Think you can take us all on, do you?" Bald Head mocked, cracking his knuckles. "You're barely more than a child yourself."

The words stung, but Belyx wouldn't let them see her falter. She drew on the memory of her family, their love and strength propelling her as she rose to her feet. "No more innocents will be hurt again," she vowed.

"Brave, but foolish," another prisoner...Big Tooth, sneered, lunging towards her.

Belyx met him head-on, her years of training kicking in as she sidestepped his clumsy attack and countered with a swift elbow to the face. He crumpled to the ground, and Belyx whirled to face the next assailant.

Eleven against one, she thought, her body tensed and ready. *I am in it now.*

She fought like a tempest, her fists and feet striking with deadly precision. But the prisoners were relentless, and Belyx soon found herself outnumbered and outmaneuvered. One prisoner managed to slip past her defenses, landing a crushing blow that sent her sprawling to the floor.

As the men closed in, their battered shoes raining down on her weakened form, images of her family flickered through her mind. Each kick threatened to extinguish the fire within her, but she clung to the memories, using them as an anchor in the storm of pain.

Through the haze of agony, Belyx spotted a glint of steel out of the corner of her eye. A fellow prisoner had produced a concealed knife, its blade shimmering like a beacon of hope. With a surge of adrenaline, Belyx lunged for the weapon, her fingers closing around the hilt just as another blow landed and she ended up on the rough floor again.

Belyx closed her eyes as the snaggle-toothed prisoner held the blade above her, tears welled in her eyes. This was the end. All she had worked for crumbled like a castle.

She was ready. Death was at her door. As she shut her eyes again, her mother's face appeared. *No Belyx,* she whispered. *You are a survivor. The true hope for the land.*

Her father appeared next. *I will always be proud. Never give up.*

Then, her grandmother. *Flower. You have more in you than you know. Never surrender to the evil that threatens you.*

Whether it was real or not, it was enough. With open eyes, the blade came down and the world slowed around her, each beat echoing through her chest like a slow rhythm. Her veins hummed, and she could almost sense the spirits of her ancestors urging her on.

Finish this!

Time snapped back into focus as Belyx rolled, narrowly missing the blade and snatching it from the brute.

The confused looks from the prisoners radiated as Belyx launched herself at the nearest prisoner. The blade sang through the air, finding its target with lethal precision. He fell without a sound, and his comrades had little time to register their shock before Belyx was upon them too.

"I told you!" she snarled. "No innocent will be hurt again!"

Her movements were fluid, a deadly dance of steel and grace. One by one, the prisoner's images blurred around her, not moving at all, as she sent a barrage of attacks. The remaining prisoners crumpled under her assault until only she and the boy remained standing.

"Are you okay?" Belyx asked, breaths tiring.

The boy shook, his eyes flickering with awe. "You saved me."

"Remember this." Belyx crouched down to look him in the eye. "Never steal from those you can't outrun. It's a lesson I learned from someone I care deeply about. He was a lot like you once."

She thought of Enzo, the mischievous glint in his green eyes as he regaled her with tales of his thieving escapades. A swell of fear threatened to overtake her at the thought of his death, but she pushed it down, channeling it into resolve instead. Enzo was okay. He was still alive.

"Find your strength," she encouraged the boy. "And use it to protect what matters most."

Belyx stood and handed the boy the shiv, all at once, a sense of confidence settling within her. She had faced her emotions and emerged victorious. The road ahead would be long and fraught with danger, but she was ready to face whatever challenges awaited her.

"Thank you," the boy said quietly as his shaking hands grasped the steel, his eyes shimmering with unshed tears.

"Stay strong...You're not alone."

With that, she turned away. She had begun to accept her grief, and though it still clung to her like a shadow, she knew she had the strength to keep moving forward. The ancient art was hers now, and although it was faint, she had enough to face the trials that lay ahead. Once she won and escaped, she would return to Aikradal...and make all who opposed her suffer.

TWENTY-FIVE

"Going somewhere?" Belyx eyed Aurelius, he had a small sack in his hand as if he was going on an elaborate trip.

He took a deep breath and gazed around the prison. "You learning the skill and letting go of your grief taught me one thing. I have been hiding away for too long. Today is the day I escape. When you win this last trial, meet me at the slave docks south of the kingdom. There will be a boat for you."

"Escape? Take me with you then!" Her hands scrunched the rough fabric of her tattered clothes. "I can barely control these new abilities. Winning looks slim right now anyway."

"Never give up. You are stronger than any challenge they throw your way. Your path is to win and show Majeria you are strong and not some coward. Show them you can beat their twisted games. That way they have no reason to disrespect your honor. Now meet me where I instructed."

Arguing with him was futile, but before she could respond, the distant bell tolled, signaling the commencement of the fourth and final trial. Sighing, Belyx closed her eyes for a moment, reminding herself of the determination and courage that had carried her this far. She knew she couldn't afford any more mistakes. "I guess I will see you then."

Aurelius nodded and disappeared into the shadows. As the trial approached, part of her wished he had taken her with him. *It is your path, Belyx. Show these bastards you can win their silly games.*

Belyx and the other remaining prisoners were led to their final task, including Luo, Soren, and Edrik. Her pulse quickened in anticipation. The guards ushered them into an open area surrounding a vast pond, its water dark and still. Prince Vincent stood at the edge, his eyes narrowed in anger upon seeing Belyx among the competitors.

"Ah, Belyx." He sneered as he approached her with his armed guards. Good. He needed them for the things Belyx planned to do to his neck. "I'm surprised to see you've made it this far."

"Your surprise means nothing to me," Belyx spat, meeting his gaze without fear. The other prisoners eyed each other with discomfort, now annoyed they were not receiving the same one-on-one attention from his Highness.

"Very well," he said with an icy chill as he stepped up to the podium. "The final trial is called The Drowning." He was addressing everyone now. Belyx only wished Zephyr and Gelina were still here. They would figure out a way for them all to win, but now Edrik was the only person she cared about and she would save him from this.

"You will race to an underwater bunker, and only one of you will make it out alive. And, as promised, that prisoner will go free." He stared at her again...a silent warning it wouldn't be her.

Heart pounding in her chest, she gazed at the pond before her. The water rippled ominously under the cold gaze of Prince Vincent, and a shiver ran down her spine. It had been a while since she last swam, but now, it was a skill that could mean the difference between life and death.

She reached for her mother's strength inside her mind, recalling the way her mom had taught her to swim when she was a child. She pictured her encouraging smile, the warmth of her touch, and the soothing sound of her voice as she guided her through the water. Belyx took a deep breath and centered herself, focusing on the memory of her.

Edrik stood next to her and she placed a hand on his shoulder which he batted away. "It will be alright. Try and stay with me," Belyx reassured.

Edrik shook in response. There was no turning back now.

"Begin!" Prince Vincent commanded.

The other prisoners dove into the freezing depths with chilled movements. A gasp left her throat as the icy liquid enveloped her, the shock making her forget to take a breath beforehand. Panic threatened to overtake her as she frantically tried to kick underneath the cold embrace, her chest burning for air.

She stilled, forcing her body to calm down and remember her mother's teachings. Her arms cut through the water, propelling her forward even as her lungs screamed for oxygen. How long would she need to hold her air in here?

As she swam deeper, Belyx caught sight of sporadic air pockets trapped beneath the surface. Desperate, she managed to gulp in a few precious breaths before continuing her descent. But just as a small measure of relief came, a hand grabbed her ankle and yanked her downwards.

Belyx recognized Soren's meaty grip as they whipped through the murky depths, arms locked in a deadly embrace. Belyx's insides felt like they were ablaze, her exhales coming in agonizing gasps. With every passing second, she was closer to her demise.

With a well-timed kick, she sent Soren away, but he was relentless and followed Belyx like a shark to the air pocket. Belyx managed one breath before he was on her again. Even through the water, she could see the look in his eyes. A look that said he would finish the job this time.

Belyx fought with her last will as he closed his muscled hands around her throat, crushing the oxygen from her lungs. The icy water sapped at her strength and she knew even a hint of a struggle was useless against him. With every second that passed, her will to survive faded away.

With gritted teeth, she stuck out her fingers into his eye sockets. A bubbled gasp left Soren as Belyx sent a knee into his groin. He fell back and Belyx returned to her treck. That wasn't nearly enough to take him down, but she just needed to swim to land.

Keeping her focus forward, Belyx maneuvered through the tricky cave ways, refusing to look back as Soren was likely on her tail.

A light reflection shone in the distance. That had to be the opening in the bunker! With her lungs pinching, she made the final push for the surface, but something grabbed her hair.

Belyx held the grip and involuntarily let out her remaining air. Soren held his grasp and pushed Belyx into a rock, a heat from his hands ebbing from him.

With failing limbs, Belyx struggled to stop him. His grip was as solid as metal.

Suddenly, a darkness engulfed her vision and Belyx's throat screamed for oxygen that was no longer there. Her body went limp and her fate became sealed—this was how she would perish; the last thing Belyx ever saw was his victorious face.

With a thrashing wave of water, Soren released his grip. A wall of thick water bubbles appeared between them as someone knocked him away. When the bubbles subsided, Luo was there, her hair wild and eyes fierce. Relief and fear flooded through Belyx. Did Luo betray her partner? But why? She had spent the whole trial trying to help Soren kill Belyx.

The expression in Luo's eyes told Belyx to swim away. Soren thought he had the advantage because he had an ally in Luo. But now, Luo was protecting Belyx from his death mission.

Soren growled in fury as he fought against Luo's unexpected betrayal.

Belyx swam forward and kicked off a nearby rock.

With a glance behind her, Luo moved as if she controlled the water instead of it controlling her. Luo was vigilant and sent a couple of quick attacks into him. Soren was not giving up; chasing Luo down.

Go! Luo gestured to Belyx again, her hand pointing to the direction of the bunker.

Belyx hesitated for a moment, watching as Luo dragged Soren further down into the depths, the two of them becoming nothing more than shadows in the murky water. She forced herself to swim upwards, her chest tightening with each stroke.

On her way, A horror struck Belyx's sight; Edrik's pale, lifeless body being pulled along the rocks by a prisoner with dark brown hair. Her fury boiled over as she swam higher and higher, determined to make the killer pay for what he did.

Every ally I make...dies.

They will not go unpunished.

Breaking the surface, Belyx gasped, filling her lungs with sweet air. Her thoughts raced with questions about Luo's actions, but now was not the time for answers. A promise had been made to Aurelius, and she would keep it.

Three other prisoners she didn't recognize were fighting to kill one another. A sealed door was just beyond. Most likely triggered when only one living body remained. The one who killed Edrik was there as well. He fought like an animal against the others, but he stood no chance at Belyx's fury. She would avenge Edrik's death.

Gasping for breath, Belyx tackled the brute, letting the rage pour out of her as she pounded his face into the ground.

She had her hands on his pockmarked throat, when another prisoner slammed her face with a rock, taking the opportunity while she was distracted.

The world spun around Belyx as she grasped for anything to defend herself. Her vision blurred as the shaky figures came closer and closer.

But in a flash, they were thrust back by a stream of water. As her sight returned, Luo sprung from the surface.

Moments later, Luo emerged in front of Belyx. With a wave of her hand, she summoned the water's power and sent swirling currents toward the remaining prisoners. Their cries were muffled by the churning water as they were dragged beneath the opening, one by one.

What ability was that? What was Luo? Was she some kind of water fae? If so, where were her pointy ears and tattoos?

"Wh—why?" Belyx stammered, unable to comprehend Luo's actions. "Why did you save me? You've done nothing but try to kill me this whole competition."

"Because..." Luo's head did a double take, as if to make sure no one was around. "I was under deep cover."

"Deep cover?" Belyx scoffed, her eyes narrowing. "For what?"

Luo shook her wet hair. "My real name is Ulo Pina. I descend from the tribe of Control Witches...able to manipulate things from the outside world...like water. I was assigned by them to infiltrate this prison."

Belyx blinked rapidly, unable to comprehend this new information. "And what about Gelina and Zephyr? Why didn't you save them?"

"I had to keep my cover. Soren had strict instructions from the prince to kill you in these trials. He would have succeeded too. Soren's family was a poor military one and the prince offered him a healthy sum for your head in this trial."

"Why not just murder me in my sleep then?"

"The prince has a specific set of rules he follows. He wanted to do it the 'right' way. If that makes any sense."

Like a math equation. "Still. You didn't have to let Gelina and Zephyr die. They were good people who didn't deserve any of this."

"We had to keep you alive," Luo said as she bent to Belyx, she batted the witch away. "I am sorry I couldn't do more for them, but I had a specific task to help you and only you. I tried my best to save them. I had a way to save Gelina, but then she trapped herself with that beast and I had to get out. Zephyr should have just stayed on the boat, I was going to get him to safety as well. I apologize."

Belyx didn't know whether to hug or kill this woman but remembered what following orders was like. "Why me?" I am nothing but a common queen."

Luo's gaze dug into Belyx. "A great danger threatens our continent, and I was instructed to find the chosen one—the one who can unite the fae and witches again."

"Me?" Disbelief colored her features. "That makes zero sense. What makes me so special?"

"You seriously haven't figured it out yet?"

"I don't feel special."

"Cut the shit."

"Wha—"

"Only you have the strength and will to bring peace between the two factions. What you did last year was the first part. Getting the fae to trust you and now…" Luo's jaw tightened, while her yellow gaze locked onto Belyx's. "We have enough to break it."

Belyx shook her head hesitantly, disconcerted by the intensity of her leer. "Break what?"

Luo or Ulo took a step towards the sealed door. "We have been waiting for quite some time. A queen with fiery hair and an unrelenting spirit. We were trying to get to you earlier, but then Majeria attacked. Our plant in your Order was supposed to tell you all this. I don't know why—"

"Amnethya." Belyx knew she was a witch, but now it made sense why she was there. *Amenthya didn't tell me because I was dating a fae and would be biased. I wish she had told me about this plan. I would've done something.*

Luo shook her head vigorously. "We knew the chosen one was from Aikradal. We originally thought it was someone else."

"My mother…" Of course, it would be her.

"At first, but now I realize it was actually you." Luo grabbed her hand firmly in her own, glancing towards the door as if she expected guards to rush in at any moment.

Belyx couldn't help but laugh despite the tension that hung heavy in the air, her thoughts turning bitter with irony. "I love the flattery, but my mother was way more competent than me. I am a second choice."

Luo squeezed her hand ever tighter. "There is no second choice, Belyx Velena. You *are* the one to unite the fae and witches. You are the one to bring peace."

"Peace?" Belyx said, overwhelmed by a cacophony of discomforting questions whirling in her mind without any answers in sight yet. "But how can I—"

"It will all become clearer soon enough," she murmured urgently under her breath before adding louder so she could hear her properly. "I must go now." She quickly released her hand and backed away towards the shadows of the room. "A witch will find you soon, but right now, escape here and save your kingdom."

"Where are you going? We both can live!"

Luo shook her head. "That door will never open for two people." She placed a reassuring hand on Belyx's shoulder before letting herself sink and fall back into the water, a knowing smile gracing her lips.

"Wait!" Belyx cried out, reaching for her, but Luo had already vanished beneath the water hole.

As she gazed into the depths, Belyx wrestled with the jumble of emotions surging through her. Although she was relieved that she had won, the revelation of Luo's true allegiance left her feeling disoriented. And now she was expected to unite the fae and witches to rebuild their world? She had enough problems to deal with trying to save her kingdom.

"Peace." That word was foreign on her tongue. *Can I really bring peace? The conflict between them was supposed to be over.* There haven't been any recent wars...

The answer remained elusive as she considered the enormity of the task at hand. With a heavy burden, she decided to ponder these revelations later. There was still an escape to be made.

Belyx raced to the edge of the bunker, her muscles aching with exhaustion and her lungs still burning from her underwater ordeal. The once-sealed door opened with a groan and Belyx charged through.

It led to an embankment of some kind and Belyx hoisted herself onto the muddy ledge, water streaming off her soaked clothes, pooling around her. The cold wind bit at her wet skin, but she couldn't afford to dwell on that now.

After she was up, the path went to an empty shore. The moon indicated it was nightfall already. Sailing in that would prove tricky. *Get to the south of Majeria, find Aurelius, find a boat, and sail away.*

She crept along the shoreline, moving through the shadows cast by the towering trees above. Her eyes twitched as she scanned her surroundings for any signs of danger.

As Belyx grew deeper into the beach, multiple Majeria guards jumped out and surrounded her. She held her arms up, ready to fight all of them if necessary.

"Going somewhere, Belyx Velena?" called a sneering voice, shattering her hope.

Belyx's body locked in place, her veins running icy. Her gaze snapped up to find Prince Vincent looming before her, his guards hemming him in with menacing weaponry. His hands were clasped behind his back. She had known it was he who arranged for Soren to take her life, and now here he was, coming to finish what he started.

"Prince Vincent," she spat, clenching her fists. "I wondered when you would show up."

Twenty-Six

The cells beneath Aikradal's palace were nothing but...inviting. Enzo as he slumped against the stone wall, the weight of his failure pressed down on him, suffocating his mind and memories. Inky shadows played across the walls as he traced the rough outline of the bricks with a fingertip, remembering how his tribe had been trapped by humans and didn't give a damn about them. *It was the king, Enzo. Not all the people.*

Enzo clutched the bars, trying to summon his flame, but he only received a flicker. The fight with The Scorpion had taken a toll on him.

Belyx's face haunted his thoughts. Enzo fervently wished she was still alive, somewhere beyond these cursed gates, fighting to free her people. He was so near to reviving The Original, and now, he had to finish the job.

His home was ablaze. Where was his family? His tribe? These things kept Enzo yearning for a way out. The locks were nothing. Belyx referred to him as an artist of escapes, which had a nice ring to it. He didn't need his powers to escape. All those years on the streets served him just fine.

He studied the lock closer. It was a basic model, one that would take time with the makeshift equipment he had.

A while into his work, a gruff voice interrupted his reverie. "Get up, fae." A guard loomed above him, his long braided gray hair falling over his shoulder as his intense gaze bore into him. Without waiting for a response, he opened the door and pulled Enzo to his feet. Enzo went to fight back when more guards appeared and bound his hands behind his back.

He gritted his teeth in frustration. "Where are you taking me?" Enzo struggled to maintain an air of defiance despite the panic rising within him.

"Princess Vivienne wants to speak with you," he replied, his expression unreadable. He led Enzo down a winding corridor, the torchlight casting flickering shadows on the ancient stone walls.

As they entered the throne room, Enzo couldn't help but shudder at the sight that greeted him. Majerian blues swathed the room in a chilling embrace, while fish skeletons hung from the high ceiling like macabre chandeliers.

"Ah, Enzo," Princess Vivienne purred, her deep blue eyes spearing him like glaciers. She sat upon Belyx's throne, now donned in the giant bones that looked like a whale. "I've been waiting for this moment."

"Let my tribe and Aikradal go." He vibrated as if he could breathe fire at this witch. "We've done nothing to deserve this."

"Your very existence is an affront to my kingdom," Vivienne replied, a small smile twitching on her lips. "But I am not without mercy. Tell me what I wish to know, and perhaps I will consider your request."

Enzo clenched his jaw as he struggled to keep his emotions in check. He couldn't give her the satisfaction of knowing she'd broken him, but he was acutely aware of the danger he was in.

"Ask your questions," he spat, meeting her glare with a fire that matched his abilities. "But know that I'll never betray Aikradal."

"Brave words." Vivienne sat up on her throne. "We shall see how long they last."

Princess Vivienne strode toward him, draped in a gown of shimmering midnight cerulean. The fabric clung to her slender frame, accentuating her sharp features and pale eyes. Enzo's heart twisted as he recognized the dress—it had once belonged to Belyx. It was modified with intricate silver embroidery that slithered across the bodice like a nest of serpents.

"Tell me, Enzo," Vivienne began, "what were you doing in the forest before we captured you and your pathetic friends?"

Fear for his allies threatened to overwhelm him. But Enzo stuck to his defiance. This merciless woman wouldn't strip him away of his self-control. She would never discover The Original. "I'll never tell you anything," he snarled.

"Interesting..." Vivienne circled him slowly, like a predator. "What about The Original? Why are you trying to revive him?"

Enzo's stood still, but she wouldn't see the terror that spiked through him. How did she find out what he was doing? He knew what the humans would do if they discovered The Original's true power. They would use it to further their agenda. "You're delusional, *Princess.*"

"Perhaps." Her lips curled into a sinister smile. The princess snapped her fingers, and a guard emerged from the shadows, carrying a small wooden box. From within, Vivienne retrieved Belyx's snake, Bruxos.

"Ah, this creature," she cooed, stroking the serpent's back as it coiled around her wrist. "Such a fascinating thing. You must know what its venom does, don't you, Enzo?" She locked eyes with him, her gaze unwavering.

His anxiety churned like a storm inside him, but he gritted his teeth and said nothing. The venom...it could kill him, or worse. Like Aydevko.

"Fine," Vivienne sighed. "I'll give you one last chance—tell me everything, or have a decadent cocktail." A laugh almost left her throat.

"Go to hell," Enzo spat with false brevity.

"Suit yourself." With a flick of her wrist, Vivienne signaled the guard, who plunged a syringe filled with Bruxos's venom into Enzo's arm.

He tried to fight it, but the toxin spread through his veins like sludge, searing him from within. As his vision blurred and his strength drained away, he heard Vivienne's cold laughter.

"I will find out what I need," she said as darkness closed in around him. "And when I do, I'll kill every last fae until I have complete control."

Flashes of his tribe burning alive reverberated in his mind. Agonizing screams and cries of children were the only vicious sounds in his emptiness. The humans towered over them, ready to deliver a fatal strike.

Enzo felt his vision shimmer and vibrate. His tongue ran along his teeth, sensitively. He had failed once more, and everything within him was intensified. With a fierce shake, Enzo's reality vanished into darkness.

223

TWENTY-SEVEN

Prince Vincent eyed Belyx like she was a dead fish, his eyes flashed a hint of jealousy as he watched her. His admiration was palpable in the air. The guards held their stances, but Belyx refused to waver. She would kill every last one of them. The taste of freedom was too close to lose now. The open breeze was a familiar song...and Belyx would hear the rest of it.

"Congratulations, Belyx," he said, making Belyx reel back. There was no way he was being sincere. "You've proven yourself to be a formidable opponent."

"Save your flattery, Prince Worthless." Belyx's eyes narrowed, refusing to accept admiration from the enemy. "Why aren't you letting me go?" Her hands clenched, assessing the guards' weapons and how to take one.

He chuckled softly, shaking his head. "I assure you, my intentions are to kill you right now, but sadly, you won fair and square, despite my efforts to stop you."

"Like Soren?" The way he killed her friends...she should gut this prince where he stood.

The prince shook his head. "And I almost succeeded. Who knew Luo would do such a thing? Terrible pity."

"You never spoke of honor before? Why now?"

"I must honor the codes of my kingdom. You are something else...Queen." Belyx went to respond when Vincent cut in again. "Before you let that get to your pious head, I will warn you, my sister won't be as forgiving. If you dare to take Aikradal back from her, she'll kill you without hesitation."

"See her try," Belyx said.

The strong wind whipped her loose hair around her face as she turned away. At that moment, her face hardened into something else. A prisoner to a queen. "I'll gut every last one of them if it means freeing my kingdom. Stand in my way again…and you will feel my full wrath."

"Best wishes to you Belyx," Vincent said. "Also know." Belyx paused. "If you ever step foot in my kingdom, you will see *my* full wrath."

Belyx shot him a rude gesture and sprinted inland, letting each crunch of sand drive her tenacity. She was free, and she had more things to take care of.

As she hurried through the markets of Majeria, her blood rushed with a mixture of adrenaline and anxiety. The marketplace bustled with activity; vendors sold their wares, children darted between stalls, and the air was filled with the aroma of exotic spices and salt-sprayed fish. Majeria's vibrant colors and cacophony of sounds were a stark contrast to the grimness their palace invokes on the rest of Keyica.

Her destination loomed in the distance—a slave ship docked at the harbor. She recognized it based on the dingy wood and the array of people hurled around it like cattle. Belyx's fists tensed at the thought of what awaited her there. She could almost feel the weight of the chains that bound the people, and she swore to herself she would set them free.

As she approached the ship, a commotion broke out near the gangplank. Guards were panicking as they scrambled to subdue an old man…Aurelius. He had escaped after all…and Belyx was just in time. Despite his obvious age, he moved with surprising agility as he took down the guards one by one.

"Need some help?" Belyx called out, already rushing towards the fray.

"You are five minutes late," Aurelius grunted as he dodged a guard's sword. "Run into trouble?"

"Just an odd conversation with his Highness," she quipped, launching herself into the fight, kicking a guard off the handrail with a splash. "Turns out he has some honor after all. I hate this damn place."

"I couldn't agree more."

Together, they made quick work of the remaining guards. As the last one fell, Belyx looked over at Aurelius, his chest heaving from exertion. She knew he had once been a fighting instructor and weapons master, but she hadn't realized just how formidable he still was.

"Let's set these poor people free," she said.

As they boarded the ship and unlocked the slaves' chains, Belyx couldn't help but think of her conversation with Prince Vincent. His warning of his sister echoed in her mind, but fear wouldn't dictate her actions. Vivienne would not hold her kingdom hostage anymore. She was on her way...for Aikradal, she would fight—and she would win.

The moon shone low in the sky behind various clouds as Belyx and Aurelius, with the newly freed slaves, readied the ship to sail. The scent of salt and brine filled Belyx's lungs as she hoisted the mainsail with practiced ease, her chapped hands protesting the strain as she gripped the rope. As she scanned the faces of the former slaves, their eyes darted. Some had burn marks on their skin, others wore worn clothing that barely covered their bodies. How can anyone treat another human like this?

"Listen up!" Belyx shouted, drawing their attention. "You are no longer slaves! We're heading for Aikradal, my kingdom, where you'll be free."

They whispered among themselves in a language Belyx didn't recognize. A secret one they used against the slavers. A girl caught her eye and her stomach churned. She was too young and reminded her the girls they saved who joined the Order. Belyx approached the doe-eyed girl and kneeled, handing her something.

Belyx put a paper rose in her open hand, which Belyx made to comfort her after all those drab nights in the prison. The girl beamed and Belyx stood again. "Surely you have heard of the great slave freer, Gelina Ossix. She died so that I could be free. Now I repay that to her. I will continue her legacy, but I must take my kingdom back. Let's sail!"

Whispers rippled through the crowd, their eyes shining. The ship began to gain momentum as they worked together, each movement bringing them closer to freedom.

"Are you ready for the next challenge?" Aurelius asked Belyx.

Belyx hesitated. "I don't know what awaits us in Aikradal." She scanned the horizon. "The thought of facing Vivienne and the state of my kingdom...it terrifies me."

Aurelius placed a reassuring hand on her shoulder. "You have the power to take your kingdom back...remember that."

"These abilities are still new to me."

"I wasn't talking about those." He sighed. "I didn't teach you that technique because you needed it. You would have won those trials without it. You will be able to take back Aikradal without it too...although it will help." A throaty rasp left his mouth.

She nodded, trying to push away the uncertainty that threatened to overwhelm her. But another question nagged at her mind. "Aurelius, what about the witch's chosen one? Is it true?"

He frowned, the lines of his face tightening. "I don't know, Belyx. But if it is, it is another obstacle you will have to pass. The witches have not chosen a person in centuries. They don't take this lightly."

"But what if it isn't me? I can't unite two fighting tribes."

Aurelius shook his head. "You may not have a choice. But know you are never alone. You have all the help you need, including those who have perished."

Belyx turned away. "They did their part, but they are no longer able to help."

"Wrong," Aurelius added. "The God had them die for a reason. That is because They knew you were strong enough to handle losing them. And you would use it to make this world a better place. Never forget who has died, and use their knowledge."

Taking a deep breath, the weight of responsibility fell upon her shoulders. As the ship cut through the waves, Belyx knew one thing for certain: she would fight with every last ounce of strength to free her kingdom and honor all the people who died for her memories.

"Let's do this," she murmured. The briny mist spattered her face as they set sail into the approaching night, a storm of change brewing on the horizon.

The moon cast an eerie glow over Aikradal's docks as their boat glided through the dark waters. Leaning against the railing, her eyes went ablaze with anger as she surveyed the scene before her. Slave ships and smuggling vessels littered her kingdom's port, their shadowy outlines a stark reminder of Majeria's corruption.

Another deep light and scent caught her attention. In the distance were rising smoke and flames, coming from the Sehrlic forest...where the fae lived. What had Majeria done? And how did they defeat the fae? Her mind raced to where her friends were...where Enzo was...and if they were still alive.

"The forest...It's on fire! What have they done? I have to help!"

Aurelius blocked her. "Don't veer from the plan. Check the dungeons first. Free anyone there. Never run toward a burning fire...and I mean that too."

Belyx paused, exhaling. "You're right."

"Remember to be strong," Aurelius said. The scarred face of the Majerian master held a solemn expression as he steered the small vessel closer to the dock. "Like your great-grandmother was."

Belyx clenched her hands into fists, recalling her great-grandmother's courage in the face of adversity. The wind picked up as if detecting the return of the queen. "I will, Aurelius. I promise."

As they reached the dock, the old master grabbed her forearm, his grip firm, yet gentle. "I have some things to handle elsewhere. You are on your own for now." Belyx went to protest as she required all the help she could find, but he raised a hand. "This is your kingdom to save. I'll find you again when the time is right. And never deny your feelings."

"What does that me—" He tilted his chin at her. "Okay. When the time is right. Thank you, Aurelius." With one last look at her mentor, she leaped onto the dock, her feet landing soundlessly on the worn wood. She waved as the vessel began to turn. Though she was alone, she felt their presence, all the wisdom from everyone she had met. This was her mission to complete.

Belyx moved like a shadow, slipping past the bustling crowds and dimly lit taverns that lined the harbor. Her eyes constricted as she spotted the unmistakable uniforms of the Majerian guards patrolling the kingdom. They were everywhere, their arrogant strides and mocking laughter making her blood steam. She longed to kill them all, to free her people from their oppressive rule. But she had to be patient, to wait for the perfect moment to strike.

The streets of Aikradal had become dingy and lifeless under the watchful gaze of the Majerian guards. The once-vibrant hues of the buildings had faded, replaced by a dull gray that seemed to seep into every crack and crevice. Belyx's couldn't believe the sight of her beloved kingdom, so broken and devoid of joy.

She cursed as she used her knowledge of the Order's secret passageways to slip through the kingdom unnoticed. Her destination was the Order hideout in the palace gardens, a place where she could regroup her plan.

With a leap and roll, she slipped by the palace guards. Someone should be fired for the horrible patrols. Although Belyx could map this place inside and out, sneaking back and forth all those nights as a Thorn. She prayed the lair remained undiscovered, or she would need to think of another plan.

The once-vibrant gardens were now desolate and colorless, a mirror of the kingdom's decay. But instead of despair, her will grew stronger at the sight, aiming to reclaim what was rightfully hers.

She found the entrance and checked around before clicking the statue switch. The small door hidden in the overgrown shrubs groaned open. The bunker was empty from any intruders. Belyx kept her guard up as she closed the door behind her.

Within the quiet confines of the bunker, Belyx allowed herself a moment to grieve for the losses her people had suffered. She shut her eyes, feeling the weight of their suffering pressing down on her like a heavy wave. But as she mourned, her spirit hardened, transforming her grief into a burning desire for justice.

Enough. Her thoughts held firm. *It's time to take back what is ours.*

Belyx knelt on the cold stone floor, her mind whirring with plans and strategies as she began to plot the downfall of the Majerians and the liberation of her people. She would need allies, but no one was here, so she had another idea.

Be strong, Aurelius's words repeated in her head like a mantra. *Like your great-grandmother was.*

Like my mother and grandmother too.

And with that, Belyx set her plan in motion.

In the dimly lit corner of the hideout, Belyx held her breath as she opened the door to her snake room, praying they were all still alive. *They have to be for my plan to work.*

The plan was foolish, but it had to be done. The four snakes slithered to her from their cages, expressions of pain and hunger written into them. When had they last eaten? Belyx had nothing for them, but they would have food soon.

Belyx approached each snake...giving a final goodbye to them. Tears cascaded down her face. It was the only way to enter undetected. She wouldn't let them rot if anything happened to her in there.

Kali, her sinuous pink cobra, flicked her forked tongue at Belyx as if sensing her unease. Jay, her blue viper, moved its head about as if knowing something was coming. Belyx stroked her water krait, Mira, and the snake fell into the glass as if craving attention after all these weeks. Last was Gwyar, her old black mamba, moving like paste, but slithering to the end of the cage as if to say she was ready to fight.

It was a miracle from The God they survived all this time. They held on too...like Belyx did. And now it was time to say goodbye.

Belyx donned her assassin leathers, filled with spare venoms, poisons, blades, and antidotes. It had been too long since she had been Doneque.

No. She was always Belyx...Queen Belyx, now ready to save her kingdom.

"Alright, everyone," Belyx said. "It's feeding time." She pulled the latches on their cages and went to open the door. They slithered out in a fury and Belyx prayed they wouldn't attack her on the way.

"Please forgive me for what I am about to do," she told them, her throat tight. In truth, she had no other choice. The fate of her kingdom depended on it. "Take care of one another." Her tears streamed down her cheeks. "You're my family, and I love you all."

With a shaky breath, Belyx opened the bunker hatch door. "Go now!" she urged, unwilling to show sadness in the next step.

As if understanding her command, the snakes slithered away toward the palace grounds, their vibrant colors disappearing into the shadows. Belyx crouched behind a statue, watching as her pets emerged into the moonlit court-yard and began to weave their deadly dance among the unsuspecting guards.

"Snakes!" one guard shouted in alarm, his scream carrying across the palace as he scrambled to avoid Kali's venomous bite. Panic erupted as more guards caught sight of Belyx's serpentine companions, fleeing in terror or drawing their weapons in defense.

Belyx seized the opportunity, slipping into the palace through a concealed passageway. She reached the door and paused for a moment, catching a glimpse of Gywar, striking down several guards before being cornered and killed by their relentless onslaught. Her black body stilled as her other snakes fled. Gwyar had stayed to make sure Belyx made it. Her old girl...who she had known for years...her venom getting her out of so much trouble. Gwyar had saved her life more times than she could count and now that was over. A sharp pain pierced her chest, but she swallowed her grief, refusing to let it control her. "Good girl," she whispered.

Determined not to let Gywar's sacrifice be in vain, Belyx rushed through the hidden corridor, heading straight for the dungeons.

Belyx's muscles hammered in her garb as she pressed herself against the cold stone wall, gripping the hilt of her knife. The Majerian guards' footsteps echoed along the path, growing louder with each passing moment. As they rounded the corner, she sprang into action.

With swift, precise movements, she dispatched two of the guards, their bodies crumpling to the floor. The remaining guard lunged at her, but Belyx ducked beneath his blade and buried her knife in his throat. He gasped, eyes wide, before collapsing beside his comrades.

Belyx took his key and entered the palace dungeons, praying she wasn't too late.

"About time you showed up," Cook grumbled, stepping out from a shadowy cell. Freyja and Onka emerged behind her, their faces sheet white. That was the answer to that.

Her relief came as a grace. "Are you all okay?" She scanned for any sign of injuries. "I need to tell you what I've discovered about—"

"Enzo is dying," Freyja interrupted.

Belyx's blood ran cold.

She opened the lock and pushed past them, dashing down the dimly lit corridor. Her thoughts swirled like a whirlwind, leaving no room for the information she had been so eager to share.

Beyond the door was Enzo lying on the stone floor of a tiny cell, shivering with force, his face ashen and slick with sweat. His green eyes were unfocused. Of course, she would return to finally save her love and he would be at death's door.

"Vivienne tortured him," Freyja said, as unshed tears welled in her eyes. "She gave him venom from Bruxos." The creature hurting venom!

"Can Amenthya do anything?" Belyx looked around, realizing Amenthya wasn't there. "Where is she?"

Freyja shook her head. "She disappeared deep into the forest after the attack and no one has seen her since."

Leave it to the one person Belyx needed to talk to about this chosen-one prophecy to be long gone. *One thing at a time, Belyx. Save your kingdom and then worry about the witch prophecy.*

Belyx's stilled, recalling how the same venom had weakened Aydevko last year. She knew the danger of keeping Bruxos around her partner, so she had come prepared. Reaching into a hidden pocket in her leathers, she pulled out a vial of antidote. The liquid inside glowed a faint, reassuring blue.

"Will it work?" Onka asked, watching Belyx closely.

"I never had to use it." Her fingers were unsteady as she popped the lid. "But I pray it works."

Kneeling beside Enzo, she gently tilted his head upward and poured the antidote into his mouth. She silently prayed to The God...or any god she could think of, that it wasn't too late.

Her mind raced to last year in the Whisper lair when he drank poison and she had to guess which antidote was the correct one. She had barely trusted him then, but the connection they shared was more potent than any toxin. After all this time and hardships, she never thought she could call him hers and now she needed him to live.

"Come on, Enzo," she murmured as his shivering began to subside. "Fight it. You're stronger than this venom."

His eyes released a feeble flicker of life. Every nerve in her body shivered, yet Vivienne's wickedness looming over her caused an icy dread to settle into her bones. Would the antidote be enough? She prayed for him to survive, but feared that it would all be in vain.

"Enzo, stay with me," she urged, knowing they were running out of time. "We have so much left to do together."

Belyx gripped his hand as she held back the panic welling within her chest. His breathing was shallow, and the color was draining from his face with every second that passed.

"Please," she begged, tears threatening to spill. "Don't leave me."

The tension in the cell thickened with each labored breath he took, the silence punctuated only by everyone's quiet prayers in the background. It felt like an eternity before the antidote began to take effect, and still, there was no guarantee it would save him.

Unable to bear the thought of losing him without a proper goodbye, Belyx leaned down and pressed her lips against his, willing every ounce of strength she had into him. She tasted the lingering traces of the dryness on his tongue, and for a moment, she feared it was too late.

Belyx pulled away in tears, thinking all was lost...until—

"Is this really the best time for a kiss?" Enzo rasped as his eyes strained to open. Of course, he would make a snarky remark, now of all times, but relief dived through her. He was alive.

"Enzo!" She threw her arms around him, sensing his fire warmth return to his body as he embraced her back. "You're okay!"

"Thanks to you, my Queen," he croaked, a weak smile forming at the corners of his mouth.

"Vivienne..." Freyja began, "she took over and burned down the forest as well."

"I saw."

"What happened to you in Majeria?" Onka asked.

"It appears Vivienne isn't the only one we need to worry about." Belyx sighed, remembering everything she had found out about that wretched place. "She has a twin brother, Vincent. They've been ruling Majeria since they overthrew their parents."

"Twins? What are the odds?" Enzo mused, trying to sit up with a wince.

"Looks like evil runs in their blood," Cook said. "And comes in twos."

"During my time in Majeria, I learned of their Trials of Rain," Belyx continued. "It's these brutal tests they put their prisoners through, but it was how I managed to escape. Only one could win...it was me."

"Trials of Rain?" Freyja's brow arched. "Sounds terrible."

"Trust me, it was," Belyx shuddered at the memory. "But it allowed me to return here, and now we need to come up with a plan to stop Vivienne once and for all."

"First things first," Enzo interjected, grimacing as he forced himself to sit up all the way. "We need to get back to my family. I have no idea what has happened to them."

"Agreed." A new pulse blazed within her. "Together, we'll end her reign of terror and free the people and fae from this violence."

Belyx was about to elaborate on her harrowing experience in the Trials when a faint sound caught her attention. Her throat clenched, and she swiftly pressed herself against the cold stone wall, peering out the cell door.

Shadows flickered along the corridor as guards approached, their armor clinking ominously.

"Guards," she whispered urgently, her eyes open. "We need to break out—now."

Enzo's face sharpened, his body full of new spunk despite his weakened state. "I have a plan, but we have to separate. Belyx, you need to confront Vivienne. Show her who the real queen is. The rest of us will head to the forest and rally the fae tribe."

Belyx hesitated for a moment, the thought of leaving Enzo behind…again wasn't an option. But she could understand the wisdom in his words; they had to divide and conquer if they were going to stand a chance against Vivienne's forces.

"Alright," she said. "But promise me we'll see each other soon."

"Promise," Enzo replied, his stare never faltering from hers. He reached and cupped her face in his hands, pulling her in for one last searing kiss that spoke of love, desperation, and hope all at once.

"Take care of yourself, thief rat," Belyx chided as they broke apart, her breath mingling with his. "After I handle the 'queen,' I will find you."

Her eyes flashed, and Enzo still cracked a smile despite the dire situation. "I wouldn't want to be in her shoes," he murmured, the ghost of a smirk playing at the corners of his lips. "Ugly shoes I might add."

"Nor would I," Cook chimed in, restless to go. "Now, let's get moving. We don't have much time."

Enzo nodded and turned to Belyx one last time. "See you soon, my Queen."

"See you soon," she echoed, swelling with love for the man who had captured it.

With a final nod, they split up—Belyx making her way through the dimly lit corridors towards the throne room, while Enzo, Cook, Freyja, and Onka slipped out of the cell and into the shadows, their destination the center of the forest where the fae tribe awaited their return.

As Belyx stalked through the palace, she thought of Enzo—her advisor, her partner—and their promise to reunite. No matter what happened, they'd find each other. They always did.

TWENTY-EIGHT

The first guard fell with a gasp, blood staining his uniform as he crumpled to the floor. The second had little time to raise his sword before Belyx's blade found its mark, slicing cleanly through his throat. Her rage only grew stronger as life faded from their eyes, feeding her lust for vengeance.

With one final push, Belyx threw open the doors and stepped into the throne room...her throne room, now decorated in the drabbest of ways. Belyx was no designer, but all the sea decor was a bit much.

Vivienne lounged on the stolen throne, her cold blue eyes staring down at Belyx with a smug smile curving her lips.

"Ah, the once queen returns," Vivienne drawled, not an ounce of surprise on her mouth. "Of course, you passed the stupid trials and wormed your way through my palace. I must admit, I'm almost impressed."

Her palace. What a joke! And also...was that *her* dress she was wearing? It was last year's collection, only she edited it with different hues and gaudy rhinestones.

Sewek towered over Vivienne, her manicured nails clacking together as she scowled at Belyx, like someone lit off a stink cloud. Vivienne turned toward the former Whisper. "Warn the guards about a jailbreak. I don't need the prisoners interfering with my plans."

Sewek locked cold eyes with Belyx and clacked out the side doors. Belyx vowed she wouldn't escape again.

"Leave us," Vivienne commanded her guards. *Over-confident bitch.*

The guards hesitated but left the throne room in a quiet shuffle.

Belyx twirled her knife. Vivienne was making it too easy now. "You might need those."

Vivienne chuckled while staying seated, checking her nails. "Yeah. I don't think so. You don't scare me. Just because you passed those dumb games doesn't mean you are anything special. You are still just the sad, pathetic little princess who always tried so hard to please others." Her cold stare locked with Belyx's and she wanted to plunge her knife in her throat. "Trying is never part of someone who rules. You either have it or you don't. You. Do. Not."

"At least I don't have to rule with fear and lock down a whole country! I saw your kingdom and the prison. What you consider 'crimes' is outlandish."

An evil twist formed on Vivienne's lips. "People need to be shown that treason is never an option. Look at how I have transformed your former pitiful kingdom in a matter of weeks. No one complains now!"

"The point of ruling is to understand the people and listen to their concerns." Her skin itched with irritation. This fool had sat on her throne for too long.

Vivienne laughed again. "And that was why you had a gang problem and were overthrown. You still worry about what the people think." A choking laughter escaped her throat. "I'm glad I declined to help you last year."

"And killed your cousin to do it?" Belyx raised an eyebrow.

"False accusations only land you in trouble...except you are correct this time."

"But...why? Why kill your own family?"

"He was a worm who hated how my brother and I ran things. He had to be taken care of and what better way than to make sure your weak gangs did it?"

Heat rose to her fingers. Vivienne's cousin had warned Belyx at the ball, but she was too consumed with getting Majeria's aid to listen. "My father was ready to sign over the kingdom. You had what you wanted. He didn't need to die!"

Vivienne shook her head, her triple braids flowing with her. "Your father was weak. I was going to kill the gangs after our rule...until you had to open that pathetic mouth. You had no right interfering...But it all worked out." Her head twisted as she looked down upon Belyx. She was seconds away from being ripped from Belyx's throne. "What a lowly princess...Maybe I can find a place for you amongst the servants after I defeat you and your precious group."

"Maybe I can find a place for you in hell. Get the fuck off my throne...or see how lowly I can be!"

"I have grown to love this throne too much and have spent too much time stealing it!"

"Is that your end game? Take over all the kingdoms?"

Vivienne nodded. "And with the help from that Whisper, I have access to all of their secrets. After I caught her and her crones in my kingdom, I offered her a deal she couldn't refuse...as long as I promised her a throne. Power is the best motivation."

"Power is the greatest illusion. It made you and your sick brother kill your parents...and my mother."

At the mention of her mother, Vivienne's lips curled into a tight smile, and her gaze softened. An intense wave of energy coursed through Belyx's body, and she knew at that moment she was determined to avenge her mother. "So, you figured it out. Yes, Belyx. It was the perfect plan. Kill the righteous bitch and incriminate the fae so your oaf of a father would do something crazy. And it worked! Your kingdom imploded from the inside!"

"But it didn't," Belyx replied, collecting her anger like shards of glass. "Aikradal stayed strong and we ended the gangs. You failed."

Vivienne gritted her teeth in a vicious sneer. "It was merely a part of a new grand plan. You are just a hindrance and hindrances must be executed. They should have killed you outright in that prison, but my brother insisted he wanted to watch you suffer...what a little sociopath. But no matter, I will do whatever it takes to keep my power—even if it means killing you."

"Then you'll find I'm not the same weak princess you once mocked." Belyx's grip tightened on her knives. "I've grown stronger, and I will take back what is rightfully mine."

"Is that so?" Vivienne smirked, unimpressed by her bravado. With a snap of her fingers, Belyx's heart stopped. "Let's see how you fare against an old friend. Remember him?"

A hulking figure emerged from the darkness, clad in black armor that covered him from head to toe. He carried the same massive spear, the tip glistening with dried blood. His presence was imposing and silent, like a predator stalking its prey—a feeling he gave off like an odor...The Scorpion

Stay strong Belyx. He may be a fierce warrior, but so are you. Don't forget Aurelius's training.

Belyx met The Scorpion's dark leer. Her mind raced, searching for weaknesses in his armor, and strategizing her next move. She circled him, her knives poised and ready. Even though she had a rough time defeating him the last time they fought, she was stronger now...braver.

Attacking with ferocity, Belyx's knives sliced through the air as she aimed for the gaps in his armor. But The Scorpion wouldn't go down, shrugging off each strike as if it were nothing more than an annoyance.

In the heat of the fight, Belyx's thoughts turned inward, reflecting on the losses she'd suffered and the obstacles she'd overcome. Her grief had been a heavy burden, but it had also made her better. She would not be defeated. Not by this monster or the cruel woman who commanded him.

Belyx kept her distance from the beast while he swung his spear, barely missing her. She struck his helm with her blade, but it reverberated right off.

The Scorpion lunged for her and she backed away from each of his strikes. Despite facing him in the past, his presence sent a crippling wave of fear down her back, like all her training would be useless against him. The monster thrust his spear, but Belyx sidestepped it and ran behind one of the pillars.

Vibrating thuds in the ground indicated he was still close.

Holding her breath, Belyx clung to the pillar as The Scorpion tried to run around it, but Belyx kept her distance, taking in deep breaths. Any mistake would lead to her death.

The air of the throne room stilled. The stomping ceased, his heavy breathing emanating. Belyx could imagine Vivienne's cold smile as if she had won. She underestimated one thing.

Belyx coated her blades in the venom, praying they would work like the last time. After waiting for a beat, The Scorpion charged through the pillar, debris and porcelain flying. But Belyx was ready. She climbed up the side and leaped at the beast. He was unprepared as Belyx slammed into his head, shoving her blade at his eye.

He was on to her tricks, for he turned his head and the steel ricocheted off. Belyx cursed as she plummeted into the ground and the beast sent a thrusting kick right into her chest, sending her vaulting across the throne room, her venom knives free from her grip. The clang of her weapons was a sad song as she struggled to get up.

Vivienne laughed as The Scorpion approached her, his signature slow walk. "Kill the princess!"

Belyx clawed the marble floor until her nails bled. She was no princess! She was a queen!

With a fierce cry, Belyx jumped up and charged her attacker. He had taken too many lives and his streak would come to an end. She had one more trick up her sleeve and it had to work.

The Scorpion swung his weapon in an arc and Belyx averted the strike. Although she was unarmed in body, her mind was equipped for attack.

She let the beast come close and he thrust his spear at her. Belyx feigned a stumble, allowing herself to fall to the ground.

Letting the stone floor ground her, she remembered Aurelius's training. She could feel The Scorpion's sharp weapon almost touching her head as he drew nearer, his breathing coming in deep gasps as a chill fear coursed through her veins. But still, she refused to let this monster rend her spirit—no more would he be able to keep her awake at night with the memory of his armored face slaughtering all she held dear. This time, it would end with her own hands.

The spear came down, and Belyx shifted back, letting the blade crack the marble.

Belyx lunged, grabbing at the spear. Once she had it in her grasp, The Scorpion tried to pull away, but it was too late. Belyx drew upon the power of the new weapon, feeling time slow around her as she moved with incredible speed.

"Enough!" Belyx shouted, leaping to her feet and snatching The Scorpion's blade from him. "This is for Aikradal!"

She thrust the steel into The Scorpion's gut with a sickening gush, sending waves of sound throughout the room. With one hard shove, she hurled him backward.

An enraged bellow ripped from his throat as he staggered up and charged Belyx once more. In one swift breath, Belyx slowed time again, trapping the beast in his grasp without warning. When time resumed, the massive creature collided with the ground in a thunderous roar. Belyx jumped on top of him and held up the spear high above her head. "Go to hell and leave my kingdom!"

She impaled him over and over again, her fury driving the spear deeper each time. The Scorpion's thick red blood seeped into the cracks between the stone tiles, a dark stain spreading across the floor.

Standing, Belyx turned to Vivienne. "Your monster has fallen." Belyx panted, throwing the spear to the ground. "Now, Vivienne, it's your turn."

Vivienne stepped gracefully down from her throne, her blue eyes hard and calculating. Tearing off the bottom of her dress to reveal leathers beneath, she was prepared for a fight the whole time. "You know," she said, a song-like quality reflecting in her voice. "I should have killed you along with your mother all those years ago."

Belyx tried to keep her rage in check. Vivienne was attempting to provoke her, but Belyx couldn't let the taunt go unanswered. "You'll regret not finishing the job."

"I don't know how you defeated my invincible general...but you just tired yourself out." Vivienne unsheathed a gleaming sword, its wicked edge catching the flickering torch light. "Let's see how well you fare now."

Belyx was unarmed and tried to focus on her newfound power, but it remained stubbornly out of reach. She had used too much of it to slay The Scorpion. It seemed she would have to rely on her other skills for this fight.

Which was good enough.

As Vivienne lunged forward with the sword, Belyx dodged, using her agility to her advantage. Vivienne's weapon rang in a symphony of steel, each strike more forceful than the last.

As Belyx was being narrowly cut in half, her thoughts rolled. She had to find a way to defeat Vivienne without relying on her new ability. She couldn't let her people down, not when they were counting on her to restore Aikradal to its former glory.

Vivienne lunged her sword and Belyx used her palms to parry the attack and elbowed the princess in the face, the satisfying sound of bone meeting flesh ringing in her ears.

After kicking the sword from her grip, Belyx went to strike when Vivienne sent a knee into Belyx, knocking the air out of her. Belyx twisted back and threw a punch, but Vivienne blocked it and thrust a counter strike into Belyx's face. With distorted vision, Belyx kept her hands up. Her grandmother always taught her to never drop her arms in a fight.

Vivienne closed the gap with a flurry of strikes, and Belyx managed to block a few of them before Vivienne sent a kick that knocked Belyx to the floor.

Spitting blood on the marble, Belyx looked at her attacker. Vivienne laughed. "Wow. It must have been lucky how you defeated my champion, but you are pathetic against me. Where did you learn to fight? Ladies tea classes?" She threw a fist Belyx's way, but Belyx jumped under her hands and directed a back knuckle into Vivienne's jaw. The princess screamed and grasped Belyx's hair. The pain rippled down to her roots, but Belyx held the hand down as Vivienne launched more attacks, Belyx blocked with her elbow and hooked her other hand around Vivienne's neck. Belyx spun toward the ground and sent a full-force knee right to Vivienne's groin.

Vivienne groaned as she pulled away, a heavy breath coming from her. Belyx's body ached. She wouldn't last much longer here.

The women stared each other down. Belyx reflected on all those years Vivienne bullied her and always put her down, saying she wasn't good enough and would never rule. All those voices of doubt circled her mind, but she refused to listen. She was in control.

Vivienne screamed as she attacked again. Belyx kept up a fortified defense and the fight raged on, taking them through the opulent halls and up the grand staircase.

Belyx sent Vivienne back with a kick and a few Majerian guards showed up, ready to kill Belyx.

"No!" Vivienne yelled with bloody teeth. "She is mine!"

The duel grew more violent as Vivienne slammed strike after strike into Belyx. She did the same, but her body couldn't take much more. Vivienne was a trained machine...preparing for this moment for a while. And Belyx had used too much energy to get here.

Vivienne put Belyx in a quick choke hold from behind, but Belyx bent down and bit Vivienne's hand. The princess screamed as she shoved Belyx into a wall, sending a kick right through it as Belyx dodged. Vivienne pivoted and sent a back hand into Belyx's eye, blurring her vision. Vivienne spat blood as she tackled Belyx through a door into a nearby room...her old room, now Freyja's.

They knocked a few candles over, the wax dripping on the carpet. Vivienne pressed Belyx's face into the wood floor near the spill. Belyx reached out with her all her might and flung a broken candle into Vivienne's perfect face.

She shrieked as Belyx jabbed at the soft spot between her thighs. Vivienne cursed and leapt at Belyx connecting her elbow with her jaw. Belyx flew into a mirror, shattering it into a million shards. That would hurt later.

Vivienne vaulted across the glass-strewn carpet, her eyes wild with rage as she grasped Belyx's hair. Belyx yelped in pain, but her adrenaline gave her strength as she wrenched herself away and felt a wave of dizzying satisfaction when her knee connected with Vivienne's stomach. Grabbing the back of Vivienne's head, Belyx launched Vivienne into the old armoire, splintering it and filling the air with its broken pieces.

A grunt left Vivienne's throat, but she stood herself up with sporadic movements. Belyx exhaled, admiring Vivienne's tenacity, but no one harmed the ones she loved. Vivienne had killed her mother, orchestrated a plot that most likely killed her father and grandmother...and also almost killed Enzo, the love of her life. She couldn't fathom how life would move on without him. Her fire fae, her muse, her everything. People like Vivienne needed to be put down.

Flower vases shattered and portraits hanging on the wall broke as Belyx stayed on Vivienne's attacks. With a solid kick, Belyx sent Vivienne out the balcony door. Vivienne caught herself before falling off to the side, charging for Belyx again.

Belyx tried to twist away, but Vivienne locked Belyx's arm in a hold and rotated her body so it hung over the ledge. The chilled air mixed with Belyx's breaths. Is this how she would die? Over her own balcony?

No.

Belyx spun around, her arm extended and a sharp clicking sound emanated from deep within her shoulder joint, but she ignored it as her elbow connected with Vivienne's chest, sending her back.

"Look at you." Vivienne said with heavy pants as she backed away, crimson caked across her cruel smile. "You're pathetic, just like the rest of your family. How does it feel to have lost everything? Your pathetic mother was weak! Just like you!" Blood soared with her words.

Belyx's heart clenched at the mention of her mother, but Vivienne would not see her pain. Her mother was not weak. She was strong. All those years of

Majeria threatening innocents and despite the warnings she was in danger, her mother never gave up.

Not too long ago, those words would have been enough to defeat Belyx, but she embraced her grief now. Grief was not the enemy, but the uncontrollable emotions that followed. Vivienne ruled with the expectation that all people would bow to her. Bowing was not an option. Vivienne would have to cut off her legs and even then, Belyx would fight with all she had.

That was a promise.

"You underestimate me," Belyx said through gritted teeth. "I've let go of my demons. Your twisted taunts mean nothing."

With a roar, Belyx launched herself at Vivienne, her fists flying through the air as she fought with renewed force. Vivienne parried her attacks, but it was clear the tide of the battle had turned.

"Your reign of terror ends tonight!" Belyx landed a solid kick to Vivienne's chest. The force sent her stumbling back, teetering dangerously close to the edge of the balcony. Vivienne growled, but she was wavering. This was the end.

Belyx stood tall, craning her neck. "This is for my mother!"

In one final move, Belyx kicked Vivienne off the balcony, and the satisfying pressure sparked through her whole body.

Vivienne's shrill scream echoed in Belyx's ears as she plummeted to the ground below. There was a thunderous thud and then silence.

And with that, Belyx knew justice had been served for her family at last.

"I did it, Mom."

A commotion took Belyx out of her victory.

There were still enemies within the palace walls, and Belyx couldn't rest until they were dealt with...Including Sewek. She rushed up the stairs, knowing full well where the Whisper leader was hiding.

Her own bedchamber.

Twenty-Nine

Enzo's lungs thundered in his chest as he sprinted alongside Freyja, Onka, and Cook. They weaved through the chaos of clashing fae, the freed Aikradal soldiers, and Majerian guards, their blades gleaming in the dim light. The air was thick with the scent of blood and sweat, the cacophony of screams and steel echoing around them.

One of Enzo's friends was cut down, the nature fae's viscous staining the ashen ground. Enzo twirled a flame in his hand and burned the attacker alive, running behind and taking out another one.

An arrow came for his head, but another one knocked it out of midair. Freyja readied another arrow and fired it through a guard's throat. The Majerian soldiers were quick to overwhelm them and he prayed Belyx was strong enough to reclaim the throne. The doubt in his mind told him he still had to do this ceremony.

The might of The Original would stop this.

Onka flipped forward, subduing a guard with her baton and whipping a sword out of another.

Cook grasped the chin of the disarmed guard and throttled him into the desecrated street.

Majerian soldiers scrambled through the passageways of the kingdom. The frightened screams of citizens filled the air as they fled from the Majerian forces, who showed no mercy. Everywhere he looked, he could see the Majerians slashing at any unlucky soul who was too slow to escape. He knew if he didn't act fast, everyone would be gone soon and Majeria would have won. A white-hot rage surged through his veins at the thought of these invaders burning down everything he had ever known and loved.

He dashed ahead into an eruption. A few Majerian soldiers brandished arm-sized contraptions that resembled miniature cannons. One launched a powerful blow that detonated the rock near Enzo.

Cook and Freyja were already on it as they took out the cannon wielders. Enzo couldn't waste any more time. Going slow wasn't an option.

"Keep going!" Enzo shouted, his voice raw from the fight. "I'll handle my part of the plan—you go save the fae!"

"Be careful, Enzo," Freyja warned. She charged forward with Onka and Cook, arrows flying from her bow with deadly accuracy.

Enzo pressed on alone, his breaths coming in ragged gasps as he neared the altar of The Original deep into the forest. The room was bathed in an eerie, flickering light from the surrounding torches. In the center stood a stone altar, adorned with ancient carvings that seemed to pulse with power.

He approached with caution, his fingers tightening around the journal, quill, and key. His mind raced, replaying the instructions he'd discovered in the ancient texts. This had to work; there was no other option. The sounds of innocents dying rung in his ears. Even if Belyx did succeed, they were still outnumbered.

He placed the journal on it, its worn leather cover creaking under his touch. Next, he positioned the quill, the ink inside shimmering like liquid obsidian. Lastly, he inserted the key into a hidden slot within the altar, feeling it click into place.

Enzo took a deep breath, steadying himself for the incantation. He raised his hands above the objects, his flame tattoos glowing in response. Closing his eyes, he focused on the words, letting them flow through him like a river of fire.

"By the power of the elements, I call upon thee," Enzo intoned, speaking the ancient language. "Return to us, The Original, and bring forth your ancient might."

The air crackled as the objects began to levitate over the altar. The journal's pages flipped open. The quill danced across the parchment in a blur of ink and magic. The key pulsed with a brilliant light, illuminating the entire room.

Enzo's pulse raced as he felt a surge of force within him, fueling the ceremony. He could sense the connection between himself and The Original, their energies intertwining like strands of a cosmic tapestry.

"Rise, The Original!" Enzo cried out. "Come forth and save our kind!"

With a final flash, the objects fell back onto the altar, each glowing a radiant gold hue.

The blinding ray burst from them and swirled in an elegant dance.

After the light faded, a tall figure emerged, his emerald-crimson eyes pulsing with an otherworldly brilliance.

"Enzo Prekaro," the figure said with a harmonious and light tone. "You have done well."

As Enzo stared up at The Original, his mind was a whirlwind—relief, fear, and hope all battling for dominance. Only time would tell if his gamble had paid off, or if he'd unleashed a force far beyond his control.

"Enzo Prekaro," The Original repeated, a smile gracing his lips as he extended a pale hand to him. "I am The Original, the purest of our kind. I owe you. You have my eternal gratitude for returning me to this world."

"Please, we need your help." Enzo clasped The Original's hand in desperation. "Our people are being attacked by Majerian invaders. Can you save them?"

"Of course, my brethren," The Original said without a hint of concern. He glanced outside of the chamber. "Let us waste no time."

The fae zoomed out of the altar toward the sounds of chaos. Enzo had to run to keep up, praying this would work.

With a flick of his hand, The Original summoned the elements at his command. Flames roared to life, swirling around him like a fiery cyclone. Water surged from the ground, forming a tidal wave that crashed through the ranks of the Majerian soldiers. The earth trembled beneath their feet, walls of stone rising to crush the enemy, while whirlwinds tore through the air, ripping apart the invaders with relentless force.

Enzo caught up and watched in awe, his body slowing as he witnessed The Original's elemental powers at work. It was a display of sheer, unstoppable might, and it sent a shiver down his spine to think that he had been the one to unleash it upon the world.

The Original moved onto the kingdom ports, with Majerian forces attempting to defend the boats. The Original lifted his immaculately tattooed arms and the sea exploded in a fury, wrapping the boats and soldiers in the water like a hug and pulling everything deep under it.

Soldiers rushed for The Original, but with a flick, a tornado of flames and sharp leaves engulfed them, they didn't even have time to scream.

The Original flew to the other part of the kingdom, and by the time Enzo reached him, the Majerian guards were half eliminated as they tried to launch their mini cannons at the fae, but with a twist, the balls ricocheted and imploded on themselves, guard bodies flying everywhere.

Any remaining soldiers who tried attacking were dealt with and soon there were none left, but the fae, and the Aikradal citizens.

The battle was over in mere moments, the Majerian forces decimated under the onslaught of The Original's fury. Enzo's chest swelled with pride and relief as he saw his tribe and Aikradal allies emerge victorious from the carnage.

They were alive, saved by the ancient might of The Original.

I did it. My plan worked. I rescued Aikradal. All that suffering was worth it.

The palace was the next location and then he would un-summon The Original. The text said all it took was to return the three objects at the altar. It was difficult to translate, but he believed The Original would be grateful to be back. It would all work out.

Enzo approached The Original and bowed. "Thank you again. My people are eternally grateful. Now we need to clear Majeria out of the palace."

"It is my pleasure," The Original replied, placing a comforting hand on Enzo's shoulder. "It is my duty to protect our kind, and I shall continue to do so until the end of time."

But their victory was short-lived. As the Aikradal guards and members of the Order stepped over, their expressions were a mix of gratitude and fear, The Original's expression darkened.

"More humans." His eyes narrowed in contempt. Before Enzo could react, The Original unleashed his elemental fury once more.

Fire rained down upon the approaching figures, while water swept them away in merciless torrents.

"What are you doing? They are on our side!" Enzo screamed, dread snaking down his chest.

"They are no different from the invaders. They must be eliminated," The Original continued his assault, burning and drowning the people of Aikradal, who were now screaming in terror.

"Stop!" Enzo roared as The Original resumed his attack. Regret strained his being as he realized he had rescued the fae from Majerians, but damned innocent humans. He couldn't accept it. This was not what he had wished for. His distrust of humans had clouded his judgment, and now an unstoppable power had been set free—one that would obliterate all in its way.

Thirty

S ewek had whispered her last secret. Belyx's hands tightened around the hilt of her knife as she dipped it in one of her venoms, reminded of her snake's downfall. The balance would be restored to her kingdom...and it started here.

Majerian guards were on her the moment she stepped out of the chamber. The fight with Vivienne left her fatigued, her shoulder refusing to move properly. A guard shoved her into a wall which hurt more than it should have. She tried to get up, but her bones throbbed and the guard grabbed Belyx by the throat. She went to stab him, but the other guard knocked it from her hands. Belyx held onto the guard's meaty grip as he slammed her against the wall again. Her whole body fell and she shook her head. *Stay in it, Belyx.* But her muscles cried for a reprieve, unable to continue.

"This is for the queen," the guard declared, pointing his weapon at Belyx. She fixed him with a stern gaze as he brought his sword down upon her—but before it could make contact, a needle flew and pierced his throat. Blood spilled from the wound as the guard gurgled in agony.

The other guards toppled over, and Belyx heaved a sigh as five women clad in leathers with rose pins adorning their shoulders approached. One helped her up. "Thank you," she stammered.

The Stem nodded. "We have cleared most of the palace, but it looks like Sewek is escaping."

A new surge of energy flowed through Belyx. "Where is she?"

The Stem pointed up. "Toward your chambers. What would you like us to do?"

"Secure the guards!" Belyx commanded as she charged forward, bloodlust clouding her thoughts. *I am going hunting.*

Belyx was certain she was walking into a trap. Sewek had no chance of fleeing up the stairs with no means of escape unless she had something planned.

As soon as she stepped into the room, a bullet whizzed past her head, confirming her suspicions.

Without even looking, she flung her blade and knocked the pistol right from Sewek's taloned grasp. Surely she had a better plan than that?

The tall Whisper leader flinched as Belyx closed in, hand pressed to her other knife. "Give it up, Sewek."

Sewek backed against the wall and held her hands up. "Okay. You got me."

Belyx slammed Sewek onto the hardwood floors, the impact reverberating through the room. She put a knife with venom-tipped edges to her face, furious that she had allowed this troll to escape last year. Belyx's heart rate spiked, desperate not to let Sewek evade her grasp again. The memories of Sewek's wicked ways flooded her mind—her use of the Whispers to infiltrate the palace, the attempt on Enzo's life, and bringing that dreadful Scorpion back into their land. Sewek would pay for her misdeeds with her head.

Sewek kept a smile on her large-nosed face. Was she happy to die? Belyx kept her down. "Is this a part of your plan? Dying with a smile?"

Sewek chuckled despite the blade near her carotid. "Why do you think *you've* won? You should really learn to open your eyes."

A bone-chilling wail echoed down the hallway, causing Belyx to freeze. Belyx knew who it was, knowing this was far from over.

"Unhand me you two timin' brute! It took me forever to get this hair right!" an accented voice bellowed as two women, cloaked in black, stormed in with Lim and Maria, knives held to their throats. The assailants looked like the Petrovkan assassins Belyx had dealt with earlier.

Tears caked their faces. "Queen," Lim said before one of the assassins jabbed the hilt of the blade into her side. Why were they not in the dungeons like the others?

Sewek yanked away from Belyx, brushing the wrinkles off her silken attire. She shot her an icy glare. "Do you like my new companions? You can learn so much while roaming around the continent, can't you?"

Belyx tried not to roll her eyes. "You have quite the influence, don't you?"

Sewek laughed and walked behind the assassins. "I am not so easily taken down. Your floozy advisors were quite helpful in their knowledge of how to run this kingdom. As long as I promised them comfortable amenities."

Belyx caught a shrug from Lim. No surprise they would bend so easily to promises of comfort. "Why does it matter? Vivienne was queen. Not you."

A smile etched on Sewek's face. "Thanks for handling her."

Belyx's jaw slackened. "You were planning to overthrow her?" She wished she'd known that before her exhausting duel with Princess Perfect.

Sewek laughed while stroking Maria's hair, the woman flinching from her touch. "Of course. The Scorpion would put her overly accented head on a spike and then I would rule. It was a foolproof plan...well until the fool returned. I must say, I continue underestimating you."

"I'm used to it."

"Well, in the meantime. Have fun with my friends. I've decided this palace isn't for me, but I will see you around." She turned to the assassins. "Kill them. And then the children. Be quick about it."

After Sewek left, the assassins readied their knives to kill Belyx's advisors, but Lim flung her head back and nailed the woman in the nose while Maria tossed a white powder in the other one's face.

Belyx acted with haste; launching herself at the assailants and sending them both tumbling to the ground. But they quickly regained their footing.

Clutching her blade, time slowed around them and Belyx moved with finesse, slicing the throat of one and then stabbing the other in the stomach. They were down before Lim could finish screaming.

"My lord!" Lim finished, gagging in the corner.

"I thought we were toast," Maria said.

Belyx scowled at them. "You couldn't have subdued the enemies while Sewek was still here?"

Lim puffed some air. "Well, sorry that some of us weren't trained to gut humans like cattle on Wakenin' Day!"

Belyx cared little for her expressions right now. "What children was she talking about?"

Maria opened her mouth, but Lim interrupted her. "They have some of the Seedlings as hostages. They were holding it over our heads if we didn't tell Sewek everything."

"Wait. So you didn't just sell our secrets for lavishes?" Belyx asked.

Lim put a hand on her hip. "I know you think lowly of us dainty ladies, Queen, but we do have a soul!"

What a relief. "We need to save them. Where are they?"

"South palace region. In the servant's quarters," Maria replied.

Belyx spun her knives. "Not for long. Follow me."

As they rushed to where the Seedlings were being held, Belyx dreaded losing Sewek, but the children were more important right now. Once she cleared the palace and Enzo secured the kingdom, then they could hunt for Sewek. The longer they waited, the more likely that snake would strike.

The servants' quarters loomed into view, and of course, they were well guarded. "I'll free them. You stay here and keep an eye out—don't leave me."

Lim folded her arms. "Fine."

Belyx dashed ahead, her fists and feet a blur of motion. She could feel the power surging through her again, and it made her faster than ever. The guards didn't stand a chance; within moments they littered the floor. With a final burst of energy, she kicked open the door and charged in.

The Seedlings were huddled together in the corner, trembling with fear. A couple of guards on the inside rushed towards them, but Belyx flung her knife and struck one of them. The other managed to reach the kids, but an older girl grabbed his arm and threw him onto the bed while the others subdued him.

The children stripped him of his weapons, one handing the thrown knife back to Belyx. "Here you are, Queen."

Belyx tucked it away and bent down. The children's frail bodies and bruises revealed their lack of sustenance, no doubt due to Majeria's torture. Belyx seethed with rage. Through gritted teeth, she asked them, "are you alright?"

The older one shrugged. "I am glad you came. They were preparing to ship us off as slaves. I would rather die than go back to that life."

Belyx remembered they had all been slaves or homeless in their old lives. She would sooner face the Pits than see them suffer again. "No one will go back to that life today," she said. "Follow me and we'll reach safety."

Lim's scream bellowed from outside. Belyx and the Seedlings ran to its source. Majerian guards had them in their grasp, and Belyx prayed this would be over soon.

"Let them go, and you can live," Belyx pleaded. No more blood had to be shed.

"Ha! We have orders," one replied as he held his sword to Maria. There were no tricks that would get them out of trouble this time.

Belyx put up her hands and walked slowly to them. No more would die.

"Stop!" A guard ordered. "Drop your weapon!"

With a grin, she squeezed her knife, before letting time slow.

They were still as trees as Belyx released her fury, cutting down every soldier. He couldn't say she didn't warn him.

After the onslaught, Lim eyed Belyx. "I don't know what kind of magic that is, but I'm more grateful than a spoon fly."

Maria went to the Seedlings, checking to make sure they were okay. "Thanks for being strong little ones." She turned to Belyx. "We will escort them in the secret bunker until it is safe."

Lim butted in. "I think we should head for the escape routes. It is faster. Come on!"

Maria froze. "No."

Lim whirled. "What?"

"We are doing my plan. Majeria will be waiting by the escape an—"

"Preposterous. I—"

"Stop!" Maria screamed. "You will listen to me now, damn it! I am tired of you always bossing me around. I am my own person too and I know losing Hannah hurt you, but you need to understand I have ideas too and we need to work together if we want to survive."

Belyx stayed silent. Maria was full of surprises. Lim stared dumbfounded, eventually folding her arms sticking up her nose, doing a bad job at hiding her tears. "I never...you're right. Let's go then."

Belyx hugged her advisors, scared to leave such inexperienced fighters with the Seedlings, but she had few options. She needed to cleanse the rest of the palace. "Stay hidden until it is safe to come out. If it is worse, go to the secure location we talked about, okay?"

The advisors agreed and Belyx went back to the throne room.

A Thorn approached as soon as she hit the main floor. "Queen. Sewek managed to evade us and escaped to the streets."

"Damn it," she muttered under her breath, resisting the urge to hurl her knife at the wall. Instead, she glanced back at the remaining Majerian forces, who had been dispatched by the Order. At least her palace was clear now.

"Are we Majeria free now?"

The Thorn stilled. "Yes, but there is something worse happening."

Her throat closed. What could be worse? Did Enzo fail his mission after all?

A flash of light from outside the window caught her attention. An explosion of fire followed. What had Majeria done? And were her allies all right?

Panic surged through her, momentarily pushing aside the worry that had consumed her since Enzo left again. They should have stayed together and now Enzo was in danger and it would be her fault if he died.

"Enzo," she whispered as she broke into a run toward the kingdom. She knew his fire powers would keep him safe, but the sudden fear of losing someone so dear to her overrode all logic.

As Belyx raced through the palace exit, her mind flashed back to the countless nights they'd spent, sharing secrets and dreams beneath the stars. She couldn't imagine a world without his quiet humor and unwavering loyalty, and the thought of failing him now was unbearable.

Please, Enzo, she prayed silently, her breaths coming out in short gasps as she sprinted with aching muscles. *Please be okay. Along with everyone else.* For her kingdom, for the Order, and Enzo—she would not give up. She had successfully taken back her throne. Now, she would secure her kingdom.

Thirty-One

Human screams clawed into Enzo's mind. His ears hammered as he witnessed the carnage unfolding before him.

The Original, once a figure of myth and legend, was tearing through the kingdom like a hurricane, wielding the elements with terrifying precision.

The buildings rose to the sky like a funeral pyre, engulfed in blazing orange and red flames. Water from swollen rivers flooded the streets and battered against the walls, while gusts of wind whipped through and left ruin in its wake. People ran for their lives, screaming as they fled the inferno that threatened to consume them all—even the children, whose screams would stalk Enzo's nightmares.

"By the gods," Enzo muttered, his eyes widening. He had never imagined that The Original would be capable of such destruction. *What have I done?*

His gaze fell on Freyja and Onka, who were desperately trying to fend off a vicious assault from the powerful fae. With each swing of their weapons, it was becoming more evident they stood no chance against him.

Freyja launched an arrow for The Original, but he batted it away like a fly and sent an earth torrent right into the captain, hurtling her into a wooden fence.

Onka charged the being, but it was too late, he shifted his hand and a gust of wind sliced the handmaiden into the same fence as Freyja.

The Original hovered closer to their unconscious bodies.

Taking a deep breath, Enzo called upon his own elemental powers, feeling the heat of the fire surge through his veins.

"Hey!" he shouted, drawing The Original's attention away from Freyja and Onka. As the villain turned to face him, Enzo unleashed a flood of flames from his hands, hoping to buy his friends enough time to escape.

The Original flung the flames away and retaliated with his own, yet Enzo held on, clinging to the fire like a sharpened sword.

It was too late, though. The Original pushed even harder and Enzo stumbled back. Freyja and Onka limped behind him, trying to escape. Enzo lashed out a tendril of flame and scrambled away from the fae. The Original stilled as Enzo rushed over to his allies. This wasn't over.

"Enzo!" Freyja cried out, her tired eyes meeting his for a brief moment.

"Get to safety!" Enzo screamed, sensing The Original looming closer and closer.

Freyja nodded, grabbing Onka by the arm, and retreated as fast as she could.

"Poor Enzo Prekaro," The Original sneered, his hypnotic swirl of eyes narrowing in disdain. "I expected better from you. Have you truly become so enamored with these humans that you would betray your own kind?"

"Betray my kind?" Enzo spat back, his fingers sparking with flames as he prepared for the fight of his life. "You're the one destroying innocent lives! You don't speak for all fae!"

"But don't I? I was chosen by the gods after all."

"You lied. You said you would protect us!"

He waved a long finger. "I said I would protect *our* kind. The humans have lived long enough—throwing around their beliefs and their 'god.' It disgusts me. Once we take the humans, we move onto the witches. Then this world is ours."

Enzo blinked the smoke out of his eyes. Aydevko tried doing the same thing last year, but it failed and The Original would meet the same fate. "We have stopped bigger threats than you!"

"Ah yes, Aydevko..." The Original mused, taking on a comically dramatic tone. How he knew about that was beyond Enzo, like he had been watching the entire time. "A tragedy, for sure. But it's hardly enough to justify your newfound allegiance to these...creatures."

Enzo's teeth clenched at The Original's genocide plan. Knowing Belyx was part of the humans made it even worse. Launching another burst of fire at The Original, he was met with a wall of water that extinguished his flames instantly.

"Pathetic," The Original taunted. "Is that really all you've got?"

But Enzo refused to back down. He dodged a gust of wind, then retaliated by sending a whip of fire snaking towards his opponent. The Original smirked and conjured a barrier of earth to block the attack.

"Your elemental control is impressive, Enzo," The Original said, almost bored. "But you forget, the gods themselves created me. Your puny flames are nothing compared to my power. It came from me!"

As if to prove his point, The Original unleashed a devastating combination of elemental attacks and Enzo was sent sprawling, his body battered by wind, water, and fire.

"Enough!" Enzo roared. Forcing himself back onto his feet, he gathered every ounce of his power and launched an inferno of flames at The Original. To his dismay, the villain merely absorbed the fire into his own body, grinning as he did.

"Thank you for the boost, dear male," The Original mocked, his eyes alight with malicious glee. "It's been a while since I've had heat like that. You *are* remarkable. Letting your power wither away and then begging for it back like a dog. The gods are truly pitiful. You should have burned this whole kingdom down for what they did to your family. You had enough power to do it. Even at such a young age. But it's fine...I will create a new world."

Realizing his powers were no match for The Original, Enzo made a desperate decision: he had to get help from the rest of the fae tribe. They would never stand with this monster.

"Mark my words, you fiend," Enzo growled, his eyes burning with unshed tears. "You will not win this war."

Enzo let out a final, fiery blast, and the explosion created a dense cloud of smoke. He whirled around and ran away, leaving behind the scorched ruins of the human wreckage. As he sped towards his fae tribe, Enzo could only ponder how many more lives would be taken before this nightmare came to an end.

Enzo's lungs thundered in his chest as he arrived at the fae camp, desperate for their assistance against this threat.

The air crackled with tension and newfound aggression that made him shudder. Their homes were nothing but ash burnt trees and other debris scattered about. His tribe held each other with their heads down. The humans may have done this, but he refused to believe they would work for such a monster.

"Listen to me!" Enzo shouted, trying to make himself heard over the clamor of murmurs. "The Original has returned, but his plans are leading us down a path of bloodshed and destruction! We must not follow him! We need to fight him! He has forsaken our gods!"

A murmur ebbed through the crowd as some looked at him with doubt, while others sneered with disdain. Enzo's fathers, however, stood resolutely by his side.

"Enzo is right," Gink said, grasping Enzo's hand. "The humans have done nothing to deserve our wrath. We are better than this."

"Then you are traitors!" roared The Original, flying forward into the center of the gathering. His eyes blazed with fury, and his voice echoed through the trees like a storm. He had made it here faster than Enzo thought...although he did fly. "Either you stand with your own kind or against them. Choose wisely, for there will be no mercy for those who betray their brethren."

Gasps and whispers rippled through the tribe, but no one spoke out against The Original. Despair mauled at Enzo's insides like sludge, and he knew he had to act quickly.

The Original was here, in front of his entire tribe, but instead of fearing him, they were beginning to rally behind him. This was unreal. What were they doing?

"Last chance, Enzo. Stand with your kind...or die."

Enzo stilled, his fathers by his side. It would be so easy to join the rest of the fae. The humans had shown nothing but malice toward him and his family. All the violence and all the harsh words were proof of that. Enzo looked down at the ashen ground...fires caused by humans...on his home.

No, Enzo. A thought pleaded. *Humans may have done bad things, but not all of them are bad. Look into your heart and find the good.*

Enzo looked up. There were good humans...and there would continue to be. That was his hope. The Original fed off of hate, but hate only brought fear and Enzo refused to be afraid.

He stepped forward, flames circling his hands. "Never. I will not succumb to hate like the rest of you. I will stand for what is good! You will all realize the danger of following such an idol too closely."

The Original laughed. "And how do you plan on defeating me when I have all your powers?"

Enzo clenched his fists, smiling. "Those three objects. If they brought you in, they can bring you out!"

He guffawed. "You mean these?" He raised his hand, and the items that Enzo had given his life for came into view: the journal, the quill pen, and the key—all whirling around before being tucked away on him. "Too bad they shall serve no purpose! The bell has been rung...as they say in human language."

Enzo lit a flame in his palm. "Stand down and leave here. I will never support those who murder innocents."

The Original tapped his fingers together as if pondering a move in a card game. "Well, if you are not with us...then you are against us. Kill him."

Multiple fae launched their elemental attacks at Enzo without so much as a thought. Like he wasn't their brethren. Before Enzo could react, a gust of wind deterred the attacks.

Thano stood behind, his wind tattoos shimmering. Gink stepped in front of Enzo and nodded. With that, his nature tattoos exploded and thick green mist surrounded the area.

The fae launched at them and his fathers drew their power away. Enzo needed to get back to Aikradal to find Belyx and explain to her what had happened. The fae would show no mercy behind the might of The Original. And Belyx, even with her impressive skill, wouldn't be able to best them in a fight. And she would die trying.

A fae warrior lunged at him from the shadows, armed with vines that twisted and writhed like live serpents. Enzo sidestepped the attack and sent a wave of flames roaring towards his assailant, who shrieked in agony before collapsing into a heap of ash. But there was no time to rest as more fae appeared, eyes blazing with a newfound purpose.

"Is this really what you want?" Enzo shouted over the cacophony of battle. "To slaughter innocent humans for some twisted sense of justice?"

The fae snarled, their loyalty to The Original unwavering as they continued their relentless assault, but Enzo refused to be deterred. He fought his way through the forest, leaving a trail of charred fae in his wake.

In the middle of the broken trees, was the fae leader, Sycamore. He ruled this tribe for hundreds of years. If Enzo could convince him to stop fighting, then maybe the other fae would listen.

He confronted the leader—towering in a cloak of scattered leaves and vines. As he met his gaze, his cold eyes were dark and deceptive.

"Enough!" Enzo demanded, panting like a flame. "Why are you doing this? Why kill the humans? The Original is a liar! He was banished by our gods for a reason! This is blasphemy!"

The tribe leader stared down at Enzo with disdain. "We have been victims of the humans for too long. We have suffered as they cursed us, desecrated our lands, destroyed our homes, and spat at us like animals."

"What about our pacifists beliefs? Why did you all refuse to fight against the invaders? Hypocrites!" Dread seethed in him. His family—those he had toiled so long to save—were now rejecting all that he had fought for.

The leader took a step forward, the ground beneath his feet split with broken roots where he stood. "Our gods may forbid violence, but The Original has shown us the truth. We should not be meek and submissive, hiding in the shadows while they take all we own. We must seize control, reclaim our birthright, and exterminate the human menace."

Enzo's heart raced, but he kept his face passive. The tribe leader's words sparked something deep within him—a seed of doubt that had been planted long ago. It was true; humans had brought suffering to the fae. But could he truly condone such violence?

"Is that really the answer?" Enzo asked, struggling to keep steady. "More bloodshed? More death? This will never solve the problem of hate! Can't you see it?" They wrote books about these things. Why don't people read it?

The tribe leader's expression didn't waver. "Once all the humans are gone, peace will be restored. It is the only way. The Original will lead us to victory, and we will finally be free from the humans' tyranny."

"Stop this madness," Enzo pleaded. "There must be another way. We cannot become the very monsters we seek to destroy."

The tribe leader sneered, baring sharp teeth. "You are weak. You are just a pathetic and sad human-fucker, Enzo Prekaro. You make us all sick when you are with that vermin. You were a traitor the moment you joined forces with that witch! You'll join her in death." He raised his arms and summoned vines and leaves to his command.

Enzo's chest ached as he dug deep within himself, igniting his fire. A vortex of embers swirled around him, providing a barrier against the vines that snaked through the air, seeking to ensnare him. He leaped forward, dodging the roots that shot up from the ground like spears, and sent a wave of fire at the tribe leader. The fae merely laughed, the flames parting around him like a light breeze.

Leaves flew through the sky, their edges as sharp as blades, heading right for Enzo. He rolled to dodge, feeling the breeze slump off of the projectiles. He launched another stream of flames toward the leader, but he sunk into the dirt below, the flame soaring right above him.

Enzo circled the area with his hands aflame. He knew he would come from the ground, but where? Screams of his fathers and the other fae filled his mind, but he quieted them. Faes had exceptional hearing, even things under the ground.

With a breath, he focused. A faint rattling started, and then it grew closer and closer. In a flash, Enzo leapt forward and blasted an arc of flame behind him.

The leader grunted as it knocked him back, teeth snarling. In an instant, the leader launched a barrage of thorns Enzo's way. Enzo twirled in the air and swung his flame around, knocking the thorns back. After landing, he fired a pellet of flames in quick succession. The leader swiftly evaded the oncoming assault and summoned thick vines around Enzo. He deftly rolled away to avoid their clutches, then unleashed a powerful wave of flames with all his strength.

Sycamore clapped his hands together and wet dirt flew in front of him, staunching the flames.

"Is that all you have?" he taunted. Trees began to bend and twist, closing in on Enzo like a cage.

Enzo gritted his teeth, sweat beading on his forehead as he strained to keep his fiery abilities above the leader's. But it was faltering, the relentless onslaught of nature proving too much for his powers alone. *I can't let this happen. I won't let Belyx down.*

Just as Enzo was about to be crushed by the encroaching trees, a gust of wind tore through the forest, slicing through the timber like knives. Thano swooped in, his green eyes beaming. Gink followed suit, his hands weaving an intricate pattern to counteract the tribe leader's control over the plants.

"Your reign of terror ends now!" Thano declared, his voice ringing through the air like an alarm call.

With a flick of Gink's wrist, the tribe leader's connection to nature was severed. Thano seized the opportunity to strike, summoning a whirlwind that lifted the fae off his feet and slammed him into the ground with enough force to crack the earth beneath him. The tribe leader lay motionless, the light extinguished from his eyes.

"The fae have gotten closer to the palace," Thano said. "It is a blood bath. There is no way we can win."

"We need to get out of here," Gink added, nodding solemnly. But Enzo caught the brief flicker of uncertainty in his father's gaze, a silent question he didn't say aloud.

"Belyx is in the kingdom! We can't leave yet!" Enzo charged ahead, avoiding the fae attacks while his fathers dealt with them.

Together, they turned their attention to the remaining fae, determined to put an end to the violence. They fought side by side, their powers combined to form a near-unstoppable force. As they made it into the desecrated kingdom, Enzo's ears picked up a sound that made his blood run cold—Belyx's screams echoing through the streets.

A few fae blocked their path, but Enzo's fathers engaged them.

Enzo plunged into battle. As dread and anxiety filled his chest, his strength and courage increased. *I must keep her safe. I'll do anything to rescue her.* He persevered, each stride bringing him closer to the one he cherished most, the one he'd do anything to protect. They felled the remaining fae, but there were more wreaking havoc throughout the kingdom.

"Go," he said to his fathers, gripping their arms tightly as he began to lead them away from the chaotic scene. They needed to find Belyx; she was their only hope now...assuming she had defeated Vivienne and secured her palace. It was Belyx—of course she had.

As they hastily scrambled into the shadows, a cacophony of violent screams burst forth. The stench of spilled blood and terror flooded Enzo's nose as the fae descended upon the humans in an onslaught far more wicked than he ever could have dreamed.

"Where do we go from here?" asked Thano, his face pale and drawn.

"First, we find Belyx," Enzo responded. "Then, we need to get those objects back from The Original and save the humans. We can un-summon him from them."

He knew it wouldn't be easy, but he couldn't stand by and watch innocent lives be torn apart. Belyx and the Order were their only chance at turning the tide of this war. Enzo refused to let her down.

As they slipped through the alleyways he memorized as a homeless kid, Enzo's thoughts raced with the enormity of their task. If Belyx could just rally enough support against The Original, then maybe, just maybe, they could put an end to this madness.

"Enzo," Gink said softly, drawing his attention back to the present. "We're with you, no matter what happens. We won't let The Original destroy everything we hold dear. We know he is fae, but we can't go back to last year. I refuse to fight my own son. I would rather have my lungs torn out of me than do that again. I am here for you."

"As am I," Thano responded. "Just with less dramatics." He nudged his partner.

"Thank you," Enzo said. Their unwavering loyalty meant more to him than anything else.

They continued their search. They were not alone in their fight, and Enzo clung to that fact like a lifeline as they plunged into the bloodied streets, ready to face whatever battles lay ahead.

Thirty-Two

Her beloved kingdom—previously filled with hope and prosperity—lay in shambles. What Enzo done? The past opulent markets were in ruin, their stands uprooted and the houses shattered and blackened. Smoke billowed from smoldering fires, painting the sky a sickly gray.

"By The God," she whispered, her nails digging holes in her palms.

All around her, fae wreaked havoc, slaughtering the innocent people who had once called this place home. What was left of the streets was now a graveyard of death and destruction.

What had happened to the fae? Were they under a curse again? Belyx's eyes flashed as she spotted a child trembling behind a fallen tree.

"Run!" she shouted, waving her arm. But it was too late—a fae swooped down from above, ending the child with a barrage of flames.

"No!" Belyx launched herself forward. Focusing on the power within her, she let the familiar sensation of time slow around her. Her enemies moved like they were swimming in molasses, allowing her to dart between them with ease.

She cut down the murderer, but...the child was dead.

As she fought on, Belyx couldn't help but recall the events of the previous year when the fae had been under a spell, their eyes glazed over and void of reason. This time, however, their eyes were clear, filled with only bloodlust. This was no obvious curse.

Enzo...please tell me you haven't turned against us, she thought, driving her knife through the heart of another fae.

Every life taken weighed like a cannon on her conscience, but she couldn't allow them to continue their massacre. Last year, she would have shown mercy because of Enzo, but this time, Majeria was no longer the enemy. How foolish she had been.

Amidst the chaos, Belyx fought with lethal grace. With each swing of her blade, she moved like a dancer, striking down her foes with precision and perseverance. But for every fae she killed, another took their place, claiming more innocent lies.

"Is this truly the path you've chosen?" she snarled at a fallen attacker. "Have you so easily forgotten the peace we once shared?"

But there was no answer, only the sounds of screams and destruction echoing through the kingdom. Belyx suspected that Enzo had been conflicted about his loyalties to both humans and his kind. She clung to the hope that he remained on their side, but she steeled herself to do what was right, even if it meant facing him in battle.

The weight of her decision settled on her shoulders—she was queen, after all. She would protect her people, no matter the cost. These were invaders and they must die.

As Belyx's blade sliced through the air, she caught a glimpse of a towering figure in the distance. A being who seemed to command all the elements. Fire danced around his fingertips; water surged at his feet, wind whipped through his long, stringy hair, and the earth trembled beneath him as if bowing to his will. It couldn't be…The Original? The fae from their legend, who was banished by their gods, for being too power-hungry.

"Stop this bloodshed or else!" she demanded, stepping closer, her eyes narrowing with suspicion. The deafening sound of battle receded as she focused on this new threat.

"Ah, the Queen of Aikradal graces us with her presence," he replied with a flamboyant, comical voice that seemed to mock her existence. His sage eyes were hypnotic, yet cruel, and a shiver raced down her spine. "This is not bloodshed, my dear...but a rebirth of fae supremacy."

"It seems we disagree there." Belyx tightened her fists on her weapons as more citizens died around her. "What have you done with the fae?" *With Enzo.*

"Ah, dear Enzo has been most useful in that regard," The Original revealed with a wicked grin. It couldn't be.

"Enzo?" Belyx's heart ebbed at the mention of him, her hope faltering for a moment. She couldn't believe that he would betray them, but she couldn't let emotion cloud her judgment. "Why are you doing this? Killing humans, turning your kind against innocents?"

He howled with laughter. Only monsters laughed at dead children. "Because we, the fae, deserve to rule!" He paused. "Innocent? You kid yourself. Any human, human-lover, or witch who dares defy me will pay the ultimate price."

Belyx's insides twisted with anger and disgust as she took action. The Original wouldn't continue this slaughter, but she also had to be strategic in her approach. She glanced around at the chaos surrounding them, weighing the odds of success against this danger.

"Your arrogance will be your downfall," she said, unwilling to back down despite the fear that gripped her. "You may have the power of the elements, but you underestimate the strength of those who stand against you."

"Bold words for a mere human queen," he taunted. "But let us see if your actions can match your bravado."

As Belyx prepared herself, she sent a silent prayer to The God for the iron will to protect her people and to bring an end to The Original's reign of terror. She would not rest until this threat was vanquished, even if it cost her everything. The God helped her do it last year and They would do it again.

"Prepare yourself. I will fight you with every ounce of strength I possess."

"Ah, such determination," he mocked. "But do not fool yourself into thinking you stand a chance against me, Queen Belyx."

With a flick of his wrist, The Original summoned a gust of wind that almost knocked Belyx off her feet. She gritted her teeth, digging her heels into the ground, and charged forward, her blade slicing through the air as she aimed for his throat.

"Is that all you have?" He laughed, dodging her attacks like nothing and retaliating with a torrent of water that slammed into her chest, sending her skidding backward across the damp earth.

Gasping for breath, Belyx pushed herself back up, her hands throbbing with pain from her old burn wound as she clung to her knife like a long-lost heirloom. Why were her palms burning now?

Her strength was waning, but she refused to back down. She had faced insurmountable odds before and triumphed; this would be no different.

"Your foolishness amuses me." The Original taunted a sinister melody as flames danced at his fingertips, and the ground beneath Belyx's feet trembled ominously. "But, alas, all good things must come to an end."

He raised his arms to unleash his full elemental fury, and Belyx steeled herself for the onslaught. In her mind, she recalled all of her dead loved one's brave faces, seeking solace in their beauty even as her world crumbled around her.

"Come then, monster," she snarled. "I will not give up my kingdom. Too many evil bastards have tried to take this crown and they have all failed. As shall you."

With a resounding roar that shook the earth itself, The Original hurled his power at Belyx, who charged forward to meet him head-on. Their two forms collided in an explosion of fire, water, wind, and earth, the air crackling as the battle raged between them.

And amid the chaos and destruction, Belyx fought with every fiber of her being against the darkness that sought to consume all she held dear.

Thirty-Three

Belyx's vision swam before her, struggling to focus as she lay still on the broken streets. These were the same roads she had once traveled, bringing hope and cheer to those she passed. But now, the streets were filled with darkness and despair; the citizens were tattered and forlorn, their hope all but extinguished.

Her throat sunk in her chest as The Original towered over her, his sick eyes gleaming with malicious intent. With a smirk that sent shivers down her spine, he stuck his hands out, a raging firestorm swirling around his person.

"Get back up, little queen. Show me all that 'power' you possess."

Belyx exhaled, her expression hardening with each painful gasp. She gripped her knife, the shape indenting her palms.

Gripping her wrist in pain, she opposed yielding, laboriously rising to her feet. "Your tirade ends today." Belyx charged forward.

The Original laughed, launching the fireball in response. Belyx gritted her teeth and dodged, barely avoiding his large attacks. The heat singed her hair as she rolled to the side, further igniting her rage. *Why is it always my hair getting ruined in these fights?*

"Is that all?" she asked, trying to slow time. Would it work on him?

The air thickened, suppressing the elemental onslaught. But it wasn't enough; the Original's abilities were too strong—she could feel her strength waning rapidly.

"You wanted power." Belyx twirled her knife around, recalling all of her training—all her training led her to this moment—this moment to save her kingdom.

The Original grunted, his multitude of elements circling his frame. "You are a mere human. The only powers you possess are how to bore me back to exile."

"Is it working?" Belyx ebbed a smile as she stalled, trying to call the sensation again.

"The queen has a humorous side. Enough games. Today you fall, along with the rest of the humans."

We will see.

In her hands, the blade vibrated. The power was back. She rushed the fae, time and everything around her stilled again. The Original was nothing but a meaningless idol...who underestimated humans for the last time.

Edging closer to the monster, Belyx stuck out her steel to slit his murderous throat when, in a flash, he twisted out of the way and launched a gale of wind that slammed Belyx into a nearby wall.

What? I had him!

As Belyx struggled to regain her posture, The Original roared with laughter. "You thought that pitiful witch trick would work on me?" He continued his chuckling as heat climbed its way up her spine. He was immune to her power, but how?

The Original twirled his hands and a stream of water surrounded Belyx, the cool mist bouncing off it. "I am an all-powerful being. Witch magic doesn't work on me. I have no idea how you were able to use such an ability—you are full of surprises."

Hands trembling, the water caved in on her. If she didn't act fast, he would drown her. *That's it!* He may be able to move in her time freeze, but could his elements?

Focusing on her blade once more, the swirling liquid froze and she darted underneath it, dashing forwards at The Original. He reacted in a swift haze, meeting her attack head-on with deft movement. Even though she lacked his abilities, she made up for it with remarkable hand-to-hand combat skills.

The Original parried Belyx's weapon and tore it from her grasp. She dodged his other strike and sent a kick for his knee, but he sidestepped the strike and flicked a palm right into her face.

Time returned as she hit the ground. Blood painted the cracked brick as she spat. She was losing this fight.

"Pathetic," The Original sneered as he tossed the knife away, conjuring a torrent of water, and hurtled it towards Belyx. She dove out of its path, gasping for breath as fatigue took its toll. Her hands snatched the knife, the weight of it leaden now. It was useless against him.

"Give up, human." he summoned vines from the stones that snaked toward her. Belyx slashed them away, envisioning her failure. *No! I have to win this!*

Exhaustion threatened to consume her. With all the fighting she had done in the last hour, she had nothing left. In a desperate attempt, Belyx lunged at The Original. But he was too fast, his eyes flashing with triumph as he swept her off her feet with a gust of wind.

"Sad." he gloated, flames licking at his fingertips as he thrust his hand forward. Droplets of liquid fire cascaded from his palm and the air around him quivered with heat. "You were quite the foe, but like all my enemies, you must burn to ash." Belyx closed her eyes, waiting for the searing pain, signaling her end.

But it never came.

Instead, she felt an intense heat radiating from her hands. Only this time, the sensation grew stronger until it surged outward, creating a barrier between her and The Original's flames. She blinked her eyes in astonishment, watching as the fire harmlessly licked at the shield.

"What?" snarled The Original, his previous cocky demeanor obliterated. "Impossible!"

Belyx couldn't believe it either. Somehow, her hands Enzo burned last year had tapped into an unknown power, saving her life. As the realization sank in, a newfound confidence returned. What kind of magic was this? Her mind shifted to how Enzo's fae abilities saved her from Scandeni's curse the prior year and perhaps this was something similar.

"I may be defeated," she said, staring up at her adversary. "But I'm still alive. And I won't stop fighting until you're gone."

The Original's laughter echoed through the air, his cocky demeanor returned. "You foolish. pathetic, little queen. Did you truly believe you could defeat the fae? Even with your magic trick, it is still too late!"

The wind whipped around Belyx, stinging her cheeks and tugging at her singed hair. She struggled to catch her breath, her lungs burning with each ragged inhale. She glanced down at her hands, still radiating an otherworldly buzz, and clenched them into fists. Whatever this was, it was ready to fight.

"Your determination is admirable," The Original continued, circling her like a hurricane. "But ultimately futile."

"I will never stop. Even if we lose today. I will come back and your pathetic head will be on a spear!" Belyx shouted. She couldn't afford to be impulsive now, but the rage simmering beneath the surface was too much to contain.

"Ah, there it is," The Original purred, delight coloring his soft tone. "The fire that burns so brightly inside you. But alas, it will not save you this time."

With a sudden burst of speed, he lunged toward her, his hypnotic grin promising pain and destruction. Belyx's heart performed a frantic ballet as she closed her eyes, bracing for impact.

The attack sent Belyx hurtling into the hard ground, her hands pulsating with power, but it wouldn't obey. Her bones and muscles ached. Any more movement caused them to retaliate.

"Give it up, Belyx," The Original jeered. "You die today, as your kingdom falls"

As her hope began to fade, a whoosh of air knocked the fae back. She turned to find the arrival of Enzo and his fathers. The trio stood united. *So Enzo wasn't on the fae's side?* Relief swam through Belyx as she continued struggling to push herself up.

"Leave her alone, you murderer!" Enzo roared, his fiery fae essence glowing around him.

"Ah, the human lover returns," The Original replied, turning his attention to the new arrivals. "You think you can defeat me after the last time? How amusing! And he brought his traitorous fathers as well. I understand fatherly love, but to go against your own kind? Sad."

"You wouldn't know!" Gink shouted back. "Being a father requires a lot more than you could ever give!"

Enzo wasted no time in engaging the fae, his fingers igniting with flames as he lunged forward. Thano joined him, his wind abilities creating forceful gusts that buffeted their enemy. Gink summoned vines that entangled The Original's limbs, attempting to hold him in place.

"Is this how you repay my kindness, Enzo?" The Original laughed. "I gave you life, and you choose to stand against me?"

"Your twisted version of kindness nearly destroyed us all!" Enzo shouted back. "I revived you to end the hate! Not cause it! If anything, you should be thankful to me!"

He sent a flurry of flames, but The Original held it at bay. "I owe you nothing anymore, human-loving worm."

As the battle raged, Belyx struggled to catch her breath, her thoughts stampeding.

He came back for me. They all did.

"Let's finish this!" Thano yelled as he unleashed a torrential gale at The Original.

"Don't need to tell me twice," Gink said, his sturdy form bracing through the power of Thano's wind as he called forth more vines to constrict their foe.

As Enzo and his fathers fought valiantly against The Original, Belyx marveled at the power and unity they displayed. The three fae moved in perfect harmony, their abilities combining into a formidable force. Together, they were unstoppable. Maybe there was hope after all?

The Original turned away and Enzo took the opportunity to direct a searing burst of flame, causing him to recoil in pain and surprise. As the villain stumbled backward, Enzo rushed to Belyx's side and offered her a hand.

"Are you alright?" he asked. His features ashen.

Belyx grasped Enzo's hand, feeling the warmth of his fire abilities envelop her again as if recharging the new power. "I knew you wouldn't betray me," she said, although she was still scared he might have.

"Never." His mouth curving upward. "We stand together."

For a moment, time froze as they shared a wordless understanding, their bond stronger than ever.

Belyx's vision drummed as she turned to witness Enzo's fathers struggle against The Original, their once fluid movements now faltering under the relentless assault. The air thickened as the elements collided, fire destroying the vines and wind tangling with plants.

"Fathers!" Enzo cried out as Thano was thrown back by a forceful gust of wind. Gink, too, was unsteady, his vines shriveling from the heat of The Original's fire.

"Go!" Enzo ordered Belyx, his voice strained. "We'll meet up with you later. You have to get away from here!"

"Enzo—" Belyx tried to protest, her chest tightening at the thought of leaving him behind again.

"Please." His eyes twinkled in desperation. "Find the rest of the Order and plan for an escape. We will meet you. This fae is my problem. I caused this." Terror laced his words, yet beneath it all was a steely boldness that held her stare.

"Trust me." He planted a kiss on her mouth before turning to aid his fathers.

Belyx swallowed, trying to look back as she sprinted away. As she ran, her thoughts vibrated with the fearful realization that she might not see them again. *They're willing to sacrifice everything for us*, she thought, *and I can't let them face this alone.* She needed to find the rest of the Order and escape the hell out of here.

Thirty-Four

A multitude of screams and the clash of steel filled Belyx's ears as she sliced through the fae with her venom-coated knives. She pushed through them with ease, slowing time, and picking them off one by one. Sweat trickled down her temple, but she barely paid it mind as she focused on the battle before her.

Freyja, Cook, and Onka fought multiple fae in the distance. Other Order assassins battled their opponents from the rafters of the disheveled homes. Belyx's breaths grew shallow. The very creatures she vowed to guard...were now slaying all she cherished. She should have listened to the people—they had been right. Though thankfully Enzo and his fathers were with her. Although it may not be enough this time.

Belyx darted towards her friends and vaulted onto a water fae's back, ramming her blade into her throat and sending her crashing down. "Thought you could use a hand."

Before Freyja could respond, she held up her bow. "Behind you!" Her voice sliced through the chaos. An arrow found its mark in the chest of a charging fae.

"Thanks," Belyx replied, her chest heaving.

To her left, Onka whirled into action, her baton smashing violently against a fae's skull. Her eyes were focused and narrowed as she executed every strike with precision. Onka gracefully transitioned from baton strikes to whip mastery, honoring the memory of her deceased sister with each whip crack.

"Stay sharp," Cook growled as she moved past Belyx, cutting down another fae with deadly efficiency. Her words were shallow. Cook was somewhat right about not trusting the fae as well, but feeling guilty wouldn't help anyone now.

They battled back to back. Any charging fae was struck down by Freyja's cat-like precision and any fae who were stupid enough to venture closer, were met with hostile retaliation.

Onka shoved a fae away, while Cook grabbed their arms and sent flames shooting into the air. Belyx plunged her blade into the fae's throat; blood sprayed as the creature collapsed.

More of the enemy advanced, but they were ready—the Order had trained them well. Despite this, Belyx found it difficult to swallow; the Order her family had worked so hard to build was rapidly diminishing. No matter how much they fought, victory seemed unlikely: her palace would soon be destroyed. How would she go on from here?

Fight, Belyx. And never stop.

That was what her mother would do.

Belyx continued their offensive strategy. Each time a fae attempted to end them, they were met with a blade to the throat. Onka managed to evade one swing and quickly disabled Cook's assailant. Freyja moved as if performing a dance, skillfully taking down the adversaries one by one.

A gust of air sent Cook into a wooden wall. Belyx threw her knife and the wind fae dropped, then she went to her.

Cook waved her off, clenching her side.

Fae's descended, but Onka's whip and Freyja's arrows vanquished them.

They fought as one, their strengths and skills complementing one another, until finally, the last of the fae crumpled lifeless at their feet.

Belyx stood panting, her body throbbing with pain, but she felt rejuvenated. This was what she trained for.

"I must speak with Belyx. Can you manage out here?" Cook commanded her captain and handmaiden. They bowed and pressed on helping other struggling Order assassins."

"Cook. We need to keep fighting we are s—"

Cook pulled her into a now abandoned home and slammed the door. What was she doing? There was no time for idle chat while her people were being slaughtered.

"We are not going to win this fight, flower," Cook said, her throat raw. Belyx went to retort when Cook held up a hand. "I admire your stubbornness, but even you know this is futile. The best we can do is try and get a head start on regrouping."

"What did you have in mind?"

Cook leaned against the wall, dirt and various other things littered her outfit. How long had she been fighting? "I am going to tell you something and I need you to keep an open mind and follow what I say?" Belyx gave a curt nod and Cook rubbed her encrusted hands. "Long ago, your grandmother and I-" Cook hesitated, "before she married the king...we were in a—relationship."

Belyx blinked in surprise, twisting with the knowledge of Cook's hidden pain. So that was why the death of her grandmother had cut so deep.

"Why didn't you stay together?" Belyx asked. Who knew her grandmother had such an unknown past?

Cook shook her head. "She had a responsibility to the kingdom. I couldn't handle it. That was why I left. I tried to stay here while we were together in secret, but Dara couldn't do it anymore. And she became so hyper-focused on the Order. After she told me she had a duty to her kingdom, I went back home. Back to Quoxia."

The weight of Cook's words was heavy on her chest. Quoxia was the northernmost kingdom. Belyx had never ventured that far north as the desert path was treacherous.

"You must retreat there," Cook explained. "You will find allies who can help you with this takeover. They have their own Order so to speak, one I used to be a part of. That was how your grandmother and I met. She was on a diplomatic mission and I was in charge of making sure she didn't betray the kingdom or something." She laughed. "What a woman she was."

"I wish you had told me sooner." Belyx frowned. "Why didn't you tell me about this? Especially after she died? I said all those horrible things to you an—"

"Child," Cook interrupted, her eyes downcast, "I too, had my grieving to do, but I didn't want it to change the way you felt about your grandmother. But now I realize, you need all of that wisdom more than ever. I'm so proud of you. You escaped that wretched place and took back what was stolen."

"It's not good enough It is being ripped from us again."

"It will be. You just need to never give up. Remember that. After witnessing your strength today, I know you are ready. Head north and find their Order. They will most likely find you first as they don't take kindly to new people. Tell them you know me. They will remember. Hopefully, Quoxia can bring an invasion force here."

"What about the desert? No man alive has ever crossed it and lived?"

Cook put a hand on her shoulder. "You are no man. You can face anything. You bested a powerful witch and a dangerous kingdom's twisted games. You can do it. I wish I had more answers for you, but our time is up."

Belyx stared at her for a moment, her mind peddling with questions about this plan she had. She wanted more, but now was not the time. Instead, she agreed, accepting Cook's advice with as much grace as she could muster.

"Thank you," she whispered, gripping Cook's hand. "I promise I won't let you or my grandmother down."

"Your courage will carry you far, Belyx." A sad smile tugged at her lips. "Now go. Find your allies and get them out of here. I'll prepare a carriage."

An explosion took them out of their moment. Cook's eyes locked with Belyx's, the intensity of her gaze burning like a steady flame. "No matter who dies, always fight for good. Aikradal has fallen, but you possess the courage to take it back." Belyx had to listen despite the gnawing in her chest

Belyx exhaled. "I won't forget your words."

"Remember, child," Cook added, her tone softening, "even when all seems lost, hold onto hope. The darkness cannot last forever as the sun always returns."

Belyx nodded, the friction of their conversation pressing down upon her like a heavy rock. She couldn't afford to fail now; not after everything she had been through.

"Promise me you'll be careful," Belyx said, tears cascading down her cheeks.

"Of course." Cook placed a reassuring hand on Belyx's shoulder.

"See you soon." The word tasted bittersweet on her lips. So much was at stake, so much left unsaid, but she knew right now, time was of the essence.

As Belyx exited the house, Freyja charged her, blood and dirt caking her face. "Belyx!" Freyja called out as she dashed towards her. "Enzo and his fathers are losing to The Original!"

Belyx grasped Freyja's hand. "Cook is getting a carriage. Tell all Order members it's time for Code Wilt."

"Queen?"

"I know, Freyja." Belyx stammered. "But we need to think about other lives here. We are outmatched and need to retreat."

"I'm with you every step, but how do we save Enzo?"

Belyx's stomach clenched at the mention of her partner in danger. Fear gripped her like a vice, threatening to suffocate her, but she pushed it aside, focusing instead on the wise words of Cook. She could do this.

"We fight," Belyx said with a straight face.

As they raced through the streets, rubble and flying debris whipped at Belyx's face, stinging her skin like a thousand tiny daggers. But the pain was nothing compared to the thought of losing Enzo to The Original. She couldn't—wouldn't—let that happen.

The acrid smell of smoke and carnage assaulted Belyx's senses. She spotted Enzo, his green eyes almost shimmering as he wielded his flames, alongside his fathers who were struggling against The Original and his fae followers. They were surrounded. Dirt lined their faces and blood oozed from their wounds. They wouldn't last much longer at this rate.

Belyx checked her own injuries. On top of the Trials, Vivienne, The Original, and all the fae, her body wouldn't hold out. The plan was to get in and get out. Retreat.

I hate retreating, but Cook is right. We need to.

"Enzo!" Belyx shouted, scanning the battlefield, taking in the chaos of the fight.

"About time you showed up," Enzo called back, spinning to lock eyes with her before sending a fireball toward an enemy fae. "We're losing ground!"

Belyx's tossed all fear aside as she dove into the fray, her love for him driving her forward. Whirling around with her knife in hand, she slashed through the air, cutting down fae after fae, her fury relentless.

Freyja ran behind her, letting loose arrow after arrow from her bow staff, her intense focus locked on her targets. No one would harm Belyx as long she was at her flank.

Onka cracked her whip and swung her baton with deadly precision.

"Push them back!" Belyx wailed as she turned her gaze towards The Original, who was closing in on Enzo's fathers, their tattoos fading in the light.

"No!" Enzo screamed, sweat dripping down his face as he deflected incoming attacks with his flames. "You will not harm them!" Enzo charged and Belyx ran close behind, refusing to separate this time.

As the fight raged on, it became apparent they were losing. The Original's elements were overwhelming, his dark elements swirled as he laughed at their efforts.

Enzo launched a fire shield in front of his fathers. Belyx helped them up.

"He is too strong!" Thano shouted, using his wind to create a barrier between them and their enemies coming from their rear. His bloodied eyes were wide as Gink attempted to slow the advancing fae with vines and roots.

"He has the objects I used to summon him," Enzo said with quick breaths. "If we can get them, there is a way to un-summon him."

Belyx liked his plan, Maybe they didn't need to retreat after all. "How—?" But she was interrupted as a flame the size of a carriage plummeted at them.

Enzo used his power and bat the flames away. "We got the Dark Tome from Aydevko last year. We can take these just as easily." He reached out his hand. "Together."

Taking his hand, Belyx shot him a look. As she recalled, it wasn't easy.

Enzo sent a barrage of fire for The Original, but he swatted it away like a fly, sending up a billow of smoke. Thano twirled his hands and the smoke lingered.

Belyx rushed to Freyja and Onka. "If we steal the objects from him, we can defeat him. Cover me."

"Always," Onka replied, readying her whip as Freyja nocked an arrow.

Belyx charged the cover with Onka as arrows buried into fae from Freyja. After ducking a strike, Belyx took a deep breath and entered the haze. The indication of The Original was his cursing as he struggled against the fumes, too busy to notice her. Enzo taught her the distracted man was a foolish one. Before he noticed, Belyx reached into his pocket and touched one of the objects. With a puff of air, she pulled it from him. It was a quill pen about the size of her palm. *One down.*

She thrust her arm in again, only to be submerged in a circle of waves. Her vision blurred and her lungs burned for air against the pressure of the water.

Fearful memories of the Trials resurfaced, and she searched for any escape, but it was futile.

The water heated and steam billowed around her as she dropped from the prison.

Coughing up what felt like her entire throat, she clutched the quill tight to her. The smoke lifted and Enzo, Gink, and Thano were pushing the snarling Original away, their tattoos fading. They barely retrieved one object and there wasn't enough time to get the rest. Cook was right. "Sorry Mom," she muttered, standing to the others.

"Retreat!" Belyx shouted frantically, her breathing strained. But as if summoned, Cook drove a double horse carriage around the corner, mowing down fae and tossing them off.

"Everyone! To the carriage!" Belyx kicked a fae away and grabbed her partner's hand, leading him to it.

"Listen to me," Cook said urgently. "Remember the plan we discussed? It's our only chance."

Belyx hesitated, her muscles crying for relief as she remembered their last-ditch effort, the quill pen in her pocket a mocking reminder of their failure. Fear washed over her as she kept her head down, knowing what had to be done.

The others jumped on and as Belyx joined, Cook suddenly sprang off. "Wait!" Belyx cried out, grasping Cook's arm. "Where are you going?"

But Cook shook her head, breaking free from Belyx's grasp. "This is my choice. Now go!"

"Come on, Belyx!" Enzo shouted, grabbing her by the shoulder and pulling her from Cook. "We need to go, now!"

As Enzo pulled her away, Belyx's eyes remained locked on Cook. She knew what was about to happen, what Cook was sacrificing for their survival. But she couldn't bring herself to accept it.

"Goodbye, Belyx," Cook saluted and charged the fray.

"No!" Belyx screamed, reaching out as Freyja and Onka joined Enzo in holding her back. She had lost enough people to this and Cook would not be another one.

"Let me go!" she hissed through clenched teeth, struggling against their tight grips.

"Look!" Thano shouted, nodding towards Cook who had already dove headfirst into the battle.

"Cook!" Belyx cursed under her breath, knowing Cook's sacrifice was essential if they were to have any chance of survival.

Cook managed to draw The Original's attention away from the rest of them. Belyx stood in horror as Cook held her ground, her small frame dwarfed by the menacing figure of the fae leader.

"Your fight is with me now," she heard Cook snarl.

The Original laughed, an unsettling sound, echoing throughout the battlefield. "You really think you can stand against me, human?" His hypnotic green eyes flashed with amusement.

"Watch me," Cook spat, her face set in grim defiance.

"Enough!" Belyx shouted, unable to bear witness to her friend's impending doom anymore. Tears streamed down her cheeks, hot and bitter.

"We need to leave, now!" Gink yelled.

"Grab the horses," Enzo ordered, his tone unsteady. "Let's get out of here before more fae follow us."

Tears blurring her vision, Belyx gasped in anguish as Freyja lashed the reins and spurred the horses to the forest. With a heavy step, she turned for one final glance back at the battle. To her horror, The Original advanced towards Cook.

"Please." She pleaded with The God. "Please let her live."

But even as she spoke the words, Belyx knew her prayer would go unanswered. As The Original struck the last blow, Cook's body crumpled to the ground, lifeless and broken.

"Bastard!" Belyx gripped the edge so tightly that her knuckles faded to white. "I will kill you all! Never forget it!"

"Faster, Freyja!" Onka shouted, her whip lashing out at approaching faes. "They are swarming us!"

Wooziness threatened to tear Belyx apart as she lashed at enemies, watching their traitorous bodies fall. Her chest tightened, and her breath came in ragged gasps as a maelstrom of emotions raged within her. She could hardly see through the tears propelling down her face, but she forced herself to focus on the path ahead.

"Keep going!" Enzo said. "We'll make it out of here, I promise."

More fae emerged, so Freyja tugged at the reins and veered towards the forest. A flurry of gusts caused the carriage to shudder, yet it didn't slow them down. Belyx peered back at the pursuing fae, but even they couldn't keep up with the horses.

"Your promises mean nothing." Belyx's eyes burned. Whether it be from the smoke or tears was beyond her now.

Retreating was their only option, but the thought of leaving Cook behind tore her very soul. Every fiber of her being screamed at her to turn back, to fight until her last step in honor of her fallen friend. But deep down, such a choice would be futile; she had to survive, to carry on the fight for Cook.

"Forgive me," she whispered, wiping the tears from her face as she forced herself to look forward. "I won't let your sacrifice be in vain." Cook was the only reason The Original hadn't been able to chase them. Without her, they would all be dead.

All signs pointed towards one thing: they were on the right path. The Original's response when she stole one of the objects further assured he was afraid of them getting those objects. They would return and steal the last two.

And when she did, she would make him pay for taking Cook's life.

Belyx gasped as she watched Enzo's hands tremble, his dirtied appearance haunted by the devastation left in The Original's wake. Though they had managed to escape with their lives, the loss of Cook would weigh heavily on them all.

"Enzo," Belyx said softly, placing a hand on his shoulder, feeling bad for her earlier snap. "You couldn't have known what would happen."

"Still." His throat cracked. "I brought him back. I'm responsible for this." A tear slid down his cheek, and he smudged it away.

"Enough." Gink's tone was firm, but not unkind. "We must focus on what we can do now. There's no going back."

"Right," Thano said, the blood dripping down his forehead caught the faint light filtering through the trees. "We need a plan."

"North," Belyx declared, her words cutting through the air like one of her knives. "We need to travel north to Quoxia."

"Through the Desert of Polakaz?" Freyja frowned. "No one has ever survived that journey, Belyx. It's a death sentence. We should go by sea."

Belyx shook her head, feeling her singed hair clap at her face...not even caring because it was just stupid hair and stupid problems. "Sea travel isn't an option. Majeria controls the seas and will find us. We'll make it, I promise."

"Are you sure Quoxia is the best place?" Onka's eyes widened.

"Positive," Belyx responded, keeping her gaze on the horses to avoid more tears. "And it's our best chance at getting the upper hand on The Original. Using Quoxia's armies. Cook used to work for them." The sound of her name sent daggers into her spine. Another wound of loss she would scrawl.

"Very well." Freyja crossed her arms, her braids all lose and in disarray now. "But if we're to attempt this, we need to prepare. The desert is unforgiving. Good thing Cook packed us a week of supplies. Bless that woman."

Belyx agreed. "That should be plenty to make it...I hope." The forest was stretching thinner now, revealing a shimmering light, leading to the desert.

"Are you sure about this?" Enzo asked, his gaze searching hers. "There's no turning back once we begin."

"Enzo," she murmured, meeting his eyes. "My heart aches for Cook, but allowing our grief to control us will only lead to more suffering. We have a duty to protect our people and defeat The Original. If traveling through the Desert of Polakaz is the way to ensure that...then it's a risk I'm willing to take."

"We are willing to take." He sighed, his shoulders sagging. "Let's go, then."

As they continued riding into the desert, Belyx couldn't help but feel the weight of her decision pressing down on her. She knew the journey would be brutal, but she refused to let fear dictate her actions. For Cook, for her friends, and herself, she would find the resources to face whatever challenges lay ahead.

THIRTY-FIVE

After hours of riding, they had to leave the horses and use another method for traversing the desert. Luckily they had a wind fae with them and turned the carriage into a sand glider. It was more efficient in the long run. It was Onka's idea. Bless her brain for its knack for structure. Belyx barely knew what a hammer did.

The glider cut through the desert, its sleek form kicking up a plume of dust as it raced across the dunes. Thano stood at the helm, his abilities guiding their course, his red hair fluttering around with each gust he summoned.

Belyx endured the sand lashing her skin as she sat in the back, not letting go of Enzo's hand. His grip was unwavering, yet no longer emanating its usual warmth. Her once powerful nation of Aikradal...now swept away in a matter of hours.

This retreat was hard but necessary for beating The Original. Any great strategy took time. They would get that aid and she would personally avenge Cook's death.

"Thano!" She raised her voice over the wind. "How much farther until we reach the kingdom?"

"We still have a couple of weeks left," Thano answered without turning around.

"Perfect." Belyx tried to sound confident for the sake of her friends. She squeezed Enzo's hand, searching for some sign of reassurance from him. But his features remained distant, lost in his own thoughts.

"Hey," she whispered, brushing her thumb against the intricate flame tattoos that adorned his hand. "We'll get through this, okay?"

Enzo met her gaze, the ghost of a smile playing on his lips. "I know. It's just...hard."

"Hard" didn't even begin to cover it. The weight of their losses hung heavy, threatening to crush her under its oppressive force. But she couldn't allow herself to succumb to the grief—not when so many lives were still at stake. He probably experienced immense guilt for reviving that monster. But Belyx knew she would have done the same if her people were in danger, so she couldn't stay angry at him.

"Once we've reached Quoxia, we'll regroup and plan our next move," she told Enzo as she pulled out the quill, marveling at how such a tiny object caused so much trouble.

"That seems so useless now," Enzo said, burying his face in his hands.

"It gives us hope."

"How so?"

"He has a weakness. If we get the other two, we can defeat him. That means there is a chance."

Enzo looked back at her, his eyes dim. "I wish I had the same determination as you right now. I am not even 100% sure of that translation. It may not have said un-summon at all!"

"Well, at least it is a start. I refuse to let Cook's and all the other's deaths be in vain. We're going to end this, and secure a future for our people." Belyx wished he had the fae lore, but not that she could read it anyways.

"She is right," Freyja chimed in from her seat across the glider. Her intense eyes were fixed on Belyx. "We've come too far to turn back now. We'll see this through to the end, no matter the cost."

"Agreed," Onka added, her gaze staying low. "We owe it to those we've lost."

The sun dipped lower in the sky as they continued through the vast desert, casting long shadows that stretched out before them like dark fingers reaching for the horizon.

But nestled within those memories was something stronger: hope. It glimmered like a flickering flame, tenuous but unyielding, burning brighter with each moment they spent with each other.

Their journey was far from over, but Belyx knew in her heart they would face whatever trials lay ahead as one. They were bound by a shared purpose, forged in fire and tempered by loss. And together, they would rise above the ashes, bringing justice to their enemies and peace to their people.

Thirty-Six

A week dragged by, and it felt like years.

As the sun dipped in the sky. Belyx stood at the edge of their makeshift camp and frowned. She gazed out at the vast expanse of sand, unable to comprehend why it was considered so dangerous aside from the scarcity of food and water. Her hand instinctively reached for one of her knives, fingers tracing the familiar curves as she contemplated the seemingly endless treck.

"Still can't wrap your head around it, can you?" Thano's melodic voice floated over to her, pulling her from her thoughts. The older fae leaned casually against a nearby rock, his eyes taking in the same view that had captured her attention.

"Do you think there is something to be afraid of out here?" Belyx scoffed, the wind whipping her sandy hair across her face. How she longed for a long rinse after all this traveling. "Aside from dehydration and starvation, of course."

Thano chuckled softly, pushing himself off from the rock to stand beside her. "Well, there are rumors." He hesitated, as if unsure whether she would believe him. "Rumors of a giant killer creature that roams these sands."

"Really?" Belyx raised an eyebrow, her eyes narrowing. "And you believe these rumors?"

Thano shrugged, his former wounds were already healing from the fight thanks to his fae healing abilities. "I've learned not to discount any possibility in my many years alive, Queen. But even if it isn't true, I think it's wise to be cautious."

Belyx sighed at the slow pace of their journey. She wanted nothing more than to race ahead, to confront The Original, and reclaim her kingdom. Instead, they were inching their way across this desolate landscape, weighed down by their dip in morale.

"Fine," she muttered, her grip on the knife handle tightening. "I suppose caution is better than a swift death. Also you don't need to call me queen. I am not one anymore."

"Apologies. But for what it's worth, I still think of you as such," Thano added, a glint of amusement in his eyes. "Besides, we have plenty of other reasons to be on our guard. The desert can be as treacherous as any enemy we might face."

The sun sank beneath the horizon, painting the sky with vibrant hues of orange and pink. Belyx couldn't help but feel a shiver of unease run down her spine. She glanced over at Thano, who was as still as a statue, gazing out at the dunes as if he could see something she couldn't.

"Let's just hope," she said, more to herself than to him, "that these rumors are nothing more than whispers in the wind."

Thano departed and Enzo arrived with roasted tree nuts Cook had prepared. He offered her some, but she refused. The others needed to eat first—it was what a good queen did.

Belyx and Enzo stood atop the dune; a mosaic of reds, oranges, pinks and purples spilling across the sky, interrupted only by a few pale clouds drifting overhead.

"Beautiful." Enzo was hushed with awe. "I've seen so many sunsets, but this one...it's different. The sand adds a pop of color."

Belyx nodded, her fingers tracing the burns on her hands. "It's like the desert is trying to remind us there's still beauty in the world, even when everything feels so dark."

Enzo sighed, the sound heavy. "I'm sorry for what I did, Belyx. I know I caused this. I brought him back, but I didn't know he would slaughter everyone." He kicked up some sand, cursing to himself.

She glanced at him. "We were all tricked, Enzo. It wasn't just you. With Majeria trying to take over and The Original offering up his power, it was tempting. I wanted to tell you earlier, but I would have done the same thing. I have no idea if that helps, but there you go." Even after all this time, words were tricky around him.

"A little bit," Enzo replied, looking down at his feet. "I should have known better. I should have trusted you to handle things. You usually do."

With the sun gone, a cool breeze swept through the air, sending a shiver down Belyx's body. She reached out and grasped Enzo's hand, giving it a reassuring squeeze...the familiar warmth clung to her veins. The mysterious shield that protected her remained a mystery, but she was thankful it came when it did. He saved her life again...in a sense. "We can't change the past, Enzo. All we can do is learn from our mistakes and move forward."

Enzo smiled, his emerald specks of eyes meeting hers once more. "Thank you, Belyx. I promise we will find a way out of this."

Her grip on Enzo's hand tightened, and rested her head on his shoulder. "What if we can't do this, Enzo? What if it's all too much?"

"Hey." he wrapped his slender arms around her in a warm embrace. "You're not alone, Belyx. We'll face whatever comes our way together."

As night fell, Enzo pulled out a weathered book from his pocket. Of course, he had one—that bibliophilic fool!

"Care for a story?" He chimed as he brushed a stray curl from his forehead. Belyx beamed and he began to read aloud, his voice soothing and rhythmic. The tale was a simple one, about love and loss, but as Belyx listened, the weight of her worries began to lift.

The desert breeze carried the scent of night-blooming flowers, mingling with the earthy aroma of the sand. It was a strange contrast—life and desolation, beauty and danger—that somehow made Belyx feel both nervous and reassured.

She had a dedicated group of friends by her side, people who would fight with her, and together, they could overcome any obstacle.

As the stars began to appear in the sky, one by one, Belyx closed her eyes and whispered a silent promise. No one else would die for her. She would make sure of it personally. No matter what happened, no matter how hard the journey became, she would never give up. For her kingdom, for her friends, and herself.

EPILOGUE

Bua Alovia grabbed a handful of grass, pulling the blades between her fingers so they left indents. She felt the energy transferring from her into the roots as she shut her eyes and visualized the Inkbara, a slender plant with an opaque center and swirling petals. With a deep breath, she opened her hand and watched as the grass slowly morphed into the shape of her favorite flower.

Clenching her hand again, the plant transformed into a new paintbrush. She grinned in delight and swept it through the vivid colors, applying them to her canvas with enthusiasm.

Focusing solely on her painting, she forgot all of the heartache and disappointment that surrounded her. Despite the solace she found in creating art, she couldn't help but think about how much she wanted to venture deeper into Keyica like the other witches—however, her mother had denied her this opportunity, citing her age and condition as reasons why she was too dangerous.

Her condition. Always a reminder of the price that was paid for her to live a life of loneliness and seclusion.

The strokes came together as one, forming a cascading symphony. In it, she was reminded of the legendary kingdom of Aikradal—a place she had only heard stories of but she always admired its strength, and how a single female sat on its throne. It echoed something within her, of her witch tribe's own ways: women ruling—the way it should be.

Alovia's concentration was broken by the pounding footsteps outside. As if on cue, witch after witch oozed out of the shadows and began to assemble around a figure, ready to hear whatever news their spy had brought.

The four witch tribes convened, and Alovia's mother tugged her along. If she spoke, Alovia would miss it—her mother still neglected to face her when talking.

Once the four witch tribes had come together, their leader, Ulo Vyx, strode into the fray. Her hands moved in a flurry as she told them the intel—Alovia was too far away and tilted her head in an attempt to catch a glimpse of Ulo Vyx's mouth. *"...news from Aikradal...listen."*

A witch, unseen for years, made her way to the center. Deep undercover in Aikradal's Order of the Rose as a healer, she had been ordered not to come back unless it was an utmost emergency. Alovia didn't hear, but she always listened.

Wara Amenthya was in disarray. Strands of her ashen hair hung over her face, and her robes were torn to shreds. The pungent smells of humans and fae alike lingered in the air around her. Could they have been involved? Wara Amenthya spoke, and Alovia intently observed, not wanting to miss a single word. *"He has returned. The prophecy has begun. We need to move."*

Alovia inhaled sharply. Could it be? The tales from her childhood were becoming reality. The leader uttered more words, but Alovia missed them. Alovia tapped her mother on the shoulder and she waved her off muttering something off her line of sight...forgetting yet again to face her.

Alovia tapped her mother again, and when she spun around with an impatient expression, Alovia asked with her hand communication, *"What? Happened?"*

Her mother gestured to the leader as all the other witches sank to their knees in prayer. Alovia joined, unable to speak, but she thought the chant.

Oh Mother, Giver of life and Taker of evil. Be with us now as we face a threat against your world.

This routine chant was crafted for the darkest moments, reserved only for when the witches prepared for war.

Alovia caught eyes with the leader and gasped at what her lips said. *"War is upon us. He has returned."*

Thank you so much for reading A Song Amidst the Storm. If you enjoyed the book, please consider leaving a short review on Amazon, Goodreads, and/or your retailer of choice. Reviews help us authors get noticed and you can help with my journey by doing so. Here is the link to Amazon where you can go to leave your review———https://www.amazon.com/dp/B0C3WS7JZP

You can also follow me on social media to get a look into my life and interests, as well as more engaging content. Instagram: @brettshafferauthor

Sign up for my newsletter to receive exclusive freebies, content, and more! As well as get an opportunity to join my ARC reader team for future books. Sign up at my website: brettshafferauthor.com or click this link: https://brettshafferauthor.com/newsletter/

ACKNOWLEDGEMENTS

They say publishing your first book is hard, but I would argue the second is a whole other beast. Like I said in my first book, the idea for this series came at a time of immense pain and anxiety. I was at an impasse in my life where I spent six years building a career that ultimately failed...twice.

At my first teaching job, I was emotionally abused by leadership and thrust into a hostile working environment of favoritism, gossiping, and intimidation. The next job, I was finally told I wasn't good enough to do what I loved and that hurt me the most.

Most people would advise me to not say anything about these occurrences in my life and "move on." I disagree. Things need to be said when we are not being treated how humans should be. What happened to me has taken years to get over and caused me to rush and make mistakes in my first book, but I am hoping to alleviate that with the rest of my series. Thank you for sticking it out with me with your continuous support.

Despite the struggles, planning and writing an entire series is a daunting task, one that requires a focus and strength to keep going. It would not be possible without all the support of these people.

First and always first, my incredible partner, Ryan. Thank you for those late-night diet coke runs and listening to my rambles about made-up stories in my head. Also thank you for waiting patiently while I finished a chapter so we could get our morning coffee. I know I can always count on you to be on the sidelines. I love you to the moon and to Saturn.

To my best friends, Amber, Olivia, and Janelle, for having my back for over TEN years and also listening to me ramble about made-up worlds. I truly cherish our last-minute road trips, blasting Tswift, and binging bad reality TV.

To my editors, KM Enright, and Lisa Shaffer. (Yes, the latter is my mother and the scariest proofreader you will ever meet) Thanks for helping my story make cohesive sense and for also removing those plentiful "that's."

To Miblart, for doing my GORGEOUS cover art that reflected my vision I had for this story, and I can't wait to use you for the rest! Always use a cover artist! It takes a village to publish a novel.

To bookstores and libraries that allow banned books and are still fighting the good fight. Banned stories are ones that need to be told and us marginalized voices will never stop creating them.

To my family, for showing me a world of literature and "forcing" me to read 20 minutes a day when I was young. Who knew that would triple in my adult life! Thank you for exposing me to books and having them around.

And lastly, to the readers. Writing a book is no joke and publishing under a small press is also no easy feat. Thank you for encouraging my stories and leaving me wonderful reviews! I encourage all of them, even the negative ones! Your support is how authors like me can do what we do.

Thank you for reading A Song Amidst the Storm. Sequels dive deeper into the story and I still feel like we are only scratching the surface on this one. I can't wait to continue this journey. Trust me, it will be worth it.

BOOKS BY BRETT SHAFFER

The Flower and Flames Saga

A Flower Amidst the Flames
A Song Amidst the Storm

ABOUT THE AUTHOR

Brett Shaffer is an author and administrative assistant, born and raised in Boise, Idaho. He has a BA in Elementary Education and Special Education. He is a writer of stories for teens and young adults. He currently lives in Boise with his partner, tuxedo cat, and bearded dragon. When he is not writing, you can find him reading the next best thing, playing tennis, and occasionally winning at Magic the Gathering. Catch up on books one and two of The Flower and Flames Saga today!

He invites you to visit his website at brettshafferauthor.com or follow him on Instagram @brettshafferauthor

Sign up for his newsletter and be the first to know about bonus content and new projects!